Praise for
Meredith Efken
and

SAHM I Am

"Can a novel consisting entirely of e-mails be enjoyable
faith fiction? Efken's charming, light debut offers
a resounding and surprising 'yes.' Efken keeps the
mood light, although she's not afraid to tackle serious
topics such as infertility, marital difficulties and chronic
illness. Christian readers will savor this fresh entrée."
—*Publishers Weekly*

"Written in the tradition of Erma Bombeck,
this fine first novel is recommended."
—*Library Journal*

"Efken's debut novel is pure delight. Infused with humor,
the touching issues reach deep into the soul
with spiritual truth and love."
—*Romantic Times BOOKclub*

"*SAHM I Am* is hysterically funny and I lost count of
how many times I laughed out loud. I loved the cast
of quirky characters and I could hardly turn the pages
fast enough. Erma Bombeck was a funny lady,
but Meredith Efken is even funnier."
—Christy Award–winning author Randall Ingermanson

"Ms. Efken has done a wonderful job portraying a typical
e-mail loop and any woman who has ever been
a member of one will get a kick out of *SAHM I Am*.
This book is going right to the front of my keeper shelf!"
—*www.cataromance.com*

Meredith Efken

@HOME for the Holidays

Steeple
Hill®

Published by Steeple Hill Books™

STEEPLE HILL BOOKS

Steeple
Hill®

ISBN-13: 978-0-373-78570-4
ISBN-10:   0-373-78570-4

@HOME FOR THE HOLIDAYS

Copyright © 2006 by Meredith Efken

www.SteepleHill.com

Printed in U.S.A.

To Stephenie, who will always be my kindred spirit
and bosom friend, no matter how many miles
are between us.

ACKNOWLEDGMENTS

I could never have written this book with any
authenticity without the help of some wonderful people:

Ethiopian Adoption: Thank you to Merrily Ripley at
Adoption Advocates International for giving me such
great information about adopting from Ethiopia.
You've inspired my husband and me to consider it for
our family. And thank you to Grant and Anna Braasch
for looking over the manuscript for accuracy. I hope
your little one from Ethiopia is doing beautifully.

Embryo Adoption: Thank you to Lori Maze, the director
of the Snowflakes Frozen Embryo Adoption Program at
Nightlight Adoption Agency. Your help was invaluable in
understanding this unique form of adoption.

Critiques: Thank you to my wonderful critique group—
Jill Eileen Smith, Tammy Alexander, Maureen Lang,
Kathy Fuller and Diana Urban—for your feedback
on the manuscript. And thank you to Randy
Ingermanson for brainstorming with me and giving
me feedback on the entire book. All of you—the book
is stronger and better for your insight and honesty.

A special thank-you goes to my editor,
Melissa Endlich, and my agent, Steve Laube,
whose support and enthusiasm for my writing
has been such an encouragement to me.

From:	Rosalyn Ebberly <prov31woman@home.com>
To:	SAHM I Am <sahmiam@loophole.com>
Subject:	**[SAHM I AM] We're in the newspaper, Ladies!**

Dearest SAHM I Am'ers,

Remember a couple of weeks ago when I asked for volunteers to be interviewed by Farrah Jensen, a reporter for our local paper, the *Hibiscus Herald,* for an article she was doing on stay-at-home moms? Well, it's been printed at last. I thought you all would like to see it, and Farrah said I could reprint it for the loop, so I'm cutting and pasting below. But as always, please DO respect the noble copyright laws of our land and don't abuse this privilege by forwarding this e-mail to anyone else. I've always felt strongly about upholding our nation's long tradition of protecting intellectual property rights, and the Internet and e-mail have really eroded those rights. So resist the urge to forward! I know those of you mentioned in the article will probably want to show your friends and family, so just e-mail me and I'll be glad to mail you as many photocopies as you'd like!

Blessings,

Rosalyn Ebberly

SAHM I Am Loop Moderator

"She looks well to the ways of her household, and does not eat the bread of idleness."

Proverbs 31:27 (NASB)

From:	The Millards <jstcea4jesus@familymail.net>
To:	SAHM I Am <sahmiam@loophole.com>
Subject:	Re: [SAHM I AM] We're in the newspaper, Ladies!

Wow, great news, Rosalyn! But...you forgot to include the article!

Jocelyn

From:	Rosalyn Ebberly <prov31woman@home.com>
To:	The Millards <jstcea4jesus@familymail.net>
Subject:	LOOP GUIDELINES

Dear Jocelyn,

According to our loop posting guidelines, you really should have sent that reply to me directly instead of the entire group. As it turns out, I really didn't "forget" to include the

article. I *meant* to send it separately, so as to keep the loop messages from getting too large. I really did! It's never a wise idea to jump to conclusions, you know.
Much love,
Rosalyn

"She looks well to the ways of her household, and does not eat the bread of idleness."
Proverbs 31:27 (NASB)

From:	The Millards <jstcea4jesus@familymail.net>
To:	Rosalyn Ebberly <prov31woman@home.com>
Subject:	Re: LOOP GUIDELINES

My apologies. I must have misunderstood what you meant by "I'm cutting and pasting below." :)
Jocelyn

From:	Rosalyn Ebberly <prov31woman@home.com>
To:	The Millards <jstcea4jesus@familymail.net>
Subject:	Re: LOOP GUIDELINES

Jocelyn Millard wrote:
<My apologies. I must have misunderstood what you meant by "I'm cutting and pasting below." :)>
Of course. That makes perfect sense. That comment was for the benefit of our good women on digest mode. You know they read a group of 20 or so loop messages by scroll-

ing through one long e-mail, and I wanted to make sure they knew to keep reading farther down for the news article.

You are completely forgiven. I know you are just over-wrought with excitement about the article. You'll LOVE it—it's a great article. I'm going to have my original framed and signed by Farrah herself.

Oh, Jocelyn, it's such an *amazing* responsibility to be in the public eye! Now that we have media attention, I imagine our loop will grow at an even faster rate. We'll need to all work together to maintain the high-quality interaction these new SAHM I Am fans will be expecting when they join.

What a *privilege* and *honor* it is, don't you think?
Rosalyn

"She looks well to the ways of her household, and does not eat the bread of idleness."
Proverbs 31:27 (NASB)

From:	The Millards \<jstcea4jesus@familymail.net\>
To:	"Green Eggs and Ham"
Subject:	**Fact Hunt, anybody?**

I'm offering the reward of undying friendship and eternal gratitude to the first one of you ladies who can find out for me what the circulation is for the *Hibiscus Herald* out of Hibiscus, WA.
Love,
Jocelyn

From:	Brenna L. <saywhat@writeme.com>
To:	"Green Eggs and Ham"
Subject:	**Re: Fact Hunt, anybody?**

What, you can't Google that yourself, Jocelyn? :) It took me like thirty seconds. The circulation is exactly 526—with two pending, apparently. Why did you want to know?

From:	The Millards <jstcea4jesus@familymail.net>
To:	"Green Eggs and Ham"
Subject:	**Re: Fact Hunt, anybody?**

Brenna wrote:
<Why did you want to know?>
   Oh, no particular reason. Just curious. 526, huh? Wow. "Privilege and honor," indeed.
Jocelyn

From:	Rosalyn Ebberly <prov31woman@home.com>
To:	SAHM I Am <sahmiam@loophole.com>
Subject:	**[SAHM I AM] The Hibiscus Herald Article**

A Woman's Place Is…In Front of the Computer
By Farrah Jensen

Hibiscus, WA— Over fifty years ago, housewives, wearing their high heels and pearls, gathered at each others' homes to bake chocolate chip cookies and exchange tips on how to keep their husbands' work shirts stain free and well starched. Politics were left to the men while the wives' pursuits consisted of weightier matters such as making sure a hot supper was on the table when hubby got home and seeing that the children finished their homework. The term "stay-at-home mom" was unknown—what other kind of mom was there?

Fast-forward to the twenty-first century. In a world where most women have now embraced the financial freedom and personal fulfillment of a career and have even outnumbered men in many universities, there is a growing number of women who have chosen to trade in their suits and PDAs for sweats and a cookbook, to follow in their mothers' and grandmothers' footsteps. Instead of hosting dinner parties, however, they gather in front of their computers for some old-fashioned female bonding with a technological twist.

Local "domestic diva" Rosalyn Ebberly is one such stay-at-home mom, or SAHM (pronounced "Sam"), as they call themselves. She and best friend, Connie Lawson, also of Hibiscus, operate an e-mail discussion loop called "SAHM I Am" where SAHMs across the nation can exchange e-mails with each other. Ebberly regales the rest of the loop with her sage advice on everything from exercise to where to find organic cotton diapers and lectures the women about having the proper "Godly" attitude toward typical SAHM trials such as potty-training and cleaning the oven. According to Ebberly, "SAHMs need a way to support each other in this highest of all callings—being a full-time mom. It truly is an art, and I use the gift of technology to help each woman aspire to ever-greater levels of domestic and parenting skills."

About five hundred women create this cyber support group, and many have formed deep friendships utilizing this unlikely tool. Lawson, the group's founder and mother of five children, says, "The women on the loop are like daughters to me. They all tend to look up to me and Rosalyn for advice and support. It gives me so much pleasure to know I am helping so many."

What do these ladies chat about in their virtual therapy sessions? Dulcie Huckleberry, mom of three from Springfield, Missouri, says discussion topics range from daily events in the lives of the women to favorite books and even the occasional current event. These SAHMs have come a long way, baby. What about those recipes, though? Huckleberry's good friend, Jocelyn Millard, a soccer mom of four in Colorado Springs, laughs at this. "Recipes? Who has time to cook?" Apparently, e-mailing her friends all day takes up too much time and energy.

The Internet has brought together a surprisingly diverse assortment of women, considering that the world of the SAHM tends to be dominated by white, Christian, middle-class, SUV-driving suburbanites. Millard and Huckleberry are part of a particularly close group of friends that include Phyllis Lorimer, a preacher's wife from Scoville, New York, Brenna Lindberg, a farmer's wife from Oklahoma, and Zelia Muzuwa, wife of British-Zimbawean immigrant Tristan Muzuwa, of Baltimore, Maryland. New to the group is earth mother Marianne Hausten, of Omaha, Nebraska, who was the college roommate of fellow SAHM, Dulcie Huckleberry.

Their interests are as diverse as their geographic locations. The Muzuwas are months away from completing an adoption from Ethiopia. Zelia Muzuwa is also active in Baltimore's art community—one would assume she excels in crayon drawings and finger paintings. The Lindbergs are working on a different type of "adoption"—the more controversial so-called adoption of leftover frozen embryos from another family's in vitro fertilization procedure.

Of the six friends, Phyllis Lorimer is the only one who has retained any educational or career aspirations. She hopes to eventually return to graduate school for a Ph.D. in English and become a professor. "I have a responsibility to nurture my children," Lorimer says, "but that doesn't negate my responsibility to also nurture my God-given talents and abilities and to strive to use them for His glory." Spoken like a truly devoted preacher's wife.

Regarding matters of faith and religion, Veronica Marcello of Houston, Texas, has keen insights. Marcello is the sister of loop moderator, Rosalyn Ebberly, and is also the token agnostic of the decidedly Christian-dominated group. She joined SAHM I Am several months ago when she decided to toss out her new promotion at a top marketing firm in favor of a crash course in Step-SAHM 101. "I don't mind the religion talk," she drawls in her Texan accent, "at least not from most people. As long as they're sincere in their beliefs, it's not my job to judge them." What people does she mind "religion talk" from? She refused to comment.

How healthy is all this housewivery and e-mailing? Psychiatrist Anna Furmin, who recently published a study about the emotional health of women who choose not to work, says, "Depression has always been most common among housewives and stay-at-home mothers. While these sort of e-mail groups undoubtedly aid in creating an illusion of socialization, they cannot negate the sad truth that the majority of stay-at-home mothers are among the most isolated and dependent cross section of American society."

Economic analysts, such as Rick McTavish of Delmar University, also point to the financial burden of this staying-home trend. "When women leave the workforce, it often means a family must make do with less buying power. For a nation that relies primarily on consumer spending to drive the economy, this is a pretty big blow. It also results in a loss of potential jobs, since these families are not utilizing child-care services."

However, the psychological risks and economic costs do not seem to deter these women in their quest of becoming perfect wives and mothers. It seems that theirs is an art for which we all should be willing to suffer. As far as their own mental health or the national economy, Huckleberry sums it up well: "I let my husband worry about that."

From:	Zelia Muzuwa <zeemuzu@vivacious.com>
To:	SAHM I Am <sahmiam@loophole.com>
Subject:	[SAHM I AM] YOUR HUSBAND, DULCIE???

"I let my husband worry about that." She says in her cute, little I-need-a-big-strong-man voice.

What on earth were you thinking, Dulcie-babe? My goodness, I choked on my own tongue when I read that! Zelia

From:	Dulcie Huckleberry <dulcie@showme.com>
To:	SAHM I Am <sahmiam@loophole.com>
Subject:	Re: [SAHM I AM] YOUR HUSBAND, DULCIE???

I WAS SOOOOOO MISQUOTED! Honest-to-goodness, I am totally innocent. What I REALLY said was, "When it comes to household chores, my husband and I share pretty equally. I do the laundry and a lot of the vacuuming and dusting. But when it comes to stuff like taking out the trash or cleaning toilets, *I let my husband worry about that.*"

Oooohhh, I'm furious! That woman deliberately took my words out of context for her stupid little mocking article. Isn't it illegal for a reporter to misquote a source? Can't I make them issue a retraction? It's so embarrassing. Now all 526 subscribers to the paper are going to think I'm some sort of Stepford Wifey-dear.

So. Not. True.

Dulcie :(

From:	Zelia Muzuwa <zeemuzu@vivacious.com>
To:	SAHM I Am <sahmiam@loophole.com>
Subject:	Re: [SAHM I AM] YOUR HUSBAND, DULCIE???

Aha! I should have known. Any person who makes cracks about my art consisting of "crayon drawings and finger paintings" is enough of a low-life, slime bucket to totally manipulate a quote like that. She's got the ethics of a…a cow!
Z

From:	Brenna L. <saywhat@writeme.com>
To:	SAHM I Am <sahmiam@loophole.com>
Subject:	**Re: [SAHM I AM] YOUR HUSBAND, DULCIE???**

Hey! Don't insult the poor bovine, okay? I'll have you know that cows, our cows anyway, are highly ethical creatures. At least, they probably would be if there was the slightest spark of intelligence in their brains. I'd compare Ms. Jensen's ethics to those of a cutworm. Ew!!!

SO-CALLED "ADOPTION"? She said my future baby was "so-called"? And she used quotes! SHE USED QUOTES! Well, I'll tell you something, Ms. So-Called "Reporter"—your article smells like our pasture after the cows have been there. And I'd like to scoop up your so-called "Article" and dump it on your So-Called "Head."

So-called "There!"

Brenna

From:	VIM <vivalaveronica@marcelloportraits.com>
To:	SAHM I Am <sahmiam@loophole.com>
Subject:	**Re: [SAHM I AM] YOUR HUSBAND, DULCIE???**

Hey, y'all, don't forget 'bout little ol' Ronnie Irene over here in Houston with my "Texan drawl." She called ME a "Step-SAHM"! As if I were somehow not in the same category as a plain-old SAHM. That woman has more issues than the magazine section of the Library of Congress, let me tell you!

And "token agnostic"??? Please tell me that ain't how y'all really think of me!

Steamed like a bathroom mirror,
Veronica

From:	Marianne Hausten <desperatemom@nebweb.net>
To:	SAHM I Am <sahmiam@loophole.com>
Subject:	**Re: [SAHM I AM] YOUR HUSBAND, DULCIE???**

And I'm NOT an "earth mother." Today, I wish I wasn't any sort of mother at all! Oh dear, another crash...wonder what Helene destroyed now? Probably nothing more than some priceless heirloom passed down from mother to daughter with love and care for centuries. The rate we're going these days, the only thing I'll have to offer as an inheritance is a giant headache and prematurely gray hair. I suppose I should get up and waddle my ever-widening pregnant body down the hall and see what disaster she's prepared for me this time.

And she said WE CHOOSE NOT TO WORK???? I hope this doesn't sound impolite, but...I beg your pardon, Ms. Jensen. You don't know the meaning of the word WORK.

Marianne

From:	P. Lorimer <phyllis.lorimer@joono.com>
To:	SAHM I Am <sahmiam@loophole.com>
Subject:	**Re: [SAHM I AM] YOUR HUSBAND, DULCIE???**

Tell me truthfully, my friends…do I really come across THAT self-righteous and pious? I am utterly humiliated. She made me sound like everything I do NOT want to be as a pastor's wife. Or any kind of wife, for that matter! Why did I even talk to her? I know jouralists can be unreliable. I should have warned everyone to stay away. It's my fault.
Phyllis

From:	Connie Lawson <clmo5@home.com>
To:	SAHM I Am <sahmiam@loophole.com>
Subject:	Re: [SAHM I AM] YOUR HUSBAND, DULCIE???

No, dear Phyllis, it is NOT your fault. And of course we don't see you as self-righteous or pious, any more than we view sweet Ronnie as our "token agnostic"! That woman betrayed us all. And she didn't even hardly talk to me, though I *am* the "loop mom." Just that one quote. And I sent her tons of great information, too! That's the last time I'm ever letting any reporter do an article on SAHM I Am!
Connie Lawson
SAHM I Am Loop Mom

From:	Rosalyn Ebberly <prov31woman@home.com>
To:	SAHM I Am <sahmiam@loophole.com>
Subject:	Re: [SAHM I AM] YOUR HUSBAND, DULCIE???

Girls! I'm shocked! Totally shocked at your reaction to this gracious, generous article! Do you know it had the honor of running on the FRONT page of our esteemed newspaper? I fail to see why you are so upset.

Dulcie, it's unfortunate if you *really* did get misquoted. However, I think it's more likely a simple misunderstanding on your part of what Farrah was asking. At any rate, it doesn't really matter, does it? There's no shame in admitting that you let your husband worry about things like finances and such while you concentrate your efforts on more "humble" pursuits at home. We all have our roles and duties.

And the rest of you—except dear Connie, of course—are being extremely petty and small-minded about this. You just must not understand the incredible pressure to be "fair and balanced" that these poor journalists are under. It's all the fault of that horrible, awful…LIBERAL media!

But, no matter the reason, I simply cannot allow you all to continue maligning Farrah's character. This discussion is OFFICIALLY CLOSED!
Your gentle moderator,
Rosalyn Ebberly

"She looks well to the ways of her household, and does not eat the bread of idleness."
Proverbs 31:27 (NASB)

From:	The Millards <jstcea4jesus@familymail.net>
To:	"Green Eggs and Ham"
Subject:	**"Officially Closed"**

What she really meant was, "Oh, no! You don't agree with ME—you evil, subversive people! You must conform! You must be…ASSIMILATED!"

Ah, girls…this is why we have good old Green Eggs and Ham as our own personal SAHM I Am subloop. It's a good thing none of us mentioned GE&H to that reporter! Can you imagine what Rosalyn would have done if she'd found out that we have our own little group dedicated to venting about HER?

"OFF WITH THEIR HEADS!!!" :)

That article made me angry, too! She all but called us emotionally unstable and isolated! Could she possibly have been MORE snotty about us "SAHMs"? Sheesh!

Jocelyn

From:	Dulcie Huckleberry <dulcie@showme.com>
To:	"Green Eggs and Ham"
Subject:	**Re: "Officially Closed"**

Well, what I don't get is why Rosalyn is so defensive of that article. That Jensen woman was clearly condescending and supercilious, and yet she has Rosalyn practically licking her boots!

Dulcie

From:	P. Lorimer <phyllis.lorimer@joono.com>
To:	"Green Eggs and Ham"
Subject:	**Re: "Officially Closed"**

"Condescending and supercilious"? I must say, Mrs. Huckleberry, I am QUITE impressed with your vocabulary. Well done! :)

Phyllis

From:	Dulcie Huckleberry <dulcie@showme.com>
To:	"Green Eggs and Ham"
Subject:	**Re: "Officially Closed"**

Well, you know, I've "come a long way, baby." I even *read books* and pay attention to one or two *current events!* Of course, that's nothing to your "educational and career aspirations" but we *isolated* and *dependent* women can expect nothing grander. :)
Dulcie

From:	P. Lorimer <phyllis.lorimer@joono.com>
To:	"Green Eggs and Ham"
Subject:	**Re: "Officially Closed"**

Meow!!! I am in awe of your scathing rhetoric, Dulcie, dear. And I heartily agree.
Phyllis

From:	The Millards <jstcea4jesus@familymail.net>
To:	"Green Eggs and Ham"
Subject:	**Rosalyn's Odd Behavior**

Hi, girls,
Brenna and I have been Googling together while you catty ladies have been purring, and I think we figured out why

Rosalyn is kowtowing to this reporter. Check out the following article that appeared in their paper about a week ago:

How The GWENCH Will Save Christmas
By Farrah Jensen

Hibiscus, WA—The "War on Christmas" is heating up again in Hibiscus, WA. Last year, retailers in the historic Market District angered tourists and residents alike with their joint refusal to bow to pressure to wish their customers a "Merry Christmas." Citing a desire to be more inclusive and acknowledge the holidays of other faiths that coincide with the Christmas season, some retailers relied on the ubiquitous "happy holidays" while others resorted to a planned rotation of various holiday greetings that included "Merry Christmas," "Happy Hanukkah," "Joyous Kwanzaa" and "Wonderful Winter Solstice."

This year, a dedicated group of evangelical women have begun a campaign to "force retailers to show more respect to the preeminence of the Christian celebration of Christmas." Calling themselves the Godly Women for the Enforcement of National Christian Holidays (GWENCH), their mission is daring: Boycott Christmas presents. Chairperson Rosalyn Ebberly leads the charge as the group has their first public forum scheduled for July 20 at the Hibiscus Community Center.

Ebberly says that the Save Christmas campaign is designed to "demand respect and consideration for the great American tradition of Christmas." Instead of buying presents, GWENCH is advocating donating money to an approved list of local charities. According to Ebberly, "Christmas is not about materialism and consumerism. It's no secret that most retailers, especially in the Market District, rely on Christmas sales to get them through the rest of the year. We will force the retailers to acknowledge that we Christians hold the true meaning of Christmas when their budgets fall short and they experience the financial cost of pandering to political correctness. Plus, we can help out some well-deserving charities. But most importantly, our aim is to take back Jesus's birthday and punish the retailers for not being more respectful of our beliefs."

A spokesperson for the Market District says the retailers doubt that any serious backlash will occur from the unconventional boycott. "This is all a tempest in a teapot. It's absurd to imply that retailers are being disrespectful of anyone's faith. It was our attempt to display respect toward all faiths that has caused this controversy. We hope that the people of Hibiscus will realize that there is nothing about giving gifts that goes against any faith, and that giving to charity can coexist peacefully with giving to friends and relatives."

Don't you see? This reporter gave Rosalyn and her "organization" some major press time. How could she possibly criticize Jensen now?

Jocelyn

From:	Zelia Muzuwa <zeemuzu@vivacious.com>
To:	"Green Eggs and Ham"
Subject:	**Re: Rosalyn's Odd Behavior**

This is the most ridiculous thing I ever heard of! Boycotting Christmas? What's next? Flying the Union Jack and singing "God Save the Queen" on the Fourth of July? Oh, wait…Tristan does that. As a joke, of course. The rest of us end up in a shout-out rendition of "My Country 'Tis of Thee." Do you think my kids will have identity crises when they grow up???

Anyway, I can't imagine anyone would be dumb enough to participate in this "boycott." True meaning of Christmas, indeed!

Z

From:	Dulcie Huckleberry <dulcie@showme.com>
To:	"Green Eggs and Ham"
Subject:	**Just. So. Wrong.**

…on so many levels I hardly know where to begin! Not only is the idea of boycotting Christmas in order to "force retailers to respect us" so utterly contrary to Jesus's example, but IT'S ONLY JULY, FOR CRYING OUT LOUD! They should all be at the pool slathering sunscreen on their children and complaining about cellulite and how unfair it is that we all have to wear swimsuits designed for tiny teenagers!

What happened to summer? I don't even want to THINK about Christmas for another five months!
Dulcie

From:	Brenna L. <saywhat@writeme.com>
To:	"Green Eggs and Ham"
Subject:	**Re: Just. So. Wrong.**

Uh, Dulcie? In five months, it will *be* Christmas.
Brenna

From:	Dulcie Huckleberry <dulcie@showme.com>
To:	"Green Eggs and Ham"
Subject:	**Re: Just. So. Wrong.**

Yep. Ho–ho–ho.
Dulcie

From:	Marianne Hausten <desperatemom@nebweb.net>
To:	"Green Eggs and Ham"
Subject:	**Re: Just. So. Wrong.**

You all have to understand about my friend Dulcie here. I have known her since college, and she never goes Christmas shopping until the stress gets so bad that she can't sleep for worrying about what to buy everyone for Christmas.

Until then, it might as well not even exist. I keep telling her she will die someday as a result of a Christmas-induced stroke, but I guess she won't believe me until it happens. Marianne

From:	Rosalyn Ebberly <prov31woman@home.com>
To:	SAHM I Am <sahmiam@loophole.com>
Subject:	[SAHM I AM] TOTW July 11: How Can We Make Our Husband's Lives Easier?

Dearest Sisters in the Lord,

During my devotions at five this morning, I was reflecting on my favorite passage of Scripture—Proverbs 31. You all know how I *strive* to model my life after this "excellent wife" described in these verses. This morning, verse 12 particularly stood out to me. Speaking of the wife's husband, it says she does him good and not evil all the days of her life.

As I thought about this verse, I wondered to myself, "How is it that I have been able to achieve this level of wifely devotion while so many others struggle to do good to their husbands?" I don't mean this to sound proud. You all know how committed I am to absolute humility and meekness. But the fact is, I treat Chad very well. I'm patient and understanding, even when his plans don't fit with mine. I just change my own plans, because his happiness is more important than my own. I never gripe when he doesn't help out around the house—after all, he doesn't expect me to help him with *his* job! And I try to make sure that our home is always a peaceful, pleasant retreat from the harsh world of the office. I never raise my voice to him, and I'm always accommodating and ready to meet his needs.

What about the rest of you? What are ways that you can do good and not evil to your husbands? If only you could grasp how deeply they appreciate it—you would take great joy in doing whatever you can to be a blessing to them.
Praying for you all,
Rosalyn Ebberly
SAHM I Am Loop Moderator

"She looks well to the ways of her household, and does not eat the bread of idleness."
Proverbs 31:27 (NASB)

From:	Chad Ebberly <chad.ebberly@henpec.com>
To:	Rosalyn Ebberly <prov31woman@home.com>
Subject:	**Meeting Tonight**

Hey, sweetie,
Hate to do this to you, but I just found out I have a meeting for work tonight. Don't hold dinner, I'll just grab something beforehand. Should be home around 9:00 p.m.
Chad
Chad Ebberly
Sr. Engineer
Henderson, Peckham, & Associates

From:	Rosalyn Ebberly <prov31woman@home.com>
To:	Chad Ebberly <chad.ebberly@henpec.com>
Subject:	**Re: Meeting Tonight**

Darling,

How could you do this to me? A meeting? It's so inconsiderate of you, dear. After I've spent the whole day grocery shopping and fixing dinner and doing laundry and catching up on filing, now you expect me to also manage the kids for the entire evening? Did it ever occur to you that I might have plans, too? Actually, I think I have a GWENCH meeting tonight. You KNOW how important it is to me to help persuade our community to take back Christmas! So now I'll have to try to sweet-talk Connie into taking my kids so I can go to the meeting.

Can't you tell those people at work that your family comes first? After all I do for you, the least you could do is let me have one evening off. ONE EVENING! Is that so much to ask?

All my love,

Rosalyn

"She looks well to the ways of her household, and does not eat the bread of idleness."

Proverbs 31:27 (NASB)

From:	Chad Ebberly <chad.ebberly@henpec.com>
To:	Rosalyn Ebberly <prov31woman@home.com>
Subject:	**Re: Meeting Tonight**

Sheesh, Rosalyn! This is the first after-hours meeting I think I've ever had. You've had GWENCH meetings 3 of the last 5 days— I had no idea there was yet another one. I'm sorry to inconvenience you. Do you want me to make the arrangements with Connie?
Chad
Chad Ebberly
Sr. Engineer
Henderson, Peckham, & Associates

From:	Rosalyn Ebberly <prov31woman@home.com>
To:	Chad Ebberly <chad.ebberly@henpec.com>
Subject:	**Re: Meeting Tonight**

Darling,
You seem to be having trouble grasping the tremendous importance of what GWENCH is about. I'm amazed at your utter indifference to it. You haven't even shown any interest in attending the meetings.

As far as calling Connie…would you? I have such a headache. You have no idea how difficult my job is. Any small thing you can do to ease my load is so appreciated!
Love,
Rosalyn

"She looks well to the ways of her household, and does not eat the bread of idleness."
Proverbs 31:27 (NASB)

From:	Chad Ebberly <chad.ebberly@henpec.com>
To:	Rosalyn Ebberly <prov31woman@home.com>
Subject:	**Re: Meeting Tonight**

Dearest,

Quite possibly the reason I haven't attended any GWENCH meetings is that they are for "Godly WOMEN Enforcing National Christian Holidays." I hardly qualify. Besides, what you ladies are trying to do seems a little extreme, don't you think?

As far as understanding how difficult your job is, yes I'm aware of it. I think it would be easier if you didn't try to do so much. But it's your decision.

Chad

Chad Ebberly

Sr. Engineer

Henderson, Peckham, & Associates

From:	Rosalyn Ebberly <prov31woman@home.com>
To:	Chad Ebberly <chad.ebberly@henpec.com>
Subject:	**Re: Meeting Tonight**

Are you just TRYING to bait me, to make me upset? It's not going to work, you know. I *never* get upset! I *never* get angry! I HAVE PERFECT CONTROL OF MY TEMPER! And don't forget it.

But I am disappointed in you, Chad. You aren't even TRYING to be supportive! Mothers Against Drunk Drivers has men working in that organization. If you really wanted to, you'd find some way of helping us out. It's embarrassing to be leading the charge on this, and find that my husband has his head stuck in the sand just like everyone else. If we don't stand up for Christmas, some Christmas morning, we'll wake up and find that it's been taken from us entirely! Rosalyn

"She looks well to the ways of her household, and does not eat the bread of idleness."
Proverbs 31:27 (NASB)

From:	Chad Ebberly <chad.ebberly@henpec.com>
To:	Rosalyn Ebberly <prov31woman@home.com>
Subject:	Re: Meeting Tonight

<If we don't stand up for Christmas, some Christmas morning, we'll wake up and find that it's been taken from us entirely!>

Yes, by a bunch of overzealous women who have boycotted Christmas presents!
Chad Ebberly
Sr. Engineer
Henderson, Peckham, & Associates

From:	Dulcie Huckleberry <dulcie@showme.com>
To:	SAHM I Am <sahmiam@loophole.com>
Subject:	[SAHM I AM] NASAL EMERGENCY!!!

I'm taking Haley into the Emergency Room. Apparently, she has two pairs of Polly Pocket shoes stuck up her nose. I discovered this when McKenzie stormed into my bedroom complaining that Haley wasn't "sharing." From the looks of it, Haley decided to put the shoes in question where big sister couldn't reach them…. Judging from the fact that she is trying to cry but can't even sniffle, I think she may be regretting her choice of hiding places. She'd BETTER be regretting it!

Update to come,

Dulcie

From:	Zelia Muzuwa <zeemuzu@vivacious.com>
To:	SAHM I Am <sahmiam@loophole.com>
Subject:	Re: [SAHM I AM] NASAL EMERGENCY!!!

Dulcie,

I guess you could say, "Her zeal burns in her nose…" Slight paraphrase from *The Second Part of Henry the Fourth,* act II, scene IV. :)

Two-year-olds…egocentric to the point of self-destruction! Hope she's okay…

Z

From:	Brenna L. <saywhat@writeme.com>
To:	"Green Eggs and Ham"
Subject:	**GUESS WHAT?**

Hey, gals,

Our social worker for the Snowflakes program just called. A genetic family is interested in us, and they want to choose us for the embryo adoption! The family lives in New Mexico, and if we like them, then we can sign the adoption agreement and move forward with the Frozen Embryo Transfer procedure. That part's a bit freaky, but I'm overall excited. We're getting a packet of information about them in the next couple of days. I hope we LOVE them.

Can you believe this is actually happening?

Brenna

From:	Zelia Muzuwa <zeemuzu@vivacious.com>
To:	"Green Eggs and Ham"
Subject:	**Re: GUESS WHAT?**

WHOOO-HOOO!!! Congratulations, Brenna and Darren!

Though I have to say, I'm just a tad jealous. We're still toodling around with our home study for Ethiopia. Our social worker got the report written, and then MESSED UP the document that verifies we aren't child molesters. So we've had to wait several weeks to redo that paper.

I'm soooooo impatient.

Z

From:	P. Lorimer <phyllis.lorimer@joono.com>
To:	"Green Eggs and Ham"
Subject:	**Update on the Lorimers**

Dear Green Eggs and my beloved Ham,
I haven't had much of a chance to let you all know how the move to New York went. And I wanted to give you an update because each of you was so supportive when Jonathan was fired from our previous church. We will never forget how you all opened your homes to us during that horrible time. I especially remember the sweet, refreshing stay at Brenna and Darren's farm.

People keep assuming Jonathan and I are bitter about what happened. After all, firing him over a miscommunication about the fact that we got pregnant with Julia before we were married was a pretty low-down thing for any church to do. But thanks to the months we spent with Brenna and Darren, God did a lot of healing of our hearts, and we can honestly say we have no hard feelings toward that congregation. We're just thankful God provided us a chance to serve Him here in darling little Scoville.

Just this evening, I was able to put up the final homey touches in our house, and it is starting to look lived-in. We've been here a whole month, and I still find myself looking around wondering whose house this is. The church is great—they seem like they'll treat Jonathan really well. You should see the nice office they gave him. The office staff even put together a box of toys for when Julia and Bennet come to visit daddy. And for my birthday a couple of weeks ago, they sent me flowers and a gift certificate for a massage at a very elegant day spa. I know we are still in the "honeymoon" stage, but everything seems to be pointing toward this being a church that really knows how to treat its pastor and family.

Oh, just to let you know...now that we're getting all settled in, I'm planning to talk to Jonathan soon about applying to the university near here. When we talked about it while we were staying with Brenna and Darren, he sounded very enthusiastic about me getting my Ph.D., so I'm hoping to apply this fall. It would still be another year before I could actually start, but one must take things one step at a time.

Thanks for asking!
Phyllis

From:	Dulcie Huckleberry <dulcie@showme.com>
To:	SAHM I Am <sahmiam@loophole.com>
Subject:	[SAHM I AM] A Shoe-In...and Out

Sorry I have been slow at giving you the update on how the shoes...came out. Tom was at work, and I couldn't reach my MIL to watch the other two girls, so all three came with me. That was an adventure! By this time, Haley was panicking and crying, which made Aidan cry, too. And McKenzie, in typical four-year-old angst was pouting, saying, "I want my Polly Pocket shoes back. They're my favorites." Whatever. Last week, she had forgotten she owned them! LOL!

I said, "No, darling, trust me. You will NOT want them back." But she didn't believe me.

So we pull up to the E.R. entrance at the hospital, and I haul in my three whimpering children and try to explain to the receptionist what the problem is. She's like, "Your daughter did what?"

"Stuck doll shoes up her nose."

"Up her nose?"

"Yes. Up. Her. Nose."

"Shoes. Plural?"

"Yes. Two pair, actually."

"She has FOUR shoes in her nose?"

"Yes, and we would like them out, please."

She takes a hard look at Haley's schnoz and shakes her head. "Are you sure?"

WHAT? "Well, on second thought, maybe we'll let her keep them in as snot collectors."

She blushed, and stopped her attempt at triage. Then we had to sit in the waiting room for another 40 minutes because our issue was not life threatening. The fact that it was sanity threatening didn't seem to strike an emotive chord with any of them.

And of course there was a soap opera on the television. The girls seemed to be ignoring it until McKenzie piped up, "Mommy, why is he taking off her clothes?" Oh, just great! I tried to change the channel, and got yelled at by a blue-haired old lady munching pretzels and muttering about how "Terrance is a &*#^% fool for—ahem, having intimate relations—with that &*%$# Angelica." Of course, McKenzie chooses that moment to have supersonic hearing, and asks me quite clearly what Blank #1 and Blank #2 meant. The other people in the waiting area sat there alternately smirking at me or glaring at Blue Hair. Blue Hair seemed to be watching me to see what I'd do, so I responded pretty loudly to McKenzie, "Those words are very naughty words that Mommy and Daddy would never use, especially around children. You are such a smart little girl, you don't need to use words like that. *Some* people just don't know any better."

Blue Hair crumpled up her pretzel bag and huffed off, hurling a few more choice words over her shoulder. Thankfully, McKenzie had already lost interest, and was looking through a kids' magazine.

When we finally were called back to a room, the nurse tried to examine the wrong twin. I told her, "That's not Haley." And she responded, "You sure?" YES! IT'S MY KID, THANK YOU!

Anyway, I'll spare you the details of how they removed the shoes. I had no idea a child's nose had so much room in it! McKenzie and Haley were both mad that I made them throw away the shoes. I suppose I could have cleaned them up, but after all the fighting, not to mention the $50 co-pay for the E.R., I didn't think either girl deserved them.

For the past two days since then, the sight of anything Polly Pocket-related has made me feel slightly ill....
Dulcie

From:	Dulcie Huckleberry <dulcie@showme.com>
To:	SAHM I Am <sahmiam@loophole.com>
Subject:	**[SAHM I AM] Addendum**

My husband... *big sigh* He arrived home from work today with a package for me. Upon opening it, I discovered it was a miniature Operation! game. But instead of all the body cavities being filled with bones and hearts and such? Yes…Polly Pocket Shoes. He says if we practice hard, we can save money by extracting toys from our daughters ourselves.

Somehow I managed not to throw it at him.

Dulcie

From:	Marianne Hausten <desperatemom@nebweb.net>
To:	Dulcie Huckleberry <dulcie@showme.com>
Subject:	The medical facilities in Omaha

Dear Dulcie,

The hospitals in Omaha are FAR superior to those in Springfield. WHY DON'T YOU MOVE BACK TO OMAHA!!! Not to whine, but it's no fun here without you, and there's nobody to listen to me complain about Helene and being bulky and clumsy. And this HEAT! Third trimester during the hottest part of the summer is just TOO unfair. I'm having dreams of running away to the Arctic and living in an igloo with a polar bear and two penguins.

Helene has found a new way to torture me. She holds her breath. If I tell her it's time to put away toys, she fills her lungs with air and clamps her mouth shut. Nothing I do makes any difference. I yell, I plead, I threaten. She just turns blue. I'm so afraid she will pass out that I usually end up compromising with her. Am I pathetic or what? I just hate conflicts! When I saw parents with naughty kids in the grocery store, I always promised myself I'd never have kids like that.

I was going to do it better, smarter. But now, I'm just like THEM. Only my child is prettier. :)

Write me soon, I'm dying up here!

Marianne

From:	Dulcie Huckleberry <dulcie@showme.com>
To:	Marianne Hausten <desperatemom@nebweb.net>
Subject:	**Give it up, dearest.**

You know I'd do anything for you, my friend. But we aren't moving back. I love our new house. I attached a picture of it to this e-mail, so check it out! It was built in 1910, and you know how I adore old houses. Isn't the porch with the pillars just yummy? It's a full two stories plus finished attic.

We're still unpacking boxes, but it's so nice to not be living with Tom's mother and her new husband. Morris and Jeanine are really nice, but they *are* newlyweds. And…well, you can imagine how awkward that is at times. I about keeled over when I went to put in a load of laundry for them a while back and picked up this barely there teddy. Trimmed in marabou, OF COURSE. With sequins, lime green, no less. EEEEEWWWWW! I flung it out of my hand and it landed on the release valve of the hot water heater, hanging there like some dead, furry, radioactive creature. So I grabbed the mop in the corner and used the handle to unhook the thing and deposit it gingerly in the washing machine before adding the rest of their clothes. It gave me nightmares for the entire weekend. You know, I'm not a prude. But there are just some mental images to which NO daughter-in-law should be subjected. And the vision of MIL frolicking around in marabou-trimmed nuclear waste for dear old Morris is one of them!

Tom is enjoying his new job. It's a pretty large company, and this is just a regional office. They have nice benefits and the pay is good. He wishes he had an office, but he's still a cube-dweller like all the rest. At least he's in town, though.

I'm sorry to hear about Helene. You REALLY have to stand up to her. So what if she passes out? As soon as she hits the floor, she'll start breathing again, and then she'll realize you mean business. I know about these things—remember last year when I was trying to get McKenzie to sleep in her own bed? I speak as a scarred veteran of the Mommy vs. Child War. Marianne, darling, please, please, PLEASE grow a backbone!

By the way, penguins do not live in the Arctic. :)

Back to unpacking boxes,
Dulcie

From:	VIM <vivalaveronica@marcelloportraits.com>
To:	Rosalyn Ebberly <prov31woman@home.com>
Subject:	**Your TOTW?**

Howdy, sis,

I just wanted to make a mention of something I been noticing about y'all's little weekly topics. NOBODY PAYS ATTENTION TO THEM! Except maybe Connie. Sometimes.

Now, I may not be the sharpest crayon in the box, but, boy howdy, I know a dud message when I see one. And this week's topic, being good to our husbands…well, that *obviously* struck a chord with the rest of the loopers. Look at all the replies you've been getting…a BIG, FAT GOOSE EGG. What is up with this?

Maybe it's time you tried some different topics. I came to the loop here for some stimulating conversation, but about all I'm getting is stories about what to do when your kid gets stuff stuck up her nose. Sure, that's entertaining as watching my husband try to line dance, but it don't answer my questions none.

Just some friendly, sisterly advice…

Veronica

From:	Rosalyn Ebberly <prov31woman@home.com>
To:	VIM <vivalaveronica@marcelloportraits.com>
Subject:	Re: Your TOTW?

Veronica, dear,

Thank you so much for your *heartfelt* concern for the quality of loop conversation. I'm sure you have only our best interests in mind. However, you have to understand that it takes a lot of experience and wisdom to craft a good weekly topic. My topics are not the problem at all. It's simply that people are terribly busy during the summer, and so naturally responses go down. Everyone has always been very appreciative of my fine facilitating of the TOTW.

Now, if you'll excuse me, I'm off to a GWENCH meeting. We've been hearing rumors that some of the retailers may be trying to thwart our efforts at promoting the boycott on Christmas presents! So typical of those greedy, grasping consumerists! All we're trying to do is promote a spirit of charity and true peace during this special time of year, and all THEY can think about is their bank accounts! The nerve!

All my love,

Rosalyn

"She looks well to the ways of her household, and does not eat the bread of idleness."
Proverbs 31:27 (NASB)

From:	VIM <vivalaveronica@marcelloportraits.com>
To:	Rosalyn Ebberly <prov31woman@home.com>
Subject:	**TOTW?**

<All we're trying to do is promote a spirit of charity and true peace during this special time of year, and all THEY can think about is their bank accounts! The nerve!>

Yeah, I hear that. It's purt near horsefeathers for retailers to try to stay in business so they don't have to go down to the local food pantry themselves just to keep the wolf outta their bellies. Disgraceful!

Anyhoo, no, I'm afraid the "it's summer" excuse has more holes in it than a block of Swiss cheese. I did a search on the Loophole archives, and your response rate to the TOTW is at an average of 37% of the membership each week. And as the membership has grown, your response rate is declining. You got yourself a major rat's nest, there, sweetheart.

VIM

From:	Rosalyn Ebberly <prov31woman@home.com>
To:	VIM <vivalaveronica@marcelloportraits.com>
Subject:	**Re: TOTW?**

Oh, okay, Ms. Statistics, you think you could do better?

"She looks well to the ways of her household, and does not eat the bread of idleness."
Proverbs 31:27 (NASB)

From:	VIM <vivalaveronica@marcelloportraits.com>
To:	Rosalyn Ebberly <prov31woman@home.com>
Subject:	**Re: TOTW?**

It'd be mighty hard to do worse!

From:	Rosalyn Ebberly <prov31woman@home.com>
To:	VIM <vivalaveronica@marcelloportraits.com>
Subject:	**Re: TOTW?**

You've always been so cocky. Let's see you do it. From now until Christmas. Every week. With better response rate than me. I'd like to SEE YOU TRY.
Rosalyn

"She looks well to the ways of her household, and does not eat the bread of idleness."
Proverbs 31:27 (NASB)

From:	VIM <vivalaveronica@marcelloportraits.com>
To:	Rosalyn Ebberly <prov31woman@home.com>
Subject:	**Re: TOTW?**

Oh, a challenge, is it? Well, hot diggedy dog! Let's place a little bet on this. If my average response rate over the next six months is higher than yours compared to last year's rates for each month—as a percentage, to account for increased membership—you have to send me a picture of you sitting on Santa's lap at Christmas. And if my response rate is the same as yours or lower, then…well, I'll let you decide.

How 'bout that?

From:	Rosalyn Ebberly <prov31woman@home.com>
To:	VIM <vivalaveronica@marcelloportraits.com>
Subject:	**Re: TOTW?**

I could NEVER place a bet! You know that. Why are you always trying to persecute me for my beliefs? And you know how I feel about Santa Claus!

"She looks well to the ways of her household, and does not eat the bread of idleness."
Proverbs 31:27 (NASB)

From:	VIM <vivalaveronica@marcelloportraits.com>
To:	Rosalyn Ebberly <prov31woman@home.com>
Subject:	**Oh GOOD GRIEF!**

I have a headache THIS BIG, and it has "Rosalyn Ebberly" written all over it! So don't call it a bet. Call it a contest. You like contests. You like being able to say you won all them important prizes and awards. It don't make no never mind to me.

As far as the Big Man himself, I know...y'all think he's in cahoots with the other guy in the red suit. Tough cookies. If I win, I want you cheesing for the camera on good old St. Nick's lap, and looking like you're enjoying it. I'll put it on my fridge and it will make me feel like I have a normal family after all.

It's either a picture with Santa or posting the world's largest "Happy Holidays" sign in your front yard. What'll it be, sweetheart?

From:	Rosalyn Ebberly <prov31woman@home.com>
To:	VIM <vivalaveronica@marcelloportraits.com>
Subject:	**Re: Oh GOOD GRIEF!**

Okay, fine. Santa, it is. If I win, you have to DROP THAT STUPID, RIDICULOUS, ANNOYING, AND UT-TERLY ABSURD fake accent. Forever. Period.

"She looks well to the ways of her household, and does
not eat the bread of idleness."
Proverbs 31:27 (NASB)

From:	VIM <vivalaveronica@marcelloportraits.com>
To:	Rosalyn Ebberly <prov31woman@home.com>
Subject:	**You're on!**

Little lady, you got yourself a deal. Bring it on, honey.

From:	Rosalyn Ebberly <prov31woman@home.com>
To:	VIM <vivalaveronica@marcelloportraits.com>
Subject:	**Re: You're on!**

Okay. FINE!

"She looks well to the ways of her household, and does
not eat the bread of idleness."
Proverbs 31:27 (NASB)

From:	VIM <vivalaveronica@marcelloportraits.com>
To:	Rosalyn Ebberly <prov31woman@home.com>
Subject:	**Re: You're on!**

FINE!!!

From:	VIM <vivalaveronica@marcelloportraits.com>
To:	SAHM I Am <sahmiam@loophole.com>
Subject:	**[SAHM I AM] TOTW July 18: An Announcement**

Surprise, y'all! It's little old me, beloved kid sister of our revered loop moderator. I'll be handling the TOTW for a while while Rossie dear takes some time off for some sabbaticalizing. Her bulb is burning dim these days and she's about a battery short of a full pack. She's as used up as an empty toilet-paper tube. So wore out, she's air-conditioned undies ready for the ragbag. If she were a carton of milk, her date stamp would be 10–18–1994. Let's summarize it like this—when it comes to freshening up, she's a roomful of wet dog in need of a Glade Plug-n.

So I've offered to be the breath of fresh air under her wings, the balm of Gilead bringing sunshine for her sore eyes, the rock of Gibraltar in the winding path of life, and a cup of cold water to warm her heart and keep her from drowning in her own hectic schedule.

In short, I'll cut to the meat of my tale—the Topic of the Week:

I'm pregnant. What do I need to know?

Ciao,

Veronica Marcello

Sister of the SAHM I Am Loop Moderator

"Signature files are a mindless waste of perfectly good computer bytes."—Veronica Marcello

From:	Rosalyn Ebberly <prov31woman@home.com>
To:	VIM <vivalaveronica@marcelloportraits.com>
Subject:	**GET BACK ONLINE THIS INSTANT!!!!**

WHAT DO YOU MEAN YOU'RE PREGNANT???
AND WHY DIDN'T YOU CALL AND TELL ME
FIRST BEFORE TELLING THE WHOLE LOOP? I
JUST TRIED TO CALL YOU BUT I ONLY GOT
VOICE MAIL. WHEN ARE YOU DUE?

So happy for you!

Rosalyn

From:	Rosalyn Ebberly <prov31woman@home.com>
To:	Connie Lawson <clmo5@home.com>
Subject:	**Ronnie's pregnant?**

And she didn't even discuss it with me first! What was she
THINKING! They've been married less than a year, and
she's got all those other stepkids, who obviously have
MAJOR issues. You can't just go popping buns in the oven
when you've already got half-baked nut bars running around
the house! But what can you expect from Veronica? She's
SO irresponsible. This whole marriage was a bad idea. I give
it three years, tops. And then it's going to fall apart, and she's
going to have some fussy, spoiled kid to support. Well, she'd
better not show up on my doorstep, that's all I have to say
about it. It's just a matter of tough love, plain and simple.
She's made her decisions and will have to live with them, I

guess. What sort of *intelligent* person marries a photographer? I don't care how rich he is. You know, I bet she got a prenup. That's the world for you, always trying to keep an escape-hatch open in a marriage. But it would have been more responsible not to bring a baby into the mess.

Sometimes, I don't know why I even try with her....
Rosalyn

"She looks well to the ways of her household, and does not eat the bread of idleness."
Proverbs 31:27 (NASB)

From:	Connie Lawson <clmo5@home.com>
To:	Rosalyn Ebberly <prov31woman@home.com>
Subject:	Re: Ronnie's pregnant?

Because you are a loving, compassionate big sister. You just keep showing her the love of Jesus, like you have been. Someday, when her dark world falls apart, you'll be there to shine the light of the Lord and show her the way home. We'll just have to pray that she reaches bottom soon, so she has nowhere to turn but heavenward.

Hey, Kurt and I want to know if you and Chad can come over for a game night Friday?
Connie
SAHM I Am Loop Mom

From:	Rosalyn Ebberly <prov31woman@home.com>
To:	SAHM I Am <sahmiam@loophole.com>
Subject:	**Re: [SAHM I AM] TOTW July 18: An Announcement**

I wanted to publicly thank my dearest sister for sharing with you all those excellent samples of similes and mixed metaphors. It was actually an example we came up with to help those of you who are homeschooling introduce figure of speech to your children. I thought it was a *hilarious* way to do it.

As far as the TOTW, we thought it would be fun to surprise all of you with Veronica's wonderful news! I'm sure she'll give more details SOON, since the rest of you are probably dying of curiosity to know the particulars. Like when she is due, and how she is feeling. You know, things that I as her sister would naturally be told, but that she might not think to mention to the entire loop.

As for what Veronica needs to know? I would say don't be expecting a Gerber baby, dear Sis. Mother says that when Veronica was born, she looked JUST like Yoda, from *Star Wars*. Needless to say, we have few baby pictures of dear Ronnie.

Love,

Rosalyn Ebberly

SAHM I Am Loop Moderator

> "She looks well to the ways of her household, and does not eat the bread of idleness."
> Proverbs 31:27 (NASB)

From:	VIM <vivalaveronica@marcelloportraits.com>
To:	Rosalyn Ebberly <prov31woman@home.com>
Subject:	**Re: [SAHM I AM] TOTW July 18: An Announcement**

At least *I* outgrew *my* ugly phase....

From:	Rosalyn Ebberly <prov31woman@home.com>
To:	VIM <vivalaveronica@marcelloportraits.com>
Subject:	**Re: [SAHM I AM] TOTW July 18: An Announcement**

You did? When? :) LOL!

Seriously, if you ever pull a stunt like those cheesy metaphors again on the loop, so help me... I promise I will nominate you for *What Not To Wear!* Just think...you in the 360 degree mirror on national television with Stacy and Clinton systematically trashing your "I wish I were still a college cheerleader" wardrobe. It'd be a huge hit.

And you'd better be thankful that I'm not the type to be bitter or vengeful. How could you tell the whole loop about your pregnancy without telling me first?

Rosalyn

"She looks well to the ways of her household, and does not eat the bread of idleness."
Proverbs 31:27 (NASB)

From:	VIM <vivalaveronica@marcelloportraits.com>
To:	Rosalyn Ebberly <prov31woman@home.com>
Subject:	**Re: [SAHM I AM] TOTW July 18: An Announcement**

You're a fine one to talk about fashion, Ros. Any woman that sews matching sailor jumpers for herself and her seven-year-old-daughter—and wears them in public—needs good ol' Stacy and Clinton MUCH more than I do!

And sorry you got your shorts in a knot about my little bit of news. Wasn't trying to leave you out. I had the e-mail ready except for the TOTW question itself when we got back from the doctor's. I just plumb got myself all in a dither and sent out the loop mail without thinking about anything else. No offense meant.

Anyways, I figure y'all and Connie probably had a good jaw about how I'm so unfit to be pregnant so soon after getting hitched. If I'd a told you first, you woulda had to wait on that—unless you told Connie against my wishes. I KNOW you'd NEVER do anything like that. So I was just looking out for you, sis, like I always do. There ya go.
Veronica

From:	VIM <vivalaveronica@marcelloportraits.com>
To:	SAHM I Am <sahmiam@loophole.com>
Subject:	**[SAHM I AM] My TOTW reply**

Dear y'all loopers,
Okey-dokey, here's the particulars about the new Marcello

baby. It was quite a shock because I'm already three months along and didn't realize what was going on. Of course, Aunt Flo ain't been to our house for a few months, but that's not much unusual for me. Been hungry as a baby bird, but no weird cravings yet. I've been a mite on the upchucking side for a few weeks, but I figured it weren't nothing but a flu bug or something. Never did occur to me to take a pregnancy test....

Anyway, I'm excited, but about as nervous as a long-tailed cat in a room full of rocking chairs. Being the baby of the family myself, I never was around younger kids much. But I figure I got six months for y'all to learn me what I need to know.

Off to dinner now to celebrate,
Veronica Marcello

From:	VIM <vivalaveronica@marcelloportraits.com>
To:	SAHM I Am <sahmiam@loophole.com>
Subject:	**[SAHM I AM] Whoops!**

I plumb forgot to tell y'all the details about my little announcement! Junior, or Juniorette, will be making an appearance around January 18. The doctor says everything looks just dandy, and I'm feeling right as rain. Frank and I are both tickled pink 'bout the whole shebang. We got outside the doctor's office and were whooping and hollering like cowboys at a roundup. Well, make that one cowgirl, and a cowboy from Venice…he rattled off in Italian for several minutes before I could actually understand a single word again.

Thank you all from the bottom of my heart for your kind

words and congratulations. I'm much obliged. So glad to be able to share this with you all.

Hugs to y'all,

Veronica

From:	Marianne Hausten <desperatemom@nebweb.net>
To:	SAHM I Am <sahmiam@loophole.com>
Subject:	Re: [SAHM I AM] TOTW July 18: An Announcement

Congratulations, Veronica! Your story made me think about how we found out we were expecting Helene. We were trying to get pregnant, and I'd been waiting anxiously for the earliest day I could take the pregnancy test. When I got the two blue lines, I could hardly believe it. So I went to the store and bought eight more tests, and spent the rest of the day drinking lots of water so I could use up all the tests. On the very last one, I only got one blue line, and was so upset that I called the company's customer service line in tears. The woman I spoke with listened very politely to me and then pointed out that because of my excessive water drinking that day, I probably had diluted the hormones to the point where they weren't registering on the test anymore. She said that if eight other tests had shown positive, more than likely I should trust the results.

Then when Brandon came home, I showed him all the tests, and his response was "You took EIGHT pregnancy tests?"

"Well, nine, including the one I already had..." I was very

nervous that he was angry. After all, those tests aren't cheap. But he just laughed, and then insisted on seeing all of them...except the negative one. He told me to burn that one. He was so happy. Of course, that was before we had really gotten acquainted with Helene... I'm sort of mostly just kidding...

As far as what you need to know? PREGNANCY STINKS, Veronica! It just does. It's a horrible, nasty experience that will leave you stretched out like an old pair of panty hose. Your complexion will be ruined, you'll get cavities in your teeth, and soon you'll be sporting a fine set of varicose veins in your previously youthful-looking legs. After the "cute widdle baby" is born, your hair will fall out and you'll spend the next two years trying to make your body remember its pre-baby shape.

All right, time to go take a nap. Computer screens make me tired. Everything makes me tired. No, *motherhood* makes me tired.... Oh, Lord, won't You *please* make this baby come soon?

Marianne Hausten, the Human Manatee

Due Date: 21 days, 4 hours, 16 minutes, and...38 seconds

From:	VIM <vivalaveronica@marcelloportraits.com>
To:	SAHM I Am <sahmiam@loophole.com>
Subject:	Re: [SAHM I AM] TOTW July 18: An Announcement

Somebody tell me she's joking. PLEASE!

VIM

From:	Dulcie Huckleberry <dulcie@showme.com>
To:	SAHM I Am <sahmiam@loophole.com>
Subject:	Re: [SAHM I AM] TOTW July 18: An Announcement

It's okay, Veronica. Marianne gets like this when she's pregnant. Today is a good day, actually. You should see her on a bad day.
Dulcie

From:	VIM <vivalaveronica@marcelloportraits.com>
To:	SAHM I Am <sahmiam@loophole.com>
Subject:	Re: [SAHM I AM] TOTW July 18: An Announcement

A GOOD day??? AAAAAAAAAAAAAAAAAAAIIIIIIIII-IIIIIIIIEEEEEEEEEEEEE!!!

From:	The Millards <jstcea4jesus@familymail.net>
To:	SAHM I Am <sahmiam@loophole.com>
Subject:	Re: [SAHM I AM] TOTW July 18: An Announcement

Veronica, here's what you need to know—CHILDREN ARE ANNOYING, IRRITATING, CONNIVING, IR-RESPONSIBLE LITTLE TWITS! And we mothers are weak, spineless creatures that can't help loving them anyway, even though they are experts at driving us insane. Case in point:

While I was in the shower, Tyler glued model car pieces to my dining table with superglue. Granted, it was unintentional, except for the part where HE CHOSE TO USE THE TABLE IN THE FIRST PLACE! The finish is ruined!

After watching *Finding Nemo* for at least the hundredth time, Cassia has flushed all our fish down the toilet because "all drains lead to the sea" and it just wasn't fair that our fishies weren't free. Do you think I could sue Disney for the cost of replacing the fish??? Poor critters....

Evelyn has another cold, so now there is an entire box of Kleenex strewn around the house. Every tissue has been blown in...once.

Audra is potty training, and pooped in her pull-ups. Decided to be a big girl about it and take care of it herself. I now have an entire bathroom and part of a hallway to clean. Not to mention the "big girl" herself....

And then I turn on the radio and the Christian station has some talk show featuring this supermom, Ms. Perfect Author who is waxing sentimental about the joys and virtues of motherhood. I can't take it anymore! It's either vent on my fellow SAHMs or...draw mustaches, goatees and horns on all the pictures of my children. I choose to vent on you, you lucky people.

Jocelyn

From:	VIM <vivalaveronica@marcelloportraits.com>
To:	SAHM I Am <sahmiam@loophole.com>
Subject:	**Re: [SAHM I AM] TOTW July 18: An Announcement**

Okay, y'all…'fess up. Y'all are just trying to yank poor Ronnie Irene's leg here, right? With all that funning about losing my hair and how irritating kids are. I mean, I got me three kids already from Frank's first marriage. They ain't so bad…

mostly…I mean, there *are* times…lots of times…at least several each day, actually…

THUNDER and TARNATION, y'all are 100% on the money! What have I done? I'm SOOOOOO toast!

Ronnie Irene crouches in a corner, whimpering
VIM

From:	Connie Lawson <clmo5@home.com>
To:	SAHM I Am <sahmiam@loophole.com>
Subject:	**[SAHM I AM] My new business!**

Dear SAHMs,

I wanted you all to be the first to know that I have made an important decision. Now that my kiddos are all past babyhood, I've decided to give up being a SAHM. No, I'm NOT going to go back to work! I'm going to be a WAHM—WORK At Home Mom. Isn't that great?

I know some of you already have a cottage industry of

some sort, and I would love to do some professional net-working with you. I've decided to do a home-party busi-ness. I've narrowed it down to two: Kerrie May cosmetics, or Gadgets for Gals. You all know Kerrie May, I'm assum-ing. But you may not be familiar with Gadgets for Gals. This is the only company that makes household tools sized and weighted for a woman's hand. There's hammers and screw-drivers, tape measures, ice scrapers, paintbrushes, you name it—all ergonomically designed and created with the female in mind. Everything even comes in beautiful designer col-ors like Raspberry Mocha and Tangerine Fluff!

The problem is, I am having a hard time choosing be-tween these two companies. I love the products in each line, and the programs both have positive aspects to them. Are any of you current consultants with either company? If so, PLEASE e-mail me and tell me what you think!

Thanks,

Connie Lawson

SAHM I Am Loop Mom

From:	Zelia Muzuwa <zeemuzu@vivacious.com>
To:	SAHM I Am <sahmiam@loophole.com>
Subject:	Re: [SAHM I AM] My new business!

Raspberry Mocha and Tangerine Fluff??? Connie, are you sure these aren't *edible* tools?

Z

From:	Brenna L. <saywhat@writeme.com>
To:	Sharla Trippit <sharla@highlightadoptions.org>
Subject:	The Gillmans

Dear Sharla,

Thanks so much for the info packet about the Gillmans. We are really interested in them. But I do have to wonder why they picked us. I mean, I'm a teen-mom married to a farmer. When I read that Tess is a reporter for their local news station and Pat is a pharmacist, I really had to question what they saw in us. Well, not that we'd be bad parents or anything. We're great parents. Madeline is very happy and well-adjusted. I don't want anybody to think that just because we live on a farm, she's deprived at all. In fact, farm life is typically very wholesome.

But do you think it will be a problem that they're vegetarians and we're not? We try to eat healthy, but we do believe in eating meat. After all, Darren's family raises cattle and if we didn't eat any meat at all, that would be a huge insult to them. They do know that we eat meat, right? I hope that's not a problem. If it was, we could try to talk about it and come to a compromise. Maybe meat just once a week, to keep up appearances with Darren's family or something. Don't think we're inflexible. We're VERY willing to compromise.

Their little boys look so cute! Darren and I would just love having a boy. But we'll be happy with whatever we have. I don't want you to think we're picky or anything. I mean, we'll love any child that God gives us. I should say, "children" because I know we might end up with multiples. And that's TOTALLY okay. We can handle that. We don't believe in selective reduction at all.

Maybe we should just become vegetarian. I wouldn't want them to think that we care more about what Darren's family thinks than we do about the health of their children. Or...our children, I guess. We totally think of them as ours. Or we will. If we end up adopting the embryos. And Darren and I are both completely committed to providing a good education to our children. I don't want the Gillmans to think that just because neither of us has a four-year degree that we don't think education is important. We will make sure our kids go to college. I'm sure they'll be really smart. Not that we wouldn't love them even if they aren't. We don't care about smarts at all. Well, we do, but not that much. I mean, it IS important, but so are other things in life, too. Does that make sense?

Okay, so what do we do next? Are you SURE they want us? You didn't get us mixed up with some other family? Not that you would do that. I'm not trying to imply that you are incompetent or anything. But it never hurts to double-check.

Thanks,
Brenna Lindberg

From:	Sharla Trippit <sharla@highlightadoptions.org>
To:	Brenna L. <saywhat@writeme.com>
Subject:	**Re: The Gillmans**

Dear Brenna,
RELAX! :) I'm glad you and Darren are pleased with the

info on the Gillmans. I assure you there is no mistake. They really loved your profile and are very interested in working with you on the embryo adoption.

Being nonvegetarians will not be an issue for them. If it was, they would have said so. They understand that their embryos will be raised in a family that may choose a different lifestyle from theirs. That's part of the counseling they go through before making the decision to place their embryos for adoption.

All you and Darren need to do is be yourself. Your level of education and your professions are perfectly acceptable to Tess and Pat or they would not have chosen you. The Gillmans are a lovely family, and I think you will enjoy partnering with them. Would you like me to ask Tess if you could e-mail her? Many of our adoptive clients find it helpful to chat directly with the genetic family. Some of them go on to form lasting friendships.

If you decide that you are comfortable being matched with the Gillmans, go ahead and fill out the paperwork and get it back to me. Feel free to e-mail or call me with ANY questions you or Darren have. That's what I'm here for.

Sincerely,

Sharla Trippit

Snowflakes Frozen Embryo Adoption Program

From:	P. Lorimer <phyllis.lorimer@joono.com>
To:	SAHM I Am <sahmiam@loophole.com>
Subject:	**[SAHM I AM] I am NOT pleased.**

Hi, ladies,

First of all, congratulations, Veronica! I'm so happy for you. Don't let Marianne, Jocelyn and Dulcie frighten you. And girls, stop it—haven't you ever heard that "Ignorance is bliss"?

Now, why I am not pleased: Some of you know that when my husband and I moved to NY this summer, it was mostly because of a pastoring position for Jonathan. However, I also had hopes of attending graduate school to get a Ph.D. in History. I *thought* my husband was supportive of this. But now, it seems he's had a change of heart. I brought up the subject this evening, and his response?

"Honey, you know I want you to get your degree. But I just don't think now is a good time. The kids are so young, and I really need you to help out around the church…" And so on.

I admit, I lost my temper and we ended up in a pretty heated discussion. But this really blindsided me. Two months ago, he was all for it. And now that he faces the reality of it, that support evaporates. I feel betrayed. I have given up so much for his dreams! I've put my own life goals on hold to care for our children and to be the "good pastor's wife." And when I ask for the one thing I really want in return, he finds it too "inconvenient" to suit him.

And I feel sad. Tonight is the first time in our married life that I don't really feel like sharing a bed with him. It makes me lonely to think about it, but that's the truth.

See…pastor's wives really aren't perfect.

Phyllis Lorimer

From:	Zelia Muzuwa <zeemuzu@vivacious.com>
To:	P. Lorimer <phyllis.lorimer@joono.com>
Subject:	Sleeping on the couch

Hey, friend. I'm so sorry to hear you're hurting right now. Trust me, I understand—Tristan and I have knockdown, drag-out arguments on a pretty regular basis. Jonathan sounds like he can be every bit as hardheaded as my own DH. Can I encourage you and give you just a little advice? Don't stay mad. He's really not the enemy. Once you both cool off a bit, try to talk about the issues he brought up and see if you can find any solutions. Work together. I know that man loves you to pieces. And I know God gave you the dream and the ability to go back to school. He will make it happen.

Hugs and kisses,

Z

From:	Dulcie Huckleberry <dulcie@showme.com>
To:	SAHM I Am <sahmiam@loophole.com>
Subject:	[SAHM I AM] A week of surprises!

Both good and bad ones, apparently. Well, I'm afraid I have to add one to the "bad" column. Tom came home from work today and told me his company lost a major contract and is having to cut back its budget. So they're sending his whole department to India. He and all the other programmers are being let go, as of next week.

I've never seen him so low, ever. We're both stunned. I

don't know what we're going to do. It doesn't seem like there's very much in the way of programming jobs around here, and the job market is terrible anyway. INDIA! How could they do that to us? How can the government let companies take away its citizens' jobs and send them overseas? I'm so mad, I'd like to slap a senator. Or maybe even the President. Definitely the company CEO.

We can't go back to Omaha. No money. It's all in the house we just bought. On which we have to make payments starting next month. Oh, you guys, I'm starting to feel sick to my stomach just thinking about it! I don't know what we're going to do! I'm trying not to freak out, for the girls' sakes, and so I don't make Tom feel worse than he already does. But I feel all shaky inside. I'm scared. Really, really scared. Why would God let this happen to us? I thought He brought us here for a reason.

We could use your prayers…thanks.

Dulcie

From:	Rosalyn Ebberly <prov31woman@home.com>
To:	SAHM I Am <sahmiam@loophole.com>
Subject:	**Re: [SAHM I AM] A week of surprises!**

Dear Dulcie,

I'm so sorry to hear your husband has lost his job. It's probably a sign from the Lord that you weren't supposed to move to Missouri in the first place. You know, it really was a very irresponsible thing to do, especially in this sort of job market. My heart just goes out to you! I was sure something like this was bound to happen after you being so flighty!

But, really, slapping the President? How could you even joke about such a thing? After all, he is the Lord's Anointed. And it's not his fault the company sent jobs off to India. In fact, it's probably the hand of God, because think about all those destitute people living in India who will now have jobs. What would you rather see—our government become completely corrupted by trying to suppress capitalism?

This is the problem with our liberal media—it's taught us to rely on the government to solve all our problems. Tom just needs to shake it off and go apply for another job. It's America—there's tons of opportunity for someone willing to work hard enough.

All my sympathy,

Rosalyn

"She looks well to the ways of her household, and does not eat the bread of idleness."
Proverbs 31:27 (NASB)

From:	Dulcie Huckleberry <dulcie@showme.com>
To:	"Green Eggs and Ham"
Subject:	**Rosalyn**

Okay, now I'd like to slap HER! Owwww...I just kicked my office door. It's solid antique oak. About as hard as Rossie's heart.

Dulcie

From:	Brenna L. <saywhat@writeme.com>
To:	"Green Eggs and Ham"
Subject:	**Re: Rosalyn**

Dulcie, I'm so sorry. I know I can speak for all of us when I say we'll be praying for you. If you need anything, just holler. We still have the extra house on the farm, if you end up needing a place to go.

Brenna

From:	Zelia Muzuwa <zeemuzu@vivacious.com>
To:	"Green Eggs and Ham"
Subject:	**Re: Rosalyn**

Hear, hear! Brenna's right. It's going to be okay, Dulcie. We're all in it together.

Z

From:	Dulcie Huckleberry <dulcie@showme.com>
To:	"Green Eggs and Ham"
Subject:	**Thanks**

You all are amazing. You make me cry…or that might be the toe I bruised.

Dulcie

From:	VIM <vivalaveronica@marcelloportraits.com>
To:	Rosalyn Ebberly <prov31woman@home.com>
Subject:	**Response Rate for Week of July 18**

Rosalyn's response for week of July 19, last year: 32.29%

Veronica's response for week of July 18, THIS year: 33.46%

Nothing like a good start, I'd say. :)

Ho, ho, ho…. Merry Christmas!

VIM

From:	Rosalyn Ebberly <prov31woman@home.com>
To:	VIM <vivalaveronica@marcelloportraits.com>
Subject:	**Good grief.**

One percentage point? You're "ho-ho-ing" over a measly one percent? I think that's a pretty poor showing for someone who thinks she can do such a better job. Pardon me if I can't restrain a big Y…A…W…N….

Rosalyn

"She looks well to the ways of her household, and does not eat the bread of idleness."

Proverbs 31:27 (NASB)

From:	VIM <vivalaveronica@marcelloportraits.com>
To:	SAHM I Am <sahmiam@loophole.com>
Subject:	**[SAHM I AM] TOTW August 1: Cravings**

Sorry, y'all!

I got me yet another rascally old pregnancy question for you. What was the weirdest craving you had when you were pregnant?

I'm asking because my DH thinks there's something mighty wrong with me, just because right now the thought of Brussels sprouts smothered in caramel sauce has me hot enough to howl. Why can't he just let me enjoy it all by my lonesome instead of cracking jokes? It's not like I'm going to share with him anyway!

Yee-haw, my sweet, sticky little heads of baby lettuce... come to Mama!

Off to fix me another bowl,

Veronica Marcello

From:	Marianne Hausten <desperatemom@nebweb.net>
To:	SAHM I Am <sahmiam@loophole.com>
Subject:	**Re: [SAHM I AM] TOTW August 1: Cravings**

OREO COOKIES DIPPED IN RANCH DRESSING!!!
Enough said.

From:	Zelia Muzuwa <zeemuzu@vivacious.com>
To:	SAHM I Am <sahmiam@loophole.com>
Subject:	**Re: [SAHM I AM] TOTW August 1: Cravings**

Ewwww! You guys are weird! I only had cravings with Cosette.

Corn nuts. Bags and bags of them.

Tristan bought me a whole case one time which I ate in two and a half days, and my breath smelled so bad, Tristan couldn't bear to come within two feet of me so he refused to get any more; and I had to resort to begging friends to smuggle me some during the day and then, before Tristan came home, brushing my teeth like three times and gargling with mouthwash which made me so sick to my stomach that I threw up, which meant I had to go through the whole process again, so finally I just told Tristan he'd have to put up and shut up. :)

Z

From:	P. Lorimer <phyllis.lorimer@joono.com>
To:	Zelia Muzuwa <zeemuzu@vivacious.com>
Subject:	**Re: [SAHM I AM] TOTW August 1: Cravings**

Zelia,

That's QUITE the sentence you've constructed there. It's even grammatically correct. I am thoroughly impressed.

Love,

Phyllis

From:	Dulcie Huckleberry <dulcie@showme.com>
To:	SAHM I Am <sahmiam@loophole.com>
Subject:	**Re: [SAHM I AM] TOTW August 1: Cravings**

Cravings with McKenzie: None.
Cravings with twins Aidan and Haley: Limburger cheese on cinnamon-raisin bread toast.

From:	J. Huckleberry <ilovebranson@branson.com>
To:	Dulcie Huckleberry <dulcie@showme.com>, Thomas Huckleberry <t.huckleberry@showme.com>
Subject:	**The Job Thing**

Dear kiddos,

I was just sitting here thinking about you both and the TRAGIC position you find yourselves in, and I just started to CRY! I feel completely horrible about it and so does Morris. After all, we helped Tom find that job, and it makes me so mad that they had the gall to send all those jobs overseas when people need them right here in the U.S.

But don't worry. I'm going to talk to Mr. Tabuchi himself and see if he could find you a job with the theater in Branson! If not, he has connections with all the other performers in Branson. I'm sure he can find something for you. And he was SO nice about letting us have our wedding in his theater. I just couldn't ask for a better boss!

Just a couple questions—Tom, does it HAVE to be a programming job? You know, you could always brush up on your dancing skills. I'm sure you could get a performing job somewhere. In fact, I think I still have that video we made of you in dance class in junior high. Don't you remember? You were SO CUTE in those little blue tights and that black leotard. Though I don't know the reason you insisted on wearing a T-shirt over it. Why you went into programming instead, I'll never understand. You showed such potential!

And, Dulcie, you could get a job, too. You could help with set design, I'm sure. I'd even be willing to cut back on my hours and watch the kids for you. They'd LOVE spending time with Gammie Jeanine, I just know it! We could play dress up—I got the most adorable little nighties and robes for the wedding. They could wear those with my sparkly high-heeled sandals, and we could wear lipstick, and eye shadow and lots of perfume and beads, and then we could all pretend we were going out for the evening to see a show. We would have the best time!

Don't you two worry for a minute about any money stuff. If you have to sell your house, you can ALWAYS move back in with us. We just LOVED having you around. We're going to help you in any way we can. So DON'T WORRY!
Love and hugs and kisses,
Mom Jeanine

From:	Dulcie Huckleberry <dulcie@showme.com>
To:	"Green Eggs and Ham"
Subject:	**My Mother-In-Law**

Great. She wants us to LIVE with them. And for Tom to wear a tutu. And she wants to dress my children up like little Jean Benet-Ramseys. All while I'm designing sets for Shoji Tabuchi and can't keep an eye on her. Methinks it's some sort of plot. Revenge, perhaps, for the food fight Tom and I had at her wedding reception....

Dulcie

From:	Dulcie Huckleberry <dulcie@showme.com>
To:	"Green Eggs and Ham"
Subject:	**We're still alive...**

Tom's been unemployed for a couple of weeks, and we are still alive! I still feel like I'm starting to hyperventilate every time I think about the bills coming due, but at least it isn't making me cry. At least not EVERY time. Thanks so much for all your e-mails and prayers. I can really feel the support and I know it's helping.

There are NO programming jobs here right now. None at all. Tom is thinking about applying in Kansas City, since some of the clients of his former company are there. But then we're back to having him gone all the time again. Only this time, I'd be stuck in a town I barely even know. Marianne, I WANNA GO HOME!!! I wish with all my heart we could, but at this point I don't know for sure that we'll have grocery money next week, much less money for yet another move. If only this had happened before we bought the house....

The thing I'm most concerned about is Tom. He is really

depressed. I think he is wondering if he made a mistake by taking the job here, and doubting if he really heard God correctly. We were so sure God wanted us to do this. But I just don't see how He would want us to be stranded here in financial ruin.

I'm seriously thinking about going back to work. I found a job opening for an interior design associate at a firm here in Springfield. I have mixed feelings—I hate the thought of leaving the girls, even though Tom can watch them. But I also am feeling a bit desperate about our joblessness. We don't have ANY cushion to fall back on. We have to do something. And this is a "something" I can do. What do you all think?

Please pray for us. I'm hoping we won't have to turn the Internet off, but if we do, I'll try to let you know in advance. Hoping for a miracle,
Dulcie

From:	Zelia Muzuwa <zeemuzu@vivacious.com>
To:	"Green Eggs and Ham"
Subject:	**Formal Declaration of Objection**

WE, the undersigned, being known henceforth and hereafter as the e-mail alias and subgroup of the SAHM I Am e-mail loop "Green Eggs and Ham" thusly comprised of the members jointly listed below in electronic attachment 46 C appendix iv, section 1, subsection a, point 2.6, do hereby affix signatures duly noted and confirmed to petition and formally register objection to the employment plans of Green Eggs and Ham affiliate, Dulcie Huckleberry, by reason of said employment opportunity provoking unprovoked and unwarranted pain and suffering upon remaining members of group, creating undue hardship for the relational stability of group, and the general consensus among group members that such a decision is ill-advised and premature given the duration of spousal unemployment. Green Eggs and Ham, therefore, to wit, and wherein, do submit this petition and request that Ms. Huckleberry immediately and hereafter abrogate any and all attempts to identify, secure, or maintain employment outside location of domicile.

From:	Dulcie Huckleberry <dulcie@showme.com>
To:	"Green Eggs and Ham"
Subject:	**Huh?**

Z, darling, all that red tape and legal documents for the adoption must be affectiong your brain. What are you talking about?

From:	Brenna L. <saywhat@writeme.com>
To:	"Green Eggs and Ham"
Subject:	**Re: Huh?**

SHE MEANS DON'T YOU DARE EVEN THINK ABOUT GETTING A JOB BECAUSE WE DON'T KNOW HOW WE WILL SURVIVE SAHM-HOOD WITHOUT YOU!

Z, see? I *told* you the legalese would be a bad idea…

From:	P. Lorimer <phyllis.lorimer@joono.com>
To:	"Green Eggs and Ham"
Subject:	Re: Huh?

We're just teasing you, Dulcie. If you need to get a job, go for it! I, for one, will be somewhat jealous. But as long as you don't abandon us entirely, I am sure I will recover.

I've been asked to take on a job, actually. A *volunteer* job, that is. The church wants me to be in charge of adult education. Jonathan thinks I should accept. It was his idea. I am not sure how to tell him or the board that the only adult education I'm interested in is my own. That sounds so self-serving. But it's the truth. I've wanted a Ph.D. since I was in high school, and instead I will be trapped into organizing Sunday school curriculum for senior citizens and planning hog roasts for middle-aged couples who have forgotten how to have fun together without their preadolescent children in tow. Not that I'm feeling sorry for myself or anything....
Phyllis

From:	Dulcie Huckleberry <dulcie@showme.com>
To:	"Green Eggs and Ham"
Subject:	Re: Huh?

Thanks, girls...I think. I'm going to send in my application. Tom agrees that it is probably the best shot we have at this point. He says he doesn't mind watching the kids if I get the

job. I told him he can check in here if he needs entertainment. He said no thanks, because Z scares him. :)
Love you,
Dulcie

From:	Zelia Muzuwa <zeemuzu@vivacious.com>
To:	"Green Eggs and Ham"
Subject:	**Re: Huh?**

<I told him he can check in here if he needs entertainment. He said no thanks, because Z scares him. :)>

WHAT? Me? Scary? Tell Tom, "Be not afraid of greatness." —Twelfth Night, Act II, Scene 5. I really don't bite. Often.
Z

From:	Brenna L. <saywhat@writeme.com>
To:	"Green Eggs and Ham"
Subject:	**I can do this!**

Hey, gals,
I'm just about to push the send button on what could be the most important e-mail of my life. I'm writing to Tess and Pat Gillman, our potential genetic family for the embryo adoption. They have two little boys, Colin and Chase. They live in New Mexico, and Tess is a TV news reporter, and Pat is a pharmacist. Oh, and guess what? They're VEGE-TARIANS! I still don't know why they chose us. We're not

anything like them. But I'm not complaining! I'm just nervous. And stalling.

Brenna

From:	Zelia Muzuwa <zeemuzu@vivacious.com>
To:	Brenna L. <saywhat@writeme.com>
Subject:	**Do it! Do it!**

Push that little send button, Brenna! You can do it! I felt the same way when I stood in front of the mailbox trying to work up courage to drop in our adoption paperwork. But Tess is going to love hearing from you, so you just go right ahead and PUSH THAT BUTTON! :)

Z

From:	Brenna L. <saywhat@writeme.com>
To:	Tess Gillman <tessty@newmeximail.com
Subject:	**Hello from Brenna**

Dear Tess,

This is Brenna Lindberg, who you are going to be letting adopt your embryos. I hope it's okay to e-mail you. Sharla at Nightlight said it was, and I was going to e-mail sooner but…okay, frankly, I was too nervous.

I just want to let you know how very grateful Darren and I are that you and Pat chose us. We're going to do everything we can to make this a success, and then raise these children the best way we can. You have no idea how much this means to us.

I don't really know what else to say, except that if you have any questions about us, feel free to ask. I'm sorry we aren't vegetarian. If you want us to be, we can talk about it.

Thank you again,

Brenna Lindberg

From:	Connie Lawson <clmo5@home.com>
To:	SAHM I Am <sahmiam@loophole.com>
Subject:	**Re: [SAHM I AM] TOTW August 1: Cravings**

Pregnancy Cravings! Oh, what a FUN topic, Veronica! During my last pregnancy with Rebecca, I could NOT get enough of this certain recipe. I forgot who gave it to me, but it was strange, to say the least. It was fish fillets—halibut or something like that, dipped in apple cider vinegar and then rolled in a spice combination of nutmeg, basil and dill weed, then baked and drizzled with a raspberry-prune juice glaze.

It's funny—that would probably make me ill now, but at the time, I thought it tasted wonderful! LOL!

Hope your pregnancy is progressing well!

Connie Lawson

SAHM I Am Loop Mom

From:	Rosalyn Ebberly <prov31woman@home.com>
To:	Connie Lawson <clmo5@home.com>
Subject:	Re: [SAHM I AM] TOTW August 1: Cravings

Connie, I GAVE YOU THAT RECIPE! It was my award-winning Halibut with Raspberry Glacé that appeared in the *Egregious Gourmet* four years ago! It would never make anybody sick!

And furthermore, HOW COULD YOU respond to my sister's topic of the week? Don't you know that every response puts me closer to having to sit on Santa's lap? *shudder* I feel like you've stabbed me in the back! Friends don't sell out like that, no matter how good the topic is. NOT that this was a good topic, mind you!!!
Rosalyn

"She looks well to the ways of her household, and does not eat the bread of idleness."
Proverbs 31:27 (NASB)

From:	VIM <vivalaveronica@marcelloportraits.com>
To:	SAHM I Am <sahmiam@loophole.com>
Subject:	[SAHM I AM] Have mercy!

Y'all's disgusting cravings are enough to make my stomach do a triple axel on the edge of the Grand Canyon! Come on, now, ya sure you didn't make them all up just to be funnin' poor Ronnie here? Anyhoo, thanks for sharing. At least now I know it's not ME who's a Coke can shy of a six-pack.

Pepto, anyone?

Veronica

From:	Tess Gillman <tessty@newmeximail.com
To:	Brenna L. <saywhat@writeme.com>
Subject:	**Re: Hello from Brenna**

Brenna,

It's so good to hear from you! Please don't feel nervous about e-mailing me. I would like us to get acquainted, if you are comfortable with that. And don't worry about the vegetarian thing. That's just the way Pat was raised, and we've basically stuck with it to avoid offending his family. Every once in a while, I get a huge longing for a nice, thick steak, so I go out to eat with girlfriends who won't tell Pat! Though I think he suspects. :)

Pat and I are very excited about this adoption. When we saw your info packet and read about your family, we both knew this was "IT." I hope this doesn't freak you out, but when I saw your picture, I just started to cry. There was a huge emotional connection, at least for me. Our lifestyles and backgrounds are very different, but I think we see in the two of you the same commitment to each other, to raising a family, the same love for God and the same values as we have. And it sounds as though even our personalities are somewhat alike! We were so excited to find another couple that seems so compatible with us. I am hoping in time we can be friends, if you two are agreeable to it.

I just want you to know that I am available if you have any questions about the IVF part of the process. It can be an emotional roller coaster, and physically, it's not the most fun thing you'll ever get to do. But I hope you will find that it is worth it in the end.

Many blessings, and please e-mail me again soon,

Tess Gillman

From:	VIM <vivalaveronica@marcelloportraits.com>
To:	Rosalyn Ebberly <prov31woman@home.com>
Subject:	**Weekly Report**

Rosalyn, Week of August 2, last year: 32.41%

Veronica, Week of August 1, this year: 29.00%

I gotta admit, sis, I'm completely hornswoggled. Thought for sure I got more responses than that. Sure enough seemed to me like a doozy of replies. But your TOTW last year on self-esteem must of hit a nerve. However, our little contest is based on the average response rate between now and Christmas, so don't be getting too big for those britches yet, ya hear?

Y'all be sweet now,

Ronnie

From:	Rosalyn Ebberly <prov31woman@home.com>
To:	VIM <vivalaveronica@marcelloportraits.com>
Subject:	Re: Weekly Report

You're being very gracious, Ronnie. I think you will find that it will not be as simple as you think. As I told you weeks ago, crafting a good TOTW takes skill and practice. Just because you had a couple of unusually responsive weeks doesn't mean that you'll be able to sustain that pace indefinitely. I would highly recommend you purchase a copy of *English Grammar For Dummies,* BECAUSE YOU WILL MOST CERTAINLY BE NEEDING IT! You and your rednecked facade are going DOWN, DOWN, DOWN!
In Christ's love,
Rosalyn

"She looks well to the ways of her household, and does not eat the bread of idleness."
Proverbs 31:27 (NASB)

From:	VIM <vivalaveronica@marcelloportraits.com>
To:	SAHM I Am <sahmiam@loophole.com>
Subject:	[SAHM I AM] TOTW August 8: Sibling Rivalry, anyone?

Dear SAHM'ers,
I'm about as aggravated as a one-legged man at a butt-kicking contest! My two girls, Ashley—age 10—and

Courtney—age 7—are waging a catfight of histrionic pro-portions. I'm talking sniping and put-downs that would im-press a whole army of reality TV contestants.

Today was just another battle in the war. Ashley turned up to go to a movie wearing her hair in a ponytail at the back of her neck, with the tail part all fuzzed up like a cat that saw itself in a mirror. Courtney took a gander at it and busted out laughing.

"Ashley," she says, "your hair's so big, they're gonna make it buy its own movie ticket."

And Ashley pulls a face that would scare Frankenstein himself, and says, "What are you—dumb as a box of ham-mers? You're too little to know anything about style. Charisse LaCroix wore her hair like this in the spring fashion show in Milan, and *Girl Power* magazine says it's THE look for summer."

"Yeah, for what—roadkill?" Courtney yanks the ratty-looking thing. So Ashley shrieks and slaps her.

And they both come hollering and yammering to me, ex-pecting me to take sides. I'm at a total loss on what to do. Do y'all have problems like this with y'all's girls? I never did hear of such a thing. Sure enough, my sis and I never acted that way. ;)

Well, if any y'all have some good advice, it would be right appreciated.

Thanks,

Veronica Marcello

From:	Dulcie Huckleberry <dulcie@showme.com>
To:	SAHM I Am <sahmiam@loophole.com>
Subject:	Re: [SAHM I AM] TOTW August 8: Sibling Rivalry, anyone?

Hey, Veronica,

My mom used to tape our mouths shut with packing tape if me and my brothers got to fighting. Hmm…probably couldn't get away with that now.

By the way, could everyone please pray for me this Wednesday? I have a JOB INTERVIEW! I applied for an interior design position with a local firm last week, and they just called this morning to set up an interview. I can't believe it happened so fast! But I'm glad, because we just paid some of our bills for this month with a credit card because Tom's unemployment was woefully short, and there was no severance package. Our parents are offering to help, but they'd have to go in debt, too, so we're going to try to keep that from happening.

I'm SO nervous about the interview! I haven't had to do one in five years.

Don't even own any business clothes anymore. I'm going shopping this evening…my parents are sending me some money. The last time they bought clothes for me was when I was a freshman in college. I HATE THIS!
Dulcie

From:	Zelia Muzuwa <zeemuzu@vivacious.com>
To:	SAHM I Am <sahmiam@loophole.com>
Subject:	Re: [SAHM I AM] TOTW August 8: Sibling Rivalry, anyone?

So odd that this should be the week's topic. So far this evening, my children have had the following arguments:

1. Bigger Is Better

Seamus: (to Cosette) I'm bigger than you!

Cosette: So what? My hair is longer than yours!

Seamus: Well, my fingers are longer than yours.

Cosette: My eyes are bigger!

Seamus: My feet are bigger!

Cosette: (sticking out her tongue) By dongue ib longah thad yahth!

Seamus: (flustered) Well...well... MY GERMS ARE BIGGER THAN YOURS!

2. He's Touching Me

Cosette: Mo-om! Griffith is hitting me!

Me: Griffith, are you hitting your sister?

Griffith: No. She pushed me!

Me: (sighing) Cosette?

Cosette: But, Mom! He touched my very special, favorite, de-li-cate doll!

Me: Okay, both of you—leaveeachother'stoysalonenopushinghittingorshoving. GOT IT?

Cosette and Griffith: (mournfully) Yes, Mom.

Cosette: (moments later) Mom! Griffith is looking at me!

Griffith: She's breathing on me!

Cosette: Was not! I was just breathing normally. He thinks I should hold my breath. And he was wiggling his finger at my doll!

Griffith: Nuh-uh! I was just waving my fingers like this. (demonstrates)

3. Hungry Hippos

Cosette: (Are you seeing the common denominator?) Moooo-ooooom!!!

Me: What NOW?

Cosette: Seamus says that Hubert ate Thor! (She's now almost in tears.)

Me: Who ate what? And why are you telling me about it?

Cosette: Hubert! He's Seamus's pretend hippo. And he ATE MY PRETEND BUNNY, THOR!

Me: You named a bunny…THOR?

Seamus: She took my name! I was going to name the hippo "Thor" and she knew it, so she used my name. So I had to name the hippo "Hubert" and that made him mad, so he ate the bunny. Hippos are pretty fierce, you know.

By this time, I am nearly having seizures. I sent them all to their rooms and told them they weren't allowed to talk to me for the rest of the evening. They tried the old "But, Mom, I have to tell you something" trick, but I stopped them with "Blood? Is there blood? I see no blood. Unless there is *blood,* I don't want to hear about it. Go to your room."

I'm telling you, police investigators ought to rent out my children. After experiencing such nerve-shredding pettiness, even the most hardened criminal would beg to talk rather than put up with any more from them!

Z

From:	Brenna L. <saywhat@writeme.com>
To:	SAHM I Am <sahmiam@loophole.com>
Subject:	Re: [SAHM I AM] TOTW August 8: Sibling Rivalry, anyone?

I did it! I did it! I found a Shakespeare quote for Zelia!!! It's not from some obscure play, like she usually finds, but it's a perfect quote for her children. It's Mercutio, from *Romeo and Juliet:*

Thou! Why, thou wilt quarrel with a man that hath a hair more or a hair less in his beard than thou hast. Thou wilt quarrel with a man for cracking nuts, having no other reason but because thou hast hazel eyes… Thou hast quarreled with a man for coughing in the street, because he hath wakened thy dog that hath lain asleep in the sun. Didst thou not fall out with a tailor for wearing his new doublet before Easter? With another, for tying his new shoes with old riband?

How's that? Is it a good fit? Did I do it right???

Brenna

From:	Zelia Muzuwa <zeemuzu@vivacious.com>
To:	SAHM I Am <sahmiam@loophole.com>
Subject:	Re: [SAHM I AM] TOTW August 8: Sibling Rivalry, anyone?

<How's that? Is it a good fit? Did I do it right???>

Bren, girl, you ROCK! It's a great quote. Very applicable. And the fact that you took the time to find it and post it totally brightened my entire evening and made me laugh.

Thank you, sweet friend. :)

Z

From:	Chad Ebberly <chad.ebberly@henpec.com>
To:	Rosalyn Ebberly <prov31woman@home.com>
Subject:	Blackberry

Hey, Ros,

If you get this e-mail before eleven-thirty this morning, could you run my BlackBerry over to the office? I got all the way here and realized I forgot it, and there are some appointments I need to check on for lunch and after work. I won't be home for supper since I have a dinner meeting. Thanks!

Love ya,

Chad

From:	Marianne Hausten <desperatemom@nebweb.net>
To:	SAHM I Am <sahmiam@loophole.com>
Subject:	**[SAHM I AM] I am officially Overdue**

Dear everybody,

It's 11:59 p.m. Monday night, and today was my due date! Am I in labor? NO! Am I happy about this? NO! My DH Brandon took me and Helene out in our SUV tonight and we drove outside Omaha until we found the most pitted, potholed, washboarded road available—to my joy, it also had a set of very rough railroad tracks. My plan was to cruise this road and hit every single bump at a minimum of 40 mph until we jostled me into labor.

But my DH, who is to blame for this condition I'm in, REFUSED to go at a decent clip. He gingerly tiptoed the SUV over the bumps and crept over the tracks at about 2 mph, and when I protested, he responded, "I don't want to damage the tires. Besides, if we flip over, do you really want to give birth while hanging upside down by your seat belt?" He's worried about his precious tires and making jokes while I'm swelled up the size of a small-town water tower?

Needless to say, the only thing useful we accomplished was getting Helene to go to sleep. And of course, the minute we drove into the garage and turned off the engine, she woke up and began to howl. Go figure.

Does anyone have any other bright ideas about how to put me in labor? My doctor says he won't induce me for another TWO weeks. I had to hang up the phone because I couldn't think of a single nice thing to say to him after that. Please, somebody, have an inspiration!

Marianne

From:	Connie Lawson <clmo5@home.com>
To:	SAHM I Am <sahmiam@loophole.com>
Subject:	Re: [SAHM I AM] I am officially Overdue

Dear Marianne,

One word—CASTOR OIL. I was overdue with all my children, and I took castor oil and within twelve hours, was on my way to the hospital to deliver. It doesn't taste the best, but it cleans out your system and it gets things going in the labor department. Hang in there—we'll be celebrating the birth of your new baby before you know it!

Connie

SAHM I Am Loop Mom

From:	The Millards <jstcea4jesus@familymail.net>
To:	SAHM I Am <sahmiam@loophole.com>
Subject:	[SAHM I AM] Castor Oil

Hi, Marianne,

I'd have to agree with Connie on this one. Castor oil worked for me, too. Of course, I only used it with Tyler. All the other ones came a few days early. So I don't know if it was the castor oil or not. It could have just been coincidence. But it's worth a try. Just hold your nose and try not to think about the taste…oh, and stay close to a bathroom. It's better than being induced.

Jocelyn

From:	Rosalyn Ebberly <prov31woman@home.com>
To:	Connie Lawson <clmo5@home.com>
Subject:	**Please tell me I'm overreacting**

Hi, Connie,

How are the kids? Did you get that recipe I e-mailed to you for edible organic play dough? Don't forget to put in the soy flour, as that really increases the protein content and makes it actually healthy to eat.

I wanted to ask you about something. I'm probably being silly, but I'm worried about Chad. He has been working really long hours recently, and it's not like him. You know how devoted he's always been to the family.

Well, yesterday, he forgot his BlackBerry at home, and he asked me to bring it to him at work. It was charging, and when I unplugged it, I noticed he had an appointment alert. So I checked it, and…well, I don't know what to make of it.

It said, "Dinner at Maddy's house, 6:30 p.m., bring dessert. Anything chocolate."

Who is Maddy? And why is she having MY husband over for dinner? Chad has never, ever given me reason to distrust him, but I can't think of a single plausible explanation for this. Should I ask him about it? Or will I just sound suspicious? I didn't say anything yet, just dropped off the Black-berry at work.

If nothing is going on, then why hasn't he told me what is going on? I'm a little scared, Connie. He was gone most of the evening yesterday. It's probably nothing. Chad would never do anything wrong. He is such a righteous, strong, good man. And he adores me. You know he does. So that's why I probably won't say anything. I want him to know I trust him implicitly. If I questioned him about it, that would be disrespectful, and you know I'm NEVER dishonoring to my husband. It's silly to even have the slightest doubt about him. I probably have been watching too much television. It's polluting my mind. I think I'll go read the entire book of Isaiah just to purify myself. Then I won't be acting so ridiculous.

Okay, then. I'll just get my own act in gear, and then I'll be fine. Thanks so much, Connie. I know I can always count on you for good advice and support. I appreciate you. Love,

Rosalyn

"She looks well to the ways of her household, and does not eat the bread of idleness."
Proverbs 31:27 (NASB)

From:	Connie Lawson <clmo5@home.com>
To:	Rosalyn Ebberly <prov31woman@home.com>
Subject:	Re: Please tell me I'm overreacting

Oh, my dear Rosalyn! I don't think you are overreacting at all! If I found something like that in Kurt's appointment book, I'd be devastated! I think you should definitely talk to Chad and find out what's going on. It's not disrespectful to ask for an explanation. You have a right to know. Oh, I'm so sad for you—I would have never DREAMED Chad could do something like that! I'm not saying he has definitely fallen into sin or anything, but it does sound like temptation is laying a snare for him. If you confront him in truth and love, then maybe you can rescue him before it's too late.

I am always here for you, dear friend.

Connie

SAHM I Am Loop Mom

From:	Dulcie Huckleberry <dulcie@showme.com>
To:	SAHM I Am <sahmiam@loophole.com>
Subject:	**[SAHM I AM] Shopping for an interview outfit**

It seems to be my lot in life to cause other people to say stupid things to me. I went shopping for an interview suit today. I stopped in at the Lady's Unmentionables because they have a barely-there underwire that is just what I needed to give the suit the right shape. The sales clerk helping me couldn't have been a day over twenty, if that. I showed her my suit and explained the situation, and she cooed, "Oh! I remember MY first job interview! I was so nervous. It must be especially hard for you, going back at *your* age. But we'll fix you right up. After all, having the right foundation garments makes SOOOO much difference in your confidence level."

My age? Tell me—when did twenty-seven become a "my age"? I knew right then she was headed for trouble, and I was right. At one point, while she was assisting me with trying on some "foundation garments," she caught sight of my stomach.

She gasped and clapped her hand over her mouth. "Oh my goodness!" she yelped. "Were you in an accident?"

"No." I looked down at my still-purple stretch marks. "I had twins."

Her eyes got round, and she shook her head. "I'm so sorry. That must have been horrible. It looks like it hurt."

I just stared at her. Speechless in the presence of such incredible witlessness. How is it fair that SHE has a job while my husband is let go? Not that I want him selling bras or anything...

Dulcie

From:	Zelia Muzuwa <zeemuzu@vivacious.com>
To:	Dulcie Huckleberry <dulcie@showme.com>
Subject:	**Selling bras**

Yeah, but think of the great employee discount he'd have! No more excuse for getting you a new coffee mug instead of some lacy, pretty thing for your birthday. :)

Z

From:	Rosalyn Ebberly <prov31woman@home.com>
To:	Connie Lawson <clmo5@home.com>
Subject:	**Re: Please tell me I'm overreacting**

Connie,

I'm crushed and horrified and EXTREMELY disappointed that you would even, for ONE SECOND, *dare* to think that

Chad would do anything "wrong." I go to you for support and encouragement, and this is what you give me? Have I done something to offend you? I'm not aware of anything. Why would you treat me like this?

Chad is a MODEL husband—devoted, kind, loving. He doesn't deserve your doubt over some silly appointment. And for your information, he explained the whole thing to me. Madeline, or Maddy as everyone calls her, is a coworker and had a working party-meeting over at her house last night. A whole group of people were there, and it was all perfectly innocent.

So you see how dangerous it is to jump to conclusions? How would you like it if I insinuated that Kurt was having an affair or whatever it was you were thinking? But I'm sure you just weren't thinking about how your message would come across. So don't worry, I'm not mad...anymore. I have forgiven you. It's done and forgotten.

But don't be surprised if I hesitate the next time to tell you about something I'm wondering about. You'll have to earn back my trust, just like we teach our kids. But I still LOVE YOU!

Love,

Rosalyn

"She looks well to the ways of her household, and does not eat the bread of idleness."

Proverbs 31:27 (NASB)

From:	VIM <vivalaveronica@marcelloportraits.com>
To:	SAHM I Am <sahmiam@loophole.com>
Subject:	[SAHM I AM] WHY DIDN'T Y'ALL WARN ME???

We just got home from our first childbirth class. What is
WRONG with you people? All y'all congratulating me,
telling me how peachy you think it is that I have to have a
baby! And all the time, y'all KNEW good and well what I'd
be in for, AND YOU DIDN'T TELL ME! What kind of
friendship is that?

The nurse teaching the class was the same sort of smug,
sadistic been-there-done-that mother like you all. She made
us watch the most freakishly horrifying video of these poor,
suffering women going through labor. LABOR! It should
be called torture! Land sake, I had no idea. I honestly
didn't, or I'd of never let Frank so much as wink at me, much
less get me pregnant!

THOSE WOMEN WERE IN *PAIN!!!* I'm gonna DIE!
DIE, I tell you!!! There ain't no way this side of the blessed
Jordan that little ol' Ronnie Irene is going to survive that
sort of trauma!

By the time they got to "transition" on the video, I had
to leave the room. Frank found me out in the hall, bawling
my eyes out. I thought I was going to be sick! It wasn't just
the blood, and the obvious agony that sweet gal had to en-
dure. It was the total lack of privacy, the "here I am in all
my womanly glory" for a roomful of people to see, the…vi-
olence of it all that did me in.

I can't do this, y'all. I really can't. And it gives me the

willies to realize I don't have a choice. The baby has to come out one way or another. I feel trapped.

Why didn't anybody tell me? Is this some sort of hazing ritual you women put each other through to be accepted into the mommy club? Why would they show videos like that to impressionable first-time mothers?

The nurse came out to the hall to talk to me and apologize for upsetting me. She persuaded me to come back in and watch the end of the video. I think she thought that seeing the couple cooing and drooling over their new cutie-pie would make me feel better. But it didn't.

That was the most disturbing part of all. Everyone says you don't remember the pain or the fear afterwards. That's NOT fair! I want to remember. Every single thing. So the next time I know to avoid it. If we don't remember, then we just keep putting ourselves through it over and over and over. Well, this lady ain't gonna forget!

You bet I'm hissy-fitting!

Veronica

From:	Marianne Hausten <desperatemom@nebweb.net>
To:	SAHM I Am <sahmiam@loophole.com>
Subject:	**[SAHM I AM] Castor oil and Childbirth videos**

First of all, those of you who recommended castor oil to me—YOU ARE EVIL! Very, very wicked people. I tried it yesterday, just like you suggested. Am I in labor? Do I have my baby yet? NO! I *do,* however, have a permanent imprint of the toilet seat on my posterior, because that is where I spent exactly six hours, twenty-four minutes and fifteen seconds…getting "cleaned out." Thanks SO much.

Secondly, dearest Veronica—take a deep breath, put your head between your knees—if you can still bend that far—and CALM DOWN! It will be okay. Those videos are shocking the first time you see them. But you will be just fine. When you use your breathing exercises, it really does help manage the pain. And you'll be so excited about bringing a life into the world that the blood and stuff won't bother you at all.

You need to go on a desensitization regimen—something to help you gradually become more comfortable with the birthing process. I'd recommend the very thing that many of us have done—watch *A Baby Tale.* It's on the cable TV during the day. You might have to start out by just watching the predelivery segment every day for a week, but gradually you can build up to where you can go through the entire labor and delivery. I think it will really be helpful for you.

But whatever you do, stay away from that castor oil!
Waiting for the conclusion of my own Baby Tale,
Marianne
Due Date: Minus Four Days, 6 hours, 37 minutes, and…18 seconds. :(

From:	Dulcie Huckleberry <dulcie@showme.com>
To:	SAHM I Am <sahmiam@loophole.com>
Subject:	Re: [SAHM I AM] Castor oil and Childbirth videos

Marianne wrote:

<When you use your breathing exercises, it really does help manage the pain.>

OR you can do as I did: As soon as you set foot—or wheelchair tire—in the hospital, say, "Gimme the epidural. Gimme the drugs. Wake me up when it's over!" :)

Dulcie

P.S. The job interview went GREAT! I should hear something by next week. *hoping, praying, the answer is yes*

From:	VIM <vivalaveronica@marcelloportraits.com>
To:	Rosalyn Ebberly <prov31woman@home.com>
Subject:	**Weekly Report**

Dearest sister,

The "sibling rivalry" topic musta hit a raw nerve, 'cause lookit this:

Rosalyn, Week of August 9, last year: 23.6 %—a record low for you, so far.

Veronica, Week of August 8, this year: 37.05%—a record high for me, so far.

Think I'm going to celebrate with a double-chocolate brownie, a glass of milk, and today's episode of "A Baby Tale." Ya know, that show has a way of growing on a person, like mold on bread.

Cheers,

Ronnie

From:	Rosalyn Ebberly <prov31woman@home.com>
To:	VIM <vivalaveronica@marcelloportraits.com>
Subject:	**They're just being kind...**

...because of your pregnancy. When are you going to have some REAL topics? That's what I'd like to know.
Rosalyn

"She looks well to the ways of her household, and does not eat the bread of idleness."
Proverbs 31:27 (NASB)

From:	VIM <vivalaveronica@marcelloportraits.com>
To:	Rosalyn Ebberly <prov31woman@home.com>
Subject:	**Real Topics?**

When will I have "real topics"??? About the same time as you have some "real" feelings. Sometimes I think you have got to be a Stepford Wife or something. Are you sure Chad doesn't plug you in at night?
VIM

From:	Rosalyn Ebberly <prov31woman@home.com>
To:	VIM <vivalaveronica@marcelloportraits.com>
Subject:	**Re: Real Topics?**

That's just mean. Even for you. I sincerely hope it was just pregnancy hormones talking. Actually, I do have real feelings, and you just bruised them. And now I have to be going, because my oldest daughter has a therapy appointment in a half hour. An appointment that's not covered by our insurance, and I have no idea how we will pay for it, since we don't happen to be up to our ears in money. After that, I have to clean my house. Unlike you, I can't afford a housekeeper. Not that I'd have one anyway, since I take pride in my own housekeeping abilities. You spend so much time being ugly toward me, one would think you were jealous of me or something. I can't imagine why. At least your husband can make it home for dinner now and then.

"She looks well to the ways of her household, and does not eat the bread of idleness."
Proverbs 31:27 (NASB)

From:	VIM <vivalaveronica@marcelloportraits.com>
To:	Rosalyn Ebberly <prov31woman@home.com>
Subject:	**Re: Real Topics?**

Well fry me up a mountain lion and serve it for dinner, honey, now you're just plain scaring the willies outta me. You almost sound like you're having a mite of a…*gasp*…BAD DAY! Impossible! The world as I know it is now coming to an apocalyptic end. Who would have thought the unthinkable was…thinkable?

Seriously, what's wrong with Suzannah that she has to go see a shrink? I'd crack some joke about it, but I kinda like the poor critter. I hope nothing too much is wrong.

VIM

P.S. Didn't mean to hurt your feelings none. Did your sense of humor stage a sick-out today?

From:	Rosalyn Ebberly <prov31woman@home.com>
To:	VIM <vivalaveronica@marcelloportraits.com>
Subject:	**Re: Real Topics?**

Don't you have anything better to do than rub your supposed "victory" in my face? Some of us are dealing with personal crises that aren't as trivial as e-mail posts and fears of having a baby.

As far as your kind inquiry after Suzannah...she had an appointment with a pediatric psychologist because she has been having stomach problems. Her pediatrician felt that it was a pre-ulcer type issue caused by stress, which is absolutely ridiculous. Our household is perfectly peaceful. There is nothing that could be causing stress in their lives, but he recommended having her speak with a therapist anyway. I consented simply because I've been taught always to respect a member of the medical profession.

But I'm afraid the therapist is an incompetent money-grubber. She had the nerve to tell me that Suzannah needs to come in for therapy on a weekly basis, that she is feeling a lot of stress at home, and that OUR WHOLE FAMILY NEEDS COUNSELING! Is that not the most insulting, presumptuous suggestion! Chad and I lead classes at church on communication, for crying out loud. We know how to communicate and how to help our children talk to us. If Suzannah was feeling stressed, she knows good and well she can come talk to me about anything. However, I think it's a lot of nonsense. Whoever heard of a seven-year-old getting stress-induced ulcers? I think she needs to toughen up. Life isn't a picnic.

Needless to say, we won't be returning to that quack shrink. We'll just try to help her cut back on some of her activities and maybe move her bedtime up a little earlier. I'm sure she'll be just fine.

Love,

Rosalyn

"She looks well to the ways of her household, and does not eat the bread of idleness."
Proverbs 31:27 (NASB)

From:	VIM <vivalaveronica@marcelloportraits.com>
To:	SAHM I Am <sahmiam@loophole.com>
Subject:	**[SAHM I AM] TOTW August 15: Ugh! In-laws!**

Okay, y'all, answer me this one, will you? What in tarnation do I say to my dear in-laws who are suddenly demanding to know when my stepkids are fixin' to start Italian lessons? They've even offered to fork over the cash for it, but I'm not gung ho about the idea at all. Sure, Frank is bilingual, but I'm not—unless you count Texan as a foreign language!

LOL! I don't want them all going around talking some language I don't understand. How do I know they aren't talking about me? It don't make no never mind to Frank, but the fact that they offered to pay for lessons puts a lot of pressure on him. He told me I could take lessons, too, but foreign languages was never really my thing, so there ya go. He never speaks Italian at home, unless he's having a conniption, so I don't see why we need to start now.

What do y'all think? Do you ever have these sort of problems with your in-laws? What do you do about it?
Veronica Marcello

From:	Marianne Hausten <desperatemom@nebweb.net>
To:	SAHM I Am <sahmiam@loophole.com>
Subject:	Re: [SAHM I AM] TOTW August 15: Ugh! In-laws

Hi, all. Still pregnant. But hopefully not for long. I've been having some contractions today, and if they ever get close enough together for long enough, it might turn into the real deal.

Veronica—maybe you could turn the lessons into a game. Go with them to class and then when you're at home, practice by making them earn a piece of candy or a prize for every household item they can name in Italian. Or maybe you could…

OKAY! WE ARE SO HAVING A BABY TODAY!!! I was just sitting here writing the above part of my e-mail when suddenly my water broke. Big Broke. All over the chair and the floor. Helene wandered in and saw me and said, "Mama, you go potty?" Which made me laugh, which didn't help matters at all. So I called Brandon and Dulcie's mom—who is taking Helene for me—and got myself cleaned up. I have my suitcase by the door, and I'm off to the hospital as soon as Brandon gets home. I'll let you know how it all turns out!

Marianne, the—soon-to-be-former—Manatee

From:	Zelia Muzuwa <zeemuzu@vivacious.com>
To:	SAHM I Am <sahmiam@loophole.com>
Subject:	Re: [SAHM I AM] TOTW August 15: Ugh! In-laws

WOW!!! That's a first. We've never had someone's water break on the loop before. GO, Marianne! Have that kid, babe! Should we pass out chocolate bars? So much better for you than candy cigars. Let's take guesses on the time of birth. Whoever is the closest gets real chocolate. I'll mail it to you!

In response to Veronica…I can UTTERLY relate. My in-laws are British, and it never ceases to amaze me how many different and varied ways that simple fact can cause problems. Today, the ANNUAL OFFICIAL CHRISTMAS VISIT ARGUMENT has begun. For you who are newer to the loop, this is the argument in which I, Zelia, try to persuade my mother-in-law that it would really be better to have them come visit us in the States this year, and where she tries to guilt-trip me for it, saying that she is much too frightened of air travel and how "dreadfully disappointing it would be" if we decided not to visit this year. My theme song for the next five months will be "I'll be HOME for Christmas"—yeah...only in my dreams. That little puddle we call the Atlantic can sure be irritating, huh?

Stay tuned for more riveting drama from *As My Mother-In-Law Makes The World Turn*...

Z

From:	Dulcie Huckleberry <dulcie@showme.com>
To:	SAHM I Am <sahmiam@loophole.com>
Subject:	Re: [SAHM I AM] TOTW August 15: Ugh! In-laws

Well, MY MIL is taking me shopping for new clothes! And you know why???

BECAUSE I GOT THE JOB! I GOT THE JOB!!!! I DID I DID I DID!!!

They just called today, and it's going to be great! Tom will still have to get a part-time job, but that should be for a few evenings a week, just to fill in the difference between what a rookie interior designer gets and what an experienced computer programmer earns. But he can stay with the girls during the day.

I can't BEGIN to describe to you how relieved I am. I was really scared. But now I'm excited. And I even get to do what I really love doing! No more being cooped up at home, withering away from a lack of adult interaction. No more reducing my total mental functioning to assessing whether the stench I smell is a dirty diaper or the garbage needing to go out. I get to do ART again! And get *paid* for it!

But, I have to tell you, the idea of shopping with my MIL for new business clothes frightens me more than a little. I didn't want to say no, because she's been so sweet through all this employment mess. But most of you remember me describing her wedding to you in May, right? With the fuchsia mermaid dress and the horse decked out in marabou? I'm telling you, my MIL has a very unhealthy addiction to marabou. I'm afraid the clothes she might pick out will be professional…but the totally WRONG profession!
Dulcie
P.S. Marianne is supposed to call me when the baby is born. So as soon as I hear anything, I'll pass it along. I'm SO happy for her. :)

From:	Zelia Muzuwa <zeemuzu@vivacious.com>
To:	Dulcie Huckleberry <dulcie@showme.com>
Subject:	**congratulations!**

Hey, Dulcie-babe,
So happy for you, girl! You'll do great. But what's with this statement?

<No more being cooped up at home, withering away from a lack of adult interaction. No more reducing my total mental functioning to assessing whether the stench I smell is a dirty diaper or the garbage needing to go out.>

Ouch! I SO resemble that remark! :) Don't forget about us SAHMs you've left behind, Okay? Promise???

Z

From:	Dulcie Huckleberry <dulcie@showme.com>
To:	Zelia Muzuwa <zeemuzu@vivacious.com>
Subject:	**Re: congratulations!**

I promise. You all are totally, wonderfully unforgettable. I couldn't even if I tried. :)

Dulcie

From:	Dulcie Huckleberry <dulcie@showme.com>
To:	"Green Eggs and Ham"
Subject:	**BABY HAUSTEN!!!**

Hey, gals, Marianne just called me! Little Neil Alistair Hausten arrived at 8:31 p.m. this evening, weighing a whopping 9 lbs. 9 oz. and he's 22.5 inches long! He and Mama are doing just fine, though Brandon's a bit worse for wear. :) I told Marianne they should have named him Neil Armstrong Hausten, but she just gave me a courtesy laugh and changed the subject.

So who wins the chocolate?

Dulcie

From:	Zelia Muzuwa <zeemuzu@vivacious.com>
To:	SAHM I Am <sahmiam@loophole.com>
Subject:	[SAHM I AM] chocolate goes to...

★Drum roll★...CONNIE LAWSON!!!!!! For her guess of 8:28 p.m. Congratulations, Connie! I guess having five kids, you ought to be a good judge of how long it will take. Your chocolate bars will be in the mail to you tomorrow. :)
Z

From:	Connie Lawson <clmo5@home.com>
To:	SAHM I Am <sahmiam@loophole.com>
Subject:	Re: [SAHM I AM] chocolate goes to...

Thanks, Zelia! I can't wait for the chocolate. But I'm just glad to hear everything went well for Marianne. It's so hard to be overdue. I was late with my oldest two, James and John, and it was NOT fun! Welcome to the world, little Neil.
Connie
SAHM I Am Loop Mom

From:	P. Lorimer <phyllis.lorimer@joono.com>
To:	"Green Eggs and Ham"
Subject:	**Congratulations, Dulcie and Marianne!**

Wonderful news, both of you! I know Marianne probably won't be checking her e-mail for a few days, but I hope she sends pictures soon. "Neil Alistair" is such a unique name! I think it's lovely. I'm so glad to know everything went smoothly.

And, Dulcie, I know you will make a wonderful interior designer! I'm so pleased for you. But do you really think Tom will be happy at home with the children? What if he wants to get a full-time job? Would your in-laws be able to watch the girls?

I'm somewhat envious. Here in Scoville, the stores are full of brightly colored spiral notebooks, boxes and boxes of pencils and crayons and back-to-school clothing sales. The aisles even *smell* like new school supplies. Everywhere I look, it seems people are preparing to return to the classroom. Except me.

I am trying very conscientiously not to pout. It's not as if Jonathan has "forbidden" me to go back to school. Our relationship doesn't work that way. But I know he feels uncomfortable with it, and it is too big a change to make without his support. Family is more important than school. And it would have been another year before I could start anyway. So I really am not resentful about it. Just…sad. I could have been filling out applications by now, but at this point the dream seems to be more distant than ever before.

I suppose it did not help a bit that I've been poring over university programs during the day while the children are napping. There are a couple of programs at schools that are within reasonable commuting distance. And there are a few programs that are mostly online with summer colloquiums or other periodic on-campus workshops. It's everything I can do to keep myself from e-mailing them to request further information.

I *should* be busy with the adult education duties for church. I'm considering starting a class on Biblical history. It's amazing how much about the Bible people misunderstand because they don't have any knowledge about what was happening in history at the time. I am looking forward to it. I love teaching.

Determined to be grateful,

Phyllis

From:	Rosalyn Ebberly <prov31woman@home.com>
To:	SAHM I Am <sahmiam@loophole.com>
Subject:	[SAHM I AM] GWENCH E-mail Message

Dear Mommies,

I'm sending you the text for our special GWENCH e-mail message. We're sending it out to our friends in Hibiscus, WA, and the surrounding area in order to get the message out about the Godly Women for the Enforcement of National Christian Holidays and our campaign to Save Christmas. I wanted to know what you all think of the e-mail. Here it is:

Dear _____,

Are you tired of retailers forcing innocent, God-fearing citizens to be "tolerant" and "respectful" of other "religions" by refusing to wish people a Merry Christmas? Have you had enough of "holiday trees" and "winter sales" and long for a return of good, old-fashioned Christmas cheer?

We, the Godly Women for the Enforcement of National Christian Holidays (GWENCH) share your frustration and concern! In the spirit of loving correction and a pure desire to see Christmas returned to its rightful state of preeminence in our culture, GWENCH is kicking off a special campaign. We will use the power of our pocketbooks to teach retailers a lesson in respect that they'll never forget!

You can help! The Christmas season is just around the corner, and what we are asking is that people "boycott" all retailers by not buying ANY Christmas presents. That's right—no presents! Now, are we suggesting anything anti-Christmas? Not at all! Christmas, as we know, is not about presents. It's about love and the Gift from God that was born that blessed December night so long ago. So what we ask is that you use your Christmas money to donate to an approved list of deserving charities—see attached. They need the money much more than we do, anyway, and this is a great way to help them AND make retailers really mad!

Instead of buying presents, if you want to do something beyond making your charitable contribution, try making homemade gifts for each other. We guarantee that this will bring your family closer together and impress on your children the importance of keeping Christmas simple and focused on those we love.

So we're counting on your support to teach our local retailers a lesson about what the TRUE meaning of

Christmas is. By the time we're done with them, they'll never want to wish anyone a "Happy Holiday" again!

Love and Peace,

Rosalyn Ebberly

Chairperson, GWENCH

"She looks well to the ways of her household, and does not eat the bread of idleness."

Proverbs 31:27 (NASB)

From:	Dulcie Huckleberry <dulcie@showme.com>
To:	SAHM I Am <sahmiam@loophole.com>
Subject:	Re: [SAHM I AM] GWENCH E-mail Message

Rosalyn,

You asked for feedback on this e-mail—well, here's mine. First, Jesus was probably born in September, not December. Second, I'm not feeling much love and peace from your e-mail. And third, how will trying to hurt the business of these retailers help show them what Christmas is all about?

Please don't try to form any local GWENCH chapters here in Springfield. Wishing people a "happy holiday" isn't against any law that I know of. I'm having a hard time imagining Jesus supporting a group like that.

Dulcie

From:	Rosalyn Ebberly <prov31woman@home.com>
To:	Dulcie Huckleberry <dulcie@showme.com>
Subject:	Re: [SAHM I AM] GWENCH E-mail Message

Dulcie, dear,

I'm surprised you, an ex-SAHM, had the audacity to post an e-mail criticizing me or my group. Has the business world corrupted you so quickly? If you can't stand up for something like Christmas, how will you ever defend your faith in the midst of a hostile, secular business world?

Anyway, I'm sure you know what a *privilege* it is for you to remain on the SAHM I Am loop, now that you've given up the at-home lifestyle. I considered having you unsubscribed, but I just couldn't bear to do that—I'm so fond of you—even though I can never condone your behavior. It's just like what Jesus always used to say, "Love the sin, hate the sinner!"

Just be more careful, okay?

Rosalyn

"She looks well to the ways of her household, and does not eat the bread of idleness."
Proverbs 31:27 (NASB)

From:	Dulcie Huckleberry <dulcie@showme.com>
To:	Rosalyn Ebberly <prov31woman@home.com>
Subject:	Re: [SAHM I AM] GWENCH E-mail Message

Uh, Ros, didn't you mean "Love the SINNER, hate the SIN"? And Jesus NEVER, NEVER "used to say" that. We made that up!
Dulcie

From:	Rosalyn Ebberly <prov31woman@home.com>
To:	Dulcie Huckleberry <dulcie@showme.com>
Subject:	Re: [SAHM I AM] GWENCH E-mail Message

That's what I said, Dulcie! And of course, it's not a direct quote. But it's what Jesus MEANT.
Rosalyn

"She looks well to the ways of her household, and does not eat the bread of idleness."
Proverbs 31:27 (NASB)

From:	Dulcie Huckleberry <dulcie@showme.com>
To:	"Green Eggs and Ham"
Subject:	Fwd: [SAHM I AM] GWENCH E-mail Message

See attached. I have GOT to learn the following lesson about that woman:

It'sNOT*worth*it! It'sNOT*worth*it! It'sNOT*worth*it! It's-NOT*worth*it! It'sNOT*worth*it! It'sNOT*worth*it! It'sNOT-*worth*it! It'sNOT*worth*it! It'sNOT*worth*it! It'sNOT*worth*it!

When will I ever remember?
Dulcie

From:	Brenna L. <saywhat@writeme.com>
To:	"Green Eggs and Ham"; Tess Gillman <tessty@newmeximail.com
Subject:	**My FATHER!**

Hi, gals,

Just got an e-mail from Dad. He and his wife have decided they are "concerned" about the embryo adoption. Get this:

"We know you and Darren really would like to have a child. But 'embryo adoptions' aren't *real* adoptions because embryos are not children! We checked, and they are considered property. You can't adopt property. And besides, why would you want to take on somebody else's leftover embryos anyway? Apparently, freezing them makes them weaker. You could have handicapped kids! Why not do your own IVF procedure, even if you have to use a sperm bank, and have a healthy kid that is at least half your own?"

It goes on, but I'll spare you the rest. I'm SO STEAMED! I know Dad doesn't think life begins at conception, and so he wouldn't understand why we believe it is important to treat embryos with dignity and respect. But his objections are so calloused and even prejudiced. I don't even know what to say! I didn't expect anybody in our family to be so rude.

Anybody got a "pick me up"?

Brenna

From:	Tess Gillman <tessty@newmeximail.com
To:	Brenna L. <saywhat@writeme.com>
Subject:	**Re: My FATHER!**

Oh, Brenna! I'm so sorry your dad and stepmom feel this way. I'm even sorrier they had the gall to say it to you. But you're going to have to expect some negative reactions. My brother and his wife were skeptical of us even doing the IVF, and the adoption part made them even more nervous. They asked me, "Well, shouldn't the rest of the family have a say in what happens to our biological relatives? What if Mom and Dad want to know ALL their grandchildren?" Needless to say, we ended up spending a lot of time talking with Nightlight Agency and our social worker to deal with some of these issues before we went ahead with the IVF procedure.

But that's part of what the agency is there for, and what I'm here for—to help you work through these issues. A lot of people don't understand. Or they have misconceptions about how everything works. Just be patient and respectful. Use this as a chance to teach your dad about how the program functions, and make sure to listen to him and let him express his feelings.

As you probably have already discovered, infertility has a way of affecting not just you and your husband, but your extended family and friends. Everybody has emotions and needs to deal with them differently. I think once your dad has a new grandchild—or two!—to cuddle and play with, most of his reservations will melt away. Love has a way of doing that.

Thanks so much for including me in your e-mailing. I hope I've helped.

Blessings,

Tess

From:	Brenna L. <saywhat@writeme.com>
To:	Tess Gillman <tessty@newmeximail.com
Subject:	**Thank you.**

Dear Tess,

I was feeling so isolated. It's hard even for my other friends to really understand what we're going through. It means a lot to me that you know and are willing to talk and listen to me.

Thanks,

Brenna

From:	Zelia Muzuwa <zeemuzu@vivacious.com>
To:	"Green Eggs and Ham"
Subject:	**I'm bored...**

...so I'm going to try to annoy Rosalyn. I've got a pile of laundry waiting to be folded, and an adoption that seems stalled in committee. So I have to do SOMETHING to entertain myself. I came up with a game for the loop, and wanted to give you all a heads-up on it. Come help me out!

Z

From:	Zelia Muzuwa <zeemuzu@vivacious.com>
To:	SAHM I Am <sahmiam@loophole.com>
Subject:	**[SAHM I AM] Favorite Holiday Songs...**

Hi, Loopers,

Since it's already August, and I know you all are hard at work making those homemade gifts for the upcoming yuletide season as Rosalyn suggested, I figured it was time to get us all in the mood by suggesting one of my favorite seasonal melodies. Please join in—the more the, uh…"merrier"! :) But here's the catch—this is a GAME. It's one of those games where there's a secret rule that you have to figure out in order to have your selection count. So once you see a few song titles posted, think about the songs and the lyrics and see if you can tell what they have in common—other than the time of year they are traditionally sung. When you think you know, then post a title of your own, and I'll give you a mistletoe kiss for yes or a lump of coal for no.

Here's my all-time favorite ditty: "You're a Mean One, Mr. Grinch." For some reason, it just popped into my head after Rosalyn sent her GWENCH e-mail. I've been trotting around my house humming it ever since. It could be because I'm avoiding the laundry: You know—unwashed socks and the hearts that are full of them. Ah, Dr. Seuss! No one could put things the way you do!

Zelia

From:	P. Lorimer <phyllis.lorimer@joono.com>
To:	SAHM I Am <sahmiam@loophole.com>
Subject:	Re: [SAHM I AM] Favorite Holiday Songs...

Great idea, Zelia! My favorite is "O Holy Night." Kiss me?
Phyllis

From:	Zelia Muzuwa <zeemuzu@vivacious.com>
To:	SAHM I Am <sahmiam@loophole.com>
Subject:	Re: [SAHM I AM] Favorite Holiday Songs...

Yeppers, Phyllis! Sending you a big old pucker for under the
mistletoe: :-x You're one smart sugar cookie. With green and
red sprinkles, of course.
Zelia

From:	Connie Lawson <clmo5@home.com>
To:	SAHM I Am <sahmiam@loophole.com>
Subject:	Re: [SAHM I AM] Favorite Holiday Songs...

How creative, Zelia! Let me play! My favorite Christmas
song is "God Rest Ye Merry Gentlemen." Do I get a kiss?
Connie
SAHM I Am Loop Mom

From:	Zelia Muzuwa <zeemuzu@vivacious.com>
To:	SAHM I Am <sahmiam@loophole.com>
Subject:	Re: [SAHM I AM] Favorite Holiday Songs...

Ohhhh, rats! Sorry, Connie, I'll have to send you a lump of coal. :-("God Rest Ye Merry Gentlemen" doesn't fit the rules. Try again!
Zelia

From:	Dulcie Huckleberry <dulcie@showme.com>
To:	Zelia Muzuwa <zeemuzu@vivacious.com>
Subject:	Your Game!

Z, I'm as much in favor of annoying Rosalyn as anybody, but oh my goodness, how can you even bear to think about *Christmas* songs in AUGUST? It's crazy!
Dulcie

From:	Zelia Muzuwa <zeemuzu@vivacious.com>
To:	Dulcie Huckleberry <dulcie@showme.com>
Subject:	Re: Your Game!

Ahhhh, but is that what they REALLY are??? What's the rule, Dulcie? Come on, girlfriend, I know you can do it. I will reel you in and hook you, August or not. :) You know you want to play....
Z

From:	VIM <vivalaveronica@marcelloportraits.com>
To:	Rosalyn Ebberly <prov31woman@home.com>
Subject:	**Weekly Report**

I just don't get it! I KNOW I had a higher response than this. But I counted it up three times, from the Loophole archives themselves. And this is what I got:

Rosalyn, week of August 16, last year: 40.2%

Veronica, week of August 15, this year: 21%

What in tarnation is going on 'round these parts?

Veronica

From:	Rosalyn Ebberly <prov31woman@home.com>
To:	VIM <vivalaveronica@marcelloportraits.com>
Subject:	**Re: Weekly Report**

I, myself, am a little surprised for you, dear sister. You had many responses this week. But there have been a lot of new members, as well, so maybe that affected the count. New people are usually slow to post—at least for the first time. Once they get started, though, you can hardly shut them up!

You may want to consider that the Lord is using this to get your attention. This topic about in-laws wasn't very respectful, you know. I'm sure I would never encourage mothers to gripe about their husbands' parents like that. Maybe God is trying to tell you that as a leader of group discussion, you need to set the example by showing honor and love to your in-laws. Even if they aren't as dear and sweet as *my* in-laws. :)

How are you feeling these days with the pregnancy? Are you taking the organic herbal prenatal vitamins I sent you? I could not have coped without those. They are so much better for you, plus they don't cause constipation. I'm also knitting you a sweater for fall out of rabbit fur yarn. I spun it myself. The fur is from my friends who raise Angora rabbits. It is SO soft, you'll never want to take it off! But I need your current sizes so I can estimate how big to make it for fall. Just e-mail them to me, okay?

Hugs,

Rosalyn

"She looks well to the ways of her household, and does not eat the bread of idleness."

Proverbs 31:27 (NASB)

From:	VIM <vivalaveronica@marcelloportraits.com>
To:	Rosalyn Ebberly <prov31woman@home.com>
Subject:	**Re: Weekly Report**

Hey, Ros, darlin',

Are you feeling okay, honey? Because that e-mail y'all just sent me made you sound almost…nice. Bizzar-o! Don't you go getting yourself run down till you take sick or nothing, you hear me?

Seriously, the sweater sounds gorgeous. Thanks. I'll be

hoping for a few chilly days so's I can wear it this fall. The pregnancy is going...swell. *grin*

You sure you aren't feeling poorly?

Veronica

From:	VIM <vivalaveronica@marcelloportraits.com>
To:	SAHM I Am <sahmiam@loophole.com>
Subject:	[SAHM I AM] TOTW August 22: The problem with cupcakes...

Y'all *gotta* help me out on this here predicament. Let's see, how to put it delicate-like... Allrighty then...

Let's picture a big, yummy piece of chocolate cake, complete with huge globs of delicious frosting. And now picture a guy—an Italian man in his upper thirties, who we'll call...oh, let's call him "Frank" for the sake of the story. Frank, now, he likes to eat chocolate cake best of anything in the whole wide world. He would eat it twenty-four hours a day, seven days a week, 365 days a year if he could. And until recently, the chocolate cake thought this was just fine. The cake likes to get eaten by Frank, and thinks Frank is pretty yummy, too. Got it?

Okay, problem is, the chocolate cake is not just a chocolate cake. The chocolate cake is also a world-renowned baker, who happens to have three little cupcakes to look after, and another one baking in the oven.

So when Frank comes 'round looking for a bite of chocolate cake lately, well...the cake has been a bit stale. The frosting ain't as sweet, and the texture is a bit flat. To put it clear as mud, the cake is TIRED. Too busy baking little chocolate cakes and watching out for them other three cupcakes, keeping them from falling in the trash can or getting washed down the garbage disposal, etc.

Here's the question, then. What can a tired piece of chocolate cake do to put the zing back into…dessert? And how can it get those rascally cupcakes out of the way? Or should it just make Frank wait until Baby Cakes is out of the oven and cooling on the stove before expecting the chocolate cake to taste the way it did before?

Stewing,

Veronica

From:	Rosalyn Ebberly <prov31woman@home.com>
To:	VIM <vivalaveronica@marcelloportraits.com>
Subject:	Re: [SAHM I AM] TOTW August 22: The problem with cupcakes...

Dear sister,

I'm responding to you privately, because I'm sorry to hear about the problem with the "chocolate cake" but in *no way* does that mean you are allowed to count my reply toward your weekly response rate!

Tell the "cake" that it won't matter when Baby Cakes is out of the oven. Once a chocolate cake becomes a baker, nobody wants another taste of it. In fact, Frank will probably end up nibbling a few bites off some cheap, store-bought Madeleine. WHY WOULD HE DO THAT when the chocolate cake is a homemade, totally organic, work of art that not only tastes delicious but is GOOD for him, too??? And the cupcakes just leave trails of crumbs around the house, and guaranteed that Baby Cakes will end up needing far more milk than the recipe called for, and the Chocolate Cake will wonder why it ever thought becoming a baker was a good idea, and end up wishing it had stayed completely uneaten on the pantry shelf until it was dried up and covered in mold rather than have to put up with things the way they are now.

Rosalyn

"She looks well to the ways of her household, and does not eat the bread of idleness."

Proverbs 31:27 (NASB)

From:	VIM <vivalaveronica@marcelloportraits.com>
To:	Rosalyn Ebberly <prov31woman@home.com>
Subject:	Re: [SAHM I AM] TOTW August 22: The problem with cupcakes...

Boy howdy, sis, I dunno whether to laugh or holler. Your note was sure cute, but for cryin' out loud, how could you even joke about Frank like that? Don't you know his first wife ran off with a professional chef at a fancy restaurant in New York? Why don't you put some of that there creativity to work on developing a sense of appropriateness when it comes to humor, okay?

Veronica

From:	Rosalyn Ebberly <prov31woman@home.com>
To:	VIM <vivalaveronica@marcelloportraits.com>
Subject:	Re: [SAHM I AM] TOTW August 22: The problem with cupcakes...

You, dear sister, are as DENSE AS A FRUITCAKE.

"She looks well to the ways of her household, and does
not eat the bread of idleness."
Proverbs 31:27 (NASB)

From:	Connie Lawson <clmo5@home.com>
To:	SAHM I Am <sahmiam@loophole.com>
Subject:	[SAHM I AM] Zelia's Game

Hi, Zelia,
I'm still working on that Christmas game of yours. Can my
favorite be the "Christmas Song"—you know, "chestnuts
roasting on an open fire" and all that?
Connie

From:	Zelia Muzuwa <zeemuzu@vivacious.com>
To:	SAHM I Am <sahmiam@loophole.com>
Subject:	Re: [SAHM I AM] Zelia's Game

Bless my bowl-full-of-jelly, NO, Connie! :) The "Christmas
Song" will get you a lump of coal. Try again!
Z

From:	Brenna L. <saywhat@writeme.com>
To:	SAHM I Am <sahmiam@loophole.com>
Subject:	**Re: [SAHM I AM] Zelia's Game**

"Have Yourself a Merry Little Christmas" ???

From:	Zelia Muzuwa <zeemuzu@vivacious.com>
To:	SAHM I Am <sahmiam@loophole.com>
Subject:	**Re: [SAHM I AM] Zelia's Game**

Have yourself a merry little lump of coal, Brenna-babe. :)
Sorry!

From:	P. Lorimer <phyllis.lorimer@joono.com>
To:	SAHM I Am <sahmiam@loophole.com>
Subject:	**Re: [SAHM I AM] Zelia's Game**

"Coventry Carol"

From:	Zelia Muzuwa <zeemuzu@vivacious.com>
To:	SAHM I Am <sahmiam@loophole.com>
Subject:	**Re: [SAHM I AM] Zelia's Game**

Pucker up, sweetheart! :-x

From:	P. Lorimer <phyllis.lorimer@joono.com>
To:	SAHM I Am <sahmiam@loophole.com>
Subject:	Re: [SAHM I AM] Zelia's Game

The rest of you should join in. This is fun!

From:	Brenna L. <saywhat@writeme.com>
To:	SAHM I Am <sahmiam@loophole.com>
Subject:	Re: [SAHM I AM] Zelia's Game

Yeah, fun when you know the rule! *Brenna pouting*
Brenna

From:	Dulcie Huckleberry <dulcie@showme.com>
To:	Thomas Huckleberry <t.huckleberry@showme.com>
Subject:	Office phone number and e-mail

Hi, Darling!

Well, I finally made it to my office this morning. I had a new-employee orientation for the first hour, and then a tour of the building. And now I'm in my very own office, and they already had my computer account set up and phone ready to go! I'm attaching a document with my phone number and work e-mail, but I think it would be better if you just e-mailed me at this address instead unless it's an emergency. You can print out the document and post it by the phone if you want.

How are things going? I miss you already. But I think I'm going to have a lot of fun. And just think—we'll probably be able to afford at least some Christmas presents after all!

If you need me, just call or e-mail. They're going to get me a cell phone to use when I'm out at clients' sites. So I'll give you that number, too, once I have it.

Thank you SO much for supporting me in this, and for staying with the kids. I don't think I could have ever brought myself to send them to day care.

Love,

Dulcie

From:	Brenna L. \<saywhat@writeme.com\>
To:	Tess Gillman \<tessty@newmeximail.com
Subject:	**Thought you'd like to know...**

Hi, Tess,

I just wanted you to know we got the adoption agreement signed and notarized, and it's going in the mail to Nightlight today. Isn't this great? Do you have your agreement and the relinquishment documents done yet? Not that I'm trying to push or anything, but I'm pretty excited. Plus, since we're in Oklahoma, we have the extra step of having to file our paperwork with the adoption court.

Hope everything is well with your family,

Brenna

From:	The Millards <jstcea4jesus@familymail.net>
To:	SAHM I Am <sahmiam@loophole.com>
Subject:	Re: [SAHM I AM] TOTW August 22: The problem with cupcakes...

<Here's the question, then. What can a tired piece of chocolate cake do to put the zing back into...dessert?>

Oh, honey, you...I mean, THAT CAKE, needs to take its hungry man on a DATE, sans cupcakes. Send the cupcakes out to a friend's cupboard for the night. And if the cake is feeling tired, then it needs to give itself the freedom to stay home. Light some candles, turn on some jazz and do something romantic, like a bubble bath for two.

As far as ideas for..."dessert," well, I just happen to have a nice list of suggestions that I'm attaching to this e-mail. They're especially designed for cakes who are in the process of baking a little cake and need to fix dessert in a more creative manner.

All metaphors aside, Veronica, it's important that you and Frank continue working to develop your relationship, apart from the kids. I'm sure you already know that, but sometimes it's hard to remember in the middle of a pregnancy. For some of us, it's hard to remember in the middle of life in general. :)

Blessings,

Jocelyn

From:	Thomas Huckleberry
	<t.huckleberry@showme.com>
To:	Dulcie Huckleberry <dulcie@showme.com>
Subject:	**Re: Office phone number and e-mail**

Hey, Dulcie,

Thanks for the contact info. I'm glad things are going good for you. The girls keep asking where you are. Maybe in a week or two I could bring them by to see your office.

What do you normally give them for lunch? I didn't see much, so I just grabbed some saltine crackers and raisins from the cupboard. Then I saw some Doritos and juice boxes, so I added that. Hope that's okay.

And McKenzie had an accident—wet her pants. I forgot to remind her to go to the bathroom after lunch, and she soaked her outfit. I couldn't find any more clean training pants, and we're all out of pull-ups. So I got a pair of your undies and safety-pinned them around her and stuck a dish towel down them for extra padding. She seemed kind of upset about it.

So then I figured I'd better do some laundry. I put in all the training pants, her wet outfit, and some of your new blouses, since they haven't been washed yet, and washed them on hot, with a couple of cupfuls of bleach—for the training pants. I'll just throw it all into the dryer when they're done washing. Who knows, maybe by the time you come home, I'll have them all folded and put away! :)

The kids are napping now, so I'm looking through the job listings again. I'm looking for a part-time evening job to sup-

plement your salary. I'm also keeping an eye out for a full-time programming job, so we can get things back to normal around here.
Love,
Tom

From:	Brenna L. <saywhat@writeme.com>
To:	SAHM I Am <sahmiam@loophole.com>
Subject:	Re: [SAHM I AM] TOTW August 22: The problem with cupcakes...

Hi, Veronica,
I sympathize. When a couple is trying consciously to bake a little cupcake, it sort of ruins dessert, as well. Some people get to the point where they don't even want dessert anymore. Darren and I learned that dessert really is an important part of a well-balanced diet, so we're trying to find ways to make it as sweet, fun and creative as possible. But when you have cupcakes already, it is hard.
Brenna

From:	VIM <vivalaveronica@marcelloportraits.com>
To:	SAHM I Am <sahmiam@loophole.com>
Subject:	[SAHM I AM] Cupcakes and Baby Stories

Y'all are *Metaphor Mavens!* Keep them dessert ideas rolling. I'm eating them up! :)

Just had to give you a little update on *A Baby Tale*. Did y'all see the one today where the daddy-to-be fainted? The mom hit transition and was whimpering "Darling? I could use some help here." And then the camera shows him laid out on the floor. I laughed so hard, I almost made myself sick. I'm telling ya, I think I'm seriously hooked on this show.

If all y'all've never watched it, you really oughtta. It's so inspiring! Makes me want to go right out and...have a baby! But I'm determined to have me a nice, quiet, respectable birth. No comedy for me!
Veronica

From:	Dulcie Huckleberry <dulcie@showme.com>
To:	"Green Eggs and Ham"
Subject:	**My daughter is wearing my underwear.**

Ohhhh, you guys, was this a good idea—me getting a job? It's my first day, and I'm already scheduled for three client meetings. It's going to be great. My coworkers are friendly, and one is even an old college classmate of mine.

But Tom seems to be having a bit of trouble. He fed our children Doritos, crackers, raisins, and juice boxes for lunch, and then put McKenzie in MY underwear when she had a potty accident because he couldn't find her training pants. And I have a feeling he just ruined about $120 worth of new blouses I bought this weekend. Washed all three of them on hot, with bleach!

Is there a *Housewifery for Dummies* book?
Dulcie

From:	Zelia Muzuwa <zeemuzu@vivacious.com>
To:	"Green Eggs and Ham"
Subject:	**Re: My daughter is wearing my underwear.**

"Oh what men dare do! What men may do! What men daily do, not knowing what they do!"
   —*Much Ado About Nothing,* Act IV, Scene 1

From:	Dulcie Huckleberry <dulcie@showme.com>
To:	"Green Eggs and Ham"
Subject:	**Re: My daughter is wearing my underwear.**

DAILY??? That's *not* comforting, Zelia!
Dulcie

From:	Connie Lawson <clmo5@home.com>
To:	Dulcie Huckleberry <dulcie@showme.com>
Subject:	**Talking Business**

Hi, Dulcie,

I remembered you said this week was your first week on the job, and I just wanted to let you know that I am praying for you! I also wanted to share with you some business advice I've gleaned from some of the books I've been reading. Businesswoman to businesswoman, you know.

Here's an excerpt from *Managing Your Dream Potential,* by Earnest Moore:

"In today's dog-eat-dog corporate jungle, you have to know how to maximize your B2B potential by staying under the radar with your risk factors, but fast-tracking your learning curve by harnessing the synergistic power of the business mentoring relationship."

Isn't that just brilliant? I know that you, being a corporate mom now, and all, would really appreciate this. It's SO nice to have another business mind to consult with. We working moms need all the support we can give each other, right?

Love,

Connie

SAHM I Am Loop Mom

From:	Dulcie Huckleberry <dulcie@showme.com>
To:	Connie Lawson <clmo5@home.com>
Subject:	Re: Talking Business

LOL! Connie, you're so sweet to encourage me like that. However, you must have far more business knowledge than I, because that excerpt made no sense to me whatsoever! But thank you anyway.

Dulcie

From:	Connie Lawson <clmo5@home.com>
To:	Dulcie Huckleberry <dulcie@showme.com>
Subject:	Re: Talking Business

Oh, Dulcie! That's kind of you to say so, but I'm really not such an expert yet. But I will be GLAD to share with you all the little nuggets of wisdom I've gleaned already. I'm starting with a recommended book list I've attached to this e-mail. The excerpt I sent you was talking about the importance of having a mentor to help you reach your dream. I would be honored to mentor you!

Connie

SAHM I Am Loop Mom

From:	Dulcie Huckleberry <dulcie@showme.com>
To:	"Green Eggs and Ham"
Subject:	FW: Re: Talking Business

See attached e-mail. I really MUST learn to keep my mouth shut. Either that, or learn to say what I'm actually thinking instead of trying to be nice all the time. LOOK WHERE "NICE" HAS GOTTEN ME!

About to have the life mentored out of me,

Dulcie

From:	Marianne Hausten <desperatemom@nebweb.net>
To:	"Green Eggs and Ham"
Subject:	**Baby Neil**

Hi, girls,

I just wanted to let you know that baby Neil and I are doing okay. I don't think he's slept yet. Or maybe he has and I missed it. All I know is that it seems like every time I so much as blink, he wants to nurse again.

I'm in that new-baby stupor. Yesterday, Brandon handed me a check from my grandma—present for the baby—for me to endorse. I sat there staring blankly at it for about two minutes, trying to remember what I was supposed to write on it. Brandon finally prompted me, in the softest, sweetest voice, "Just sign your name, honey. Marianne L. Hausten. You can do it." Pathetic, isn't it? :)

He is home with me all this week and next. I'm glad, because I don't know what I'd do with Helene by myself. She does NOT like little brother. She keeps asking me when we're taking him back to the hospital. And she's doing stuff she knows I don't like, just to get attention. Her latest trick is to strip off her diaper and run around the house naked. I TRY telling her to put her clothes back on, but she can't do it herself yet. She just gets mad and starts to cry.

It's very discouraging. And right now, my hormones are all amuck, so I end up crying, too. ★Sigh★ Mothering would be so much easier if I didn't have children to worry about.

Love,

Marianne

From:	The Millards <jstcea4jesus@familymail.net>
To:	"Green Eggs and Ham"
Subject:	**Re: Baby Neil**

Oh, Marianne, I TOTALLY empathize. I'm glad Brandon is able to take some time off to be with you. Sleep as much as you can. It WILL get better. You know that.

As for Helene, all my older kids were jealous of new babies the first time they got a younger sibling. It's normal. The best thing you can do, though, is show a lot of love and set some boundaries. Helene needs to know you and Brandon are still in charge and still have a safe routine and expectations for her. The next time she strips, why not apply a firm swat to that cute little rear end and tell her she must keep her clothes on? Then get her dressed and give her a big hug. She needs to know that her world is still stable, even with all these changes.

Gotta run! Have three places to be, and haven't figured out how to clone myself yet.

Jocelyn

From:	Zelia Muzuwa <zeemuzu@vivacious.com>
To:	"Green Eggs and Ham"
Subject:	**I AM GOING INSANE!**

That's it! I give up! We are NEVER going to complete this adoption! Never, never, never, never, NEVER! God must not want us to do it. I can't see what else it could be. We've been working on the home study since JANUARY and it's still not done, and we have yet another setback!

It turns out that our fingerprints, which we did in June, didn't come out clearly enough, and now they tell us we must have them REDONE! Like, they couldn't have figured that out WEEKS ago??? The office claims they will have them expedited for us, since it's the last thing we need for our paperwork. But it's still going to cost us a couple of weeks.

I am SO mad! Hopping, boiling, steaming, kicking, screaming MAD! I want my baby! I want it NOW, and I'm tired of government red tape, incompetence and complacency getting in my way!

Tristan isn't happy, either. He's retreated to the study and has his nose buried in some book. But for me, books are not the catharsis I want or need. Give me that fingerprint officer, and let me FINGERPRINT HIM!
With what is probably not very righteous indignation,
Z
P.S. Dulcie, babe, sorry to hear about your panties and blouses. Hopefully poor Tom's learning curve won't be too steep. I hope you still have clothes left after he's up to speed on keeping house. :)

From:	Dulcie Huckleberry <dulcie@showme.com>
To:	Zelia Muzuwa <zeemuzu@vivacious.com>
Subject:	**Re: I AM GOING INSANE!**

Poor Z. I'm sorry it's not going as smoothly as you'd like. Just remember that someday, you'll have your baby in your arms, and all this is going to fade into a distant dream. And that baby will be yours FOREVER.

Hugs,

Dulcie

From:	Rosalyn Ebberly <prov31woman@home.com>
To:	SAHM I Am <sahmiam@loophole.com>
Subject:	**[SAHM I AM] GWENCH Update**

Dearest SAHMs,

I just know you all have been waiting patiently for more news on my GWENCH group's efforts at taking Christmas back from those nasty retailers. I have some good news, as well as a prayer request.

The good news is that our e-mail outreach has caused over a thousand people to sign up for our Saving Christmas campaign. Of course, over half of those people are from outside Hibiscus, but it just goes to show how much support we have in the area.

The prayer request is this—it seems that some of the retailers have bribed a few of the weaker-minded charities into helping them COMBAT our efforts! Can you believe it? The charities say they are worried that if the retailers suffer, then corporate charitable donations will also suffer! That's nonsense, of course. Why would charities want to take money from businesses that are only giving in order to get a tax write-off? To me, it's tainted money from the start, and they'd be much better off only to accept donations from people who actually care about their causes.

But never fear, our GWENCH ladies aren't scared off by the big, evil businesses. We're planning a float for the Hibiscus Harvest Parade on Thanksgiving Day, and we're going to send out press releases and everything. People know that the time has come to stand up for what we believe—and we believe retailers are bad for Christmas!

Rosalyn

"She looks well to the ways of her household, and does not eat the bread of idleness."
Proverbs 31:27 (NASB)

From:	Zelia Muzuwa <zeemuzu@vivacious.com>
To:	SAHM I Am <sahmiam@loophole.com>
Subject:	**Re: [SAHM I AM] GWENCH Update**

Gee, Rosalyn, since those "big, evil businesses" are so naughty, why don't you bend your rules and at least give them all a lump of coal for their stockings? That'll teach 'em!

Z

From:	Rosalyn Ebberly <prov31woman@home.com>
To:	SAHM I Am <sahmiam@loophole.com>
Subject:	**Re: [SAHM I AM] GWENCH Update**

Zelia, what a TERRIFIC idea! Oh, I just *knew* I could count on my SAHM sisters for support and inspiration.

Thank you SO much! I'm going to call our other GWENCH'ers right now!

Rosalyn

"She looks well to the ways of her household, and does not eat the bread of idleness."
Proverbs 31:27 (NASB)

From:	Zelia Muzuwa <zeemuzu@vivacious.com>
To:	"Green Eggs and Ham"
Subject:	**Re: [SAHM I AM] GWENCH Update**

sigh Some people just don't get sarcasm.

Z

From:	P. Lorimer <phyllis.lorimer@joono.com>
To:	"Green Eggs and Ham"
Subject:	**Re: [SAHM I AM] GWENCH Update**

Poor Z! I'll cheer you up by posting the following to the loop:

"For all of you who are trying to play Zelia's Seasonal Song Game, remember…your favorite song can be 'Jingle Bells' but NOT 'Carol of the Bells.' Have fun!"

Phyllis

From:	The Millards <jstcea4jesus@familymail.net>
To:	"Green Eggs and Ham"
Subject:	Re: [SAHM I AM] GWENCH Update

OOOOHHHH!!!!! I get it! I'm going to post that my favorite is "O Come All Ye Faithful."

Jocelyn

From:	Zelia Muzuwa <zeemuzu@vivacious.com>
To:	"Green Eggs and Ham"
Subject:	Re: [SAHM I AM] GWENCH Update

Aw, you girls are sweet. I'll be happy to send you both a kiss on-loop!

Zelia

From:	Brenna L. <saywhat@writeme.com>
To:	"Green Eggs and Ham"
Subject:	Re: [SAHM I AM] GWENCH Update

GGGGGRRRRRRRRRRRRRRR!!!!!!!!!!!!!!! It's not fair! I want to play! >:-<

Brenna

From:	Brenna L. <saywhat@writeme.com>
To:	Tess Gillman <tessty@newmeximail.com
Subject:	**Are you getting my e-mails?**

Hi, Tess,

I don't mean to bother you, but I was just wondering if you're getting my e-mails? I think I've sent about three this week, and I haven't heard back from you. I'm not trying to be pushy, but I really would like to know if you've gotten the adoption agreement and relinquishment papers signed and notarized yet? Could you let me know as soon as possible?

Thanks,

Brenna

From:	Tess Gillman <tessty@newmeximail.com>
To:	Brenna L. <saywhat@writeme.com>
Subject:	**Re: Are you getting my e-mails?**

Dear Brenna,

Yes, I got all four of your e-mails so far this week. Did you know that's about one e-mail every other day?

I know you are anxious to get going with the adoption and embryo transfer and all, and I'm anxious for you. But you need to realize that I've got two little boys, and I work full-time at the news station. Plus, Pat is working nights at the pharmacy right now. So it's really hard for us to find time for both of us to go to a notary and get the papers signed.

So I'm not forgetting you, but I do think you need to be aware that even though this is *your* top priority right now, it can't be ours. My family and career have to come first. I think we can get the papers notarized next week and in the mail. Okay?

I'm not mad. Just want you to know what's going on over here.

Blessings,

Tess

From:	Brenna L. <saywhat@writeme.com>
To:	"Green Eggs and Ham"
Subject:	**Re: I AM GOING INSANE!**

I will go with you, Z! I heard one of the other adoptive moms at our home study agency talking about how people tell her, "Well, adoption is the easy way out. You just didn't want to go through the hassle of pregnancy." That's a bunch of…cow manure. Adoption is just as hard, if not more so, than pregnancy. The trouble for me is that I have to do BOTH!

Being patient really STINKS!

Brenna

From:	VIM <vivalaveronica@marcelloportraits.com>
To:	Rosalyn Ebberly <prov31woman@home.com>
Subject:	**Weekly Report**

There ya go. The numbers for this week. Not so bad. Mighty respectable, actually.

Rosalyn, week of August 23, last year: 25.5 %

Veronica, week of August 22, this year: 26.06%

I guess people really like talking about…dessert. And it's helped me a lot. In fact, I'm feeling kinda hungry-like. Think I'll go have me something sweet. :)
Veronica

From:	Rosalyn Ebberly <prov31woman@home.com>
To:	VIM <vivalaveronica@marcelloportraits.com>
Subject:	**Re: Weekly Report**

Could we PLEASE stick to the numbers? All those editorial comments are completely irrelevant, unnecessary and serve absolutely no redemptive purpose whatsoever. I think "dessert" is highly overrated, anyway. I don't want to think about it anymore.
Rosalyn

"She looks well to the ways of her household, and does not eat the bread of idleness."
Proverbs 31:27 (NASB)

From:	VIM <vivalaveronica@marcelloportraits.com>
To:	Rosalyn Ebberly <prov31woman@home.com>
Subject:	**Re: Weekly Report**

<I think "dessert" is highly overrated, anyway. I don't want to think about it anymore.>

Not getting any these days, sis? Too bad. You really need some sweetening up. :)

From:	VIM <vivalaveronica@marcelloportraits.com>
To:	SAHM I Am <sahmiam@loophole.com>
Subject:	[SAHM I AM] TOTW September 5: What I Wish My DH Understood...

This here's my topic, so I'll start it off—

I wish my DH understood that when I've had to leave the kitchen because the sight of raw hamburger has suddenly made me feeling like hurling, that is NOT the time to swoop down on my belly and give it a big old hug and go ga-ga at the baby inside. 'Course, now he probably knows that, since he had to go take a shower to wash the results out of his hair. Ain't MY fault he got in the way of forces beyond my control!

Top that, if you can!

Veronica

From:	Zelia Muzuwa <zeemuzu@vivacious.com>
To:	SAHM I Am <sahmiam@loophole.com>
Subject:	Re: [SAHM I AM] TOTW September 5: What I Wish My DH Understood...

…that my idea of a FAMILY Christmas does NOT include his parents, his brothers, his nieces, nephews, or anyone else on that side of the Atlantic! I love them all, but for once, JUST ONCE, I want Christmas MY way! I don't want to spend Christmas Eve yawning with my eyes watering because I'm so jet-lagged that I can hardly stay awake! No more Yorkshire pudding and strange Zimbabwean dishes! No more getting teased because all the rest of them speak a language I can't understand! I'm American, for crying out loud. We only know English! And they don't even speak "normal" English! I want to stay home!

I'm talking hauling out the holly, and putting up a tree before my spirits fall again! I'm going to fill the stockings, deck the halls and put candles in the windows and sing carols at the spinet. I'm going to put up the brightest string of lights I've ever seen! I'm going to slice up the fruitcake! There's going to be tinsel hanging from that evergreen bough! We need a little music, a little laughter and a snappy "ever after"! I need a little Christmas, NOW!!!

Okay, THAT'S IT! Zelia Muzuwa is PUTTING DOWN HER FOOT! Both feet, even! I am staying home for Christmas! If Tristan wants to jaunt off to England like normal, let him. I'm not going! I'm going to stay home and "have myself a merry little Christmas" right here in good old U.S. of A.

Feliz Navidad! And pass me the fruitcake!

Z

From:	Brenna L. <saywhat@writeme.com>
To:	SAHM I Am <sahmiam@loophole.com>
Subject:	Re: [SAHM I AM] TOTW September 5: What I Wish My DH Understood...

Wow! Speaking of fruitcakes... :)
Brenna

From:	The Millards <jstcea4jesus@familymail.net>
To:	SAHM I Am <sahmiam@loophole.com>
Subject:	Re: [SAHM I AM] TOTW September 5: What I Wish My DH Understood...

Hah, Z! Good for you...I think??? Make sure you have a camcorder running when you make THAT announcement—I would hate to miss out on the fireworks.
Jocelyn

From:	VIM <vivalaveronica@marcelloportraits.com>
To:	SAHM I Am <sahmiam@loophole.com>
Subject:	Re: [SAHM I AM] TOTW September 5: What I Wish My DH Understood...

I'm sorrier than an old swaybacked cow for you, Z. Maybe I can perk you up a bit, and say that MY favorite holiday song is "Frosty the Snowman."
VIM

From:	Zelia Muzuwa <zeemuzu@vivacious.com>
To:	SAHM I Am <sahmiam@loophole.com>
Subject:	Re: [SAHM I AM] TOTW September 5: What I Wish My DH Understood...

Frosty, baby! Oh, yeah! Thanks, Ronnie. That cheers me all sorts of "up." Here's a mistletoe kiss for you— :-x
Z

From:	Rosalyn Ebberly <prov31woman@home.com>
To:	SAHM I Am <sahmiam@loophole.com>
Subject:	[SAHM I AM] Topic of the Week

Girls,

PLEASE don't muddy up the TOTW with posts that relate NOTHING to it! And just as a reminder, replies to a person's post should go to the *individual,* not the whole group.

I'm not convinced that Zelia's sweet little game has much to do with being stay-at-home moms, but I do so LOVE Christmas that I just can't find it in my heart to say no. But we need to make sure to keep replies to a minimum, all right?

That said, here's my favorite Christmas song, in light of the mission of GWENCH: "We Wish You a Merry Christmas."
Rosalyn

"She looks well to the ways of her household, and does not eat the bread of idleness."
Proverbs 31:27 (NASB)

From:	Zelia Muzuwa <zeemuzu@vivacious.com>
To:	SAHM I Am <sahmiam@loophole.com>
Subject:	**Re: [SAHM I AM] Topic of the Week**

Whoops! Coal for Rosalyn! Sorry, Ros.
Z

From:	Rosalyn Ebberly <prov31woman@home.com>
To:	VIM <vivalaveronica@marcelloportraits.com>
Subject:	**Zelia's TOTW posts**

Okay, Ronnie, you CAN'T count Zelia's TOTW posts. It wouldn't be fair. They have nothing to do with the TOPIC!
Rosalyn

"She looks well to the ways of her household, and does not eat the bread of idleness."
Proverbs 31:27 (NASB)

From:	VIM <vivalaveronica@marcelloportraits.com>
To:	Rosalyn Ebberly <prov31woman@home.com>
Subject:	**Re: Zelia's TOTW posts**

Y'all are just mad because I figured out her little game and you didn't! I'm keeping those two posts safe and sound in my tally column, thank you very much.
Ronnie

From:	Rosalyn Ebberly <prov31woman@home.com>
To:	Chad Ebberly <chad.ebberly@henpec.com>
Subject:	**Where were you???**

Chad,

I tried to call you over lunch, but your cell phone was turned off. Where were you, and why didn't you answer your phone??? Don't tell me you had another meeting, because I talked to the secretary and she said there was nothing on the schedule.

I'm really getting tired of this. You're supposed to make me a top priority, and I feel like I am at the bottom of the list. It's not like I was just calling to chat, either. Suzannah has a stomachache again, and Jefferson drew this really creepy picture of all of us in coffins, and then he scribbled over the entire thing in black crayon. I'm thinking about calling the therapist back and scheduling some appointments after all. I know it's probably normal kid stuff, but at least if Jefferson's teachers find something like that and get all weird about it, we can tell them he's in counseling. I wouldn't want them to think there are any problems or that we aren't paying attention.

I hope you have enough time to at least respond to this e-mail.

Rosalyn

"She looks well to the ways of her household, and does not eat the bread of idleness."
Proverbs 31:27 (NASB)

From:	Connie Lawson <clmo5@home.com>
To:	SAHM I Am <sahmiam@loophole.com>
Subject:	Re: [SAHM I AM] TOTW September 5: What I Wish My DH Understood...

Great topic, Veronica! LOL! I wish my DH understood that he can't hang his underwear to dry on the hall tree in the foyer! There is a big window there, so it gets warm and things dry quickly, but I had unexpected company this morning, and it was so embarrassing to bring them in past my hubby's laundry. He has this quirk where he doesn't like his clothing to be dried in the dryer, so I told him that it's his job to hang it out on the line. But he gets in a hurry and doesn't bother taking it all the way outside.

By the way, I've been talking to several Kerrie May consultants, and I'm very impressed with the company. I think it would be a great step in my professional development. They think I have real potential, too. I already have excellent skin. It's like a canvas, and all I need to do is learn to apply the right colors artistically to bring out my natural beauty. They said that when you are a Kerrie May consultant, your own face is the best billboard you could have. I think that shows real marketing savvy, don't you?

Well, off to fold some underwear and put it away. I will have to have a talk with Kurt when he gets home and see if we can work out a compromise. That's the key to a good relationship, I always say—compromise. It's also key to a good client-consultant relationship. I'm reading a book about it right now, called *Compromise: The Win-Win Strategy*

for Getting What You Want. It's fabulous! All of us businesswomen really need to read it.

TTFN! Ta-ta for now, from Tigger

Connie Lawson

SAHM I Am Loop Mom

From:	Zelia Muzuwa <zeemuzu@vivacious.com>
To:	SAHM I Am <sahmiam@loophole.com>
Subject:	Re: [SAHM I AM] TOTW September 5: What I Wish My DH Understood...

So, Connie, you're leaning toward Kerrie May, huh? What
happened to the fruit-flavored hand tools?

Z

From:	Connie Lawson <clmo5@home.com>
To:	SAHM I Am <sahmiam@loophole.com>
Subject:	Re: [SAHM I AM] TOTW September 5: What I Wish My DH Understood...

That's Gadgets for Gals, and they were *never* fruit flavored!
Just brightly colored. And I'm still considering them. But
the makeup looks so fun. And I'd be able to buy it at consultant cost which is 50% of retail. Of course, the business
books I've been reading all say that an entrepreneur like myself has to have real passion for their product. So I'm trying

to decide what I feel more passionate about—cosmetics or tools?

But then, the books also advise going with a business franchise that is compatible with the business owner's lifestyle and personal goals. And Kerrie May, as great as it is, has a lot of meetings. GFG doesn't have as many. GFG also gives a higher percentage to the consultant from sales. But I might not sell as much product right off because it's not as well-known a company.

Ah, the many questions and decisions one must face when starting a business! But the entrepreneurial spirit runs strong in my family. My great-aunt's sister-in-law sold farm eggs door-to-door when she was a girl. And I have a second cousin who always had annual garage sales that were a huge success. Business is in our blood. So I know I can do it.

Connie

SAHM I Am Loop Mom

From:	Zelia Muzuwa <zeemuzu@vivacious.com>
To:	SAHM I Am <sahmiam@loophole.com>
Subject:	Re: [SAHM I AM] TOTW September 5: What I Wish My DH Understood...

Yeah, Connie…sounds like you have a long and productive entrepreneurial family history. I wish you lots of luck! :)

Z

From:	Chad Ebberly <chad.ebberly@henpec.com>
To:	Rosalyn Ebberly <prov31woman@home.com>
Subject:	**Re: Where were you???**

Hi, Ros,

Sorry you were upset about the phone being off. I had to run to the library over lunchtime, and I didn't want the phone to disturb anybody. You know how librarians like to hush noisy patrons! You didn't have to drag in the whole "Priority Tirade." You've made your point on that clear enough over the past several weeks. I don't know what else I can do to make you feel like a priority. It seems to me if I'm not chained to your wrist twenty-four hours a day, I'm not paying enough attention to you.

I think you should talk to that therapist about Jefferson. Make an appointment for yourself, too, while you're at it. I promise I will make time to stay with the kids while you're gone. But you seem very stressed out recently, and there's nothing else I can say to help, it seems. So if talking to someone else will be productive, please do it.

I will be in a meeting this afternoon with the marketing consultant, the CFO, my supervisor and the product development team. The meeting will be in the conference room on third floor, and will last approximately from two o'clock to four-thirty. I will be sitting in the fifth chair from the door, on the left side of the table. If you need to get hold of me, please tell the secretary that you've been diagnosed with paranoia and obsessive compulsive disorder, and therefore must be allowed to interrupt my meetings at any time, under doctor's orders. She'll be glad to come get me.

Happy now?

Chad

Chad Ebberly

Sr. Engineer

Henderson, Peckham, & Associates

From:	Rosalyn Ebberly <prov31woman@home.com>
To:	Connie Lawson <clmo5@home.com>
Subject:	**The TOTW**

Connie! I spent all morning and most of the afternoon trying to track down Chad and contact Suzannah's therapist, with very little success whatsoever. Then I turn on my e-mail to find that you've been skulking behind my back by PARTICIPATING IN THE TOTW!!! You KNOW how I feel about that! And what's worse—you didn't change the subject heading with your little chitchat with Zelia, so now all those messages count toward Ronnie's response rate, too! Because of course my sister can't be sporting enough to play fair! I'm going to have to go fix that, and I don't appreciate having that to do on top of everything else!

Chad claims he "went to the library" over lunch, and that's why he had his phone turned off. Likely story. He probably is planning some sweet surprise for me and didn't want to let on. That's more probable, don't you think? He's never been interested in spending time at the library before....

Have any of your kids ever drawn pictures of you dead in

a coffin? I seem to recall reading that that's some sort of a phase most children go through about age six. Isn't that right? It's all perfectly normal, I'm sure.
Rosalyn

"She looks well to the ways of her household, and does not eat the bread of idleness."
Proverbs 31:27 (NASB)

From:	Brenna L. <saywhat@writeme.com>
To:	"Green Eggs and Ham"
Subject:	**Another step forward!**

Hey, gals,
Tess just e-mailed me! They turned in their adoption agreement and relinquishment papers, finally! Now they have to get their blood work done. More hurry up and wait, I guess. But we're making progress.
Brenna

From:	Zelia Muzuwa <zeemuzu@vivacious.com>
To:	"Green Eggs and Ham"
Subject:	**Re: Another step forward!**

That's great, Bren! Why do they have to do blood work, though?

From:	Brenna L. <saywhat@writeme.com>
To:	"Green Eggs and Ham"
Subject:	Re: Another step forward!

Zelia wrote:
<That's great, Bren! why do they have to do blood work, though?>

It's a requirement before they can ship the embryos. To make sure there are no diseases that could be passed to me through the embryos. It's actually the second set of blood work they've had to do.

Brenna

From:	Connie Lawson <clmo5@home.com>
To:	Rosalyn Ebberly <prov31woman@home.com>
Subject:	Re: The TOTW

Oh, Rosalyn, I'm SO sorry! I figured since Veronica is getting a much bigger response than you, that you'd pretty much given up by now so it wouldn't matter. I'll try to be more careful, though I don't see that it matters much.

As far as coffins go, no...I don't remember any of my kids ever drawing anything like that, at any age. Josiah is six, and his favorite thing to draw is bridges and buildings. I bet he'll be an engineer or architect! :) Maybe Jefferson is going to be an undertaker. LOL!!!

If you're worried about it, call that therapist and talk to her about it.

Connie
SAHM I Am Loop Mom

From:	Rosalyn Ebberly <prov31woman@home.com>
To:	Connie Lawson <clmo5@home.com>
Subject:	**Re: The TOTW**

Why is everybody suddenly pushing me to go see a therapist??? You all act like I have psychological issues or something! I am JUST fine.

And I really think my children are, too. They're just creative. They're artists, and we all know that many artists like to explore the darker feelings in life. It doesn't mean there's anything wrong with them.

As far as the TOTW goes, Connie, I do NOT know where you get the idea that Veronica's response rate is higher than mine. In fact, I can show you the reports she sends me weekly. Her rate has been lower than mine for three out of the past four weeks. I don't call that winning. But I need you to be on my side in all this, and help me out. Please—you'd do that for a friend, wouldn't you?

Rosalyn

"She looks well to the ways of her household, and does not eat the bread of idleness."
Proverbs 31:27 (NASB)

From:	Thomas Huckleberry
	<t.huckleberry@showme.com>
To:	Dulcie Huckleberry <dulcie@showme.com>
Subject:	**Something wrong with Aidan?**

Dulcie,

Aidan is crying—something about her bottom? I checked, and she doesn't have a rash or anything. Do you think she has a bladder infection? No fever, I don't think. I checked her forehead with my hand because I can't find the thermometer.

Tom

From:	Dulcie Huckleberry <dulcie@showme.com>
To:	Thomas Huckleberry <t.huckleberry@showme.com>
Subject:	Re: Something wrong with Aidan?

The thermometer is actually in my purse. Do you want me to come home over lunch and take a look at her? I had a client lunch at noon, but I can reschedule if you think she's really sick.

Dulcie

From:	Thomas Huckleberry <t.huckleberry@showme.com>
To:	Dulcie Huckleberry <dulcie@showme.com>
Subject:	Thermometer

Yes, please come home. She's really fussy and keeps crying about her bottom, but I can't understand what she's saying. And what is the thermometer doing in your purse?

Tom

From:	Dulcie Huckleberry <dulcie@showme.com>
To:	Thomas Huckleberry <t.huckleberry@showme.com>
Subject:	**Re: Thermometer**

Okay, I'll be right home. It was in my purse because McKenzie had gotten into the medicine cabinet Sunday morning and took the thermometer to church with her and was trying to stick it in all the other kids' mouths to take their temps. So I put it in my purse. I told you about that, didn't I?
Dulcie

From:	Dulcie Huckleberry <dulcie@showme.com>
To:	"Green Eggs and Ham"
Subject:	**My husband...*sigh***

Okay, so I come home for lunch and cancel a client appointment because Tom says Aidan is crying about her bottom, and he can't take her temp because the thermometer is in my purse. I get home, and Aidan runs to me, looking as healthy as can be, and says, "Wah ba-tum, Mama." Well, as EVERYONE knows, "ba-tum" is two-year-old speak for "vitamin." Duh! Tom forgot to give it to her at breakfast, and she's been asking for it all morning.

I don't know how I'm going to explain to Mrs. Wallace that I canceled our lunch because of a missing vitamin. :(
Dulcie

From:	Rosalyn Ebberly <prov31woman@home.com>
To:	Chad Ebberly <chad.ebberly@henpec.com>
Subject:	**Re: Where were you???**

Dear Chad,

I'm sorry if my e-mail seemed nagging or clingy to you. It's nothing to me if you want to go to the library. Why shouldn't you go to the library? Just because you've never gone before, and don't even own a library card, there's no time like the present to try something new, right? In fact, just to show you how supportive I am of your new literary endeavors, I'll be glad to read with you whatever book you checked out. I simply cannot WAIT until you get home to take a look at it!

As far as the therapist goes, I think what I need instead is just some time away from the children. As much as I adore them, with your work schedule being so busy lately—not that I'm complaining, okay?—I'm afraid I might be feeling a bit stir-crazy. A night out would be a welcome break. Is there a night this week that you'll be home?

Much love,

Rosalyn

"She looks well to the ways of her household, and does not eat the bread of idleness."
Proverbs 31:27 (NASB)

From:	Zelia Muzuwa <zeemuzu@vivacious.com>
To:	"Green Eggs and Ham"
Subject:	**Re: My husband...*sigh***

Poor Dulcie! You need to create a dictionary of two-year-old language for Tom. So how is the job going?

Z

From:	Dulcie Huckleberry <dulcie@showme.com>
To:	"Green Eggs and Ham"
Subject:	**Re: My husband...*sigh***

The job is going great! And Tom seems to like being home with the girls. He's still applying for programming jobs, but there aren't many available.

Oh, did I tell you? Morris—who married Tom's mom—hired him part-time for his woodworking business. Tom is so excited. He's always wanted to do something like that but never had anyone to teach him. And now, he gets to learn and get paid for learning. So that's good. The pay isn't much, but it helps some. I know Morris did it just because he knows we're in a tough situation right now. He's such a nice man. And to think I was SO worried when he and Jeanine decided to get married! LOL! :)

Dulcie

From:	Rosalyn Ebberly <prov31woman@home.com>
To:	Connie Lawson <clmo5@home.com>
Subject:	**The Library**

Hi, Connie,

Well, Chad must have been telling the truth. He came home with some Grisham novels, and some celebrity biographies. Odd choices, since he's never shown much interest either in legal thrillers or famous people, but whatever. Do you think he's too young to be going through a midlife crisis?

Ros

> "She looks well to the ways of her household, and does not eat the bread of idleness."
> Proverbs 31:27 (NASB)

From:	The Millards <jstcea4jesus@familymail.net>
To:	"Green Eggs and Ham"
Subject:	**I messed up BAD.**

Oh, you guys, I don't know what I'm going to do. I had promised Shane that we'd go out last night, and I totally stood him up! I didn't mean to. But I forgot to change the date because I had a meeting for the homeschool co-op. So I already had a babysitter, and I left the kids and went to the meeting. Poor Shane got home to find the babysitter, and no me. He was SO mad!

I'd love to try to make it up to him, but I just don't know

when I'm going to find the time! I wish he wasn't this upset. It was an honest mistake. It's not like I did it on purpose. Jocelyn

From:	Zelia Muzuwa <zeemuzu@vivacious.com>
To:	"Green Eggs and Ham"
Subject:	Re: I messed up BAD.

Jocie, babe, I'll join you in that doghouse of yours. I gave Tristan the news of my Christmas Revolt, and let's just say it went over like a lead… No…that's too cliché. It went over like a loaf of his mother's fruitcake, which would be worse than a lead balloon.

He says he'll take the kids and go without me. But I know him too well. He will go ahead and order our plane tickets and figure he can sweet-talk me into changing my mind. But not this time! I just saw that one of our department stores has Christmas trees on sale. I'm going to go buy me a TREE! Z

From:	Dulcie Huckleberry <dulcie@showme.com>
To:	"Green Eggs and Ham"
Subject:	Re: I messed up BAD.

Ewwww!!! First we got carols in August, and now Christmas trees in SEPTEMBER??? What happened to back-to-school sales? What happened to Columbus Day and Thanksgiving? Not to mention that bad, wicked holiday at

the end of October that us Good Christians never talk about?
I mean, those stupid Christmas-in-July sales are bad enough.
But actual, real, Christmas stuff in September???

From:	The Millards \<jstcea4jesus@familymail.net\>
To:	"Green Eggs and Ham"
Subject:	Re: I messed up BAD.

Well, you know, the poor retailers have to start early in order
to make up for the GWENCH boycott. :)
Jocelyn

From:	VIM \<vivalaveronica@marcelloportraits.com\>
To:	Rosalyn Ebberly \<prov31woman@home.com\>
Subject:	Weekly Report

How do you figure this? Folks must not have been raring to
gripe about their hubbies this week.

Rosalyn, week of September 6, last year: 35%

Veronica, week of September 5, this year: 22.05%

Ronnie

From:	Rosalyn Ebberly \<prov31woman@home.com\>
To:	VIM \<vivalaveronica@marcelloportraits.com\>
Subject:	Re: Weekly Report

Ronnie,

I don't know why you are always so amazed when you fall short of my response rates. Didn't I warn you that it's not easy to craft a good TOTW? But you were so sure that you could do a better job. I hope you are coming to realize that there are some things at which I excel.

Why don't we just call off our entire contest? I hate to see you go through the humiliation of losing. My sisterly love just rebels at the thought. And I think you've gotten the point now, so let's just let it go, shall we?

I'm only thinking of you, dear.

Rosalyn

"She looks well to the ways of her household, and does not eat the bread of idleness."
Proverbs 31:27 (NASB)

From:	VIM <vivalaveronica@marcelloportraits.com>
To:	Rosalyn Ebberly <prov31woman@home.com>
Subject:	Re: Weekly Report

Well, now, if you ain't the sweetest little thing all the sudden… CAN IT, Rossie! You WILL be sitting on Santa's lap this Christmas if I have to PAY people to gab about the TOTW. Sisterly love, my eye!

Veronica

From:	Rosalyn Ebberly <prov31woman@home.com>
To:	VIM <vivalaveronica@marcelloportraits.com>
Subject:	**Re: Weekly Report**

Suite yourself... "Ronnie Irene." :)
Ros

"She looks well to the ways of her household, and does
not eat the bread of idleness."
Proverbs 31:27 (NASB)

From:	VIM <vivalaveronica@marcelloportraits.com>
To:	SAHM I Am <sahmiam@loophole.com>
Subject:	**[SAHM I AM] TOTW September 26: Looking...**
	cute. :(

I put it off as long as I could, y'all. I did the rubber-band
trick, the husband's shirt and pants trick, the jogging pants
trick and the fat clothes trick. The rubber band snapped,
right in the grocery store and gave me a welt across my belly.
Plus, I hollered like a screech owl and had to hold my pants
together until I got home...totally humiliating. Frank's shirts
look all wrong, and his pants are too small. The jogging pants
only work when I don't have company, and fat clothes???
Never had any. I know, makes y'all sick, don't it? Sorry...

But now, I can't avoid it any longer. I gotta get me some
MATERNITY CLOTHES! So I took a girlfriend, and we
went out shopping yesterday. How did/do y'all stand to

wear that stuff??? I kept trying on one outfit after another, and the store clerks took one look at me and said, "Well, now, don't you look CUTE!" Ugh. Even my girlfriend couldn't resist, "Yeah, Ronnie Irene. You look real… SWEET."

SWEET??? CUTE??? Give me a great, big, Texas-sized BREAK! Y'all know what folks round these here parts mean by "sweet" and "cute," don't you? Means I look like a freaking COW, for crying out loud. Me—Veronica Irene Marcello. Looking cute? I don't THINK SO!

It used to be that people said I looked hot, or classy, or gorgeous. My friends would wait for me to go shopping so's they knew what clothes they should be buying. But now… now I look "sweet." And I don't see my girlfriend all in a dither to get to the store before me so she can brag about how she's wearing the trends first. No. She says I look "sweet." SWEET, I'm telling you!

What am I going to do? I gotta wear *something,* I suppose. But why do maternity clothes have to look so…*maternal?* Either that, or they make me look like *I'm* the baby! I'm telling y'all, one blouse was blue-and-white striped, with DUCKIES on it! Why didn't they just throw Bert and Ernie in for good measure???

I want to look attractive, fashionable, edgy. Not matronly or like an overgrown Shirley Temple in baby-doll blouses.

Have any of y'all found any places to shop for COOL maternity clothes?

Veronica

From:	Zelia Muzuwa <zeemuzu@vivacious.com>
To:	SAHM I Am <sahmiam@loophole.com>
Subject:	Re: [SAHM I AM] TOTW September 26: Looking...cute. :(

Hey, Ronnie, babe,

You are so NOT cute or sweet. And I mean that in the nicest, Southern-est way. :) I'm attaching a list of my fave online maternity stores.

But let me warn you—if you decide to trade in dorky for daring, be prepared! I had this totally awesome belly top that showed just a tiny bit of my "bump"—Tristan couldn't keep his eyes—or hands—off me when I wore that outfit. But I had a couple of older women, total strangers, come up to me and huff and puff, "That's SO disgusting! Nobody wants to see your pregnant stomach!" One even went as far as saying, "It's obscene, that's what it is. Completely indecent. Go put some clothes on!"

Well, Tristan wasn't going to put up with that. He put his entire six-foot three-inch frame between me and the self-righteous hags and said, in his deepest, most intimidating voice, "You shall not speak to my wife that way. Did no one teach you to respect and admire the beauty of a woman who is with child?" Then, he turned, put his hands on my belly and leaned down and KISSED it! Right in front of them. They looked very ashamed of themselves and slunk away, glaring at us. But I didn't care. I gave Tristan a huge kiss, and he had to brush away the tears in my eyes.

sigh I wish he was home from work. Now I feel all cuddly.

Z

From:	Brenna L. <saywhat@writeme.com>
To:	SAHM I Am <sahmiam@loophole.com>
Subject:	Re: [SAHM I AM] TOTW September 26: Looking...cute. :(

<"You shall not speak to my wife that way. Did no one teach you to respect and admire the beauty of a woman who is with child?" Then, he turned, put his hands on my belly and leaned down and KISSED it! Right in front of them.>

SIGH Oh, I can't just do one… *ANOTHER SIGH* And one more… *SIGH* What a guy!

Brenna

From:	VIM <vivalaveronica@marcelloportraits.com>
To:	SAHM I Am <sahmiam@loophole.com>
Subject:	Re: [SAHM I AM] TOTW September 26: Looking...cute. :(

Oh yeah, honey, definite *SIGH* All together now, girls…. *S**I**G**H* What's the emoticon for floaty hearts???

If Frank ever did something so romantic, I'd melt right into a puddle. Then he'd think my water up and broke and he'd call an ambulance. But it'd be worth every second…

Veronica

From:	Rosalyn Ebberly <prov31woman@home.com>
To:	SAHM I Am <sahmiam@loophole.com>
Subject:	Re: [SAHM I AM] TOTW September 26: Looking...cute. :(

Well, not all of us are going to join in on swooning over
Zelia's husband's romantic gesture. After all, those women
did have a point—even if they ought not to have expressed
it quite so rudely. A pregnant belly is a private thing, and I,
for one, detest this new trend of showing it off to the whole
world! There's something sweet and innocent about a loose,
flowing top that hides the "bump." After all, emphasizing
the belly is like an "in your face" reminder of how that
woman got pregnant in the first place! Who wants to think
about that? It's embarrassing! Not to mention depressing....
Rosalyn

"She looks well to the ways of her household, and does
not eat the bread of idleness."
Proverbs 31:27 (NASB)

From:	Connie Lawson <clmo5@home.com>
To:	Rosalyn Ebberly <prov31woman@home.com>
Subject:	???

I thought you weren't going to reply to any of Ronnie's
TOTW.
Connie
SAHM I Am Loop Mom

From:	VIM <vivalaveronica@marcelloportraits.com>
To:	Rosalyn Ebberly <prov31woman@home.com>
Subject:	**Nice of you to join us...**

I needed that extra response to count for my weekly rate.
Thank you, kindly, ma'am. :)
Ronnie

From:	Rosalyn Ebberly <prov31woman@home.com>
To:	Connie Lawson <clmo5@home.com>
Subject:	**Re: ???**

I was TRICKED! She knows how I feel about the topic of
maternity clothes. She did this on purpose because she is ma-
nipulative, conniving and underhanded!
Ros

> "She looks well to the ways of her household, and does
> not eat the bread of idleness."
> Proverbs 31:27 (NASB)

From:	Connie Lawson <clmo5@home.com>
To:	Rosalyn Ebberly <prov31woman@home.com>
Subject:	**Re: ???**

Ahhh, what can rival the love between sisters? It's *so* refreshing.

Connie

SAHM I Am Loop Mom

From:	Rosalyn Ebberly <prov31woman@home.com>
To:	Connie Lawson <clmo5@home.com>
Subject:	**Re: ???**

Who's side are you on, anyway?!?

"She looks well to the ways of her household, and does not eat the bread of idleness."

Proverbs 31:27 (NASB)

From:	Connie Lawson <clmo5@home.com>
To:	Rosalyn Ebberly <prov31woman@home.com>
Subject:	**Re: ???**

It's "whose." "Who's" stands for "who is." And yours, of course. I'm just not used to you being so nasty. That's all.

Connie

SAHM I Am Loop Mom

From:	Rosalyn Ebberly <prov31woman@home.com>
To:	Connie Lawson <clmo5@home.com>
Subject:	**Re: ???**

Gee, thanks for the grammar lesson. *sigh* I'm sorry, Connie. I'm just frustrated with a lot of things right now. You missed all the excitement at the GWENCH meeting. We found out that the rumors about the retailers working with the charities are TRUE! Can you believe it? They've even formed their own group—Shops And Nonprofits Together Alliance. SANTA. Awww, how cute. :(I mean, seriously, is that not the dumbest name for a group you've ever heard? And it spells SANTA. Ugh! They're just trying to shove their Godless ways in our faces! We were all so mad, we spent an extra twenty minutes interceding with God to *crush* them. And I know He will. After all, He's on OUR side. How dare they, with their anti-Christmas ideas, try to steal innocent people away from us? I hope God makes them PAY, now that they have their fancy new organization with its ridiculous acronym. WE had an acronym first, thank you very much. They're just mean little copycats.

Rosalyn

"She looks well to the ways of her household, and does not eat the bread of idleness."
Proverbs 31:27 (NASB)

From:	Connie Lawson <clmo5@home.com>
To:	Rosalyn Ebberly <prov31woman@home.com>
Subject:	Re: ???

At least you're all being grown up about it.
Connie
SAHM I Am Loop Mom

From:	Zelia Muzuwa <zeemuzu@vivacious.com>
To:	SAHM I Am <sahmiam@loophole.com>
Subject:	[SAHM I AM] Adoption update

Hey, babes,

I was always one of those kids that at Thanksgiving, when all the pies came out and my mama would ask me what kind I wanted, would tell her "a little of each, please." Apparently that trait has withstood the years and followed me into adulthood.

What does that have to do with adoption? So glad you asked. Well, Tristan and I have decided NOT to adopt a baby from Ethiopia after all....

Instead, we're going to try for a sibling group! There is a brother and sister—an eighteen-month-old boy and a three-year-old girl—waiting for a family. We've had the baby experience three times already, and these darlings might never get a home because they're older and because sibling groups are harder to place. And that way, we can use both the names we picked out, and maybe Cosette and Seamus will stop arguing over whether they get a brother or a sister. How about one of each? :)

Hopefully, this will not require too much extra paper-work. But after all the setbacks we've already had with our documents, if this causes another delay, who cares anymore? The moment we saw these two, Tristan and I both knew they were OURS.

Z

From:	Dulcie Huckleberry <dulcie@showme.com>
To:	Zelia Muzuwa <zeemuzu@vivacious.com>
Subject:	Re: [SAHM I AM] Adoption update

Oh, Z! I'm so happy to hear this. I was about two years old when my parents adopted me from Guatemala. I was always so thankful they chose a ragtag toddler instead of a baby! :) Your sibling group is so lucky to have a family like yours willing to take them in. You have no idea what it will mean for their lives.

Sending you a BIG, BIG hug!

Dulcie

From:	Zelia Muzuwa <zeemuzu@vivacious.com>
To:	Dulcie Huckleberry <dulcie@showme.com>
Subject:	Re: [SAHM I AM] Adoption update

AWWWW!!!! I could just come all the way to Missouri and hug you to pieces. Thanks, Dulcie.

Z

From:	Marianne Hausten <desperatemom@nebweb.net>
To:	"Green Eggs and Ham"
Subject:	**Busy Day**

Hi, girls,

The good news is that Neil didn't wake up until 8:30 this morning. The bad news is that he'd been up at 10:45, 12:20, 1:30, 4:50 and 6:30, too. Crying. But he didn't want to eat, which is good, because I didn't want to feed him. I stuffed toilet paper in my ears so I couldn't hear him and let Brandon take care of it.

Sometimes I look at him, and it's like seeing a total stranger. I just stare, wondering, "Where did you come from?" I know I should feel bonded to him, so I sit there concentrating, trying to work up some maternal emotion. And just when I think something might come, even the smallest spark of recognition, it sputters and dies. I'm just too tired to feel anything.

Only, sometimes I feel emotions that I'd rather not feel. Like this morning, I was getting him dressed, and I realized his little newborn socks don't fit anymore. And I got mad! Mad at his feet for growing, and mad at myself for being too tired to notice. His babyhood is slipping away, while I sit here in a fog, and I'm missing out! So I took a pair of scissors and cut the tips off each sock. But when I saw his little toes sticking out, I realized what I'd done and I started to cry. I ruined his first pairs of socks!

So then, I gathered up all the socks and their cutoff ends, and I held them to my heart, apologizing and crying. Then I got my needle and thread, and spent the rest of the morning stitching each sock and end back together. Helene kept trying to grab my needle, and when she finally poked her finger on it, I was too tired to care. And besides, at least the two-hour tantrum she threw kept her busy until lunchtime.

I fed her leftover macaroni and cheese, and I even went through the extra trouble of heating it in the microwave. But I ate a slice of pizza cold. Using the microwave twice would have been too exhausting. Then I let her watch a video because it's easier than reading her a book, and that way, if I give her a pillow, she sometimes falls asleep in front of the TV, and I don't have to move her for a nap.

Then I fed Neil, and now I think I might take a nap, too. Only maybe I'll just put my head down on the desk here. The bedroom is awfully far away, and I've already done so much work today.

Marianne

From:	P. Lorimer <phyllis.lorimer@joono.com>
To:	"Green Eggs and Ham"
Subject:	Re: Busy Day

Dear Marianne,

I'm sorry to hear about the socks. It sounds like you are still a bit depressed. Have you spoken to your doctor about this? I think I can safely say that all of us are rather concerned about you. Please, dear Marianne, please go see your doctor.

Love,

Phyllis

From:	Marianne Hausten <desperatemom@nebweb.net>
To:	"Green Eggs and Ham"
Subject:	Re: Busy Day

Phyllis wrote:
<Have you spoken to your doctor about this?>
No. He died.
Great news from Zelia, though. I hope you'll be very happy.

From:	Dulcie Huckleberry <dulcie@showme.com>
To:	"Green Eggs and Ham"
Subject:	Re: Busy Day

What do you mean "he died"??? He was alive six weeks ago
when he delivered your baby! You're talking about Dr. Colvert,
right? He delivered all my kids, too! He can't have died.
Dulcie

From:	Marianne Hausten <desperatemom@nebweb.net>
To:	"Green Eggs and Ham"
Subject:	Dr. Colvert

Yep, he's dead. Happened last week. Evidently, he was ad-
dicted to painkillers and died of an overdose. I'm disappointed. If I'd known he was capable of something like this,
I would have gone in to see him right away.
M

From:	Dulcie Huckleberry <dulcie@showme.com>
To:	Marianne Hausten <desperatemom@nebweb.net>
Subject:	**Capable???**

What do you mean, you'd have gone to see him right away? Marianne, you're scaring me. I know things seem bleak to you, but this is NOT the way to handle it! I'm going to try calling you. Maybe I should take some time off work and come visit you. Or you could come down here.

Hugs,

Dulcie

From:	Marianne Hausten <desperatemom@nebweb.net>
To:	Dulcie Huckleberry <dulcie@showme.com>
Subject:	**Re: Capable???**

What are you talking about? I just meant that if I'd known he was going to OD, I would have gone in to ask him about this whole baby blues issue before he checked out. Now I have to go through all the trouble of finding a new OB. That's an overwhelming thought right now. I refuse to go back to our family doctor, because he had the nerve to tell me that I was "hysterical." And not in the sense of being sidesplitting funny, either! I was waking up at night, gasping for air and unable to breathe, the first week after Neil came home. Went to the E.R. and everything, and the chauvinistic jerk had the nerve to say it was "all in my head."

What did you think I meant?

Marianne

From:	Dulcie Huckleberry <dulcie@showme.com>
To:	Marianne Hausten <desperatemom@nebweb.net>
Subject:	**Re: Capable???**

Marianne, why didn't you tell me about all this? I had no idea! Are you okay? Did the breathing thing get better?
Dulcie

From:	Marianne Hausten <desperatemom@nebweb.net>
To:	Dulcie Huckleberry <dulcie@showme.com>
Subject:	**Re: Capable???**

You've been so busy with your job. I didn't want to bother you. And sometimes, just talking about it or writing about it makes me cry. It's easier to not say anything. The breathing problems went away after a week or so. I think I was just too fatigued and my body didn't know what to do.
Marianne

From:	Dulcie Huckleberry <dulcie@showme.com>
To:	Marianne Hausten <desperatemom@nebweb.net>
Subject:	**Re: Capable???**

Listen, Marianne—I am NEVER too busy for you. Okay? It doesn't matter if I have ten jobs, my friends are still more important.

I never knew how hard it would be to work outside the home. I come home and the kids all want me, and Tom wants me. In different ways, of course. And I want to be there for them. Sometimes during the day, I think about them and I get this empty, sad ache inside. The first few days it happened, I thought I must be hungry, so I had a candy bar. But I think the truth is…I miss them. At least I hope that's the problem. If I keep up with the candy bars, I'm going to gain back all the weight I lost earlier this year.

And the house is looking a bit cruddy. I'm no neat freak, but I saw Tom cleaning up the kitchen cabinet after supper last night. And would you believe he didn't clear out the sink snot from under the faucet handle?
Dulcie

From:	Marianne Hausten <desperatemom@nebweb.net>
To:	Dulcie Huckleberry <dulcie@showme.com>
Subject:	**Sink Snot?**

Okay, Dulcie, I have to know. I have a degree in home economics, and not one of my professors ever used this term. What ARE you talking about?
Marianne

From:	Dulcie Huckleberry <dulcie@showme.com>
To:	Marianne Hausten <desperatemom@nebweb.net>
Subject:	**Re: Sink Snot?**

You know, it's that blackish gummy stuff that collects under the faucet handles and around the base of the faucet. It's made from all the grease and dust and old food that end up getting slopped in the sink. My mom used to call it that. You've never heard of it? Maybe you don't get sink snot at your house.
Dulcie

From:	Marianne Hausten <desperatemom@nebweb.net>
To:	Dulcie Huckleberry <dulcie@showme.com>
Subject:	**Re: Sink Snot?**

I think Helene frightens it away. :)
Marianne

From:	Dulcie Huckleberry <dulcie@showme.com>
To:	Marianne Hausten <desperatemom@nebweb.net>
Subject:	**Re: Sink Snot?**

Woo-hoo! Was that a SMILE I just got from you??? And an attempt at humor???
Dulcie

From:	Marianne Hausten <desperatemom@nebweb.net>
To:	Dulcie Huckleberry <dulcie@showme.com>
Subject:	**Re: Sink Snot?**

I suppose so. But it wore me out and now I need my bed. Good night.
Marianne

From:	Dulcie Huckleberry <dulcie@showme.com>
To:	SAHM I Am <sahmiam@loophole.com>
Subject:	**[SAHM I AM] Christmas game**

In celebration of having just made Marianne smile, I am going to attempt Zelia's game, though I am philosophically opposed to celebrating Christmas—or even acknowledging it—before Thanksgiving.

Here's my attempt: "All I Want For Christmas Is My Two Front Teeth."
Dulcie

From:	Zelia Muzuwa <zeemuzu@vivacious.com>
To:	SAHM I Am <sahmiam@loophole.com>
Subject:	**Re: [SAHM I AM] Christmas game**

Oh, sorry, Dulcie, my friend. All you'll be getting for Christmas with that song is a lump of coal. Try again!
Z

From:	Dulcie Huckleberry <dulcie@showme.com>
To:	Zelia Muzuwa <zeemuzu@vivacious.com>
Subject:	**Re: [SAHM I AM] Christmas game**

Aw, come on, Z! I'm your friend. Just tell me what the secret is. I'm so bad at these games.

Dulcie

From:	Zelia Muzuwa <zeemuzu@vivacious.com>
To:	Dulcie Huckleberry <dulcie@showme.com>
Subject:	Re: [SAHM I AM] Christmas game

Nope, I am resolute. Do what you will...I won't talk! Ever! :)

Z

From:	VIM <vivalaveronica@marcelloportraits.com>
To:	Rosalyn Ebberly <prov31woman@home.com>
Subject:	Weekly Report

Rosalyn, week of September 27, last year: 29.04%

Veronica, week of September 26, this year: 21.95%

Alrighty, sis, there's something mighty funny going on. I kept ALL the TOTW responses I got this week, and then figured out the percentages based on what I had. And then I went to the official archives and counted the responses there. Officially, my response rate was lower than y'alls for this week. But according to the messages I kept in my inbox, I was three percentage points HIGHER than you from last year. That's a difference of 10%! What in the name of Texas is going on???

Veronica

From:	Rosalyn Ebberly <prov31woman@home.com>
To:	VIM <vivalaveronica@marcelloportraits.com>
Subject:	**Re: Weekly Report**

I don't know what's going on, dear sister. But it's late and I'm headed to bed. I would think you'd have had your fill of such juvenile nonsense by now. Apparently not. I'll have Connie look into it tomorrow....
Rosalyn

"She looks well to the ways of her household, and does not eat the bread of idleness."
Proverbs 31:27 (NASB)

From:	VIM <vivalaveronica@marcelloportraits.com>
To:	SAHM I Am <sahmiam@loophole.com>
Subject:	**[SAHM I AM] TOTW October 10: Got myself "carded."**

Howdy, y'all! Well, scoop me out of the garden, mix me with water and let the kiddos make pies outta me, because my name is officially MUD. :(

I'm a mite befuddled about how it happened, but somewhere between me saying "I do" and the preacher saying "You may kiss the bride" I got saddled with the Mother-In-Law Birthday Card. Last year, it wasn't such a big deal, because we still had amnesty under the Newlywed Clause, and they were planning to visit soon. But this year? *Ay carramba!* Mama Tiziana's birthday was yesterday, and did I get a card sent? No.

When Frank realized it, he rushed to the phone to call her. I don't know what all she said, but she sure was raising an awful ruckus. And what did Frank do? Why, the sorry wad blamed it on me! I'm not kidding. They were yakking a mile a minute in Italian, but he kept pointing at me and shaking his head. He explained later, "I told Mama that you were very tired with the baby and with caring for the other children, and did not have time to go buy a card."

ME buy a card? For HIS mother? What's *that* all about? I asked him why he didn't go get a card himself. "Oh," he said, waving it off with his hand, "I am no good with finding the birthday greeting card. Women are better at such things."

Well! Just 'cause a chicken's got wings don't mean it can fly! Problem is, *this* woman might not be better at "such things." I go to the card section and stand there looking at all those choices like a calf looks at a new gate. Can't never make up my mind! And remembering dates? Shewwee! That's plumb near impossible for me.

To make matters worse, NOW I'm also in charge of the Christmas cards! Who in their right mind sends out Christmas cards anymore? I don't have time for all that jazz! I'm going to have me a baby, and they expect me to get cards sent out? Frank dumped on me a list that's a country mile long— over five hundred names on the thing! I don't even know half these people, but I did recognize the name of a great-aunt of his that DIED last year! He also handed me a boxful of returned cards from two years ago that I'm supposed to track down addresses for. Yeah right! I shoved the whole rat's nest back at him and told him that if he didn't want to be getting

"Nuttin' For Christmas" he'd sure enough better manage his own mountain of Christmas cards. I'm bearing his child, and he wants Christmas cards? I. Don't. Think. So.

So this here's the TOTW: do y'all send cards to y'all's in-laws and out-laws and up-laws and down-laws, and if so, how do you manage to keep them all straight and on time?
Tuckered out,
Veronica

From:	Rosalyn Ebberly <prov31woman@home.com>
To:	Connie Lawson <clmo5@home.com>
Subject:	**The loop TOTW**

Do you see what she's trying to do, Connie? She thinks she can LURE me into answering the TOTW. She knows I have a superbly efficient system for keeping track of greeting cards. But I'm not going to post it! I am NOT!
Resolutely,
Rosalyn

"She looks well to the ways of her household, and does not eat the bread of idleness."
Proverbs 31:27 (NASB)

From:	The Millards <jstcea4jesus@familymail.net>
To:	SAHM I Am <sahmiam@loophole.com>
Subject:	**Re: [SAHM I AM] TOTW October 10: Got myself "carded."**

Hi, everybody,

I know I said I was taking some time off from the loop, but I just couldn't stay away. I missed you all so much. It's been extremely hectic around our house. With all the activity, I've had to stay up late and haven't gotten much sleep. But it's not as bad as having a newborn, right Marianne? :) However, I did get a pretty nasty cold, and am still feeling tired. Guess that's the life of a mom, though. We baby everybody else when they get run down, but just keep pushing ourselves forward no matter what.

Veronica, I can totally relate to your TOTW. I end up doing all the greeting cards in our house because Shane just can't handle it. They always arrive about three weeks late, but at least they get sent out. I do wish there was a better system to handle it, though.

If I had more time, I would try buying all the cards in January, and then writing in them, addressing and stamping the envelopes and filing them by month. But I know I'd never remember to put them in the mail on the right days!

Gotta run—it's about time for piano lessons.

Jocelyn

From:	Rosalyn Ebberly <prov31woman@home.com>
To:	Connie Lawson <clmo5@home.com>
Subject:	**Greeting Cards**

Now she's dragged Jocelyn into it! I can't stand it! All those misguided, disorganized mothers out there. They need me!

Who else is going to be able to bring order into their chaos? The pressure is too great, Connie. I have to post. I NEED to post!

Help me!

Rosalyn

"She looks well to the ways of her household, and does not eat the bread of idleness."
Proverbs 31:27 (NASB)

From:	Connie Lawson <clmo5@home.com>
To:	Rosalyn Ebberly <prov31woman@home.com>
Subject:	**Re: Greeting Cards**

Stand firm, Rosalyn! After Christmas, you can take over the TOTW again and fix all this. January would be a great time to discuss your Hospitality and Correspondence Cabinet. Just wait her out. Don't give in.

But, since you aren't able to post about the HCC system yet, could I just give a couple of little highlights? Teasers, really. Just to whet their appetites? Surely one little post won't make that big of a difference. Would that be okay?

Connie

SAHM I Am Loop Mom

From:	Rosalyn Ebberly <prov31woman@home.com>
To:	Connie Lawson <clmo5@home.com>
Subject:	**Re: Greeting Cards**

NOOOOOOOOOOOOOO!!!!!!!!!!!!

"She looks well to the ways of her household, and does not eat the bread of idleness."
Proverbs 31:27 (NASB)

From:	hr@smartech.com
To:	Thomas Huckleberry
	<t.huckleberry@showme.com>
Subject:	**Thank You for Interviewing**

Dear Mr. Huckleberry:

We at SmarTech would like to thank you for interviewing with us. Though your credentials and experience are impressive, they are not the best fit for our company. We wish you great success in your career, and we thank you for thinking of SmarTech.

Sincerely,

Carol Hopper

Human Resource Assistant

SmarTech Solutions, Inc.

From:	Thomas Huckleberry
	<t.huckleberry@showme.com>
To:	Dulcie Huckleberry <dulcie@showme.com>
Subject:	**Lunch today?**

Hi, Dulcie,

The kids are really rowdy today, and with the rain there's no way to take them outside. I think we need to get out of the house. How about lunch with us today? We could go to Burger Dreams—they have an indoor play place.

Love,

Tom

From:	Dulcie Huckleberry <dulcie@showme.com>
To:	Thomas Huckleberry
	<t.huckleberry@showme.com>
Subject:	**Re: Lunch today?**

Hi, Darling,

I'm sorry. I have a design presentation at one o'clock this afternoon. I'm going to have to work through lunch so I'm ready for it. How about tomorrow?

If the kids are being rowdy, let them build a blanket fort in the living room. That usually works to divert their energy.

Love,

Dulcie

From:	Marianne Hausten <desperatemom@nebweb.net>
To:	The Millards <jstcea4jesus@familymail.net>
Subject:	**Welcome back to the loop!**

Hi, Jocelyn,

I'm glad you came back to the loop. We missed you. Sorry to hear you are feeling ill. Sounds like you need to rest more. I am probably resting more than is good for me these days. Seems as if all I want to do is sleep. But I can't this morning. I need to pick up all the pieces for about twenty wooden puzzles that Helene dragged out. It will take me a good hour to sort them all out and get them put back together. And then I have to fold and put away all the clothes from her dresser, which she emptied after she dumped all the puzzles. I just keep telling myself that if I get all that done this morning, I can reward myself with a nap in the afternoon. At least for a few hours until Neil gets hungry.

Hope you have a better morning than me.

Marianne

From:	Zelia Muzuwa <zeemuzu@vivacious.com>
To:	SAHM I Am <sahmiam@loophole.com>
Subject:	**Re: [SAHM I AM] TOTW October 10: Got myself "carded."**

Hi, Babes!

Sorry to hear about the greeting card snafu, Veronica. I don't know that I have a good solution for remembering all the dates, but I get tired of buying greeting cards. I'd make them myself if I had the time, but instead, I let the kids make them. I don't know if your kids are too old to find that fun or not, but mine love it. Just give them some construction paper, crayons, and maybe some catalog pictures to cut out and glue on, and you're set. And your in-laws will probably like that better than a store-bought card anyway. Mine do.

Oh, speaking of in-laws, an e-mail just came in from my MIL. Wonder what she wants.

Z

From:	Dulcie Huckleberry <dulcie@showme.com>
To:	SAHM I Am <sahmiam@loophole.com>
Subject:	Re: [SAHM I AM] TOTW October 10: Got myself "carded."

Hi, all,

I'm at work, so can't write long, but just wanted to say FORGET the paper cards. Just do an e-card! They're free, and you can send them immediately, which means you never have to admit you actually forgot to plan ahead. They've rescued my neck on countless occasions.

I have a design presentation in just a few minutes. Better go.

Dulcie

From:	Rosalyn Ebberly <prov31woman@home.com>
To:	SAHM I Am <sahmiam@loophole.com>
Subject:	Re: [SAHM I AM] TOTW October 10: Got myself "carded."

E-CARDS? Homemade kids' cards? Buying, addressing and stamping in bulk? What are you girls thinking? Is this the way to show our love and appreciation of our relatives? Is this the self-discipline and orderly lifestyle we want to demonstrate as Christian mothers? This is taking shortcuts! It's impersonal and sends the message that our family is not actually the high priority it ought to be.

You may feel that it is the only way to cope with your haphazard existence. But if you all would simply order your priorities correctly and use a good organizational system, you would find that sending a *personal,* heartfelt greeting on a birthday or anniversary is really not so difficult as you all are making it. I certainly never have been guilty of forgetting a birthday or sending a generic store-bought card, much less an *e-card.*

In January, I will present to you all my Hospitality and Correspondence Cabinet, a system that will help you all manage your personal correspondence better, IF you will put it into practice. Until then, please take a look at the attached tip sheet for making homemade greeting cards that do NOT look like a child's work. Not that encouraging your children to make cards is a bad thing, but you should not use them to get out of sending your own greetings.

Happy greetings,

Rosalyn

"She looks well to the ways of her household, and does
not eat the bread of idleness."
Proverbs 31:27 (NASB)

From:	Marianne Hausten <desperatemom@nebweb.net>
To:	"Green Eggs and Ham"
Subject:	**The Voice In My Head**

I just figured it out! It's Rosalyn! She's what I hear almost
every waking moment. "I know you can't achieve this, but
it's really how things SHOULD be done." And "If you only
tried harder to follow my example, you wouldn't be such a
pathetic mother."

Anyone know how to shut her up?

Marianne

From:	Zelia Muzuwa <zeemuzu@vivacious.com>
To:	"Green Eggs and Ham"
Subject:	**Re: The Voice In My Head**

Are you just now figuring that out, Marianne-babe? Why
do you think Jocelyn, Dulcie and I came up with our own
subgroup? It was mainly to try to talk louder than Rosalyn's
Voice of Doom. What I found out is that the off button is
somewhere in my own head. Hope you find yours soon!

Z

From:	Connie Lawson <clmo5@home.com>
To:	Rosalyn Ebberly <prov31woman@home.com>
Subject:	**You caved!**

So much for being resolute! You just couldn't resist playing Martha Stewart, could you?

By the way, I'm still trying to decide between Kerrie May and Gadgets for Gals. I've been to a meeting for both of them, now, and there's things I like about both. Which would you be more likely to host a party for if I became a consultant? You know I wouldn't dream of letting anybody but you have the honor of hosting my first home party.

Love,

Connie

SAHM I Am Loop Mom

From:	VIM <vivalaveronica@marcelloportraits.com>
To:	SAHM I Am <sahmiam@loophole.com>
Subject:	**[SAHM I AM] No more television**

Well, it's a pretty big mess of fish I'm in now. Just got done reading me an article in *With Child* magazine that says the radiation from the television can hurt a growing fetus. I can't barely imagine how much danger I've already exposed my little tyke to, just with watching *A Baby Tale* for all these weeks!

So no more TV for this mama! How am I ever going to

cope without that show? Y'all are going to have to help me
through this.
Veronica

From:	The Millards <jstcea4jesus@familymail.net>
To:	SAHM I Am <sahmiam@loophole.com>
Subject:	Re: [SAHM I AM] No more television

Veronica, you are so cute! Don't you know there's radiation
from the computer monitor, cell phone and microwave,
too? Are you going to stop using all of them? I've heard this
thing about the TV and such, and it's silly. All it does is scare
first-time moms like you. Trust me, I've had four kids, and
I've watched TV, used the microwave, and so on, with all
four pregnancies, and my kids are just fine. Relax and go
watch your show if you want to. You deserve it. :)
Jocelyn

From:	VIM <vivalaveronica@marcelloportraits.com>
To:	SAHM I Am <sahmiam@loophole.com>
Subject:	Re: [SAHM I AM] No more television

Thank you kindly, Joc, for the reassurance. But it don't
change my mind none. I've already stopped using the microwave, and I got me a wireless keyboard so I can sit farther away from the computer monitor, and I only use my
cell phone with a hands-free headset. So the TV's gotta go,
too. Can't take no chances with my little precious munchkin.

But *Baby Tale* will be on in just a few minutes. It's all I can do to not go turn on the TV. I'll miss it SO much!
Veronica

From:	The Millards <jstcea4jesus@familymail.net>
To:	Marianne Hausten <desperatemom@nebweb.net>
Subject:	Re: Welcome back to the loop!

Hi, Marianne,
Sorry to hear that Helene is making such a mess of your house. You know, you should watch *Super Nanny* on TV. Or get her book. It sounds to me like Helene needs to become acquainted with the Naughty Seat.
Jocelyn

From:	Zelia Muzuwa <zeemuzu@vivacious.com>
To:	"Green Eggs and Ham"
Subject:	E-mail from my MIL

Hi, girls,
You'll never guess what Tristan's mom e-mailed me about. The adoption. We told her we wanted to try for that sibling group. Now she's all worried that because the kids are older, they won't bond with us, or that they'll end up psychopathic because of being deprived in early childhood.

I wish we could just send our parents to some remote planet until after the adoption is completed and then invite them back after we're all adjusted to our new life. I'm getting so tired of defending our decisions to them and having them offer advice we NEVER asked for! Does she think we're not grown-up enough to know better than to jump into something like this uneducated? We have talked to many adoption professionals and other families and have read a small library's worth of books on older child adoption and adoption issues. We KNOW what we're getting into! Why can't they just be supportive instead of trying to burden us with their worry and fears?

Then she has the nerve to slip in at the end, "By the way, we hope all this fuss about the adoption hasn't caused you to forget about Christmas. Don't let's forget to set aside a bit of money for visiting those who are already part of your family, shall we?" I'm not even going to respond. It's Tristan's gene pool, so he can deal with it. He still doesn't believe that I'm not going to England for Christmas this year—even after I hired a professional Christmas lights company to decorate our house. He's SO in denial!

Z

From:	Thomas Huckleberry
	<t.huckleberry@showme.com>
To:	Dulcie Huckleberry <dulcie@showme.com>
Subject:	Saying hi

Hi, sweetie,
The blanket fort worked well. You should have seen it—we had blankets clothespinned together and strung across most of the living room and over the dining table. I made it into

a maze for them, and we had races to see who could crawl through the fastest. They're all down for naps now. The house is really quiet.

Did you know that SmarTech turned me down? That's three for three now on interviews, not to mention the stack of applications that have been totally ignored. Am I doing something wrong?

Maybe we could go out tonight, if I can find a babysitter. I don't think Mom is working this evening, so I can ask her to babysit for us. I think I'm going a little stir-crazy shut up in the house like this. I don't know how you ever managed it.

Guess I'll check out the job listings again. I hate this, Dulcie. I really do. If God really works things out for good, then where is the good in any of this?

Love,

Tom

From:	Dulcie Huckleberry <dulcie@showme.com>
To:	Thomas Huckleberry <t.huckleberry@showme.com>
Subject:	Re: Saying hi

Hi, darling,

My design presentation went great! The clients loved it, and my supervisor said that she's gotten several compliments about my work recently.

I'm sorry about SmarTech. I know you're disappointed. But how can you say you hate everything about this? Aren't you glad I'm getting a chance to do what I love? And what about the great morning you had building blanket forts and playing with your kids? Don't you know that's a memory you'll treasure for the rest of your life?

I know being home is hard. It was hard for me, too. But sometimes I sit here at my desk and stare at the picture of the three girls, and I get a lump in my throat just thinking about being home with them. Sure, the diapers and the dishes and cleaning and such get boring. But I love reading them books, and cuddling them and tickling them, and taking them for walks and seeing the glow on their faces when they find a leaf with a fuzzy-wuzzy caterpillar crawling on it. Those memories are priceless. Don't miss out on it.

Suddenly, I wish I could trade places with you! Silly, huh? I'm really loving my job. But I do miss being with them, even though they drive me crazy. Tell you what, let's plan on having lunch together as a family tomorrow. I don't have any meetings or appointments. Does that sound good?

Love,

Dulcie

From:	Dulcie Huckleberry <dulcie@showme.com>
To:	"Green Eggs and Ham"
Subject:	**What have I done?**

You guys, I just got the saddest e-mail from Tom. He got turned down on yet another interview, and I think he's feeling lonely at home. He wanted to have lunch with me today, but I had to say no. So he spent the morning building blanket forts with the girls.

He's obviously unhappy. Do you think I made the right decision to go back to work? I don't think we really had any other choice, but I'm afraid the kids are going to know that Tom doesn't really want to be there. Do you think it will scar them emotionally?

I feel guilty. Being home wasn't so hard on me. I had lots of friends to connect with. Tom has nobody. I knew how to keep house. Tom never had to learn. I have all those mommy instincts. Tom is a good dad, but he has no intuition when it comes to how to keep the girls occupied.

And here I am, with my dream job going great, and I find myself thinking about *them* all the time. Of course, when I was home, I dreamed of the day that I'd be able to go back to work. What is wrong with me? Am I really that discontent? I should be grateful that God provided a way for me to support the family, not wishing I could be home playing with them. And I am grateful, mostly....

Dulcie

From:	Marianne Hausten <desperatemom@nebweb.net>
To:	The Millards <jstcea4jesus@familymail.net>
Subject:	Re: Welcome back to the loop!

Hi, Jocelyn,
Thanks for the TV-book recommendation. But I really don't think a TV show is going to help with my daughter. She doesn't mean to be naughty. She's just energetic, and I have a hard time keeping up with her. I hate to make her settle

down because she just gets mad and throws a fit. Besides, I know things are hard for her right now with a new baby brother and with me being so tired. It's really not her fault if she gets a little naughty now and then. Poor thing has had so many changes. It's common for children to regress when a new sibling is added to the family. I just can't stand to make things get ugly just for the sake of keeping the house neat. I'm sure once things get back to normal, she'll settle down. If I was doing a better job at playing with her and being more active, she'd likely be just fine.

Marianne

From:	VIM <vivalaveronica@marcelloportraits.com>
To:	Rosalyn Ebberly <prov31woman@home.com>
Subject:	**PICK UP YOUR PHONE!**

You deceitful, scheming shrew! You're as crooked as a barrel of snakes! Mean as a wolverine! And too cowardly to answer the phone and talk to me.

How could you do this to me, your sister? Know what? Forget the phone. Don't pay no never mind to the voice message I left, neither. I don't WANT to talk to you none. I'm through.

Veronica

From:	Rosalyn Ebberly <prov31woman@home.com>
To:	Connie Lawson <clmo5@home.com>
Subject:	**Re: You caved!**

Yes, I caved. I couldn't help it. It's all been too much pressure. The kids, Chad, Veronica, the loop. I must be going crazy, Connie. Veronica sounds like she'd like to kill me, and I have no idea what I've done now, but you know, it's always something with her. I just wish I could go far away somewhere where no one could see or bother me.

Rosalyn

> "She looks well to the ways of her household, and does not eat the bread of idleness."
> Proverbs 31:27 (NASB)

From:	Rosalyn Ebberly <prov31woman@home.com>
To:	VIM <vivalaveronica@marcelloportraits.com>
Subject:	**Re: PICK UP YOUR PHONE!**

Dearest sister,

Thanks for the encouraging note and voice mail. It was a great addition to an absolutely charming week. What on EARTH has gotten into you? I don't have any idea what your problem is. Would you mind letting me in on the secret before you proceed with tearing me to shreds?

Warmly,

Rosalyn

> "She looks well to the ways of her household, and does not eat the bread of idleness."
> Proverbs 31:27 (NASB)

From:	VIM <vivalaveronica@marcelloportraits.com>
To:	Rosalyn Ebberly <prov31woman@home.com>
Subject:	**Re: PICK UP YOUR PHONE!**

Sister,

Don't act so innocent with me. You can put your boots in the oven but that don't make them biscuits. You ought to know exactly what I'm talking about.

I'm talking about how YOU MESSED WITH THE LOOP ARCHIVES! You deleted a bunch of my TOTW responses, which is why I've been losing week after week on my response rate. I knew something smelled fishy last week when my totals didn't add up with the loop archives, so I started reading through the archives. Started noticing gaps in the numbers. Posts are MISSING, Rosalyn, and the only two people who have the ability to delete loop posts are YOU and Connie! And Connie ain't got the motive.

Y'all KNEW you couldn't win honestly, so you CHEATED! And you talk about loving Jesus and being such a "good" Christian. And yet playing dirty against your own flesh and blood don't bother you none at all.

Is that why you wanted to call off the contest a few weeks ago? Is that why you knitted me that sweater? I bet you were feeling mighty guilty, weren't you? And so you thought you'd throw me off the track with your phony attempts at being nice. Why do you hate me so much, Ros?

Veronica

From:	Rosalyn Ebberly <prov31woman@home.com>
To:	VIM <vivalaveronica@marcelloportraits.com>
Subject:	Re: PICK UP YOUR PHONE!

You're right. I cheated. It was wrong. It wasn't setting a good example of Christ's love. You have every right to be mad. I'm sorry.

I don't hate you, Ronnie. This isn't even really about you. I mean, it started out that way, just a competition, like when we were kids. But then all the rest of this stuff started happening, and I just couldn't stand losing this contest, too. I feel like I'm losing everything else. So I thought if I tweaked the archives, you'd never know, and then I wouldn't have to add yet another failure to my heap.

But that doesn't excuse what I've done. Is there any way to make it right?
Rosalyn

"She looks well to the ways of her household, and does not eat the bread of idleness."
Proverbs 31:27 (NASB)

From:	VIM <vivalaveronica@marcelloportraits.com>
To:	Rosalyn Ebberly <prov31woman@home.com>
Subject:	Re: PICK UP YOUR PHONE!

What do you mean "all the rest of this stuff started happening"? I appreciate the apology, but I'm not buying it yet.

You've been big hat and no cattle before, and I ain't letting you pull the wool over my eyes again.
Veronica

From:	Rosalyn Ebberly <prov31woman@home.com>
To:	VIM <vivalaveronica@marcelloportraits.com>
Subject:	Re: PICK UP YOUR PHONE!

What I MEAN, Ronnie, is that my marriage is falling apart and my children are having emotional problems. And to top it all off, I THINK CHAD IS HAVING AN AFFAIR!

So you see, the loop and our stupid contest are really the least of my worries! I'm sorry I lied to you. I'm sorry I deleted those posts. But most of all, I'm sorry I ever agreed to the contest. I might as well go have my photo taken on Santa's lap. While I'm at it, why don't I just ask him out for dinner? I could slide down our chimney with him, and I doubt Chad would even notice!

Oh, Ronnie, how could he do this to me? To us? I cheated by deleting a few loop posts. He's cheating by destroying our wedding vows. I'm not trying to make light of what I did to you, but I honestly don't have the energy at the moment to spend being too emotional about it. My life is crumbling. Does a silly contest really matter?
Rosalyn

"She looks well to the ways of her household, and does not eat the bread of idleness."
Proverbs 31:27 (NASB)

From:	VIM <vivalaveronica@marcelloportraits.com>
To:	Rosalyn Ebberly <prov31woman@home.com>
Subject:	**Re: PICK UP YOUR PHONE!**

THAT NO-GOOD, TWO-TIMING, DOUBLE-CROSSING, PLUG-UGLY COW PATTY! Ain't nobody going to do that to MY sister!

All right, Rosalyn, here's what we're gonna do. No arguing, got it? I want you to *jump* when I say *frog!* It's time to paint y'all's rump white and run with the antelope, darling, 'cause I won't take no for an answer.

My Frank has a good friend who's a private detective. He handles this sort of stuff all the time. Just last week, he busted a guy who was cheating on his wife with one of the city councilmen. Or councilwoman in this case. Got himself quite the reputation for tracking down straying spouses. Frank taught him how to take better pictures and develops some of his photos for him, so he owes us a favor. I'm going to send him in there to track Chad awhile and he'll figure out what's going on.

All you gotta do is meet with him once he gets up there, and he'll explain everything to you and keep in contact with you.

As far as the loop goes, forget about the contest. I'll keep doing the TOTW until the end of the year, just so's you don't have to worry about it. And I forgive you for deleting those posts. Don't make no never mind about it. You got bigger problems, sure'nuff. But don't you worry none about nothing. That's what you got a sister for.

Love,

Veronica

From:	Rosalyn Ebberly <prov31woman@home.com>
To:	VIM <vivalaveronica@marcelloportraits.com>
Subject:	**Re: PICK UP YOUR PHONE!**

Thanks for being so supportive and forgiving, Veronica. It means a lot to me. But I don't know about hiring a detective. That makes it look like I don't trust Chad. Well…I don't. But it seems so drastic. Then again, adultery is pretty drastic, too. I don't know…I've never had to make these sort of decisions before.

Rosalyn

"She looks well to the ways of her household, and does not eat the bread of idleness."
Proverbs 31:27 (NASB)

From:	VIM <vivalaveronica@marcelloportraits.com>
To:	Rosalyn Ebberly <prov31woman@home.com>
Subject:	**FROG!**

I say "frog" and you jump, remember? Ain't nobody likes to have to do stuff like this, but you want to know what Chad's up to, don't you? If he's having an affair, then Stephen will get you all the proof and documentation you need to confront him with it. Plus, if y'all end up in divorce court, it'll strengthen your case. And if he's not having an affair, then at least you'll know what IS going on, and Stephen can disappear, and Chad never has to know. Stephen is very discreet about stuff like that.

Trust me on this, Ros. You are in NO condition to be making these sort of decisions. You got your kiddos and marriage to worry about. Let me help you out, okay? I'll talk to Stephen, make all the arrangements, and let you know what to expect. It's the least I can do.

Veronica

From:	Rosalyn Ebberly <prov31woman@home.com>
To:	VIM <vivalaveronica@marcelloportraits.com>
Subject:	**Re: FROG!**

Okay, okay. We'll try it. I don't see how it could make things any worse.

Jumping,

Rosalyn

"She looks well to the ways of her household, and does not eat the bread of idleness."
Proverbs 31:27 (NASB)

From:	VIM <vivalaveronica@marcelloportraits.com>
To:	Rosalyn Ebberly <prov31woman@home.com>
Subject:	**Re: FROG!**

There ya go. Good girl.

Veronica

From:	VIM <vivalaveronica@marcelloportraits.com>
To:	SAHM I Am <sahmiam@loophole.com>
Subject:	[SAHM I AM] TOTW October 17: What can I do besides watch TV?

Help, y'all! I'm going plumb stir-crazy without the TV! I tell you, I'm in withdrawal. Got the jitters, feel depressed, anxious, ain't sleeping well. I admit it—I was a reality-TV junkie! Especially *A Baby Tale.* It was so therapeutic. This can't be any better for the baby than the radiation was. What am I gonna do?

And don't any of y'all even bother telling me to do stuff like baking cookies or that housecleaning routine. I just AIN'T that type of SAHM. Not even sure what goes in chocolate chip cookies—'cept for the chocolate, of course! And I have no idea where the housecleaning ladies have stashed the toilet-bowl cleaner. I'd go shopping, but I don't want to buy maternity clothes, and the kids always gripe about what I get for them.

Veronica

From:	P. Lorimer <phyllis.lorimer@joono.com>
To:	SAHM I Am <sahmiam@loophole.com>
Subject:	Re: [SAHM I AM] TOTW October 17: What can I do besides watch TV?

Veronica Marcello wrote:

<And don't any of y'all even bother telling me to do stuff

like baking cookies or that housecleaning routine. I just AIN'T that type of SAHM.>

WAAAAHHH!!! I don't want to be that sort of SAHM, either, but I am. The household laundry propagates in the basement when I am not looking, and the dryer eats the socks. Either that or there really is a wormhole in my dryer, and in some distant universe, the natives are standing around scratching their heads at the growing pile of assorted stockings falling from the sky. In the meantime, I am going to have to go buy yet another package of socks for Jonathan and for Julia. Bennet's and my socks seem to have escaped that fate, though the washer shredded another pair of my underwear and a T-shirt I especially liked. I kicked both offending appliances, and have ended up with a jammed toe and a dent in the washer for my efforts. Let that be a lesson to you all in self-control…straight from the pastor's wife.

Speaking of, if you want something to do, Veronica, I urge you to get involved in a church. Yes, I know you aren't into the "church thing," but hear me out. I want you to go find a church. Not a big, flashy church, but a tiny community church where the pastor's wife is also the office manager, the children's ministry director, the adult education coordinator and the women's ministry director. Find the overworked woman. You'll know her because she's the one who looks like she hasn't slept in ten years, who is frantically bustling around trying to do eight jobs at once, and who has at least two board members trailing after her at all times, asking, "Well, who's going to take care of_____? What do you think about such and such?" while her young children tug at her, begging to be sent to their rooms, which are actually the church nursery and the toddler room, but they don't know that. Go up to this woman, wrap your arms around her, and say, "Honey, I'm here to help" in your sweetest Texan drawl. And then stand back and watch her fall to pieces in gratitude. I guarantee reality television has no drama comparative to the life of a pastor's wife.

Sorry. Ten years of no sleep will make a person rather punchy. Well, it *feels* like ten years, anyway. :)
Going stark raving mad,
Phyllis

From:	Zelia Muzuwa <zeemuzu@vivacious.com>
To:	SAHM I Am <sahmiam@loophole.com>
Subject:	Re: [SAHM I AM] TOTW October 17: What can I do besides watch TV?

"That she's mad, 'tis true, 'tis true, 'tis pity, And pity 'tis, 'tis true."
—*Hamlet,* Act II, Scene 2

From:	The Millards <jstcea4jesus@familymail.net>
To:	SAHM I Am <sahmiam@loophole.com>
Subject:	Re: [SAHM I AM] TOTW October 17: What can I do besides watch TV?

Hi, Veronica,
I think Phyllis's idea of getting involved at church is great. Though I'm sorry she's so stressed! I just was asked to direct our church Christmas program for the kids. I know I've got

a lot going on already, but I just LOVE the Christmas pro-gram, and since I've had four kids in it the past several years, I figure it's my turn to give back.

I'm really excited about it. It's the Christmas story as seen through the unlikely viewpoint of a spider. Sort of a *Charlotte's Web* meets Luke 2 concept. Creative, no? A lady in our church wrote it, complete with six original Christmas songs and, of course, all the favorite carols. I wanted Tyler to try out for the part of the spider, but he said he didn't want to be in the program this year. Odd. Last year, it was all he could talk about. Maybe he thinks he's too "cool" for that now. :)
Jocelyn

From:	Brenna L. <saywhat@writeme.com>
To:	The Millards <jstcea4jesus@familymail.net>
Subject:	**Re: [SAHM I AM] TOTW October 17: What can I do besides watch TV?**

And how do you think you're going to manage a Christmas program on top of everything else you've got happening? Are you insane? Does the concept of moderation mean nothing to you?

You know I'm crazy about you, but you are seriously scaring me.
Brenna

From:	The Millards <jstcea4jesus@familymail.net>
To:	Brenna L. <saywhat@writeme.com>
Subject:	Re: [SAHM I AM] TOTW October 17: What can I do besides watch TV?

Oh, you don't have to worry about me, sweetie. I can handle it. I've never been one to sit around much. Life is too short to spend in the recliner knitting afghans, no matter how trendy that is right now. :) *Carpe diem!*
Jocelyn

From:	Brenna L. <saywhat@writeme.com>
To:	The Millards <jstcea4jesus@familymail.net>
Subject:	Carpe Diem?

I think that was my brother's high school senior class motto. Wasn't it from some movie that was popular way back then?
Brenna

From:	The Millards <jstcea4jesus@familymail.net>
To:	Brenna L. <saywhat@writeme.com>
Subject:	Re: Carpe Diem?

Yikes! You're SO young! Please tell me you've seen *Dead Poets' Society,* and that you were just making fun of my age! :)
Love you...
Jocelyn

From:	Brenna L. <saywhat@writeme.com>
To:	The Millards <jstcea4jesus@familymail.net>
Subject:	**Re: Carpe Diem?**

Dead Poets' Society? Never heard of it. ;)
Brenna

From:	Rosalyn Ebberly <prov31woman@home.com>
To:	SAHM I Am <sahmiam@loophole.com>
Subject:	**[SAHM I AM] Exciting GWENCH news!**

Joyous news, SAHMs!

I was just interviewed on the news! I'm going to be on television, talking about our Save Christmas campaign. I know you'll all want copies of the video, so just e-mail me with your addresses and I'll snail mail it to you.

Plus, we have had five hundred people so far who have actually signed a pledge to participate in Save Christmas. It's really catching on. People have started putting up Save Christmas signs in their yards, and we even had a bunch of bumper stickers made that are starting to make an appearance around town.

It's SO gratifying to see what a difference we are making already. It is a great encouragement to me, despite some concerning news we also heard. The SANTA group is also gaining traction. They just got some brilliant PR guy as their second-in-command, and he is getting all the businesses riled up. The problem is, we can't go after him because everything is hush-hush. We suspect that some of our approved charities are trying to play on both sides of this—supporting us so they get donations, and yet working with SANTA in order to keep the corporate donations coming in, too. They are backstabbing, two-timing, unethical... PSEUDO charities who aren't being very "charitable." Anyway, SANTA is keeping all their activities top secret because of it, to make it harder to tell who is working against who. I always knew there was a reason that you can rearrange "SANTA" and get "SATAN." :(

But we will press on and persevere! God has not given us a spirit of fear, but of power! And we intend to use it.

Rosalyn

"She looks well to the ways of her household, and does not eat the bread of idleness."
Proverbs 31:27 (NASB)

From:	Brenna L. <saywhat@writeme.com>
To:	SAHM I Am <sahmiam@loophole.com>
Subject:	**[SAHM I AM] GET It!!!**

Rosalyn's GWENCH post did it for me!!! I understand Zelia's song game! How's this:

My favorite holiday song is "The First Noel." Right?

Brenna

From:	Zelia Muzuwa <zeemuzu@vivacious.com>
To:	SAHM I Am <sahmiam@loophole.com>
Subject:	Re: [SAHM I AM] GET It!!!

Yay, Brenna!!! You did it! Or, should I say, GWENCH did it? Yes, you get a kiss.

   :-x

Love ya, babe!

Z

From:	Rosalyn Ebberly <prov31woman@home.com>
To:	SAHM I Am <sahmiam@loophole.com>
Subject:	Re: [SAHM I AM] GET It!!!

Wait a minute! What does my GWENCH group have to do with Zelia's game?

Rosalyn

"She looks well to the ways of her household, and does not eat the bread of idleness."
Proverbs 31:27 (NASB)

From:	Zelia Muzuwa <zeemuzu@vivacious.com>
To:	SAHM I Am <sahmiam@loophole.com>
Subject:	Re: [SAHM I AM] GET It!!!

As we used to say in grade school, Rosalyn, FOR ME TO
KNOW AND YOU TO FIND OUT! :-P
Tee-hee,
Z

From:	Zelia Muzuwa <zeemuzu@vivacious.com>
To:	"Green Eggs and Ham"
Subject:	**On being manipulated**

My mother-in-law is at it again. She's determined to get her
way about all of us coming for Christmas. Here's the latest
attempt:

Dear Tristan,
I had just a lovely idea! Let's not spend money on
Christmas presents this year, especially with the cost of
shipping them to and from America if you are all staying home. I would much rather spend the money on
airline tickets for your family. I know you said Zelia
wanted to stay home, but it is my dearest wish that I
should have my family all together for this most special
of holidays. I am certain she is only trying to practice
economy in light of the financial troubles America is
having, and I want to reassure you that we would be
more than happy to pay for the trip. Your father and I
are getting on in years, you know, and I remember how
devastated your poor father was when his mother passed
away suddenly in Zimbabwe without us being able to
return for a final goodbye. I would never want you to

undergo such emotional pain, and surely Zelia would not want that for you, either. How does business class sound to you? I know you always wish for more legroom. Shall I book for a whole week before Christmas, or perhaps only three days and then you could stay on through New Year's?
Lovingly,
Mum

Laying it on thick, isn't she? What do I do? Tristan says he doesn't like being caught in the middle between me and his "mum." I told him I didn't like "Mum" interfering in OUR business. That if he didn't want to feel caught in the middle, to tell her to lay off already. Sheesh, he's smart—how hard can it be to tell his mother no?
Z

From:	Dulcie Huckleberry <dulcie@showme.com>
To:	"Green Eggs and Ham"
Subject:	Re: On being manipulated

Poor Zelia. What is it with guys and their moms? Honestly, it's as if the umbilical cord is still attached! Case in point: Tom's mother got it in her head that what my girls need for Christmas is everything under the sun related to a certain fashion doll with bullet-shaped double Ds who has a thing for the color pink. I can't stand that smug, plastic fashion plate with her skinny little thighs and pinched-in waist. And it *really* bothers me that all the "ethnic" versions of that doll are nothing more than darker-colored Caucasians—and pretty unrealistically-shaped ones, at that. Same nose, same eyes, same face shape. Even the hair—Caucasian hair dyed black. It's rather insulting. I'm Guatemalan, and our beauty doesn't come in that prepackaged shape, thank you very much!

I think it sends the message that all women should look like that. And that is NOT a healthy message to give to my little girls! I have explained this SOOOO many times to Tom, but what does he do as soon as his mom brings it up? I heard him on the phone with her yesterday—

"Well, I don't know, Mom. I think Dulcie doesn't really like all that stuff. You know she's pretty conscious about her weight. So we've never given the girls any of those sort of dolls."

ARGH! I grabbed the phone from him and said, "Mom, it's not about my weight! Those dolls are way too sexed up for a four-year-old to play with. And they promote materialism and an emphasis on outward beauty. Not to mention an unrealistic portrayal of women of color. I don't want my girls playing with them at all!"

"Oh, Dulcie," she crooned, "I do wish you wouldn't be so sensitive about your appearance, dear. I hear that men like women with larger rear ends and full hips. It's a sign of fertility, you know. And look! You have twins!"

I. Couldn't. Breathe. Fortunately, Tom saw my about-to-erupt expression and snatched the phone back. "Mom," he said, "it'll be okay. Whatever you want to give the girls for Christmas will be just fine. Don't worry about it."

During my strangled gasp for air, she said something, and he responded with, "I know. Really, she didn't mean it… Yes, you have color, too. It's just an expression…no, we don't think you're 'oversexed.' …I know, I know…you are a very loving, caring grandma. The girls adore you."

And so on. Finally, he got off the phone, after practically promising to buy stock in that toy manufacturer. Then, he went on a tirade to ME about how hurt his *mommy* was that I implied that she had poor taste in toys and how dare I suggest that she would ever buy something inappropriate for them! Give me a BREAK! I never said any such thing!

But at least the Nightmare In Pink and her cloned minions aren't likely to make any appearances at our house this Christmas. Despite Tom almost begging his mom to go ahead and get the dolls, she has apparently decided to take the martyr's high road. She said she "certainly would never dream" of giving my children something I found "so offensive." So would we please provide her with a list of "approved items" so that she can get her shopping done.

Fine. Okay. Swell.

But it just irks me that Tom didn't back me up on this. And I told him that, too. He just doesn't get why it's a big deal to me and thinks we should have just humored his mom. *sigh* Guys can be so clueless sometimes.

Dulcie

From:	Brenna L. <saywhat@writeme.com>
To:	"Green Eggs and Ham"
Subject:	Re: On being manipulated

Hey, Dulcie, I'm afraid it doesn't get any better as your girls get older. In addition to the dolls getting brattier and more rebellious-looking, then you have to deal with the clothes. I just went Christmas shopping with my mom, and she was looking for an outfit for Madeline, who is nine now. She wanted to buy my baby girl a red rhinestone-trimmed T-shirt that said One Hot Chick on it! And she'd picked out jeans to go with it that were skintight and had open lacing all the way up the sides!

"You really think for one second I'm going to let my little girl wear something so…"

"But it's just adorable!" my mom protests.

"There are streetwalkers dressed more modestly, Mom! She's NINE."

"Well, I let you wear stuff like this when you were nine. It made you feel grown-up."

She just doesn't get it! "Yeah, so grown up that I decided I was ready to sleep with my boyfriend and have a baby at age sixteen."

That shut her up.

For a second.

Then it was, "Are you trying to blame ME for your mistakes? I thought you had matured more than that."

Sometimes you just have to sigh. I definitely don't blame her for the decisions I made. But I really don't think that she helped matters any. Any time any little boys came over to the house, she referred to them as my "boyfriends" and she was constantly dressing me in clothes not even a teenager should be wearing, and she thought it was cute when I started "going with" boys in my class at age twelve. And then she was surprised that I ended up a teen mom? Get a clue! We reaped what we sowed! And I love Madeline dearly, but she was the final death knell for a childhood that never really existed.

I want better for Madeline. She should NEVER, NEVER, NEVER have to label herself as a "hot chick" or dress to kill like that—whatever the age. I'm going to teach her to have more respect for herself than I did, and to expect and demand it from those around her.

Sorry for the rant…I was about to explode.

Brenna

From:	Zelia Muzuwa <zeemuzu@vivacious.com>
To:	"Green Eggs and Ham"
Subject:	**Re: On being manipulated**

You go, Brenna-girl!!! Sheesh, you guys, I feel so small and petty. Here I am taking a stand about where we spend Christmas, while you and Dulcie are fighting for the innocence of your kiddos. Maybe I'm being selfish. Maybe I should just give it up and go to England.

Z

From:	Dulcie Huckleberry <dulcie@showme.com>
To:	"Green Eggs and Ham"
Subject:	**Re: On being manipulated**

You are NOT selfish, Z! I think wanting to have your own family traditions for Christmas is a very healthy thing to do for your children. At the very least, if you do decide to go

to England, it should be because you *want* to, not because you feel forced into it. No false guilt, okay?
Dulcie

From:	Brenna L. <saywhat@writeme.com>
To:	"Green Eggs and Ham"
Subject:	**Embryo update**

Okay, girls, this is big. The Gillmans got their blood work done last week, and our little tot-cicles shipped out TODAY! Once we found out that the embies would be arriving this week, I contacted our RE at the fertility clinic, and she said that since AF started last week, if I went in to have my lining tested, and blood tests later this week to track my LH, that as soon as it surges, then we can do the FET! I'm so excited! And scared. We're doing a natural cycle, so at least I don't have to be on all the drugs. But there's no promises. Our clinic has about an 80% thaw rate, and then there's only about a 20% chance of a live birth, if I get a BFP at all. Well, except we're doing a blast transfer 5dt, so our chances are a little better. We won't know, though, until after the 2ww—well, only about 10d for me—and my first Beta.

So, please, please pray lots of sticky prayers for our little frosties. I'm so nervous. I want this to happen so much, and it's hard to see the hope in Darren's eyes. I don't know that he really understands what a long shot this could be. Thanks for being such great support for us through all this. You gals are the best.
Brenna

From:	Zelia Muzuwa <zeemuzu@vivacious.com>
To:	"Green Eggs and Ham"
Subject:	**Re: Embryo update**

Brenna, babe, I'm thrilled for you! I don't have a CLUE what you are talking about, but if you're happy, then I'm happy.

Does anybody else understand what she just said? Just teasing you, girl. :)

Z

From:	Dulcie Huckleberry <dulcie@showme.com>
To:	"Green Eggs and Ham"
Subject:	**Re: Embryo update**

Zelia Muzuwa wrote:

<Does anybody else understand what she just said?>

Hmm… I sense exhilaration mixed with apprehension. But beyond that, nope. I'll be praying for you, Brenna. I know God understands it all perfectly.

Love and hugs,

Dulcie

From:	Brenna L. <saywhat@writeme.com>
To:	"Green Eggs and Ham"
Subject:	**Re: Embryo update**

Sheesh! I forgot you gals don't know the lingo. So sorry! Basically I was just trying to say that the embryos are being
shipped out today, and that because my period started last
week, I'll be having blood tests done to see when I ovulate.
Five days after that, they will thaw the embryos and transfer
the surviving ones to me. Then I have to wait two weeks,
or about ten days, and then have a blood test—the Beta—
to see if there's an increase in the pregnancy hormone that
will tell us we're pregnant.
Get it now? :)
Brenna

From:	Zelia Muzuwa <zeemuzu@vivacious.com>
To:	"Green Eggs and Ham"
Subject:	**Re: Embryo update**

Hey, that's cool! I'm excited for you! Just one more question…what exactly are "sticky prayers"???
Z

From:	Brenna L. <saywhat@writeme.com>
To:	"Green Eggs and Ham"
Subject:	**Re: Embryo update**

LOL! The goal of a FET is to get the embryo to implant,
or "stick," in the womb, causing a successful BFP—Big Fat
Positive—on the pregnancy test. So women in the infertility community like to send each other "sticky thoughts"—

meaning they're hoping with all their might that you have a successful transfer cycle. Since I'm the praying sort, I like to send and ask for sticky prayers instead of just thoughts. :)
Brenna

From:	Dulcie Huckleberry <dulcie@showme.com>
To:	"Green Eggs and Ham"
Subject:	**Re: Embryo update**

This is fascinating, Brenna! Thanks for explaining. Well, I'm going to do my part. My prayers will be stickier than McKenzie's body the time she poured an entire bottle of school glue all over herself! Stick, little frosties, stick like sand burrs on a long-haired dog!
Love,
Dulcie

From:	Brenna L. <saywhat@writeme.com>
To:	Tess Gillman <tessty@newmeximail.com
Subject:	**They just don't understand!**

Hey, Tess,
So excited to hear that our snowbabies are on their way. I told my Green Egg gals about it, and I made the mistake of using all the acronyms and stuff I'm used to using with you and on the IVF discussion boards. They were happy for me, but they didn't get a word of what I was saying. And even after I explained, I still think they didn't really understand. It

makes me feel isolated from them, and I don't like it. They're so supportive, and yet, they really don't know what it's like to go through all this. Jocelyn has four kids and is too busy running them and herself places that she hardly takes time to appreciate them; Dulcie had twins without fertility drugs; and Marianne usually acts as if her kids are more of a burden than a blessing. None of them know what it's like to want so desperately to give their husbands a child that they dream about it almost every night. They don't know how painful infertility is, whether it's your own or your husband's. They support me because they're my friends, but they don't really *know.*

I'm not sure what my point is to all this. I just wanted to talk to someone who does understand.

Brenna

From:	Tess Gillman <tessty@newmeximail.com
To:	Brenna L. <saywhat@writeme.com>
Subject:	**Re: They just don't understand!**

I *do* know, Brenna dear. I understand completely. And I know you are grateful for your friends, too. But it does feel isolating at times. Just remember you aren't alone. You have me, your friends on the discussion boards, and most importantly, you have a God who is walking beside you every step of the way and who loves our little snowflakes even more than we possibly could. The next few weeks could be very stressful for you. Try to relax and remember Who is in control.

Hugs,

Tess

From:	Rosalyn Ebberly <prov31woman@home.com>
To:	VIM <vivalaveronica@marcelloportraits.com>
Subject:	**Meeting with Mr. Drake**

Dear Ronnie,

I just thought you might like to know how my meeting with Mr. Drake went. We met at a coffee shop this morning. He tried to convince me to call him "Stephen" but I would never be so familiar with a man I barely know. And I felt it important to keep everything strictly professional. It's bad enough to have a private meeting with a man other than Chad. But it just served to remind me of the reason why I was doing it.

He's not at all what I thought a private investigator would be. No code names, no pen case for secret messages, no walkie-talkie watch. Just an ordinary businessman with a leather notebook, a laptop and a briefcase. I had to bring all of our personal information, like descriptions of our car and our license plate numbers as well as photos of Chad. He also wanted Chad's work address and contact information.

I feel so sneaky. I, who have prided myself on my absolute integrity and honesty, am putting my husband under surveillance. It makes me feel so...secular. *shudder* Like I could be on an afternoon talk show about "Cheating Men and the Women Who Spy On Them." Blech! Maybe it would be better to just confront Chad myself.

Rosalyn

"She looks well to the ways of her household, and does not eat the bread of idleness."
Proverbs 31:27 (NASB)

From:	VIM <vivalaveronica@marcelloportraits.com>
To:	Rosalyn Ebberly <prov31woman@home.com>
Subject:	Re: Meeting with Mr. Drake

Don't you dare, Rosalyn! Think about it—you even make one tiny ol' peep about it, and Chad's gonna get so mad it'll just push him farther away. Forget about talk shows—you don't watch them anyways. Now, if y'all had to pay for Stephen's services, I could see why you wouldn't be particular happy about it. He ain't cheap. But since he's doing this as a favor for dear Ronnie Irene, the wife of his best friend, you couldn't ask for a better way to find out what's going on. As I said before, if he finds out Chad ★is★ cheating, then you'll be able to confront him with evidence. If he's not cheating, at least you can figure out what in tarnation he's been up to, and then you won't further damage your relationship with false accusations.

And for your information, sweetheart, there are worse things in this here life than feeling a bit "secular." Things like your DH pickin' flowers that ain't growing in his own garden. Glad your meeting went well. Tell Stephen that Ronnie Irene and Frank send him a big Texas howdy and hope everything goes well.

Veronica

From:	Zelia Muzuwa <zeemuzu@vivacious.com>
To:	SAHM I Am <sahmiam@loophole.com>
Subject:	**My new babies!**

We just got the call—we're getting the sibling group! It's official, they're ours!

Check out the attached photo! The one on the right is little Duri. He's nineteen months old. The little girl on the left is his sister, Lishan, who is three years old. Aren't they just the yummiest kiddos? I can't wait to throw my arms around them, kiss their little cheeks and tell them, "Mommy loves you, baby."

I'm crying and shaking, and SO very happy! Tristan is taking the afternoon off work and we're picking the kids up from school, and we're going out to CELEBRATE!

Oh, and get this—we're traveling over CHRISTMAS to get them! Yep—God's perfect solution to the Christmas Conundrum. There's no way my in-laws can complain about us going to Ethiopia to adopt our children over Christmas. And I don't have to be selfish! Can you believe it? I finally get to spend Christmas *my* way—and I can't think of anything I'd rather do more. I wish we could bring the children with us, but we're going to drop them off with Tristan's parents in England and then go to Ethiopia. So everyone will be happy.

I think I hear Tristan in the driveway. Better go. I just LOVE you all!

Hugs,

Z

From:	Dulcie Huckleberry <dulcie@showme.com>
To:	"Green Eggs and Ham"
Subject:	**Z and Brenna**

Wow! Do the two of you have some sort of adoption race going on here? Referrals and embryo shipments are flying everywhere! I'm so excited for the both of you. Z, your new little ones are absolutely precious. I'm rejoicing with you. Bren, I've still got those sticky prayers headed up to heaven for you. Soon, we'll be getting attachments of your ultrasounds, and then we can go ga-ga over those, too. It's going to happen, I just know it. And I can't wait!

Love to all,

Dulcie

P.S. I checked my e-mail and got Z's note right before I had to meet with some new clients. My office is right near the waiting area, and I guess I got so caught up in the excitement of the announcement that I shrieked...rather loudly. Next thing I know, my office is full of my coworkers and the new clients oohing and ahhing over the referral photo. It was great! :)

From:	Thomas Huckleberry <t.huckleberry@showme.com>
To:	Jordan and Becky <schwartz@ozarkmail.net>
Subject:	**Just saying hello**

Hey, Bec, how's my little sis?

I know it's been a couple months since I e-mailed you.

Getting used to being at home is taking more time than I thought. Seems as though my days are busier now than when I was going to work. Being home isn't so bad, really. As long as I don't ruin any more of Dulcie's clothes in the wash, I just might live to see grandchildren.

And it's fun to be with the kids. Mostly. Though now I understand why Dulcie used to be so frazzled by the time I got home sometimes. This morning McKenzie gave both twins a haircut while I was trying to clean up a shattered juice glass from breakfast. She cut their ponytails clean off. Dulcie's going to have a cow when she sees it. They both look awful. And I sliced my finger on a glass shard, but I don't think I'm going to get much sympathy about it. Plus, I'm going to have to do some plumbing this afternoon because when I found McKenzie, she was rinsing the remainder of the ponytails down the drain on the tub, so now it's plugged. Those tails were likely a good six inches long. I'm waiting for Morris to call me back, since I have no idea how to unplug a tub drain and we can't afford a plumber.

So, as I said, it's fun to be home. But I tell you, Becky, it's LONELY! And I'm feeling totally lost, as if I don't even know who I really am anymore. I'm trying not to show it to Dulcie, because I don't want to make her feel guilty. But sometimes it really bugs me that she got a job that she loves, and I can't even get one that I'd hate. But at least when I had a job and people asked me, "What do you do?" I could tell them, "I am a programmer." And they looked at me with that glazed over, yet respectful, look that folks reserve for those of us in the technical fields. Now, I hardly know what to say. Tell them I'm out of work, and they think I'm a bum. But I can't bring myself to say "I'm a stay-at-home dad" because then it will sound as though I'm giving up on getting a real job. And they'll still think I'm a bum.

I don't know if you'll understand or not. Career people seem to have a lot more respect for moms who stay home. All the women I used to work with would claim they'd love to stay home if they could. And yet, they never wanted to actually try it. But I don't even know of any dads who ever stayed home, and nobody talks about a SAHD with respect. I just feel so isolated. I take the girls to the park, and there's moms and kids and minivans everywhere. But the moms look at me as if they half expect me to molest their children or abuse my own. They won't even say hello. I'm used to adult interaction. And now, the only adults I've spoken with this week are my wife and the grocery clerk. This is not good.

Got any ideas for me, sis? I hope you are all doing okay. I'm having a blast working for Morris in his woodworking shop. It's real part-time, just on his days off from Shoji. But he says I'm a fast learner. And it's fun. If Dulcie's not home, I bring the girls over and Mom plays with them. So I guess there are two more adults that I get to interact with. Okay, maybe not two. Morris is definitely an adult, but Mom... I don't know sometimes. :)

Stay out of trouble,

Tom

From:	Jordan and Becky <schwartz@ozarkmail.net>
To:	Thomas Huckleberry <t.huckleberry@showme.com>
Subject:	Re: Just saying hello

Hi, Tom!

It's so good to hear from you and get caught up on how things are going with you all. I'm sorry you're feeling isolated. Poor brother! :(I know it's hard to make that transition home. I don't know what to do about the snotty moms at the park, other than maybe freak them out someday by showing up in drag. :) But I did find something for you on the Web. It's called "Full-Time Father" and it's an online community for stay-at-home dads. Dulcie has her SAHM I Am loop, so I figured you might like to check out their discussion boards. They looked pretty active, and I saw that there were a lot of dads feeling the same way you are. It might be a little help, anyway.

I don't know if it makes you feel any better or not, but I think what you're doing is wonderful. Even if you were sort of forced into it. Those girls are going to grow up with a concept of "father" that is totally different than what you and I had. I think you're giving them a real special gift.

Hugs,

Becky

From:	Thomas Huckleberry
	<t.huckleberry@showme.com>
To:	Jordan and Becky <schwartz@ozarkmail.net>
Subject:	**Thanks**

Thanks, sis. I checked out that site. It's really great. And you're right—our girls are going to know what it's like to have a dad who is home and who loves them. No matter what I have to do to show them. Thanks for the reminder. Tom

From:	Dulcie Huckleberry <dulcie@showme.com>
To:	"Green Eggs and Ham"
Subject:	**WAAAAAAAHHHHHHHHHH!!!!!!**

My twins' hair! Their long, beautiful dark brown tresses with the little bit of curl...GONE! I got home today and they both ran up to me, and I hardly recognized them. I found the culprit—that imp, McKenzie, hiding behind the sofa, looking much like Adam and Eve must have when God came to check up on them in the garden. Tom just stood in the middle of the living room, cringing, waiting for my re-action.

"WHERE DID SHE GET SCISSORS FROM?"

"I'm so sorry, sweetheart," he said. "She did it while I was cleaning up some broken glass." Smooth evasion of the scissor question, but I was so distracted by the glass news that I let him get away with it.

"Broken glass???"

He held up a bandaged finger. "Let's just say it's been a long day…"

And I can't even put the ponytails in their baby books because McKenzie STUFFED THEM DOWN THE TUB DRAIN! Plumbers are frightfully expensive, I found out.

I should just turn around and go back to the office. That's what I should do. :(My poor little girls' hair! No more bows. No more braids. No more ribbons. I told McKenzie I should cut off her hair, too, so it matches. That made her cry, so now I feel like a bad mom, too. But why should she get to keep her pretty hair when her sisters will look like shaggy refugees for months?

Heartbroken,

Dulcie

From:	VIM <vivalaveronica@marcelloportraits.com>
To:	SAHM I Am <sahmiam@loophole.com>
Subject:	[SAHM I AM] TOTW October 24: What makes me blush…

Oh my stars, gals! I don't even remember what I was going to post about this week, but it's about 5:30 a.m. here in Houston, and I just got home. My face is gonna be the color of a flaming Texas sunset for weeks!

See, about 3:00 this morning, I woke up to use the "little girls' room" like most prego mommies-to-be, and as I was climbing back into bed, I had this mighty weird cramping feeling in my belly and around to my back. Thought maybe I pulled a muscle or something. Anyways, I went on to bed. But couldn't sleep. A few minutes later the cramping started again! This continued for about twenty minutes, when suddenly, it hit me—*contractions!*

I was sure I was having preterm labor, so I woke up Frank. He started to panic and insisted we go to the hospital immediately. So we got the kids up, put their grumpy selves into the car, and dropped them off at a friend's house. Friend was a mite on the grouchy side, too, but she's a peach and was glad to help.

We drove to the hospital, and by this time, I'd only had a couple more contractions, but I was scared, too. Frank rushed right up to the E.R. receptionist and said, "My Nica, she's having the baby too early!" Of course that spurred them into motion, and I got lots of attention.

To make a humiliatingly long story short…the E.R. doctor finally comes into my little cubicle and pulls up a stool. "Mrs. Marcello," he says, "first, I want to assure you the baby is fine. You are not in labor. Have you ever heard of 'Braxton Hicks' contractions?"

I could have just up and died. Felt as dumb as an armadillo! The doc assured me that lots of women make this mistake, but that doesn't explain why he looked like he was trying not to laugh.

Is there anything about being pregnant that ain't just plain difficult? Anyways, I thought maybe y'all could help me feel a tad better by sharing some of y'all's most embarrassing moments. I'm gonna go take a nap.

Veronica

From:	P. Lorimer <phyllis.lorimer@joono.com>
To:	SAHM I Am <sahmiam@loophole.com>
Subject:	Re: [SAHM I AM] TOTW October 24: What makes me blush...

Hello, everybody,

Veronica, I can help you out. Here's a story from yesterday at church. I've been teaching our adult Sunday school class about church history. It has been going beautifully, and we are just reaching the schism between the Eastern and Western church. Class yesterday had only been going a few minutes when my daughter Julia, age three and a half, came running through the door. Apparently, the teenager who is assigned to get our children to the nursery at the right time had let her slip away. Julia toddled straight to me, so a bit chagrined, I stopped class and bent down.

"Where's Katie?" I asked.

She apparently couldn't have cared less where the babysitter was. "Mommy!" she exclaimed, her nose wrinkled and her mouth turned down. "Micah say I'm a girl!"

"Well, he's right." I wasn't sure why this had made her so indignant. But I could tell I now had the entire roomful of adults, including Micah's parents, listening in rapt attention.

Julia crossed her arms and stuck her chin out. "He say girls don't have a—"

You know how in a bad dream, when you are about to get hit by a semi truck and are trying to dive off the road, but suddenly you are moving in triple slow motion? That's how I felt at that moment. I saw her lips come together to form a *p* and the realization hit me of what she was about to say, and who was about to hear it. I reached toward her and as the first part of the word emerged from her mouth, I wrapped my arms around her. Before the rest of it could echo off the now-silent walls, I hugged her head against me, hoping to muffle it. At the same time, I said, "Micah was wrong, darling. Girls have a penchant for causing mischief, too!"

About that time, the lost babysitter put her head in the door and called to Julia, and apologized profusely for losing track of her. Julia gave me a sloppy kiss and ran out the door. I was left to face the twenty or so adults who were either blissfully unaware of what had nearly transpired or who were smirking at me in the knowing way only other parents can.

Overall, teaching is going quite well. I'm finding it a bit of a challenge, however, to keep up with Julia and Bennet and still prepare my lessons. I'm quite worn-out some days. Phyllis

From:	Zelia Muzuwa <zeemuzu@vivacious.com>
To:	SAHM I Am <sahmiam@loophole.com>
Subject:	Re: [SAHM I AM] TOTW October 24: What makes me blush...

Poor girl, Phyllis! Reminds me of the time a couple of years ago when Cosette was about the same age as Julia. We were visiting Tristan's family for Christmas, and everyone was sitting around after Christmas dinner, talking. Cosette was sitting on my lap, and suddenly, in a lull in the conversation, put her hands on my chest and asked, "What are those,

Mommy?" I pulled her hands away and tried to distract her, but she was insistent. She pulled up her dress and looked down over the top. "I don't have bumps."

I finally had to drag her into another room. But the whole way, she kept saying, "But what ARE they, Mommy? Why don't I have them? I want to know!"

sigh When you become a mom, might as well toss the old ego right out the door, because it's either that, or let it get trampled by the "pitter-patter of little feet."

Z

From:	Rosalyn Ebberly <prov31woman@home.com>
To:	SAHM I Am <sahmiam@loophole.com>
Subject:	Re: [SAHM I AM] TOTW October 24: What makes me blush...

Dear Mommies,

I'm saddened to read of how obnoxious your children are in public. This is why I always insist on my children learning proper social skills before they are allowed out in public. There is no reason to be humiliated by your offspring, if you simply exert the effort to instruct them in proper etiquette.

I'm off to have lunch with my dearest, hardworking husband, who simply can't bear to go all week without seeing us during lunch.

Love to all,

Rosalyn

"She looks well to the ways of her household, and does not eat the bread of idleness."
Proverbs 31:27 (NASB)

From:	VIM <vivalaveronica@marcelloportraits.com>
To:	Rosalyn Ebberly <prov31woman@home.com>
Subject:	**What?**

Are all y'all really having lunch with Chad? I don't believe it.
VIM

From:	Rosalyn Ebberly <prov31woman@home.com>
To:	VIM <vivalaveronica@marcelloportraits.com>
Subject:	**Re: What?**

Are you suggesting I would lie to our e-mail group? Of course we're having lunch with Chad. I had to work to arrange it, though, because he didn't seem to have the time to spare for us. But Stephen wanted to be able to observe how Chad is around the family, so he's going to be sitting a few tables away. I'm not supposed to even act like I see him. I hate this. I've never been able to be an actress. I'm always perfectly genuine, perfectly myself, and I never put on any masks or acts. So I don't know how well this will go.
Rosalyn

From:	VIM \<vivalaveronica@marcelloportraits.com\>
To:	Rosalyn Ebberly \<prov31woman@home.com\>
Subject:	**Re: What?**

Honey, if you're so genuine and real, what's with this state-ment?

\<I'm off to have lunch with my dearest, hardworking hus-band, who simply can't bear to go all week without seeing us during lunch.\>

Yeah, that's sure not an act. Whatever.

VIM

From:	Rosalyn Ebberly \<prov31woman@home.com\>
To:	VIM \<vivalaveronica@marcelloportraits.com\>
Subject:	**Re: What?**

You obviously don't know a thing about leadership, Ron-nie. A good leader should never show any weakness. The loop ladies are looking to me for advice and to set a good example for them. I'm just thinking about what it would do to them if I revealed what was going on with Chad. I'd never be able to forgive myself if I caused any of them to stumble or crushed their fragile spirits by my personal troubles. I have to be strong and confident, for their sakes. Don't you un-derstand that?

Rosalyn

"She looks well to the ways of her household, and does not eat the bread of idleness."
Proverbs 31:27 (NASB)

From:	VIM <vivalaveronica@marcelloportraits.com>
To:	Rosalyn Ebberly <prov31woman@home.com>
Subject:	**Re: What?**

You're right, darlin' sister, I must not understand anything at all about y'all's concept of leadership. Don't make no sense whatever.
VIM

From:	Thomas Huckleberry <t.huckleberry@showme.com>
To:	Dulcie Huckleberry <dulcie@showme.com>
Subject:	**Just saying hi!**

Hi, sweetheart,
I was just getting the girls ready to "help" me rake leaves, but I wanted to tell you that I love you and was thinking about you. Also, I'm going to try making something new for dinner tonight. When a recipe says "julienne cut" what does that mean?
Love,
Tom

From:	Thomas Huckleberry
	<t.huckleberry@showme.com>
To:	Dulcie Huckleberry <dulcie@showme.com>
Subject:	**Julienne cut**

I looked it up on the Internet, so never mind. Why don't they just say "cut in long slivers" instead of all this fancy jargon? You'll have to see the leaf rubbings McKenzie is doing from what we raked up. She's really something!

Oh, and the twins probably ate about two leaves each. Sorry.

Tom

From:	Thomas Huckleberry
	<t.huckleberry@showme.com>
To:	Dulcie Huckleberry <dulcie@showme.com>
Subject:	**Tried to call you**

Are you in a meeting or something? I just thought you'd love to hear the cute thing that McKenzie said this afternoon when I put her down for a nap. She didn't want to take a nap, but I told her she had to. She said, "I'm going to get out of bed." And she stuck her bottom lip way out like she does when she's pouting. I said if she did get out of bed, Daddy would have to give her seat a swat. Then she crossed her arms and said, "Then I will tell Mommy." I said, "Fine, go ahead. Mommy will give you a little swat, too." She scrunched up her face tight, like she was thinking hard, and then she said, "Then—then…I will tell…MYSELF!" And she flopped over and faced the wall. I just had to laugh. Isn't she great?

Hope you're having a good day.

Tom

From:	Thomas Huckleberry <t.huckleberry@showme.com>
To:	Dulcie Huckleberry <dulcie@showme.com>
Subject:	**Guess what?**

Where ARE you? I haven't heard from you all day! Okay, I'm kind of proud of myself. We got the lawn raked, the girls did their leaf project, I got dinner started—julienne cuts and all, and I'm caught up on the laundry. Then, I was sort of worn-out, so I decided to check out my Full-time Father discussion boards, and found out that there's another dad here in Springfield who is staying home! His name is Flynn Sawyer, and he has a son and daughter who are both pre-school age. We've been e-mailing this afternoon, and I think we're going to start our own playgroup, since none of the moms will let us join them. :)

Tom

From:	Thomas Huckleberry
	\<t.huckleberry@showme.com\>
To:	Dulcie Huckleberry \<dulcie@showme.com\>
Subject:	**More good news!**

I just got a call from Morris. He said I'm doing a really good job with learning the woodworking business, and he wants to increase my hours to fifteen a week and my pay by $1.50 an hr. I know that's still not much, and I have a lot to learn. But I'm really enjoying it. In fact, I wish I could just do this full-time and not worry about going back to programming. You know I never really liked it anyway. But I love working with wood. And I think I have talent for it, if that's not prideful for me to say.

Anyway, I'm still trying to reach you because I thought maybe we could go out to dinner and celebrate tonight. I'll just freeze what I cooked for later. I guess you'll be home in about a half hour, so we can discuss it then.

Love,

Tom

From:	Dulcie Huckleberry \<dulcie@showme.com\>
To:	"Green Eggs and Ham"
Subject:	**Good grief!**

I just got a whole boatload of e-mails from Tom! None of them are of earth-shattering importance. But he sounds impatient for an answer. Doesn't he know that I'm at WORK?

It's not like I can just sit around all day and play on the computer as he does. I'm really busy.

I know he doesn't mean to be so annoying...I just had to vent.

Dulcie

From:	Zelia Muzuwa <zeemuzu@vivacious.com>
To:	"Green Eggs and Ham"
Subject:	**Re: Good grief!**

Uh, Dulcie-babe...listen to yourself, will you? Can we say "R-O-L-E R-E-V-E-R-S-A-L"? Cut the poor guy some slack. Us stay-at-home parents may not have anything better to do than play on the computer, but it gets a bit lonely at times. REMEMBER?
Z

From:	Dulcie Huckleberry <dulcie@showme.com>
To:	"Green Eggs and Ham"
Subject:	**Re: Good grief!**

OUCH! That smack-down stung, Z! Ugh. I hate it when you're right. I'm sorry, I don't mean to be so high-and-mighty about it. I just feel really stressed, and it makes me jealous that he has time to sit around looking up how to julienne-cut carrots on the Internet while I'm holed up in BORING meetings all day. :(
Dulcie-with-foot-in-mouth

From:	Zelia Muzuwa <zeemuzu@vivacious.com>
To:	"Green Eggs and Ham"
Subject:	**Re: Good grief!**

Aw, don't sit there sucking on your feet like that. Go home and have a bubble bath. It's good for whatever ails you. Sorry for stinging you. :)
Hugs and love,
Z

From:	Dulcie Huckleberry <dulcie@showme.com>
To:	Thomas Huckleberry <t.huckleberry@showme.com>
Subject:	**Re: More good news!**

Hi, Tom,
I'm so sorry I've been incommunicado today. I had a staff meeting this morning and then a steady stream of client appointments all day. I'm thrilled to hear about the potential playgroup, and the news from Morris. I'm so proud of you!

But I'm afraid that dinner won't work out tonight. I have to work late. Lorissa, my supervisor—you remember her, right?—e-mailed me about fifteen minutes ago and said that the Jeffersons—my newest clients—wanted to move their consultation from tomorrow to this evening. I'm so steamed about it, too! I tried to tell Lorissa that I had family plans tonight, and you want to know what she said? She got all stiff and cold on me and stuck her nose a bit in the air.

"Dulcie," she said, all sweet and fake, "you have so much potential here. All the clients love you because they know you are creative as well as reliable. But you don't have an established reputation yet. If you want to succeed, you're going to have to prioritize. If your clients feel like you don't have time for them, they'll request other designers, which means you won't really be maximizing our investment in you. Until you get established and can afford to set your own schedule, you really need to think about being as flexible as possible."

How do you like that for a veiled warning? "Be our slave or we'll throw you out!" Ugh! The Furniture Mart was never that snooty about things. Of course, we were both working and didn't have children yet, so it was different. But still...

So, I'm sorry, I'm going to have to meet with them. But it shouldn't take long. How about if I stop on the way home and pick up something decadent for dessert? :)
Love,
Dulcie

From:	Thomas Huckleberry <t.huckleberry@showme.com>
To:	Dulcie Huckleberry <dulcie@showme.com>
Subject:	Re: More good news!

Hi, Dulcie,
Sorry to hear about the last-minute meeting and Lorissa's response. Used to happen to me all the time. Now you know why I was so hesitant to ditch the overtime and come home.

The thing is, they pretty much DO own you, in a sense, especially if you're salaried. You can try for compensated time off, but I wouldn't hold my breath if I were you, since you're so new there.

Don't worry about dinner. We'll just eat what I cooked, and then I'll reheat it for you when you get home. Dessert would be great, though. How decadent were you thinking? :)

Love,
Tom

From:	Dulcie Huckleberry <dulcie@showme.com>
To:	"Green Eggs and Ham"
Subject:	**My husband**

Hey, girls,

I'm so tired! I worked late today, and then got home just in enough time to kiss the girls good-night. Tom reheated dinner for me, and I had brought home some cheesecake from our favorite restaurant here in town.

I just had to let you all know I'm so sorry for griping about Tom earlier today. I have a wonderful husband! He wasn't mad at all that I had to work late today instead of going out to dinner to celebrate his getting a raise from his stepfather. He was so sweet about it, and encouraged me. It was like he really understood the dilemma I was in, and he gave me good advice. You all *know* how I reacted when the tables were reversed! I was such a shrew about it. I'm still a shrew at times.

Actually, he's probably a better at-home parent than I was.

Today he raked leaves and did laundry and cooked, and he even came up with the idea of having the girls do leaf rubbings! It looks like he found another SAHD to connect with, too, which I think is great. And I love my job. Really. But when he e-mails me and tells me all about what they're doing, I feel a little empty inside. I miss them. And then I have to work late, and all I want is to get home to them.

But I'm not complaining! I'm thankful for my job, and I'm glad Tom is getting to spend time with the kids and learn woodworking. Life is never perfect, and I shouldn't expect it to be. I must just be tired....

Dulcie

From:	VIM <vivalaveronica@marcelloportraits.com>
To:	SAHM I Am <sahmiam@loophole.com>
Subject:	**[SAHM] TOTW October 31: Out of Control**

Hey, y'all,

Well, I reckon I'm about as recovered from the humiliation of my false alarm last week as I'm gonna get. Frank thinks it's the best laugh he's had in years. I don't like these "practice contractions" one little bit. And the baby seems to be doing somersaults in me, too. All that gyrating and contracting's got me feeling a mite dizzy these days. I was at the mall yesterday, and all of a sudden had to sit me down on a bench while my baby finished its little workout. And then, guaranteed Baby will go to sleep for the whole day, but once I lie down, it's "jitterbug in Mama's belly" time. That rascal kicks HARD, too! Gave Frank a bruise on his hip the other night. If the kid can do that much damage to somebody else, just imagine what kind of pulverization is happening to ME! But do I get any old sympathy? NO. Everyone is like, "Ooohh, Ronnie Irene! We just saw your belly jump clear into the next county! That's SOOOO sweet!" Why do they find it cute? I mean, I thought it was just amazing the first few times I felt the baby move. That was pretty cool. But this…it's gonna get mighty old by the time D-day comes.

Anyways, that ain't my topic for today. Well, sorta. I had me a tad bit of an altercation yesterday with Ashley, my nine-year-old stepdaughter. I swan, that child is nine going on nineteen these days. She's all het up because Frank and me told her she can't go to a party tonight. It's a school night, for crying out loud! I may be a brand-new stepmom, but even I know you don't go around letting nine-year-olds go to parties on a school night! Plus, I found out that the host of this party is Ashley's classmate's half brother who's basically an eighteen-year-old Bubba-in-training and known for his wild parties. Ain't NO way I'm letting her go to some shindig hosted by somebody like that. What ARE this kid's parents thinking, even allowing a party like that? For fourth graders?

So we had the oh-so-pleasant task of telling our little Texas tornado, "Nuh-uh." She got this mean, glittery look in her eyes, like a badger that's been cornered. But she didn't pitch a fit. Just stuck her little nose in the air and minced to her room, like the martyr she thinks she is. Frank and I looked at each other and I said, "Ain't she sweet?" But I realized me something that gave me shivers. We can tell her no. We can send her to her room. But I have absolutely no control over that inside part of her. She may have to obey us on the outside, 'cause we're bigger and stronger and have the ability to lock down her freedom. But that child don't have to obey us on the inside. In her heart, she's going to that party tonight, no matter what we think. And the scary thing is, someday, we won't be able to control her outside behavior, either. Someday, she'll up and go to any party she pleases, just 'cause she can.

Maybe the rest of y'all already knew this long ago. And I guess I did, too. But seeing's believing. I just hope I can figure out a way to bring her around to a responsible way of looking at stuff. I don't expect her to always choose the same things I would, but I just hope she'll let us teach her some sense about things.

Don't know exactly what question I got for you to discuss, but there ya go.

Veronica

From:	Rosalyn Ebberly <prov31woman@home.com>
To:	VIM <vivalaveronica@marcelloportraits.com>
Subject:	[SAHM I AM] TOTW October 31: Out of Control

Hi, Ronnie,

This was a good topic. Well done. You're right—we can't control anybody's will. Not our kids, not our spouse. I should know. I can't figure out why I'm so driven to make everything perfect, but the more I try, the more I see that only Jesus can do that. And even He doesn't do it by controlling people. But I've been trying for so long, I think I do

it without even realizing. And that makes me see that I can't even control the person I should be controlling—myself.
Rosalyn

"She looks well to the ways of her household, and does not eat the bread of idleness."
Proverbs 31:27 (NASB)

From:	VIM <vivalaveronica@marcelloportraits.com>
To:	Rosalyn Ebberly <prov31woman@home.com>
Subject:	Re: [SAHM I AM] TOTW October 31: Out of Control

Wow, Ros, you just blew me clean away! Never heard you mention Jesus before without preaching at me. It was kind of nice. But why are you being so open with me all of the sudden? Not that I don't trust you, but...I sorta, kinda don't trust you. :) Thanks for the thumbs-up on the TOTW.
Veronica

From:	Rosalyn Ebberly <prov31woman@home.com>
To:	VIM <vivalaveronica@marcelloportraits.com>
Subject:	Re: [SAHM I AM] TOTW October 31: Out of Control

It's easy to be vulnerable with somebody who already has a rock-bottom opinion of me. Nothing I say is going to make me look worse in your eyes. :)
Ros

"She looks well to the ways of her household, and does not eat the bread of idleness."
Proverbs 31:27 (NASB)

From:	VIM <vivalaveronica@marcelloportraits.com>
To:	Rosalyn Ebberly <prov31woman@home.com>
Subject:	Re: [SAHM I AM] TOTW October 31: Out of Control

Uh…thanks…I think.
Veronica

From:	Marianne Hausten <desperatemom@nebweb.net>
To:	SAHM I Am <sahmiam@loophole.com>
Subject:	Re: [SAHM I AM] TOTW October 31: Out of Control

Hi, Veronica,
I know exactly what you mean! Helene is like that, only at two years old, she's still tantrum prone, not snooty. In fact, she threw a huge tantrum at church yesterday. Apparently, a little boy took the fire truck she was playing with. So she grabbed his arm, knocked him over and bit his shoulder. At least that's what the nursery worker claimed. I don't think she was that malicious. I think they lost their balance as they were tussling over the truck, and she fell over on top of him and knocked her teeth against his shoulder. But the nursery workers don't seem to like Helene very much, so she tends

to get blamed for a lot of things. They've accused her of biting on a couple of other occasions, so this time she got KICKED OUT of Sunday school for the rest of the year!

I was so embarrassed. I'm sure word will get around to the entire church why the Haustens are out walking the halls with Helene. They made me feel like I have a juvenile delinquent and she's only two! I know Helene can be feisty, but they don't call it the "terrible twos" for nothing! So why is she being singled out? I don't know what I'm going to do with her now. I might as well stop going to church entirely, between Neil's feedings and now watching Helene. Brandon says we'll just have to trade off with Helene, but I'm thinking I might just stay home. It's all I can do to drag myself out of bed on Sunday mornings. And all the sermons make me feel like such a loser anyway.

So it's true—a parent really can't control what their kids do. It's pretty much hopeless. Makes me exhausted just thinking about it.

Cheers,

Marianne

From:	The Millards <jstcea4jesus@familymail.net>
To:	Marianne Hausten <desperatemom@nebweb.net>
Subject:	Re: [SAHM I AM] TOTW October 31: Out of Control

Marianne, Marianne, Marianne…when are you going to stop excusing your child and take some action? You don't have to put up with that kind of behavior from her! Really

you don't. But you've got to stop making excuses and start calling it what it is—BAD behavior. Did you watch the nanny as I suggested?
Jocelyn

From:	Marianne Hausten <desperatemom@nebweb.net>
To:	The Millards <jstcea4jesus@familymail.net>
Subject:	Re: [SAHM I AM] TOTW October 31: Out of Control

<Marianne, Marianne, Marianne…when are you going to stop excusing your child and taking some action?>

When are YOU going to start learning to say "No" and stop overcommitting yourself?

And, yes, I did watch *Supernanny*. Brandon thinks we should send in an application to be on the show. I told him when pigs fly. There is no way on earth I'd ever agree to let the whole country watch my parenting struggles for entertainment! Besides, she has some good ideas, but they're awfully simplistic. I don't think they'd work well on Helene—she's very high-strung. And putting her in a "naughty seat" just seems so unfair. I'm sure she's too young to understand why she has to sit there.

I think I just need to spend more time with her. If I gave her more attention I bet she would calm down. When she's having a tantrum, if I go to her and hold her or play with her, she always stops crying. I just am so busy trying to keep up with caring for Neil, too, that sometimes I have to let her scream. I think she resents that, and it makes everything worse. But I'm pretty sure it's mostly my own fault. If I weren't so tired all the time, I could spend more energy on her.

Marianne

From:	P. Lorimer <phyllis.lorimer@joono.com>
To:	SAHM I Am <sahmiam@loophole.com>
Subject:	[SAHM I AM] Men are such babies...

...when they are sick!

Jonathan has a sore throat today, so he stayed home. It is irritating because he is lying on the couch, wrapped in a blanket, with TWO TV trays in front of him, stocked with every home remedy imaginable. He has herbal tea with honey in it, a bag of cough drops, a little ice pack to put on his throat because he claims his glands are swollen, a thermometer and ibuproferen tablets. And guess who fetched this entire apothecary for him?

So then he calls for me, in this pathetically weak, scratchy voice, sounding for all the world like he's on his deathbed. "Phyllis? Honey? Could you please get me a book?"

I got him a book.

"Darling? So sorry to bother you. But my feet are chilly. Could you find my slippers?"

I found his slippers. I put them on his feet.

"Sweetheart??? My tea is cold. Could you reheat it for me?"

I. Reheated. His. Tea.

"Dearest, my head hurts. I don't think I can read this book

after all. Maybe I'll watch a movie. I don't mean to trouble you, but could you put in a DVD and hand me the remote?"

Shoved in DVD. Gave him remote. Made the children go upstairs to their rooms because movie was not child-friendly. Stomped back to office.

And just as I thought things were quiet again… "Phyllis? Could you just run and get me my pillow?"

GRRRRR! What is it with men and illness? And what is it about wives that make us able to nurture and pamper our children when they are sick, but the minute our DHs get ill, we turn into some sort of begrudging nag about it?

It's just a tiny little sore throat. Why can't he take a cough drop and get back to work? It's convenient that he was feeling fine yesterday—Mondays are always his day off. But now that it's Tuesday, I feel like he's shirking. Would he have taken a day off and stayed home with me for a sore throat? I think not. I'd have to be pretty much incapacitated for him to stay home and take care of me.

Grumpily,

Phyllis

From:	Dulcie Huckleberry <dulcie@showme.com>
To:	SAHM I Am <sahmiam@loophole.com>
Subject:	Re: [SAHM I AM] Men are such babies...

Poor Phyllis! I think we've all been there. Guys really are weird when they get sick. And yet they'd NEVER dream of actually going to see a doctor! :)

Tom is healthy, thankfully. But Aidan is sick. She has a fever and a cough and is really cranky. I wish I could go home and help Tom out, but I can't. He says everything is going fine, but I can hear the stress in his voice. He's never had to deal with sick kids on his own before. I told him what to try, and to make sure to call the pediatrician, but he's still going to have to take her in to the doctor's with the other two in tow. Jeanine won't let them come over there because, "What if they're contagious? I didn't get my flu shot this year!"

To make matters worse, Aidan keeps asking for me. Good for my ego. Bad for my conscience. That horrible little voice in my head keeps whispering, "If you were a good mom, you'd be home with her. If you were a good mom, you'd make time to take your own child to the doctor. You're just putting your work first. That makes you a BAD mom." I keep telling it to shut up, but it's not being very obedient this morning.

Dulcie

From:	Brenna L. <saywhat@writeme.com>
To:	"Green Eggs and Ham"
Subject:	IVF

Hey, gals,

Today's the day. Please pray for us. I'm going in to have the FET—frozen embryo transfer—done. It will only take a few hours, but then there's the TWW—Two Week Wait—to find out if it works. The doctor says about half the embryos he thawed survived the process, and several of them look really good. We kept some frozen in case we have to try again.

Madeline knows we're going in today, though she doesn't totally understand what it's about. We've had to give her a lot more information about how babies are made and grow than we would have preferred for her age, but this isn't something we could really leave her out of. So she's off to school, and we're headed out in about a half hour, and Darren's mom will watch her after school if we're not home yet. Madeline gave me a big hug and whispered in my ear, "Don't be scared, Mom. God already has a good baby picked out for you." She's such a sweet girl!

I can't tell if I'm actually scared or not. Darren thinks it's all going to go just fine and we'll have a BFP—Big Fat Positive—on the pregnancy test in two weeks. I'm really afraid to hope. I don't know how I'll be able to bear the look in Darren's eyes if we fail. If I fail.

Brenna

From:	Dulcie Huckleberry <dulcie@showme.com>
To:	Brenna L. <saywhat@writeme.com>
Subject:	**You won't fail!**

Brenna, I'm praying for you today. I know you won't read this until you get home, but I'm pulling for you both. Please don't feel like it's up to you whether this works or not. We all want you to have your BFP, but ultimately, it's not in your hands. The good news is that we both know Whose hands it is in, and They're a LOT bigger and stronger than ours.

Hugs,

Dulcie—who is late for yet another meeting!

From:	Thomas Huckleberry
	\<t.huckleberry@showme.com\>
To:	Dulcie Huckleberry \<dulcie@showme.com\>
Subject:	**Aidan**

Hi, sweetheart,

Just thought you'd like an update on how things went at the doctors. I know you were nervous about leaving it to me, but you really need to trust me more. We did just fine. The only problem we had is that I need to remember to always bring an extra set of clothes for McKenzie wherever we go. She was getting wiggly while I talked with the doctor, but I didn't pay too much attention to it. She climbed behind the rocking chair in the corner of the room, and the next thing I heard was what sounded like a glass of water being spilled. And then McKenzie started to cry. I pulled her out from the corner, and saw a nice yellow puddle on the floor, and her pants were SOAKED. Figures. Why didn't she just say she had to go potty? The nurse gave her an examination gown to wear home.

And Aidan has the flu. The real flu. But she's not in any danger apparently, so we're supposed to just keep an eye on her, give her lots of fluids and make her comfortable. The rest of us will probably get it, too, so I hope you don't have any huge projects scheduled for the next three to four weeks.

I'm just going to let them watch *Veggie Tales* the rest of the afternoon. Right after I take McKenzie potty.

Love,

Tom

From:	Dulcie Huckleberry <dulcie@showme.com>
To:	Thomas Huckleberry
	<t.huckleberry@showme.com>
Subject:	**Re: Aidan**

Oh, Tom, I'm sorry about the potty accident. I will be SO glad to be past the toilet training stage! How any of us managed to learn that particular skill is a mystery to me, after going through all the trouble of trying to train our kids. It's obviously NOT instinct or intuitive. Why can't kids be like kittens? You just shut them in the room with the litter box until they learn to use it, and then they're fastidious about it. That would work for me!

About Aidan—poor kiddo. Make sure you get a humidifier going in whatever room you park her in. If she gets really croupy, you can sit with her in the bathroom with the shower on hot and let it steam up. But not if her fever is too high. Did you give her some children's ibuprofen?

I'm having just a fun old time at work today. Cranky older couple who can't agree on any of the design options I've given them. They argue with each other during the entire meeting, and then they BOTH turn on me and gripe that I haven't gotten more accomplished. Well, maybe I would, IF THEY'D MAKE UP THEIR MINDS! Ugh.

And then there's Mrs. Jeffrey. She wants her bedroom suite redesigned at their home on Table Rock Lake, by Branson. It's a huge house, already professionally decorated, but she wants something more unique. So I started by asking her what sort of tone or mood she would like her suite to convey. But she didn't want to talk about all that. Just wanted to know what designer furniture and artwork I would recommend, and wanted to see all the most expensive upholstery fabrics and faux painting treatments. So I'm having to do a lot of guesswork, and right now, I think I'm guessing entirely wrong. If I try for a classic look, she says it's not unique enough. If I go for more funky and contemporary, she says she's not into that "modern art" look. I think she's just a very discontented woman who doesn't know WHAT she wants! But she likes the attention. Maybe she doesn't want her room decorated at all. Maybe she just likes having somebody show an interest in her. Sad, isn't it?

Guess I'd better get back to work, so I can get home on time for once.

Love you,

Dulcie

From:	P. Lorimer <phyllis.lorimer@joono.com>
To:	SAHM I Am <sahmiam@loophole.com>
Subject:	[SAHM I AM] Men are such babies, part two

Okay, I'm taking him for a doctor's appointment. His throat is much worse, and now he really does have a fever. But for being such an invalid, he certainly did put up a mighty protest about going to see a doctor! Thing is, it's Friday now, and he's supposed to PREACH in two days. I don't see how that's going to happen. I think this is the first time that he will have been sick over a Sunday. This will be interesting, to say the least.

Phyllis

From:	Brenna L. <saywhat@writeme.com>
To:	"Green Eggs and Ham", Tess Gillman <tessty@newmeximail.com>
Subject:	**FET Update**

Hey, girls,

Well, the FET went well. It was a bit uncomfortable, but not as bad as I thought it might be. I had to lie there for a couple of hours to let gravity help things out a bit. And even when I could get up, Darren keeps treating me like I might break with the smallest breeze. I'm not supposed to take any hot baths for the next couple of weeks, or do anything too strenuous. But they decided not to give me any progesterone either, since I don't have a history of miscarriages or infertility. I keep trying to picture those little embryos. I hope they're doing okay. They transferred three. I have no idea what we'd do with triplets, but if Dulcie can manage twins...

It's silly, I guess, but I feel sort of an emotional attachment to these little lives. I shouldn't, because the odds are definitely against them attaching and surviving. I know that in my head, but my heart keeps reminding me that there are, in fact, three tiny lives in me, that could develop into our children. I really hope they make it.

Time for some sticky prayers, my friends.

Brenna

From:	Tess Gillman <tessty@newmeximail.com
To:	Brenna L. <saywhat@writeme.com>
Subject:	Re: FET update

Yay, Brenna! This is an important milestone. Keep me posted. I'm sending up the stickiest prayers possible for you, because I know how long the next two weeks will be. Hoping for your BFP, dear.

Blessings,

Tess

From:	The Millards <jstcea4jesus@familymail.net>
To:	"Green Eggs and Ham"
Subject:	Grrrrrrr!!!

Okay, I screwed up. I admit it. I got myself not just double-booked, but TRIPLE booked tonight. I'd told Shane we'd do some early Christmas shopping, and the kids had won tickets to a show at the children's theater for this evening, and I had also agreed to help decorate the church for my friend's wedding tomorrow. I figured the wedding, being a—hopefully—once-in-a-lifetime event for my friend, had better get top billing on my priority list. Well, then I canceled Christmas shopping with Shane and asked him to take the kids to the theater.

So the only thing that didn't get done was the shopping. And we can do that another time. But Shane and the kids are miffed at me now. Why can't they be more flexible and understanding? I can't be at their beck and call ALL the time! Toss me a bone and a bale of straw, won't you? It's going to be a long night in the doghouse.

Jocelyn

From:	P. Lorimer <phyllis.lorimer@joono.com>
To:	"Green Eggs and Ham"
Subject:	**Jonathan**

We just got the results back from Jonathan's doctor visit yesterday. It's as the doctor suspected—Jonathan has strep throat! So now I feel REALLY guilty for being so snippy about his illness earlier this week. He really is sick. He's got a pretty high fever, and he says his throat feels like it's on fire. To make matters worse, the doctor gave him a penicillin shot this morning, and he is now turning red and swelling up all over, and itching. I thought he was having an allergic reaction, so I called the doctor. He said that sometimes the penicillin reacts this way, especially if it happens to be mononucleosis, which apparently can mimic strep throat. We have to take him in on Monday for more tests. In the meantime, he's supposed to bathe in baking soda water and rub hydrocortisone all over his body. As long as his fever isn't going up and he isn't having problems breathing, or losing consciousness or anything, they said he should be fine. He'll just be miserable until the penicillin leaves his body.

I'm feeling like a total heel now. But if it is mono, how in the world did he catch it? And what are we going to do about church tomorrow? He is in NO shape to go anywhere.

He is really swollen up. Julia saw him and said, "Daddy looks like Bob!" Bob who? Jonathan didn't hardly have the energy to ask, so I did. She rolled her eyes and said, "Bob 'Mato, Mommy!"

Ah. Bob the Tomato. My husband looks like a *Veggie Tales* character. Great. The bad thing is, I nearly laughed, right in front of him because Julia is right. He does look like "Bob." But he is in a lot of pain, and he's NOT being a baby about it. Poor guy. He's almost purple. I did not know people could turn purple.

I suppose we will have to cancel church tomorrow, or just let people come for a worship service. We don't have anyone who can fill in on such short notice.

Off to nurse this strange, puffy red creature who is my husband,

Phyllis

From:	Zelia Muzuwa <zeemuzu@vivacious.com>
To:	"Green Eggs and Ham"
Subject:	**Veggie Tales**

Waltzing with tomatoes, are you?

Just teasing, Phyllis. I hope your poor DH feels better soon.

Ham

From:	P. Lorimer <phyllis.lorimer@joono.com>
To:	"Green Eggs and Ham"
Subject:	**Re: Jonathan/Veggie Tales**

Ham, darling, it's *talk* to tomatoes, and *waltz* with potatoes. You ought to know that. My poor "Bob" isn't up to doing either at the moment, unfortunately.

Remember how I said we had no one to fill in for preaching on such short notice? I guess I was wrong. Jonathan just now took my little hand in his hot, swollen-up purple one, and asked me if I would preach for him. My jaw dropped. I've never preached in my life! And it's 7:00 in the evening! How am I supposed to come up with a sermon between now and tomorrow morning?

But he said that he had notes he was working on this week, and that with my teaching experience, I'm the only one he can think of who could pull it off.

Girls, I'm begging you… PRAY for me! It's not as if I can turn him down, even if he wasn't deathly ill. After all, I'm the one who has been pushing to become a professor. Professors give lectures all the time, with considerably less prep time, too. If I can't handle this, then I suppose I have no business trying to get a Ph.D. But the word *sermon* has so much more emotional baggage than the word *lecture* does. A poorly done lecture will hinder a person's academic growth. A poorly done sermon will hinder their spiritual growth. Not to mention that Jonathan is a fantastic preacher, even though he's still relatively inexperienced. There's no way I can imitate him. If I manage to get up and read from his notes without stumbling all over myself, it will be an accomplishment. I've never felt so intimidated in my life.

Jonathan thinks I can do it. He says I just have to be myself. He trusts me. What if I let him down? I think I could deal with almost anything but that. Guess I'd better get busy. I have a sermon to preach tomorrow.

Phyllis

From:	VIM <vivalaveronica@marcelloportraits.com>
To:	SAHM I Am <sahmiam@loophole.com>
Subject:	**[SAHM I AM] TOTW November 7: I would like to resign...**

...from being a mom, please. Particularly if it means ending up like Frank's mom. I've had me just about enough of Mama Tiziana. Bad enough that Frank compares my cooking with hers. So I ain't no Italian cook—SUE ME! Not my fault he don't appreciate a good Texas BBQ. He's got her constantly sending me his favorite recipes. "America don't have decent food. You gotta feed a man something that will stick to his bones without causing the heart attack. I was just reading in a magazine...the tomato got lots of...how you say in English—lycopene?"

I been handing the recipes over to Frank and telling him if he wants his mama's food so bad, he'd better start learning how to cook it himself, because, boy howdy, I ain't his personal chef!

Aside from the apron-string issues, Frank's okay. But Mama Tiziana is gonna make me crazier than a mad cow in just about two seconds. See, Frank and me got this idea of doing a special pregnancy photo shoot. We're planning to use his studio, and do it up right nice—flowers and gauzy white fabric draping my maternal form, a gentle breeze courtesy of a couple of fans, soft, artistic lighting, and a few belly shots for good measure. If it turned out well, we was gonna put it in Frank's next show. Pregnancy portraiture is a huge hit right now. But Frank was dumb enough to tell his mama about it, and she went off like a bottle rocket.

"What you mean, you gonna take *photos?* I raised you to be a decent boy. You no going around taking pictures of a pregnant lady, even if she is your wife. Especially if she's your wife! When I was a girl, we no talk about pregnancy. We got the modesty, and we know better than to parade about. But you young people! *Bah!* You no got the sense of a brick! You go making the thing public that should have been private, and you got no business making the art out of a woman's condition!" And then she lapsed into a stream of hissy-fittin' Italian.

I don't get it. I mean, it ain't like he was planning to photograph me in any "state of indecency." Lots of women get belly pics. I expected Frank to blow the whole thing off and tell his mama to mind her own business. But now he's wondering if his mama is right! He's rethinking the entire plan, just because MAMA said so.

I'm steamed! First off, I was looking forward to those photos. Second, I just hate it that he'd take his mama's advice over mine. That sticks in my craw. I told him, "Well, Frankie-boy, I don't know how you ever managed to be raising three kids with one on the way, when your own umbilical cord obviously ain't been cut yet." That made him mad, and he stormed out of the house, leaving a trail of untranslatable Italian in his wake.

What is it between men and their mothers?
Veronica

From:	Marianne Hausten <desperatemom@nebweb.net>
To:	SAHM I Am <sahmiam@loophole.com>
Subject:	Re: [SAHM I AM] TOTW November 7: I would like to resign...

Hi, Veronica,

I don't know what it is with men and their mothers, but whatever it is has affected my husband, too. He talked with his mom this evening, and happened to mention how tired I've been, and how hard things have been with Helene, etc. and his mother has now convinced him that I'm DE-PRESSED! He wants me to go see a counselor!

Hmmm, let's see. Why might Marianne be a bit less than cheerful these days? Could it possibly be because she has the world's most difficult daughter and most demanding son to care for? Could it be because her position in life has become a combination of dairy operation, sewage management and animal control? Or maybe it's because between 3:00 a.m. feedings and an episiotomy that still hurts, her libido has become as mythological as the Lost City of Atlantis?

I've come to the conclusion that I am not really enjoying having two children. I think I'd like to put one back, thank you. Only the hospital doesn't take returns, even with a receipt. I told Brandon that he'd be grumpy, too, if he had to…only he didn't let me finish. Said he already had night-mares about doing all the stuff I'm doing, and didn't want me to put it into words in the daylight. Coward. And yet he has the nerve to suggest I'm depressed!

I'm sorry, but they're both wrong. I'm not depressed. Overwhelmed to the point of probable death, yes, but not depressed.

Marianne

From:	Zelia Muzuwa <zeemuzu@vivacious.com>
To:	SAHM I Am <sahmiam@loophole.com>
Subject:	[SAHM I AM] We need a break from all this seriousness...

So here's another Carol Conundrum for you:

"Here Comes Santa Claus" is okay, but NOT "Up On The Housetop."

Hint: Read the lyrics!

So far, about half of our loop has figured it out, and the other half is awfully close. Come on, you can do it!

Zelia

From:	Connie Lawson <clmo5@home.com>
To:	SAHM I Am <sahmiam@loophole.com>
Subject:	Re: [SAHM I AM] We need a break from all this seriousness...

Oh, I think I got it! How about "We Three Kings"? VERY clever, Zelia!
Connie
SAHM I Am Loop Mom

From:	Zelia Muzuwa <zeemuzu@vivacious.com>
To:	SAHM I Am <sahmiam@loophole.com>
Subject:	Re: [SAHM I AM] We need a break from all this seriousness...

How about a "wee three kisses"? :-x :-x :-x And, thanks, Connie. :)
Z

From:	Rosalyn Ebberly <prov31woman@home.com>
To:	Connie Lawson <clmo5@home.com>
Subject:	Re: [SAHM I AM] We need a break from all this seriousness...

Oh, come on, Connie. TELL ME! That stupid game of hers is driving me nuts. I have half a mind to shut it down, only I don't want to put up with all the griping from the loop if I do.
Ros

> "She looks well to the ways of her household, and does not eat the bread of idleness."
> Proverbs 31:27 (NASB)

From:	Connie Lawson <clmo5@home.com>
To:	Rosalyn Ebberly <prov31woman@home.com>
Subject:	Re: [SAHM I AM] We need a break from all this seriousness...

And where would be your personal sense of achievement if I told you? You know, we businesswomen know that struggle is part of the journey to success. It's not good to shortcut that process. Just think about the clue she gave. That's what helped me.

Besides, when I was in high school and all the girls would play these sort of games, I was ALWAYS the last one to get it. It's fun to be on the other side, finally. :)
Connie
SAHM I Am Loop Mom

From:	Thomas Huckleberry <t.huckleberry@showme.com>
To:	Dulcie Huckleberry <dulcie@showme.com>
Subject:	An Idea

Hey, Dulcie,
Since you've got to work late this evening, I was thinking about taking the girls to Silver Dollar City. Mom and Morris gave us those guest passes, and I thought it would be fun to use them before all the rides shut down for the winter.
Love,
Tom

From:	Dulcie Huckleberry <dulcie@showme.com>
To:	Thomas Huckleberry <t.huckleberry@showme.com>
Subject:	**Re: An Idea**

Tom, are you sure it's a good idea to take them all by yourself? Keeping track of two-year-old twins and a four–year-old is a bit of a challenge, even for me. Maybe we should take them on Saturday when we can divide and conquer.
Dulcie

From:	Thomas Huckleberry <t.huckleberry@showme.com>
To:	Dulcie Huckleberry <dulcie@showme.com>
Subject:	**Re: An Idea**

Oh, come on! Flynn takes his kids everywhere by himself. In fact, he was going to go with us today, but his youngest has a cold. We'll be fine. Trust me.
Tom

From:	Dulcie Huckleberry <dulcie@showme.com>
To:	Thomas Huckleberry <t.huckleberry@showme.com>
Subject:	**Trust me**

Them's famous last words, pardner. :)
Dulcie

From:	P. Lorimer <phyllis.lorimer@joono.com>
To:	"Green Eggs and Ham"
Subject:	**Sunday**

Sorry, ladies, here it is almost the end of the week already and I never got a chance to tell you how the sermon went....

First of all, it's always a chore to get the kids ready and dropped off at the church nursery. I'm used to doing it myself because usually Jonathan is running about doing his pastor routine. But when I had to do the child routine in addition to substitute pastor routine, I was exhausted already! I probably had to stop at least fifty times to explain why Jonathan wasn't here, and Julia kept telling everyone he had turned into a giant "Bob 'Mato" which necessitated me explaining what had happened and that we suspect it may be because he actually has mono—which the tests confirmed this week. So THEN they either snickered about how a pastor could get *mono,* or they acted slightly offended about the idea. You can get it from other ways besides kissing, you know!

I remember nothing at all from worship, except that I felt sick to my stomach the entire time. I had horrible visions of getting in front of the microphone only to have the entire congregation walk out on me, *en masse.* But Cathy, one of the church board members "introduced" me and was very sweet. She got them to applaud me for my church history class—which I cancelled for that day—a girl can only handle so much at once! And then before I knew it, I was standing up in front of all of them, with Bible and notes in hand, looking like a pastor and feeling very much like a fraud.

Jonathan's sly sense of humor had inserted itself into the text he had prepared for me. Evidently, he'd suspected all week that this might happen. So he had me start out by reading a "letter" from him to the congregation:

"Dear brothers and sisters,
I find myself, like the Apostle Paul, to be unable to come to you this morning. So I thought I would follow his fine example and send you a letter instead. In Romans, the 16th chapter, verses 1-2, we read, 'I commend to you our sister Phoebe who is a servant of the church which is at Cenchrea; that you receive her in the Lord in a manner worthy of the saints, and that you help her in whatever matter she may have need of you; for she herself has also been a helper of many, and of myself as well.' If we changed 'Phoebe' to 'Phyllis' and 'Cenchrea' to 'Scoville' you would have my instructions regarding how to receive my lovely wife this morning. And if I get a negative report back, you may want to reference Paul's ire in Galatians to get an idea of how I will respond. But I know that you love her as much as I do and will be greatly blessed by what she has to share this morning. I miss you all, Jonathan Lorimer."

I did not want to read it, but Jonathan made me promise. And they all got a good chuckle out of his implied threat, and to be honest, it *did* break the ice some and gave me a few minutes to get used to being up there before I began the sermon.

The sermon itself went very well, actually. I stumbled over a few words, and nearly over my own feet a couple of times. And there was once where I completely lost my place in my notes and had a pause that seemed to last for about fifteen minutes. But it wasn't even five seconds when I listened to it on CD.

The thing is, Jonathan is out of commission for at least the next six weeks. The mono will leave his energy sapped, and his voice is pretty much shot. So who do you think the board has asked to fill in for him until he is able to return? Yep. Me.

I can hardly believe it. What do I know about sermons? Jonathan says he'll work with me on preparing them, but it's going to be a challenge because I can't just quit the church history class. And he's in no condition for a while to help out with the children, so I'll have to keep up with that, too. But we're a small independent church, so there's not many people to substitute for Jonathan, especially at this busy time of year. Before we came, they had the board members taking turns doing the sermons.

I want to help my husband. I just feel so unqualified. At least this is a pretty casual church, and they're used to having people speak who aren't ordained ministers. So it's no big deal to them. Just to me.

Yet, I'm looking forward to it, too. After I got past the nervousness, I realized I was having a bit of fun preaching. It really isn't so different from giving a class lecture after all, except for the spiritual impact it has on people. That knowledge is enough to totally paralyze me if I think about it too much, so I'm trying not to. But knowing that people are taking my

words for spiritual guidance is a weighty thing to me. I'll be
spending a lot of time praying over the next several weeks.
Love to you all,
Phyllis

From:	Zelia Muzuwa <zeemuzu@vivacious.com>
To:	"Green Eggs and Ham"
Subject:	**Re: Sunday**

I always said you'd make a GREAT preacher, Phyllis! Good
for you!
Z

From:	Thomas Huckleberry <t.huckleberry@showme.com>
To:	Dulcie Huckleberry <dulcie@showme.com>
Subject:	**We're home!**

Hi Dulcie,
Well, we're all home in one piece. Had fun.
Tom

From:	Dulcie Huckleberry <dulcie@showme.com>
To:	Thomas Huckleberry <t.huckleberry@showme.com>
Subject:	**Re: We're home!**

So how did it go? You sound exhausted!
Dulcie

From:	Thomas Huckleberry
	<t.huckleberry@showme.com>
To:	Dulcie Huckleberry <dulcie@showme.com>
Subject:	**Re: We're home!**

Oh, it went just fine. We had a great time! We spent a lot of time in Tom Sawyer's Landing and at some of the shows. McKenzie got to help with a magic show. I'm sure the girls will want to tell you all about it when you get home. Have you had a good day? I miss you.
Tom

From:	Dulcie Huckleberry <dulcie@showme.com>
To:	Thomas Huckleberry
	<t.huckleberry@showme.com>
Subject:	**Re: We're home!**

My day has been horrible. Lorissa has been a total grump, and I had to tell one client there was no way to do a coffered ceiling within her desired budget. I'm tired. But I should be home shortly. Just finishing up here.

Glad everything went so well for you. I have to admit I was a little worried. But I guess I shouldn't have been. You're braver than I would be.
Dulcie

From:	Dulcie Huckleberry <dulcie@showme.com>
To:	"Green Eggs and Ham"
Subject:	**GREEN**

That's me, girls. GREEN. Here I've had an awful day at work, and what did Tom do? He took the girls to Silver Dollar City to play the whole day. Had a great time. And not only am I jealous because they got to go have fun without me, I'm jealous because HE DID A BETTER JOB THAN I'D HAVE DONE! It's not fair! You know the disasters that would have awaited me if I'd had the nerve to take my girls to a theme park by myself? It's the stuff nightmares are made of. But he just waltzes off and has a great time, and everyone is happy. It's SAHD, I tell you! Totally SAHD! :)
Pouting,
Dulcie

From:	Thomas Huckleberry
	<t.huckleberry@showme.com>
To:	Flynn Sawyer <flynn@showme.com>
Subject:	Today

Hey, man, thanks for bailing me out today. I'm glad you were able to find a babysitter for Lena—hope she feels better soon. I don't know what I'd have done if I hadn't been able to get a hold of you. Who'd have figured that three little kids—and their dad—could single-handedly shut down the entire Tom Sawyer's Landing? That's like, what, four rides plus the climbing nets? But I've learned some important lessons:

1. McKenzie's chili-dog and the Skychase Balloon Ride do not mix well.

2. The ride operators for the Carousel have this nifty powder stuff that absorbs the puddle left from toddlers who have leaky diapers while riding. This stuff also worked wonders on the Balloon Ride. I need to get some of it for at home.

3. The Sand Station and the Climbing Nets are difficult to clean blood off of. Kids should be wrapped in bubble wrap before being allowed to play there.

4. The Runaway Ore Cart, though only a kiddie roller coaster, can make a grown man pass out, forcing the ride to be stopped midtrack, and for park security and EMTs to do an emergency exit of the ride to extricate said man.

5. Meanwhile, while woozy dad is recovering, the fastest way to find a lost two-year-old is to follow the crowd to the cotton-candy booth and the dozen or so security officers about to issue a parkwide APB.

Anyway, I just wanted to tell you thanks for meeting us and loaning us some fresh outfits.

That's a real friend. Next time, we'll have to all go together, only they've asked me not to bring the kids back to Tom Sawyer's Landing for a while. Go figure.

Tom

From:	VIM <vivalaveronica@marcelloportraits.com>
To:	SAHM I Am <sahmiam@loophole.com>
Subject:	[SAHM I AM] TOTW November 14: Ultrasound

All right, y'all, listen up here! After a couple week's delay, I had me my very first ultrasound today! What a fascinating experience, too! They told me to come on in with a full bladder, which I did. The nurse said, "Oh, you've reached the waddling stage. Good for you!" And I said, "Sweetheart, this ain't a baby-waddle. This is how a water balloon would walk like if it had legs." And then they pressed all over my sloshing belly with their little probe and that jelly stuff which is really cold. Could've kicked them!

But I sorta forgot to be mad at them when I saw the image of our baby pop up on that screen. Our baby! Sucking a teeny little thumb! It was love at first sight, I'm telling you.

We wanted to find out if it was a boy or girl, but the rascal was being all shy like. But for the first time, he or she actually seemed REAL to me. I really felt like a mama today. A real mama to this real baby that has a real heart and lungs and sweet little feet and hands with real fingers.

So I wanted to ask y'all this: when did you first feel that sense of being a real mom? It's a great feeling, ain't it?
Veronica

From:	Marianne Hausten <desperatemom@nebweb.net>
To:	SAHM I Am <sahmiam@loophole.com>
Subject:	[SAHM I AM] Feeling like a real mom

I'm not sure I've ever felt like a real mom. I don't think I know what being a real mom is supposed to feel like. Is it this never-ending feeling of total inadequacy? Or utter inferiority? Or helplessness? Or all three?

I am TRYING to be firmer with Helene. Really I am. Today, I had to go to the grocery store, which I HATE doing anyway, especially with the kids, but Neil was out of diapers and I was out of lunch food for Helene and me. So I took both of the children and went to the health food store we always shop at. I always tell Helene before we go into the store that "Mommy doesn't want you to touch anything. If you're a good girl, Mommy will let you have a cookie when we're all done shopping."

But of course the minute we get into the store, she runs off to the display of little bananas, and then over to the fresh produce stand, where she sticks her head under the spray of water and gets soaked. I tried to make her sit in the back of the cart, but she kept standing up and holding on to the edge so she could jump up and down. So I told her, "No, no. Do you want a cookie? Then you have to be Mommy's good little girl."

And to my amazement, she responded, "Cookie now! Good later!" I was so impressed, I gave her the cookie right then. I couldn't believe she had said something so clever. Then I realized I probably shouldn't have given her the cookie, since then she was really naughty. She took the scoop from the nut bin and poured almonds all over the floor, she pulled the handle on the honey dispenser and got herself and the counter and the floor completely gooey, and she took a big bite out of about four peaches and then put them back in the crate.

What was I supposed to do? I kept telling her, "Mommy will be very mad if you don't stop it, Helene." But she didn't seem to care. So I just tried my best to keep her by the cart.

294   @ *Home for the Holidays*

We got our shopping done, FINALLY, and I was at the exit doors, trying to shift my bags into one hand so I could carry Neil's baby carrier in the other. Helene was over by the automatic sliding doors, making them open and close. I was only a few steps away, but I had my hands full. I told her to come away from the doors, but of course she didn't listen.

Then this guy who had to have been only about my age, dressed in snazzy business clothes, walks by and totally starts freaking out about Helene. He sees her playing with the sliding door and gasps, "Look out! You could pinch your fingers!"

Then he turns to me and says, "She could pinch her fingers!"

I knew she wouldn't, and even if she did, it would serve her right, so I just sort of nodded and said, "Yeah, I know." I was still trying to figure out how to carry Neil and the groceries, so I wouldn't have to return the cart after I put the kids in the car.

So this guy, who obviously has NEVER had children, says even more loudly, "She could get hurt!"

I say, "Yes, I *know* that!"

"Well, aren't you going to do something about it?"

Was he blind? I had a baby in one hand and about three bags of groceries in the other. What did he expect me to do, use my teeth? "Look, my hands are a bit full, okay?"

He glared at me and stuck his nose in the air, and in this martyred tone, says, "I was just trying to look out for the safety of your child, not your ego." And then he spins around and struts off.

Ugh! I was so mad! I just love how people, especially

MEN, who obviously have zero experience with kids, think they can offer a critique on my parenting skills. Did he know what I'd been through already with her? No! I almost wish she HAD pinched her fingers. Maybe she'd learn not to do that anymore.

So I guess I'm not much of a mother. The Know-It-All Grocery Freak would probably do a much better job than me. He certainly would be able to handle three bags of groceries, a baby carrier and a toddler without causing any other busybodies any alarm.

Marianne

From:	Rosalyn Ebberly <prov31woman@home.com>
To:	SAHM I Am <sahmiam@loophole.com>
Subject:	**Re: [SAHM I AM] Feeling like a real mom**

Dearest Marianne,

Thank you for sharing that very informative story with all of us. It serves to illustrate an important point. You must see yourself as an authority figure before anyone else will believe it, whether children or nosy strangers. This means you must set firm boundaries and follow through with what you tell your children. If you say, "Don't touch" then there needs to be consequences if they DO touch. If they spill honey all over the store, they need to be helped to go to a clerk and confess what happened and be made to help clean it up.

My children have learned that I always mean what I say,

and I give them clear boundaries. As a result, they are very well-behaved, well-mannered young people whom I never have to worry about.

You might also consider why you are having a hard time being firm with Helene. Is it because you had a harsh mother and are trying not to be like that? Is it because you are needing your daughter's affection and approval? Perhaps it is some other emotional issue. I believe in the importance of facing that sort of baggage in our lives, if one happens to have baggage, of course. Some of us travel much lighter than others.

Hope this advice is helpful for you,
Rosalyn

"She looks well to the ways of her household, and does not eat the bread of idleness."
Proverbs 31:27 (NASB)

From:	Marianne Hausten <desperatemom@nebweb.net>
To:	"Green Eggs and Ham"
Subject:	Help!

That Rosalyn-voice is haranguing me again! I need you all to start shouting at me to drown her out. And help me find the OFF button!
Marianne

From:	Dulcie Huckleberry <dulcie@showme.com>
To:	Marianne Hausten <desperatemom@nebweb.net>
Subject:	**Re: Help!**

We've all been there, my friend. I LOVE YOU AND YOU
ARE A GOOD MOM AND A WONDERFUL HUMAN
BEING! SOMEDAY YOU WILL FIND THE OFF BUT-
TON, AND THEN YOU WILL BE FREE! There, did I
shout loud enough?

Hugs,

Dulcie

From:	VIM <vivalaveronica@marcelloportraits.com>
To:	Rosalyn Ebberly <prov31woman@home.com>
Subject:	**What on earth HAPPENED today?**

Y'all want to tell your sweet, loving sister what in the world
was going on today? I got me an e-mail from Stephen, who is
quite concerned about you and the kids. He tells me you took
them to their counseling appointment, where Suzannah deliberately pulled the fire alarm and set off the sprinkler system?
And Jefferson stuck his tongue out at one of the firemen? And
Abigail climbed on top of the fire truck and refused to come
down until you promised her a milk shake? And you have the
nerve to lecture Marianne on how to keep her kids in hand?
Are you a few Cheerios short of a full box all of a sudden?

Worried,

Veronica

From:	Rosalyn Ebberly <prov31woman@home.com>
To:	VIM <vivalaveronica@marcelloportraits.com>
Subject:	**Re: What on earth HAPPENED today?**

I would prefer not to discuss today, if you don't mind. I'm going to take about eight pain relievers for my massive headache, and I'm putting on a movie for the kids, and then I'm going to bed. I'm even going to skip my GWENCH meeting, which makes me mad, because we were going to firm up our talking points to present to the Mayor on why he needs to declare December 1 the official Save Christmas day. I've been looking forward to it for weeks, and my children messed everything up. They are officially grounded until they are forty.

Rosalyn

"She looks well to the ways of her household, and does not eat the bread of idleness."
Proverbs 31:27 (NASB)

From:	VIM <vivalaveronica@marcelloportraits.com>
To:	Rosalyn Ebberly <prov31woman@home.com>
Subject:	**Re: What on earth HAPPENED today?**

Honey, you really oughtta let me post this to the loop. Folks out there NEED to know your little kiddos are actually human.

VIM

From:	Rosalyn Ebberly <prov31woman@home.com>
To:	VIM <vivalaveronica@marcelloportraits.com>
Subject:	**Re: What on earth HAPPENED today?**

You do that, "honey," and I'll tell them all about how Frank likes to paint his toenails pink.
Rosalyn

> "She looks well to the ways of her household, and does not eat the bread of idleness."
> Proverbs 31:27 (NASB)

From:	VIM <vivalaveronica@marcelloportraits.com>
To:	Rosalyn Ebberly <prov31woman@home.com>
Subject:	**Re: What on earth HAPPENED today?**

Well, at least this incident today didn't take the acid outta you none. I was starting to worry. You been way too sweet lately.
VIM

From:	Rosalyn Ebberly <prov31woman@home.com>
To:	VIM <vivalaveronica@marcelloportraits.com>
Subject:	**Re: What on earth HAPPENED today?**

I was worried about the same thing with you, dear Ronnie.
Ros

"She looks well to the ways of her household, and does not eat the bread of idleness."
Proverbs 31:27 (NASB)

From:	Dulcie Huckleberry <dulcie@showme.com>
To:	"Green Eggs and Ham"
Subject:	Tom has an interview!

Can you believe it! He is really excited. It's the first one he's had since getting laid off. So I'm home today with the girls. It's weird being home! I feel like I've never left, and yet everything seems so unfamiliar. The girls are out of sorts because we've upset their routine with Daddy, and evidently Tom has done some rearranging, because suddenly I am having problems finding McKenzie's underwear and any of their socks. Plus, apparently, Tom washed another load of laundry with a red crayon in a pants pocket. I now need to buy a new skirt and blouse for work. WHY doesn't he ever remember to check pockets? It's not that hard!

I can't decide if I like being home or not. Part of me feels restless because I know I'm going to be behind on my work tomorrow. But it's fun to be home. Or it would be if I didn't have three pouting girls who are disappointed that Daddy's not here. That's a bit hard on my ego.
Dulcie

From:	Zelia Muzuwa <zeemuzu@vivacious.com>
To:	"Green Eggs and Ham"
Subject:	**Re: Tom has an interview!**

So, Dulcie-babe, are we rooting for Tom to get the job or not to get the job? Just let us know.

Love ya!

Z

From:	Dulcie Huckleberry <dulcie@showme.com>
To:	"Green Eggs and Ham"
Subject:	**Re: Tom has an interview!**

Ugh! Don't ask me that question! I honestly don't know. I guess I just want him to be happy. But I'm not sure if going back into programming would make him happy or not.

Dulcie

From:	P. Lorimer <phyllis.lorimer@joono.com>
To:	"Green Eggs and Ham"
Subject:	**Re: Tom has an interview!**

And what would make you happy, Dulcie? If he got the job, would you give up yours?

Phyllis

From:	Dulcie Huckleberry <dulcie@showme.com>
To:	"Green Eggs and Ham"
Subject:	**Re: Tom has an interview!**

Again, I don't think I can answer that, Phyllis! I think it's kind of an understood thing that if he got a job, I'd probably have to quit because somebody needs to be with the kids. But I hate the thought of quitting so soon. And yet, it would feel selfish of me to insist on staying. So I DON'T KNOW! :(
Dulcie

From:	Brenna L. <saywhat@writeme.com>
To:	"Green Eggs and Ham"; Tess Gillman <tessty@newmeximail.com
Subject:	**no subject**

My period just started.
Brenna

From:	Tess Gillman <tessty@newmeximail.com
To:	Brenna L. <saywhat@writeme.com>
Subject:	**Re: no subject**

NOOOOO!!!!!!!! Oh, Brenna, sweetie, I'm so sorry. Listen, I'm available all morning if you want to talk. Just call me. I don't have to be at the station until this afternoon.
Hugs,
Tess

From:	Zelia Muzuwa \<zeemuzu@vivacious.com\>
To:	"Green Eggs and Ham"
Subject:	Re: no subject

So, does that mean the transfer didn't work? Are you sure it's actually your period? Maybe it's just implantation bleeding.

Z

From:	Brenna L. \<saywhat@writeme.com\>
To:	"Green Eggs and Ham"
Subject:	Re: no subject

No, it's definitely my period. I have to go in for a blood test anyway, just to make sure, but I'm not holding out any hope. I have to go—Darren is sobbing on our bed.

Brenna

From:	Dulcie Huckleberry \<dulcie@showme.com\>
To:	"Green Eggs and Ham"
Subject:	Re: no subject

I'm crying, too, Brenna. I wish I could say something to make you feel better. Please know that we all love you.

Dulcie

From:	P. Lorimer <phyllis.lorimer@joono.com>
To:	"Green Eggs and Ham"
Subject:	**Re: no subject**

I can hardly believe it. I felt so sure it would work out,
Brenna. I'm so terribly sorry, dear. Can you try again?
Phyllis

From:	Brenna L. <saywhat@writeme.com>
To:	"Green Eggs and Ham"; Tess Gillman <tessty@newmeximail.com
Subject:	**Re: no subject**

Sorry for taking so long to reply to you all, girls. Thanks for
the support. We told Madeline when she came home from
school today, and she burst into tears and won't come out
of her room. I've spent so much of the day crying that I don't
have any more tears left.

Yes, we could probably try again. It would cost a lot of
money. But I'm not sure I want to. This is TOO HARD!
We should have just done a regular adoption. Being pregnant wasn't that fun anyway. But it meant so much to Darren. He's completely crushed. I don't know if he will want
to try again, either.

Brenna

From:	Tess Gillman <tessty@newmeximail.com
To:	Brenna L. <saywhat@writeme.com>
Subject:	**Trying again**

Brenna, I know how you and Darren are feeling. Pat and I had six miscarriages and one failed IVF before we got pregnant with Colin. It's one of the most horrible experiences you can go through. I know. But please don't give up. You knew the statistics were against you on the first try, but guess what—the chances of you getting pregnant with a FET are actually HIGHER than the average woman's chance of getting pregnant in any given month. Pregnancy is a one-in-five chance. And you have almost a 30% chance with the FET. Since you didn't have to take any drugs this cycle, they will probably be able to try again next month, if you let them. There were a few embryos still frozen from what we shipped, right?

Please don't let this setback discourage you from trying again. It's okay to grieve, but if you don't move past it, you'll become bitter. I would hate to see that happen.

Much love,

Tess

From:	Brenna L. <saywhat@writeme.com>
To:	Tess Gillman <tessty@newmeximail.com
Subject:	**Re: Trying again**

It just hurts so bad, Tess! I know you know, but I don't see how you got through it!
Brenna

From:	Tess Gillman <tessty@newmeximail.com
To:	Brenna L. <saywhat@writeme.com>
Subject:	**Re: Trying again**

YES, it hurts! Life is excruciatingly cruel, Brenna. But look at how many generations of women have faced pain even bigger than yours. And they survived. You are strong, and so is Darren. You can weather this storm. But if you quit now, you will never know if God has planned a healing blessing for the next attempt. You will spend the rest of your life wondering what could have been. Don't do that to yourselves. At least give the remaining embryos a chance to prove themselves. I care about you and Darren. I'll be praying that God helps you make the right decision.
Love,
Tess

From:	Brenna L. <saywhat@writeme.com>
To:	Tess Gillman <tessty@newmeximail.com
Subject:	**Thanks**

I don't know how we could have ever made it through all this without your support, Tess. Thank you. We're going to just take a few days to think and pray about all this before deciding whether or not to try again. I think right now I'm going to go to bed and not wake up until tomorrow afternoon.

Hugs,

Brenna

From:	VIM <vivalaveronica@marcelloportraits.com>
To:	SAHM I Am <sahmiam@loophole.com>
Subject:	**[SAHM I AM] TOTW November 28: Who all of y'all went shopping this weekend?**

Okay, gals, 'fess up now, who went Christmas shopping this weekend? Day after Thanksgiving sales and all that? Who got up before Rosalyn to brave the malls? Did y'all get some good bargains?

Sorry for the shallow-type TOTW, but being prego this year, I was just too tuckered out to drag myself anywheres that early in the morning. And seen as how after-Thanksgiving shopping is one of my favorite times of the year, I gotta live it vicariously through the rest of y'all.

My most fantastic bargain was last year—got me a pair of Prada pumps with gorgeous brocade embroidery for 40% off at Neiman Marcus. Still nearly maxed out my credit card, but it's well worth it.

Veronica

From:	The Millards <jstcea4jesus@familymail.net>
To:	SAHM I Am <sahmiam@loophole.com>
Subject:	Re: [SAHM I AM] TOTW November 28: Who all of y'all went shopping this weekend?

Veronica, I read your e-mail, and I understood all the words, but the message itself made no sense to me. Prada? Neiman Marcus? What are those? Honey, my idea of an upscale shopping trip is getting to go to Target and buy something brand-new instead of shopping at a thrift store.

But I did manage to make it to Wal-Mart this weekend. Got a LOT of Christmas shopping done. And I'm so happy—Strawberry Shortcake has made a comeback! I used to love SS when I was little. That funny pseudostrawberry plastic smell of her hair, the Purple Pie Man, the dollhouse shaped like a strawberry…ahhh. And now I can get all that stuff for MY daughter! Okay, I confess, I got a new doll for me, too.

Jocelyn

From:	Zelia Muzuwa <zeemuzu@vivacious.com>
To:	SAHM I Am <sahmiam@loophole.com>
Subject:	Re: [SAHM I AM] TOTW November 28: Who all of y'all went shopping this weekend?

Jocelyn,

Are you just NOW discovering the updated version of Strawberry Shortcake? Where have you been the past couple of years? I used to love her, too. Did you ever have the lunch box? I also had this adorable little record with a picture of her on it. And a sticker book. And pajamas. And a bedspread. As well as all the dolls, of course. Oh yeah, those were the days….

I did not go Christmas shopping this weekend. All our money is going toward travel expenses for the adoption. Getting ready to go to Africa for ten days is a crazy undertaking! We have to take clothing and medications and donations for the orphanage and all sorts of stuff. PLUS we have to keep our bags under the weight limit. We even found special teddy bears, one each for Duri and Lishan. I couldn't help getting a little teary-eyed when we bought them.

We're feeling like human pincushions since we are getting all our rounds of shots. All three hepatitis vaccines, and a booster shot, and a polio vaccine, and I don't remember what else. I come home from a shot appointment and my arm aches so badly I can barely move it. But it's worth it.

This is really going to happen! I can hardly believe it, but we're going to be leaving in less than a month!
Zelia

From:	Dulcie Huckleberry <dulcie@showme.com>
To:	SAHM I Am <sahmiam@loophole.com>
Subject:	Re: [SAHM I AM] TOTW November 28: Who all of y'all went shopping this weekend?

Um, Veronica, I thought the point of going shopping after Thanksgiving was to buy Christmas presents for OTHER PEOPLE???
Dulcie

From:	VIM <vivalaveronica@marcelloportraits.com>
To:	SAHM I Am <sahmiam@loophole.com>
Subject:	Re: [SAHM I AM] TOTW November 28: Who all of y'all went shopping this weekend?

Dulcie Huckleberry wrote:
<Um, Veronica, I thought the point of going shopping after Thanksgiving was to buy Christmas presents for OTHER PEOPLE???>

Sure-shooting? Well whaddya know. Is that why they keep asking me if I want my purchase gift wrapped?
Veronica

From:	Dulcie Huckleberry <dulcie@showme.com>
To:	SAHM I Am <sahmiam@loophole.com>
Subject:	Re: [SAHM I AM] TOTW November 28: Who all of y'all went shopping this weekend?

Could be, Veronica dear. Could be.

I did a little Christmas shopping. It's frightening out there! I showed up at 5:30 a.m. at the toy store, and there was already a crowd of people waiting outside. It was like a land rush when they opened the doors. I got shoved into a wall and a woman yelled at ME for it! Then I just about got in a fight with another woman over the last two Baby Bubble Bath dolls. She wanted mine because hers had a small scratch on the face. She claimed she was there ahead of me and that gave her the right to pick which doll she wanted. And that made me mad, so I can't say I behaved any less childishly. But just about the time she started to yell at me, another woman came over and handed her another doll. "I'll take the scratched one—my kids will rough it up much more within five minutes of opening the dumb thing." Honestly, why couldn't I have been that adult about it?

But that wasn't all! I got TACKLED in aisle five! It was a setup job, I'm sure. The wife bumped into me and tripped me while her husband grabbed the VERY LAST Teddy Fairy Tree House! McKenzie will be heartbroken. And why is it that on the biggest shopping day of the whole year, at such an unearthly hour of the morning, THERE WAS ONLY ONE HOUSE LEFT? I mean, what sort of incompetence was that?

It wasn't fair—if Tom had come with me, then I could have competed better. But he refuses to go shopping with me the day after Thanksgiving. Says he's too tired. Truth is, he's too chicken!

So that's my shopping story for this year. Not as exciting as stopping the package thief in Kansas City last year, but still…adventurous. However, I also have a great Thanksgiving dinner story, if you don't mind me hijacking this discussion thread.

Dulcie

From:	The Millards <jstcea4jesus@familymail.net>
To:	SAHM I Am <sahmiam@loophole.com>
Subject:	Re: [SAHM I AM] TOTW November 28: Who all of y'all went shopping this weekend?

Uh, Dulcie, after your Thanksgiving story from LAST year, when McKenzie threw up, I'm not sure we *want* to hear any more T-giving stories from you! :)
Jocelyn

From:	Dulcie Huckleberry <dulcie@showme.com>
To:	SAHM I Am <sahmiam@loophole.com>
Subject:	Re: [SAHM I AM] TOTW November 28: Who all of y'all went shopping this weekend?

Har, har, Jocelyn. Just for that, I WILL hijack this thread! I'll have you know that we hosted Jeanine and Morris, and Tom's sister Becky and her husband, Jordan, and their kids as well as a couple from the church we've been attending, and NOT ONE person got sick! Not even a sniffle.

Of course, that's probably because of Tom's mashed potatoes. He was determined to show how much he has improved in his cooking skills since being a SAHD. And, being a meat-and-potatoes kind of guy, he thought mashed potatoes would be practically fool-proof. But he wanted to do garlic mashed potatoes. So we found a recipe that called for eight garlic cloves. He insisted on doing the shopping and everything by himself, so I didn't know how it went until I tasted them on Thursday.

He had complained about how long chopping the garlic took. I figured he just was inexperienced and didn't know the squash-it-with-a-knife trick or something. But I put a bite into my mouth and just about shot out of my chair. GAR-LIC! Wow! It was eye-poppingly strong stuff. Not inedible, just overpowering.

But everyone else was very, very complimentary about it, so I figured I was just being picky. Until after dinner when about three tins of Altoids appeared in various places and people were consuming them with great gusto. I casually mentioned the potatoes to Tom. I believe my exact words were, "Tom, those mashed potatoes were VERY flavorful."

He grimaced a bit and said, "Thanks. Didn't you think they were a little too garlicky though?"

"Well…it did seem a little stronger than normal."

He shook his head. "I thought I was never going to be done chopping up those garlic cloves. There were eight of them, you know."

"Um, eight isn't really all that many. For the size batch of potatoes you were doing. Did you squish them with the flat side of a knife first?"

He gave me a funny look. "How am I supposed to do that? They're too big. Plus, I had to peel them and cut each section separately."

Section? "What sections?"

"Well, you know, all those smaller pieces."

I was finally getting it. Smothering a smile, I said, "Tom, show me a clove of garlic."

He took me to the refrigerator and pulled out an entire bulb and handed it to me. I burst out laughing. I couldn't help it. He'd put eight BULBS of garlic into those stupid mashed potatoes. We should be cold and flu-free for the rest of the winter after all that! And you'll be able to smell us from coast to coast.

He felt really dumb, poor guy. But we never told anybody else. Except you all. And now, at least he knows what a garlic clove is. And is not.

Dulcie

From:	VIM <vivalaveronica@marcelloportraits.com>
To:	SAHM I Am <sahmiam@loophole.com>
Subject:	Re: [SAHM I AM] TOTW November 28: Who all of y'all went shopping this weekend?

Oh my stars, Dulcie, suddenly those mashed taters sound irresistible! Mind if I borrow your recipe and make Tom's alterations on it? That man must be a genius in the kitchen!

Veronica

From:	Dulcie Huckleberry <dulcie@showme.com>
To:	SAHM I Am <sahmiam@loophole.com>
Subject:	Re: [SAHM I AM] TOTW November 28: Who all of y'all went shopping this weekend?

Well, sure, Veronica. I'll e-mail it to you. But I thought you were all about Brussels sprouts?
Dulcie

From:	VIM <vivalaveronica@marcelloportraits.com>
To:	SAHM I Am <sahmiam@loophole.com>
Subject:	Re: [SAHM I AM] TOTW November 28: Who all of y'all went shopping this weekend?

Aw, honey, Brussels sprouts are SO two months ago. You gotta stay on top of the trends, darlin'.
Veronica

From:	Thomas Huckleberry <t.huckleberry@showme.com>
To:	Dulcie Huckleberry <dulcie@showme.com>
Subject:	Phone call

Dulcie,
I tried to call you at your office, but you must be in a meeting. I just got a phone call from the company I interviewed at a couple of weeks ago. They offered me the job! I told them I would need to think it over and talk with you about it. We didn't really discuss what to do if I actually got the job. I guess we weren't very hopeful it would happen.
Tom

From:	Dulcie Huckleberry <dulcie@showme.com>
To:	Thomas Huckleberry
	<t.huckleberry@showme.com>
Subject:	**Re: Phone call**

WOW! I'm so proud of you, honey! Way to go! Yes, we will definitely have to talk this evening. I'm not sure what to do, but I know you've got to be feeling really encouraged about all this.

Hugs and kisses,

Dulcie

From:	Dulcie Huckleberry <dulcie@showme.com>
To:	"Green Eggs and Ham"
Subject:	**What do I do?**

Girls,

This is an emergency! Tom got a job offer, which I'm thrilled about, but now I have to go home and we have to talk about what to do. They're offering him nearly twice what I'm making, so it would really make the most sense for me to quit. But I don't WANT to! I'm just starting to feel like I'm getting into the rhythm here at work, and I'm enjoying actually doing what I trained to do. But how can I say that to him?

Oh look, it's 4:43. And I don't even have a "need to work late" excuse for putting this off. What am I going to do?

Dulcie

From:	The Millards \<jstcea4jesus@familymail.net\>
To:	"Green Eggs and Ham"
Subject:	**Re: What do I do?**

Hi, Dulcie,

You wouldn't actually consider putting your kids in a day care, would you? I hope not. You know, kids in day care are several times more likely to have serious colds and flu than kids who are at home. And you couldn't possibly expect Tom to give up his career just so you can have yours, would you?

Jocelyn

From:	Dulcie Huckleberry \<dulcie@showme.com\>
To:	"Green Eggs and Ham"
Subject:	**Re: What do I do?**

No, we would not consider day care! And why is it any worse to ask Tom to give up his career than it is to ask me to give up mine? Are you turning all Rosalyn-and-Connie-ish on me, Jocelyn?

Dulcie

From:	The Millards \<jstcea4jesus@familymail.net\>
To:	"Green Eggs and Ham"
Subject:	**Re: What do I do?**

Sorry, Dulcie. Didn't mean any offense. I just know that careers are really important to most guys. Seems like most women are more wired to stay home.
Jocelyn

From:	P. Lorimer <phyllis.lorimer@joono.com>
To:	"Green Eggs and Ham"
Subject:	**Re: What do I do?**

Jocelyn Millard wrote:
<Seems like most women are more wired to stay home.>
Speak for yourself, Jocelyn. I don't really feel wired for it. Dulcie, stop panicking. Just wait and talk to Tom about it. Be honest with how you are feeling and see if you two can come up with a good compromise. I'll be praying for you.
Phyllis

From:	Dulcie Huckleberry <dulcie@showme.com>
To:	SAHM I Am <sahmiam@loophole.com>
Subject:	**[SAHM I AM] Announcement**

Hi, everyone,
Guess what? Tom got a job offer yesterday! It's a really great company, and the pay is good. I'm really happy for him as it was a sorely needed boost to his ego. We went out to dinner to celebrate, and to talk about it.

I expected him to be full of plans for what we were going to do once he was making a decent paycheck again, and how best to go about giving my two-week notice at work. I had really mixed feelings about quitting my job. I absolutely am loving doing the interior design work. But he can make so much more programming than I can in interior design at this point, and we won't put our kids in day care if we can avoid it. So the only sensible thing to do seemed to be for me to quit.

But just as I was about to deal with this elephant in the room, Tom looked at me over his key lime pie and said, "Dulcie, you don't want to quit your job, do you?"

At first, I tried to hedge. I assured him I wanted to do whatever would be best for the family. But he insisted on getting the truth out of me. So finally, I looked down at the table and said, "No. The idea of quitting makes me want to cry."

He grabbed my hand and said, "No need to cry. I'm not going to take that job."

WHAT? I thought he must be going crazy! And I told him so. But he explained that he didn't have the passion for computer programming that I have for interior design.

"I actually am liking being home with the girls and working part-time with Morris. I love woodworking, and I think I'm good at it."

I tried to argue with him. Told him that I didn't mind being home, really. But he finally interrupted. "Honey, listen. For once in my life, I have the chance to really put my family and my relationships first. I'm tired of my world revolving around my tasks. Let me learn to be relational, okay?"

Well, when he put it that way, how could I say no? So he called the company back today and turned them down.

They were speechless. I get to stay at my job, and he gets to stay home.

I'm so thrilled! Really I am! But I'm torn, too. I want to be "relational"—and I have more natural talent for it than Tom does! But the office really is quite task-focused, even though I work closely with clients and other people. They tell me what to do and when to do it by and I have to comply or face the music. There are no sticky-faced kisses before naptime or crayon drawings of stick-figure Mommy and Daddy to put on the fridge. No Elmo to sing the song of the day to the tune of Jingle Bells. No Eric Carle books or *Veggie Tale* sing-along CDs. On the other hand, there is lots of adult conversation and a sense of accomplishment I never had at home.

Why can't I just be content?

Dulcie

From:	Rosalyn Ebberly <prov31woman@home.com>
To:	Dulcie Huckleberry <dulcie@showme.com>
Subject:	Re: [SAHM I AM] Announcement

Dear Dulcie,

I'm disappointed in your decision. I know that's blunt, but I don't see any reason to put sugar on this. How do you expect to fulfill your motherly duties if you are constantly gone? Do you realize what sort of example you are setting for your GIRLS? Do you want them to grow up thinking that Mommy can go off and do whatever makes her feel good while Daddy is forced to stay at home and give up his career aspirations for them? I know you said that Tom SAYS he wants to be home, but we all know that no man really wants to be domestic. They NEED the challenge of the workplace. They need the thrill and adventure of conquering the corporate jungle. Trust me, even then a man can get bored and start looking somewhere else for some excitement. You wouldn't want Tom to end up wandering off, would you?

I'm just so worried about you. There will be so many dire consequences if you continue making such selfish choices. Please reconsider.

Rosalyn

"She looks well to the ways of her household, and does not eat the bread of idleness."
Proverbs 31:27 (NASB)

From:	Connie Lawson <clmo5@home.com>
To:	SAHM I Am <sahmiam@loophole.com>
Subject:	**Re: [SAHM I AM] Announcement**

Hi, Dulcie,

How exciting for Tom to have received such a great job offer! It's a pity he turned it down so soon. Perhaps he can call them back and convince them he has changed his mind.

I know you are enjoying your job. But have you forgotten how wonderful it is to be a SAHM? Not to have to keep to someone else's schedule, nobody to boss you around and complete freedom to come and go as you please. To have the pleasure of knowing you are training up the next generation of leaders. Isn't that a wonderful feeling?

Maybe you need to think about a home-based business. Gadgets for Gals is wonderful. I've thoroughly researched it, and am so impressed. And tools are sort of related to home decorating, you know. Just let me know if you'd like a consultant info packet. I'd be glad to send you one.

Connie

SAHM I Am Loop Mom

From:	Marianne Hausten <desperatemom@nebweb.net>
To:	Dulcie Huckleberry <dulcie@showme.com>
Subject:	Re: [SAHM I AM] Announcement

How could you make a decision like that without even talking to me about it? I feel abandoned and betrayed. We always talked in college about how we were going to stay home with our kids, and now you're going all corporate on me. Maybe you shouldn't even be on the loop anymore. After all, it's called SAHM I *AM,* not SAHM I Used To Be.

Marianne

From:	Zelia Muzuwa <zeemuzu@vivacious.com>
To:	Dulcie Huckleberry <dulcie@showme.com>
Subject:	Re: [SAHM I AM] Announcement

Well, girl, I guess I'm not surprised. But I'm majorly bummed. Things just haven't been the same since you went

back to work. I know things change, but I feel as if we don't have as much in common anymore. I miss you, Dulcie. I'm happy for you, if you're really happy about this decision. But it doesn't sound as though you totally are. I hope you find what you're looking for. Do you even know what that is?
Z

From:	Dulcie Huckleberry <dulcie@showme.com>
To:	Zelia Muzuwa <zeemuzu@vivacious.com>
Subject:	**Re: [SAHM I AM] Announcement**

"Et tu, Brute?"

From:	Zelia Muzuwa <zeemuzu@vivacious.com>
To:	Dulcie Huckleberry <dulcie@showme.com>
Subject:	**Hey!**

I'm sorry, Dulcie. I know you want me to be more supportive. But I'm getting kind of tired of hearing from you how being a SAHM is just second choice, and then you ditch it the first chance you get. You're starting to sound like all the rest of those working moms out there who thing we SAHMs are odd, pathetic sorts of creatures who sit around baking cookies and cleaning house all day. Only you should know better.

Then again, you're getting to do what you really love doing. And I can't begrudge you that. Maybe I'm just being a grouch about it. I don't have a right to judge you. Give

me a few days to get used to the idea, okay? I'm sorry. I'm
not being much of a friend about this.

Z

From:	The Millards <jstcea4jesus@familymail.net>
To:	Dulcie Huckleberry <dulcie@showme.com>
Subject:	**Re: [SAHM I AM] Announcement**

DULCIE! I'm really surprised at you. I thought you were
committed to being home with your kids. I'm sure Rosalyn has already sent you the Guilt Trip, so I'll try to avoid
that. But I do think you aren't going to find the sense of
fulfillment you're seeking at a job. God made you a
mother, and until you accept that, you'll never be totally
at peace.

Jocelyn

From:	Dulcie Huckleberry <dulcie@showme.com>
To:	P. Lorimer <phyllis.lorimer@joono.com>
Subject:	**Are you mad at me, too?**

Seems like everybody else is, so didn't want you to feel left
out of the party. Why can't anybody be happy for me? It's
not as if I'm forcing Tom to stay home. He WANTS to.
What is so wrong with that?

Dulcie

From:	P. Lorimer <phyllis.lorimer@joono.com>
To:	Dulcie Huckleberry <dulcie@showme.com>
Subject:	**Re: Are you mad at me, too?**

Ah, Dulcie, my friend. No, I'm not mad at you. A tad envious, perhaps, but never angry. :) You are doing something new, unique and unconventional. Most people are VERY conventional. They don't understand why anybody would even want to try something original. Or they are people like Zelia, who are very free-spirited themselves, but think that their passion is everyone's passion.

Such people find change to be very scary. And tradition is what gives them security. You've challenged both issues, and it's only natural for them to react. But just remember—on this issue, you and Tom answer only to God. Not to any of us. Do you feel at peace with this? Then go and enjoy what God has given you grace and freedom to do.

I'm happy for you, dear.

Peace and blessings,

Phyllis

From:	Dulcie Huckleberry <dulcie@showme.com>
To:	P. Lorimer <phyllis.lorimer@joono.com>
Subject:	**Re: Are you mad at me, too?**

Thank you, Phyllis! I needed to hear that from somebody. Glad it was you.

Dulcie

From:	VIM <vivalaveronica@marcelloportraits.com>
To:	Dulcie Huckleberry <dulcie@showme.com>
Subject:	Re: [SAHM I AM] Announcement

Dulcie,

Is my sister being a jerk about this? If so, just tell me and I'll give her what-for. I'm really proud of you. I took a lot of flak from my coworkers when I decided to stay home with my kids, so I understand what it feels like to swim against the current, so to speak. I hope things with your job go really well. And if you ever need to talk over any work stuff, I was in advertising for many years. I know it's not exactly like interior design, but working with clients is not so different no matter what industry it is.

Hugs,

Veronica

From:	Dulcie Huckleberry <dulcie@showme.com>
To:	VIM <vivalaveronica@marcelloportraits.com>
Subject:	Re: [SAHM I AM] Announcement

Thanks so much, Veronica! That's so sweet of you. I do have ONE question, though…

WHAT HAPPENED TO YOUR TEXAS ACCENT???? :)

Dulcie

From:	VIM <vivalaveronica@marcelloportraits.com>
To:	Dulcie Huckleberry <dulcie@showme.com>
Subject:	**Re: [SAHM I AM] Announcement**

My accent? What—y'all think I actually TALK like this? Honey, I was born and raised in Chicago, for goodness sake. This here "accent" is strictly to annoy Rosalyn. Gotta do something for entertainment these days!

Veronica

From:	Dulcie Huckleberry <dulcie@showme.com>
To:	Thomas Huckleberry <t.huckleberry@showme.com>
Subject:	**Our decision**

Darling,

Several of my e-mail friends, including Marianne, are barely speaking to me. They think I've tied you up and forced you to stay home by locking you in the closet or something. They think we are screwing up our children for life and ruining our marriage. Let's prove them all wrong, shall we?

Thanks for being you.

Love always,

Dulcie

From:	Thomas Huckleberry
	<t.huckleberry@showme.com>
To:	Dulcie Huckleberry <dulcie@showme.com>
Subject:	**Re: Our decision**

Hi, Dulcie,

Yeah, Mom is throwing a fit, too. But we'll show them. Flynn says this is very normal. Being countercultural is never easy. But at least we're in it together.

Love,

Tom

From:	VIM <vivalaveronica@marcelloportraits.com>
To:	SAHM I Am <sahmiam@loophole.com>
Subject:	**[SAHM I AM] TOTW December 5: Weirdest Christmas gift?**

Howdy, all y'all Christmas Critters,

'Tis the season, and I must confess I ain't nearly as jolly as normal for this time of year. Getting to that point where moving around is cumbersome, and I'm afraid to go shopping because I'm so bulky, I might just tump over an entire display of dolls and leave disaster in my wake!

But I was just thinking this morning of the strangest Christmas gift I ever did see. I actually just received it, as an early present for the baby. It's a microwavable TEDDY BEAR! That's right, you just pop that bear in the nuker for a minute or two, and it comes out toasty warm. Perfectly safe. And cute. But…*weird.*

What's your strangest gift so far?

Veronica

From:	Dulcie Huckleberry <dulcie@showme.com>
To:	SAHM I Am <sahmiam@loophole.com>
Subject:	Re: [SAHM I AM] TOTW December 5: Weirdest Christmas gift?

I once got a set of glow-in-the-dark kitchen knives. The box said, Guaranteed To Cut Darkness by 25%.

Dulcie

From:	Zelia Muzuwa <zeemuzu@vivacious.com>
To:	SAHM I Am <sahmiam@loophole.com>
Subject:	Re: [SAHM I AM] TOTW December 5: Weirdest Christmas gift?

We have a friend who is a taxidermist. He gave Tristan a pair of stuffed ferrets one year for Christmas. I took them to Tristan's office one day when I knew he was in a meeting, and left them sitting on his desk. Unfortunately, the admin. assistant saw them before he did, and she screamed so loudly that somebody called security, and soon half the office was involved. Tristan hardly spoke to me for a week, he was so mortified.

Z

From:	Marianne Hausten <desperatemom@nebweb.net>
To:	SAHM I Am <sahmiam@loophole.com>
Subject:	Re: [SAHM I AM] TOTW December 5: Weirdest Christmas gift?

Why do we even have to give Christmas gifts? Half the time nobody wants what they get anyway, and they don't even care about the person giving it. And the other half, all they DO care about is the gift, and not the thought behind it. So why do we bother?

I have to take both children shopping with me next week because I can't go in the evening—too tired to drive—and nobody will babysit Helene for me during the day. I don't see how this is ever going to work. I'm trying to create a list and organize it according to where I have to go. But it's so overwhelming that all I do is sit and cry all over the notebook. Why do I have to buy Christmas presents anyway?

And just to make matters worse, the radio just played "It's the Most Wonderful Time of the Year." They LIE! They are big, fat liars dressed in red suits and white beards. I'd like to make them go shopping with a baby and a preschool terror and see if they're still singing so cheerfully when they're done! IF they survive…

Speaking of songs—I think I figured out Zelia's game. Only I need to work it backward. Z, my LEAST favorite holiday song—because it reminds me of Helene—is "Nuttin' For Christmas." I've been singing that song under my breath for the past three days… "She's been nothing but bad!" And then I sit and bawl for an hour because I don't deserve anything for Christmas, either. I must be the worst mom in the world to even sing such a song in my head to my daughter. I LOVE her so much! So why does she drive me SO CRAZY?

Anyway, Z, can I still get a kiss? If you want me to e-mail you privately and prove that I know "the rule" I will. I just really need to know I've gotten SOMETHING right today! Marianne

From:	Zelia Muzuwa <zeemuzu@vivacious.com>
To:	SAHM I Am <sahmiam@loophole.com>
Subject:	[SAHM I AM] Marianne's guess

Aw, Marianne, honey, of course you get a kiss. Here you go: :-x Don't beat yourself up so much, okay? I think we've all probably read those lyrics or heard that song and cringed… because WE'VE ALL BEEN THERE! Well, except Ros, perhaps… I know there have been LOTS of times when I've been convinced my children wrote that song. :)
Z

From:	P. Lorimer <phyllis.lorimer@joono.com>
To:	SAHM I Am <sahmiam@loophole.com>
Subject:	Re: [SAHM I AM] TOTW December 5: Weirdest Christmas gift?

My strangest Christmas gift was two years ago when my great-aunt gave everybody in the family sushi candy. Looked like sushi, tasted like gumdrops. Very strange. We asked my aunt why on earth she had purchased such a thing, and she said she got them from a door-to-door salesman who said he was working for a charity that raises money for food poisoning victims. They had fudge that was decorated to look like uncooked meat, and a sweet syrup-drink that looked like raw eggs. Very strange.

Phyllis

From:	Dulcie Huckleberry <dulcie@showme.com>
To:	P. Lorimer <phyllis.lorimer@joono.com>
Subject:	**Eeeewww!**

Okay, that gift is WAY worse than my glow-in-the-dark knives. Sushi candy…ugh. Hey, how is preaching going? Is Jonathan feeling better?

Dulcie

From:	P. Lorimer <phyllis.lorimer@joono.com>
To:	Dulcie Huckleberry <dulcie@showme.com>
Subject:	**Re: Eeeewww!**

Hi, Dulcie,

Preaching is going GREAT! Thanks for asking. I love it. Jonathan is feeling better, but he still gets tired very easily. At least the swelling and redness went away, finally.

It's very hectic, though. I knew Jonathan always spends a lot of time in sermon prep, but I had no idea just how much! And he is too tired to watch the children, so I end up with my notes spread out on the kitchen table, with Julia and Bennet running around under my feet. I'm sure they are getting away with a bunch of naughty stuff, but there isn't much I can do about it. It is difficult enough to remain focused on my sermon prep. I'm not sure how I would ever manage graduate study, as loathe as I am to admit that. But I am having a fun time of it.

Phyllis

From:	Dulcie Huckleberry <dulcie@showme.com>
To:	P. Lorimer <phyllis.lorimer@joono.com>
Subject:	**Re: Eeeewww!**

I'm glad to hear it's going well. Would you do me a huge favor? I would LOVE to have a recording of you preaching. Does your church record sermons?

Dulcie

From:	P. Lorimer <phyllis.lorimer@joono.com>
To:	Dulcie Huckleberry <dulcie@showme.com>
Subject:	**Re: Eeeewww!**

You sweet thing! Of course I would love to send you a CD. You have just made my day by asking. It will be your Christmas present from me, all right?

Hugs,

Phyllis

From:	Connie Lawson <clmo5@home.com>
To:	SAHM I Am <sahmiam@loophole.com>
Subject:	**[SAHM I AM] A prayer request for Rosalyn**

Dear friends,

I think our beloved Rosalyn could use some encouragement and prayers today. You all have heard about her Save Christmas campaign through the group she founded, Godly Women for the Enforcement of National Christian Holidays. The Save Christmas program was gaining a lot of momentum, but that local reporter, Farrah Jensen, wrote a new article today that has the GWENCH gals pretty discouraged. I'm not saying I totally agree with GWENCH's goals, but my friend is feeling glum, and I do want to be supportive of her.

Here's the newest news article:

SANTA Claims GWENCH "Stealing Christmas"
by Farrah Jensen

Hibiscus, WA—It's the latest in a dogfight where the celebration of Christmas is the contested bone. For any who have not been following this drama since it began this summer, the Godly Women for the Enforcement of National Christian Holidays, or GWENCH, has been conducting a campaign called "Save Christmas" to boycott buying Christmas presents from local retailers in retaliation for some of those retailers' refusal to exclusively wish customers a "Merry Christmas" last year. They advocate giving the money to approved local charities instead.

The campaign appeared to be resonating with the community. Several rallies and peaceful demonstrations have shown a growing support for GWENCH. The group boasts a pledge list of nearly one thousand supporters. Retailers and charities alike have expressed concern over the proposed boycott. Several have admitted after-Thanksgiving sales were much lower than expected, and the effect is being felt the hardest in the Market District where tiny, independent shops depend on the annual holiday revenue for survival.

However, the shops and even some concerned charities are fighting back. SANTA, or Shops And Nonprofits Together Alliance, has come to town, and its arrival has GWENCH worried. The secret SANTA group has hidden the names of its leadership, citing concerns of reprisal by GWENCH since some of the organizers are on staff with the "approved" GWENCH charities. As mysterious as it is, SANTA is making its presence felt with the introduction of an aggressive public relations campaign. In a press release and radio ad campaign, SANTA asks the question, "Why is GWENCH trying to steal Christmas?" They cite the economic impact that the boycott may have on not only retailers but also the very charities they claim to want to support. The press release points out, "Local retailers donate nearly eight million dollars to charity each year. Can GWENCH replace that with their 'Save Christmas' campaign? The answer is a resounding no. GWENCH is 'stealing' Christmas from not only the families of Hibiscus but also the charities they claim to support."

The message is hitting home. Several former GWENCH supporters say they have withdrawn their pledge of support, and there have been many others coming out against the campaign. One opponent, Cindy Lou Hu, says, "At first, I thought GWENCH was the real deal and was trying to really save Christmas. But then I realized that its heart was several sizes too small. It just doesn't seem like GWENCH really knows what Christmas is all about."

In a statement released yesterday, SANTA responds, "It's good to see that the citizens of Hibiscus are realizing that boycotts and retaliatory tactics are not part of the true Christmas spirit. SANTA urges everyone to be fiscally responsible both in donations to charities at this time of year as well as in purchasing gifts for friends and loved ones. But let it all be done with love and peace, in the true spirit of the story of Jesus's birth."

Stay tuned for further updates on the struggle between GWENCH and SANTA.

From:	Rosalyn Ebberly <prov31woman@home.com>
To:	Connie Lawson <clmo5@home.com>
Subject:	Re: [SAHM I AM] A prayer request for Rosalyn

Connie, I didn't ask you to send that article to the loop! I don't need prayer. I need to know who that PR person for SANTA is! I WANT HIS HEAD ON A PLATTER!!! Rosalyn

"She looks well to the ways of her household, and does not eat the bread of idleness."
Proverbs 31:27 (NASB)

From:	Connie Lawson <clmo5@home.com>
To:	Rosalyn Ebberly <prov31woman@home.com>
Subject:	Re: [SAHM I AM] A prayer request for Rosalyn

Uh, don't you think you're taking this a bit too seriously? I mean, you gave it a good try, but do you really want to ruin your own Christmas by getting so upset about all of this?
Love,
Connie
SAHM I Am Loop Mom

From:	Rosalyn Ebberly <prov31woman@home.com>
To:	Connie Lawson <clmo5@home.com>
Subject:	Re: [SAHM I AM] A prayer request for Rosalyn

Obviously, Connie, SANTA has brainwashed you.
Rosalyn

"She looks well to the ways of her household, and does not eat the bread of idleness."
Proverbs 31:27 (NASB)

From:	Brenna L. <saywhat@writeme.com>
To:	"Green Eggs and Ham"
Subject:	**Trying again**

Hi, gals,

Well, we're going to try the FET again. Today. I still feel numb and slightly hopeless, as if it's pretty much an exercise in futility to even try it. But we thought it over and prayed a lot, and we've decided to go for it. Please don't make a big deal out of it, though. I don't really want to talk about it or think about it. I just want to get it over with. Pray for us, please.

Brenna

From:	Zelia Muzuwa <zeemuzu@vivacious.com>
To:	Brenna L. <saywhat@writeme.com>
Subject:	**Praying for you**

Just wanted you to know I love you, Brenna.

Z

From:	Dulcie Huckleberry <dulcie@showme.com>
To:	SAHM I Am <sahmiam@loophole.com>
Subject:	**[SAHM I AM] Okay, you all can say "I told you so"**

I'm in the doggie house big-time. My darling little McKenzie was the Star of Christmas for our church Christmas program tonight. Her costume was a star wired with Christmas lights, and she was going to wear almost an entire bottle of hair glitter. I knew I had a big meeting that was going to go a little late tonight, but I figured if I went straight from work to the church, I'd still be there in enough time to help her get ready.

But then my clients got angry because I didn't have the upholstery swatches they'd requested—due to a shipping error—and they decided they wanted to completely redo the look of the room, or they would take their business elsewhere. They also happen to be one of the biggest accounts for our company, so my boss would have been livid if I'd been unable to appease them.

By the time I FINALLY got them out the door, there was only ten minutes left in the program. I got to church just as they were taking their curtain call. McKenzie doesn't realize I missed the whole thing, but Tom knows. And he was MAD!

"You used to ream me up and down when I couldn't be at a family function! And now you missed your daughter's entire Christmas program!" He got all quiet on me. "She was great. Remembered all her lines and even sang her solo like a pro. And you weren't there."

I feel like such a heel. I tried to explain what had happened, but he wouldn't even listen. "Don't try those excuses on me, Dulcie. I know them all, and I know there are ways to get out of client meetings when you really need to. Family comes first!"

Thing is, he's right. And it's not like I wanted to miss it. I honestly didn't know how to get around it. I'm not experienced enough to know all the tricks to managing clients yet.

But maybe I'm a fool for even trying to learn when I have young children at home. Maybe it's true that you can't pursue your own dreams and be a good mom at the same time. I don't know. I'm not sure about anything anymore. I have a job I love, but I feel like the biggest failure in the world.
Dulcie

From:	VIM <vivalaveronica@marcelloportraits.com>
To:	Dulcie Huckleberry <dulcie@showme.com>
Subject:	Re: [SAHM I AM] Okay, you all can say "I told you so"

Oh, I'm so sorry, honey. That's the sort of dilemma that drove me to quit my job last year. I know it's hard. But it doesn't mean you're a bad mom. Those things happen sometimes. Tom shouldn't be so hard on you.
Veronica

From:	Marianne Hausten <desperatemom@nebweb.net>
To:	Dulcie Huckleberry <dulcie@showme.com>
Subject:	Re: [SAHM I AM] Okay, you all can say "I told you so"

Okay, Dulcie, I'll say it: I TOLD YOU SO! I'm sorry it happened, but what did you expect? The business world doesn't care two licks about your family. All they care about is making money. Why would you even want to be part of it? Just go home and let them have their stupid meetings and snotty clients.

Marianne

From:	Dulcie Huckleberry <dulcie@showme.com>
To:	Marianne Hausten <desperatemom@nebweb.net>
Subject:	Re: [SAHM I AM] Okay, you all can say "I told you so"

You just don't get it, do you, Marianne? I LOVE doing design work. You know how you feel when you make a quilt? That's how it is for me and interior design. I was created for this! And you want me to just throw that all away?

Dulcie

From:	Connie Lawson <clmo5@home.com>
To:	SAHM I Am <sahmiam@loophole.com>
Subject:	[SAHM I AM] New Loophole Opinion Poll

Hi! I've created a new opinion poll for this loop. To access this poll, click here. I hope you will take the time to participate.

Question: Which home-based business should Connie choose?

A. Kerrie May

B. Gadgets for Gals

Poll created by Loop! Loophole for the SAHM I Am loop. Not to be used for scientific purposes.

From:	Rosalyn Ebberly <prov31woman@home.com>
To:	VIM <vivalaveronica@marcelloportraits.com>
Subject:	**Emergency!**

Veronica,

I knew it! I knew your little Dick Tracy routine was going to create a disaster! And I was right. You have RUINED MY LIFE!!!

Rosalyn

> "She looks well to the ways of her household, and does not eat the bread of idleness."
>
> Proverbs 31:27 (NASB)

From:	VIM <vivalaveronica@marcelloportraits.com>
To:	Rosalyn Ebberly <prov31woman@home.com>
Subject:	**Re: Emergency!**

What on earth are you talking about, sis? What did Stephen do?

VIM

From:	Rosalyn Ebberly <prov31woman@home.com>
To:	VIM <vivalaveronica@marcelloportraits.com>
Subject:	**Re: Emergency!**

He didn't DO anything! We were meeting at the coffee shop we normally go to for our updates. He was giving me yet more bad news about Chad, but nothing conclusive yet, and I was getting frustrated. So he just patted my hand and told me to be patient, that sometimes it takes a bit of time. Well, at that oh-so-convenient moment, CHAD WALKED IN AND SAW US!

He was confused, since he didn't recognize Stephen, of course. And then Stephen did this melting away into thin air routine, and I was left to try to explain why I was having coffee with another man without giving away the whole plan. Well, THAT made him suspicious. And angry. So now, he thinks I'M having an affair! I told him I'm not, but I wasn't able to think of a convincing excuse. I told him that Stephen was a friend of yours in town for a few days, so I wanted to be hospitable and make him feel like he wasn't totally alone in a strange city. But I don't think he bought it.

What do I do now? I knew I should have never agreed to this plan! What was I thinking, listening to you?
Rosalyn

"She looks well to the ways of her household, and does not eat the bread of idleness."
Proverbs 31:27 (NASB)

From:	VIM <vivalaveronica@marcelloportraits.com>
To:	Rosalyn Ebberly <prov31woman@home.com>
Subject:	Re: Emergency!

Oh, for good grief and crying out loud into a dozen feather pillows! I never did see such absolute idiots in all my born days! And what was Stephen thinking? He should have had a female updating you, so this sort of thing wouldn't happen!

That's it. There's only one thing to do. Y'all need me. I'm coming up to Washington. And when I arrive, y'all are gonna sit down and we're going to have a sweet little chat about all this.

Veronica

From:	Rosalyn Ebberly <prov31woman@home.com>
To:	VIM <vivalaveronica@marcelloportraits.com>
Subject:	**Re: Emergency!**

You're crazy! You can't travel 33 weeks pregnant! I forbid it! You come up here, and I won't even pick you up from the airport. I mean it!

Rosalyn

"She looks well to the ways of her household, and does not eat the bread of idleness."
Proverbs 31:27 (NASB)

From:	VIM <vivalaveronica@marcelloportraits.com>
To:	Rosalyn Ebberly <prov31woman@home.com>
Subject:	**Re: Emergency!**

Sweetheart, you are SO bluffing! I'll be just fine. No reason to worry. And you are WAY too goody-goody to leave your pregnant sister stranded at the airport. I'll e-mail you my itinerary!

Ta-ta!

Veronica

From:	VIM <vivalaveronica@marcelloportraits.com>
To:	SAHM I Am <sahmiam@loophole.com>
Subject:	**[SAHM I AM] Taking a little trip**

Well, all y'all Sahmmies,

Looks like I'll be flying to Washington for an impromptu visit to my dear sister, Rosalyn. She and Chad are having a bit of a misunderstanding, and it'll be easiest to clear it all up in person. So I'll try to send a TOTW on Monday from her house. Y'all be sweet, now, 'kay?

Veronica

From:	The Millards <jstcea4jesus@familymail.net>
To:	SAHM I Am <sahmiam@loophole.com>
Subject:	**[SAHM I AM] STOP WHINING**

I'm sick and tired of all the whining and complaining on this loop! You all think you got problems? Did your church nearly get dropped from its liability insurance because of a program you directed? I think not!

Marianne, GROW A BACKBONE! Stop being such a

jellyfish when it comes to Helene, unless you plan at some point in the very near future to sting back a little. She is just a child!

Connie, nobody gives a rip what home-based business you do! Pick one and stop dithering!

Dulcie, either quit whining about your job or quit your job! You want to be a business woman? Then cope with the challenges. Or go home.

Veronica, you are stupid to travel this close to your due date. And even stupider to try to reason with people as thickheaded and stubborn as Rosalyn and Chad!

Our Christmas program at church was a disaster. The live camel stepped on our pastor's foot and broke it, and apparently one of the wise men—a fifth grader—is deathly allergic to sheep and nearly died onstage. So the paramedics came, and one slipped in a pile of debris left by the donkey and twisted his ankle. The two and three year olds all started pulling their shirts and dresses up while they were singing "Away In The Manger," and our seven-year-old Mary got mad at Joseph—her older brother—and threw the Jesus doll at him.

Guess I won't have to worry about directing the Christmas program next year! After this, it'll be amazing if I can even show my face at church again. I'm so mad, I could scream! All this work, and then it all got messed up. But that just seems to be how my life is going right now.

I've had it. HAD IT! I'm tired of all the running around and nobody appreciating it, I'm tired of petty griping and complaining, of the utter meaninglessness of everything we do! I WANT TO QUIT!!!

Jocelyn

From:	Dulcie Huckleberry <dulcie@showme.com>
To:	Zelia Muzuwa <zeemuzu@vivacious.com>
Subject:	**Jocelyn?**

Well, somebody is a bit grumpy, huh? What got into her?
Dulcie

From:	Zelia Muzuwa <zeemuzu@vivacious.com>
To:	Dulcie Huckleberry <dulcie@showme.com>
Subject:	**Re: Jocelyn?**

I'm not sure. And unfortunately, I don't have a lot of time
to find out. But I'll try calling her and see. Sorry she blasted
you and Marianne. That wasn't cool.

And I'm sorry, Dulcie, for not being more supportive of
you. It wasn't cool of me, either. I think I'm a bit jealous.
Forgive me?

Z

From:	Dulcie Huckleberry <dulcie@showme.com>
To:	Zelia Muzuwa <zeemuzu@vivacious.com>
Subject:	**Forgiven!**

{{{Zelia}}} And I don't think you have much to be jealous
about. :)

From:	VIM <vivalaveronica@marcelloportraits.com>
To:	SAHM I Am <sahmiam@loophole.com>
Subject:	[SAHM I AM] TOTW December 12: Crisis at the Ebberly House

Hey, everyone,

Sorry I don't have the world's best TOTW for y'all this week. Got my hands kinda full here. Since y'all are the praying sort of gals, you might want to shoot a few mental e-mails to the Man Upstairs about my sister, Rosalyn. Things are pretty tough right now. She's planning to send an e-mail soon I think, so I'll let her tell you more details.

A few of you were kind enough to ask how I was feeling after my little plane ride. I'm fine as frog's hair, just a bit tired is all. The flight made me feel a tad woozy, but overall, I'm great.

So the TOTW is this: Why does it seem that personal crises always happen around the holidays?

Veronica

From:	Rosalyn Ebberly <prov31woman@home.com>
To:	SAHM I Am <sahmiam@loophole.com>
Subject:	Re: [SAHM I AM] TOTW December 12: Crisis at the Ebberly House

Dear sisters,

Why indeed do crises happen around the holidays? I think it's because people are selfish and uncaring. I have busted my backside for this family for years! I gave up a perfectly promising career to stay home and be a great wife and mom. I learned how to cook purely organic food, how to sew, how to provide the finest quality for all our household needs, on a *shoestring budget,* I might add. And this is how I'm repaid!

Veronica has mentioned the unfortunate circumstances occurring in our household. It's true—things are not good. Chad is under the mistaken impression that I am having an affair, when in reality, he saw me with the private investigator who is trying to find out who Chad is having an affair with. But Chad won't even speak to me right now, and is staying at a friend's house. How do you like that? How convenient for him that he's found a reason to be angry with ME!

Not only is my marriage crumbling, but my children are going crazy. Suzannah has stomach ulcers, Jefferson is preoccupied with death and dying, and Abigail is having nightmares and can't sleep. How's that for gratitude for all the maternal care I've given them?

I am at a complete loss to explain why all this is happening! I have spent my entire adult life devoted to my family, and yet somehow it's all falling apart. How could this be?

Because of everything that's happening, I need to take a break from my moderating duties. Connie will be running the loop until I'm able to return to my post. I'm sorry for setting such a poor example for you all. I know that you rely on me for guidance and support, and I'm not sure what happened, but right now I'm not in a position to offer either to you. For that, I'm sorry.

Love,

Rosalyn

"She looks well to the ways of her household, and does not eat the bread of idleness."
Proverbs 31:27 (NASB)

From:	VIM <vivalaveronica@marcelloportraits.com>
To:	SAHM I Am <sahmiam@loophole.com>
Subject:	Re: [SAHM I AM] TOTW December 12: Crisis at the Ebberly House

Moms,
Yes it's bad here. No, it's not quite as dire as my sis is making it out to be. Just hang in there and let me see if I can fix it. I never did see such a knotted, tangled mess as these two have gotten themselves into. It's ridiculous! But if they'd stop being so hardheaded, we'd have it all talked out in no time flat. Stay tuned...
Veronica

From:	Dulcie Huckleberry <dulcie@showme.com>
To:	SAHM I Am <sahmiam@loophole.com>
Subject:	Re: [SAHM I AM] TOTW December 12: Crisis at the Ebberly House

Rosalyn and Veronica,
I'm so sorry to hear that things are such a mess there right now. Is there anything we can do to help? You're in our prayers, of course.

Everyone Else,

I'm really doing a lot of soul-searching about my job. When I asked McKenzie what she wanted for Christmas yesterday, this was her response, "I just want you to come home and not work anymore, Mommy."

OWWWWW! I wasn't sure how to feel! Part of me was overwhelmed with guilt, and the rest of me was elated because I really thought the kids preferred being with Tom. I told her, "But honey, if I stay home, then Daddy will have to work." To which she said, "Why can't you both stay home with us?" I tried to explain, but she's only four. It just didn't make sense to her.

Will it be this way my whole life? Will I always be torn between desires and duties—both at home and at work? It's a depressing thought, to be sure.

Dulcie

From:	Connie Lawson <clmo5@home.com>
To:	SAHM I Am <sahmiam@loophole.com>
Subject:	**[SAHM I AM] If anyone is interested...**

I don't know how many of you share Jocelyn's opinion about my business decisions. I certainly did not mean to annoy anybody with my "dithering." But you'll be happy to know, then, that I finally have chosen a company. If anybody cares, it's Gadgets for Gals. Kurt is getting me the starter kit for Christmas. I've been dreaming for weeks of being able to make that announcement to all of you, but I feel now like maybe I shouldn't have said anything at all.

Connie

SAHM I Am Loop Mom

From:	Zelia Muzuwa <zeemuzu@vivacious.com>
To:	SAHM I Am <sahmiam@loophole.com>
Subject:	[SAHM I AM] Getting ready to go to Africa

We leave in a week! My house is a wreck of new outfits and packing lists and travel-size everything and electrical adapters and adoption documents. And that's just for the new children. Then we have everything for our kids to go to England. They pack their luggage and then I have to go unpack it because all they've thought to put in is their favorite toys. Seamus actually said if he had to choose, he'd rather leave his underwear at home than his chemistry set. I told him he could NOT bring the chemistry set in his luggage, and I took it out. He put it back in. I took it out. He separated all the pieces and tried to hide them in his pockets and socks, so then I had to take everything out and start over.

Plus, I have this recurring nightmare that we arrive in Africa, and our new children take one look at us and start screaming and insisting they'd rather live at the orphanage. Or what if the plane crashes and orphans the children we already have? Or what if all our paperwork has been lost and, even though the children love us, we have to leave them behind? I can't let myself even start to think about the what-ifs. I'd have a nervous breakdown!

Rosalyn, I'm praying for you and Chad. We love you.

Veronica, the reason that crises occur during the holidays is because we've had to listen to one too many repetitions of "Have a Holly, Jolly Christmas" and it makes us all slightly psychotic. Or maybe we've just licked too many Christmas card envelopes, and are being subtly poisoned by the nasty adhesive.

This is why e-mail ROCKS!

Z

From:	The Millards <jstcea4jesus@familymail.net>
To:	SAHM I Am <sahmiam@loophole.com>
Subject:	**[SAHM I AM] Apology**

I've been placed under house arrest. By my family. They cornered me last night and took away my car keys, my wallet and my winter coat. Tyler said, "It's for your own good, Mom." And Cassia piped up with, "Yeah, Daddy says you're overcommitted."

It's a good thing for Shane that he'd strategically placed the children between him and me because otherwise I probably would've thrown something at him! He pulled out his cell phone and systematically proceeded to cancel all my appointments, right in front of me!

"Consider this a crisis intervention, honey," he said as he dismantled my entire appointment book.

Thing is, as mad as I was, there was a part of me that watched the whole thing and wanted to cry. With relief. I know I've been too busy, and it's not like I enjoy it. Not to that extreme, anyway. But it all seemed like it needed doing. And if I think about the things that will not get done between now and Christmas, I can feel myself start to hyperventilate. But Shane assures me the world will still be in existence whether or not I attend our homeschool group's fund-raising Christmas party or get all the cookies made for our neighbors that we normally do.

As I said, house arrest. So I'm taking time this morning to repair some friendships my whirl of activity has damaged. My e-mail last week was inexcusable and rude. I'm very sorry, and I'm asking you all to forgive me. Especially my good friends who were targeted. Connie, I'm really proud of you for starting your own business. Send me a catalog when you get your stuff.

I guess what I'll be learning this holiday season is that Jocelyn Millard really cannot save or run the entire world. Not even her own corner of it. I thought I'd learned this lesson already, but apparently I need a refresher course. If my children do not take every class offered, and are not proficient in a variety of skills and talents, they will still become successful, well-adjusted adults. Probably more so if we actually spend some time together at home as a family. If I do not serve on every committee or volunteer for every job that needs doing, things will still get done, and life will still go on.

As Tyler pointed out to me, "Mom, we don't really need you to do all this stuff. Half of it you're not even very good at." For which Shane thumped him on the head. "We just need you to be our mom."

And my very good husband added, "We just need you to be yourself. Not fifty other people."

So now I'm sitting here at my computer, sipping coffee and watching the flames flicker in the fireplace. The kids are outside, and Shane is at work, and I'm wondering why I ever thought running around crazy was a better alternative than this.

But I'd better wrap this up. I have a special Christmas project to do for my family. And NO, it doesn't involve leaving the house or making anything elaborate. It's very simple.
Blessings,
Jocelyn

From:	Dulcie Huckleberry <dulcie@showme.com>
To:	The Millards <jstcea4jesus@familymail.net>
Subject:	**I forgive you**

I knew you were just stressed, Jocelyn. I'm glad your family put you in a "time-out" though. I was getting worried about you.

Why don't you take up a hobby that is relaxing? I've discovered knitting. Very peaceful, and the feel of the yarn in my hands is therapeutic.
Love,
Dulcie

From:	Marianne Hausten <desperatemom@nebweb.net>
To:	SAHM I Am <sahmiam@loophole.com>
Subject:	**Re: [SAHM I AM] Apology**

I forgive you, Jocelyn. I know I've needed a swift kick in the rear where Helene is concerned. You all have been trying to tell me I needed to be more firm with her. Well, I have an update about that which might encourage you.

I took her and Neil shopping yesterday, at the mall. I knew

it was going to be a disaster in the making when the first thing Helene did once we got past the food court was knock over a toy-donation display. A big wall of gift-wrapped boxes, and she hurtled herself against it, screaming. It was like a scene out of *Josh and the Big Wall,* only without the grape slushies. So Jericho came tumbling down, and soon we had a mall security officer rushing over to see what was going on.

My daughter was lying on the floor, flinging boxes in every direction, kicking and screaming. I saw looks of disgust and disdain from other shoppers, and I knew what they were thinking. "Why can't she keep her kid under control?" "People like that shouldn't be allowed to have kids." "Thank goodness *my* children never act like that!"

I was so embarrassed. And then, I got angry. I'm TIRED of Helene humiliating me! I'm so sick and tired of her running the show and calling the shots. She makes me feel stupid because I can't even handle a two-year-old! I am the adult! And she is ruining my life with her tantrums and bad behavior.

So I put the brakes on Neil's stroller and stormed over to Helene. Before I even knew what I was doing, I'd grabbed her and held her face-out, toward the security officer. "Helene is VERY sorry for knocking down the boxes," I grunted, trying to avoid her flailing parts. "And now, we are going home."

"Don't wanna go home!" she yelled.

"Too bad!" And I tucked her under my arm and pushed the stroller with my other hand. Somehow I made it back to the car, and I got Helene into her car seat. Once Neil was loaded in, too, I drove home, listening to Helene scream all the way, and wondering what I was going to do.

At home, I put Neil in his playpen for safety. Then I decided to try the *Super Nanny* technique. I set a little chair in the corner and put Helene on it. "You were very naughty at the mall. You knocked down all those boxes and you kicked and screamed. That is *not* okay to do that. You will sit here quietly for two minutes."

It took forty-five minutes for her to stay in that chair! But every time she got up, I made her go back. And I did it without losing my own temper, even after she threw the chair at me. Finally, she sat in the chair quietly for two minutes, and then I gave her a hug and let her go play.

I AM SO STINKING TIRED! But I feel better than I have in months. I know we have a LONG way to go with her, but all of your prodding helped me to find the inner strength to finally become Helene's mother, not just her caregiver. And I feel a bit proud of that accomplishment.
Merry Christmas,
Marianne

From:	Dulcie Huckleberry <dulcie@showme.com>
To:	Marianne Hausten <desperatemom@nebweb.net>
Subject:	**HURRAH!!!**

It is about time, my friend! I'm so proud of you! In fact, you'll notice I just sent you an e-card. No, I didn't get my calendar mixed up. It is actually a Mother's Day card. But you acted like a real mom today, and I thought we needed to celebrate that. Congratulations, and Happy Mother's Day, dear Marianne!

Love,

Dulcie

From:	Marianne Hausten <desperatemom@nebweb.net>
To:	Dulcie Huckleberry <dulcie@showme.com>
Subject:	Re: HURRAH!!!

Thanks for the card. You know, I've realized something through all this. Being a good wife and mom doesn't have a whole lot to do with cooking or sewing or any of the other stuff I studied in college. All that was nice to learn. But being a good mom doesn't even mean staying home with your kids. You're a GOOD mom, Dulcie. Better than I am, but I'm going to try to catch up to you on that. I'm sorry I was only looking at all those other things. I hope you figure out what to do with your job. But either way, I'm rooting for you.

Love,

Marianne

P.S. Tell the other Green Eggs that I think our little episode at the mall helped me find the off button for the Rosalyn Voice. Finally!

From:	Dulcie Huckleberry <dulcie@showme.com>
To:	Marianne Hausten <desperatemom@nebweb.net>
Subject:	**Thank you.**

I needed to hear that, especially from you, my dear friend.
And woo-hoo on finding the off switch!
Hugs,
Dulcie

From:	The Millards <jstcea4jesus@familymail.net>
To:	Marianne Hausten <desperatemom@nebweb.net>
Subject:	**Re: [SAHM I AM] Apology**

Thanks for being so gracious, Marianne. And WAY TO GO
on dealing with Helene! I knew you had it in you! Keep it
up, and be consistent. She'll come around.
Love,
Jocelyn

From:	P. Lorimer <phyllis.lorimer@joono.com>
To:	"Green Eggs and Ham"
Subject:	**Could really use your prayers**

Hi, friends,
Marianne, well done with Helene! Very well done! Jocelyn,

I'm glad to hear your family benched you. It was for your own good, you know. :)

I could probably do with some benching myself, but there's no help for it right now. Taking on Jonathan's preaching duties has been terrific fun, but as a result, it's now December 18, and I haven't done any Christmas shopping yet. I'm about ready to say forget it, and just move our own Christmas to December 26 so I can catch the after-Christmas sales.

I'm also having to prepare for our special Christmas Eve service, and since Jonathan is still not supposed to be speaking above a whisper, I've had to field all the phone calls and questions about it. I don't know how I'm ever going to be ready for that *and* our family Christmas. But can you imagine how disappointed Julia and Bennet will be if there is NO Christmas for them on Christmas morning? I can't do that to them! So then the guilt comes back in triple measure—if I was a good mom, I'd have bought gifts back in July, if I was a good mom, I would be saying "forget the church" and putting my kids first. And so it goes until I have a raging headache and feel as if everything I do is terribly substandard at best.

How did I ever think I'd be able to handle school and a family? That was pretty foolish of me, wasn't it? :(
Phyllis

From:	Zelia Muzuwa <zeemuzu@vivacious.com>
To:	"Green Eggs and Ham"
Subject:	If I was a good mom

Seems like we say this a lot. It's like a syndrome or something. We should call it the "Iiwagm" Syndrome. Or Iiwagmitis. Symptoms include drooping heads, intense feelings of guilt, depression and general sense of fatigue. Best relieved by a good dose of chocolate and a hug from your child, who must give slobbery kisses and say, "You're my very favoritest mommy in the whole entire world!"

Okay, back to packing. We leave tomorrow morning.
Love,
Z

From:	Marianne Hausten <desperatemom@nebweb.net>
To:	"Green Eggs and Ham"
Subject:	**Iiwagm?**

What in the world? What does that mean?
Marianne

From:	Zelia Muzuwa <zeemuzu@vivacious.com>
To:	"Green Eggs and Ham"
Subject:	**Re: Iiwagm?**

It's an acronym: If I Were A Good Mom—IIWAGM.
Z

From:	The Millards <jstcea4jesus@familymail.net>
To:	"Green Eggs and Ham"
Subject:	Re: liwagm?

And how would you pronounce this new disease?
Jocelyn

From:	Zelia Muzuwa <zeemuzu@vivacious.com>
To:	"Green Eggs and Ham"
Subject:	Re: liwagm?

Sigh Work with me, people! I'm trying to get ready to go
to Africa to expand my family. I can only be so creative right
now. Try pronouncing it "I-wahg-um," I guess. I don't
know! :)
Z

From:	The Millards <jstcea4jesus@familymail.net>
To:	SAHM I Am <sahmiam@loophole.com>
Subject:	[SAHM I AM] Where is the TOTW for December 19?

Hi, everyone,
I e-mailed both Rosalyn and Veronica, but they never responded. It's now Dec. 20, and no TOTW. I'm guessing that

they are too busy dealing with their family issues, but I am surprised not to have heard from Connie.

So I'm taking the liberty of posting a topic for our holiday week. What gift are you most excited about giving this week?

Here's mine: I'm giving each of my kids and my husband coupons for a "gift of time." I made the coupons on the computer, and they're my way of saying I'm sorry for getting too busy the past several months. Some of the coupons are for thirty minutes of cuddling—well, Shane's is for an hour—reading out loud from a book of their choice, doing something fun together—again, their choice—and listening to them talk for thirty minutes. Do you think they'll like them, or just think they're cheesy?

Jocelyn

From:	Brenna L. <saywhat@writeme.com>
To:	SAHM I Am <sahmiam@loophole.com>; Tess Gillman <tessty@newmeximail.com
Subject:	**Re: [SAHM I AM] Where is the TOTW for December 19?**

Hi, Jocelyn,

No, your coupons aren't cheesy. They'll love them.

The gift I'm looking forward to giving is telling Darren that…

WE ARE GOING TO HAVE A BABY! I just got back from the doctor, and Darren isn't home right now, so I have to wait to tell him. But I am indeed pregnant. The doctor says that my hormone levels look good, but I'm supposed to come in for an ultrasound in about a month. I know this doesn't guarantee that we won't have a miscarriage or something, but I have a good feeling about this. I think we'll end up with at least one baby. They transferred two embryos this time, and it appears that both have made it.

That is the best present I could give my family this Christmas—a BFP: Big Fat POSITIVE! I have to go now…can't type when I'm bawling. But it's all 100% happy tears.
Brenna

From:	Tess Gillman <tessty@newmeximail.com
To:	Brenna L. <saywhat@writeme.com>
Subject:	**BFP!!!**

Congratulations, Brenna! I'm so thrilled for you! Aren't you glad you went ahead and tried again? Pat and I can't wait to hear how it goes for you. Would you be willing to share ultrasound photos and such with us? We don't want to intrude, but we've come to feel like you and Darren are sort of an extension of our family. We're telling our boys all about "Aunt Brenna and Uncle Darren" and now I can tell them that they're going to have "cousins" soon. Unless you want me to wait to tell them?

Again, I'm so incredibly happy for you!
Love,
Tess

From:	Marianne Hausten <desperatemom@nebweb.net>
To:	SAHM I Am <sahmiam@loophole.com>
Subject:	Re: [SAHM I AM] Where is the TOTW for December 19?

Dear SAHMs,

I'm so happy for Brenna that I'm sitting here crying. Of course, that also is partly due to the fact that I've finally admitted that I am indeed suffering from depression. My best gift to Brandon is that I'm going to get some counseling and see a homeopath for the depression. I didn't want to go on antidepressants since I'm still breastfeeding Neil. But Brandon thought a homeopath sounds like a good alternative. And I'm going to get on an exercise regimen as well.

My other gift to my family is that Brandon and I will be enrolling in a parenting class at church in January. It's the same program that Jocelyn and Shane teach through their church. We will meet in small groups in the leaders' home, and it will go for about eighteen weeks.

Thanks, everyone, for putting up with me the past several months, and for continuing to encourage me to face up to my problems, even when I didn't want to. You've all been true friends, and I'm so glad I'm part of this group. Have a blessed Christmas!

Marianne

From:	P. Lorimer <phyllis.lorimer@joono.com>
To:	SAHM I Am <sahmiam@loophole.com>
Subject:	**[SAHM I AM] Happy Christmas Eve**

To my SAHM family,

It's Christmas Eve, and in just a few hours, I have to conduct our church's Christmas Eve service. But I had to let you know what happened this morning. I was so nervous about everything! Our church does communion on Christmas Eve, and I've never led something like that before. And we have a candlelight service, and I was afraid that I wouldn't be able to read my notes in the dim lighting. Plus, our pianist got sick yesterday, so I had to try to find somebody to replace her on terribly short notice. There was nobody, which meant that we'd be doing all our songs a cappella.

So all this crashed on me at once, and Jonathan found me huddled on the couch in our living room, sobbing. He held me and let me cry. Then he told me that he would be glad to play the guitar, as long as he didn't have to sing. And he told me not to worry about the dim lights or the communion or anything. He reminded me that the important thing was to celebrate Jesus's birth, not to have the program go perfectly. He's right, of course. I tend to be rather a perfectionist, and I don't enjoy admitting that I can't always be perfect.

Those of you who think of it, at five-thirty this evening, Eastern Time, please say a prayer for me. Pray for my own peace, but more importantly, that the people who come tonight will feel God's love for them.

Blessings,

Phyllis

From:	VIM <vivalaveronica@marcelloportraits.com>
To:	SAHM I Am <sahmiam@loophole.com>
Subject:	**[SAHM I AM] Sorry to disappear on y'all**

Happy Holidays, SAHMmies!

Sorry I went incommunicado the last few days. I've been…in the hospital. We should be able to leave today, but it depends on baby Stephenie's vitals.

Oops, speaking of, somebody is hungry…BRB. Be Right Back!

Veronica

From:	Dulcie Huckleberry <dulcie@showme.com>
To:	SAHM I Am <sahmiam@loophole.com>
Subject:	**[SAHM I AM] BABY WHO???**

Oh my goodness!!! Veronica, did you have your baby? Isn't she about three weeks early? Are you okay?

Girls, how are we going to celebrate this? I thought we had another couple weeks to come up with something!

Dulcie

From:	Connie Lawson <clmo5@home.com>
To:	SAHM I Am <sahmiam@loophole.com>
Subject:	**Re: [SAHM I AM] BABY WHO???**

Hi, ladies,

Yes, Veronica had her baby. Stephenie Irene Francesca Rosalind Marcello—yes, they went a bit overboard with the names, but I'm told there's a good story behind it—was born December 20, at 1:22 a.m. and weighed 4 lbs, 1 oz. She's doing well, but they are monitoring her to make sure everything is completely developed before releasing her from the hospital. They kept Veronica a couple of extra days, too, for monitoring. But they released her shortly after she sent that e-mail to you, and now she's home with Rosalyn. They're hoping to send Stephenie home tomorrow, which would make a great Christmas present.

I'm sorry about the TOTW. I was kept busy finishing up our family Christmas preparations, plus shopping for Veronica and Stephenie, since Veronica had no baby items with her. Frank is flying up with their other kids this evening, so they'll all be together for Stephenie's surprise first Christmas.

I'm sure Veronica or Rosalyn will pop back in with more details as they can.

Merry Christmas!

Connie

SAHM I Am Loop Mom

From:	Zelia Muzuwa <zeemuzu@vivacious.com>
To:	SAHM I Am <sahmiam@loophole.com>
Subject:	**[SAHM I AM] My own update**

Merry Christmas, SAHM I Am!

Okay, so now I find myself competing with Veronica for most exciting Christmas story for our loop! Oh, well.

We are in Addis Ababa, Ethiopia. The land is semi-arid, but beautiful, and we can see the Entoto Mountains towering in the distance from our hotel room. Everything has a sense of the ancient here. Even the expressions in the eyes of children look old and wise.

I love our hotel. It's fancier than anything I ever stayed at in America. I feel guilty for enjoying it when I see the poverty of the shantytowns in the north part of the city. And when we went to the orphanage, I cried. Why didn't we opt to camp out on the street and give our lodging money to the orphanage? But it wasn't actually our money to give. Tristan's parents covered our hotel expenses as their gift to us this year.

We received the best Christmas presents of our lives today. At the orphanage, we sat in a tiny, shabby reception room, and a worker brought in two shy, round-eyed children. The worker nudged the older one forward and said something in Amharic. Then she looked at us and said, "This one is Lishan." Then she handed the smaller one to us and said, "This is Duri."

Lishan stood solemnly a few feet from us, staring at us with chocolate-drop eyes. It was all I could do not to cry, but I didn't want to scare her. I held out my hand and said, "Can I be your mama, sweetie?" At first, I didn't think she would answer. Then, ever so slowly, she reached out and put her little brown hand in mine. I couldn't stop the tears after that, but they were quiet and gentle, like mist.

The worker handed Duri to Tristan, who had to brush away a few tears of his own. Unfortunately, Duri wasn't as quiet and solemn as his big sister. He started screaming, which had the effect of dampening the magic of the moment. A crying child is a crying child, no matter what country or what circumstances. And parents tend to react pretty much the same, even if they've only been parents to this particular child about sixty seconds.

Now, they're both taking a nap in the hotel room. They look like two little beautiful dolls jumbled together on the mattress. We're leaving them in their orphanage clothes for today, so that we won't overwhelm them further by taking away the last bits of familiarity they have. The rest of the week, we'll take it easy and get to know each other and do some sightseeing. We had an opportunity to visit the Blue Nile Falls, but it would have involved a full day on a tour bus, and I don't think the children are up to that. So we'll just have to settle for Niagara Falls when we get back to the States. But Addis Ababa has some amazing sights of its own, and we can't wait to go shopping at the Merkato—a huge market place. We brought an extra suitcase just for souvenirs and gifts.

The children know a few phrases in English. And we learned a few phrases in Amharic before we came. But it is hard to communicate anything but the basics.

Oh my goodness, Lishan just woke up and said, "Mama!" Merry Christmas, everybody!

Z

From:	P. Lorimer <phyllis.lorimer@joono.com>
To:	SAHM I Am <sahmiam@loophole.com>
Subject:	[SAHM I AM] My Christmas

Merry Christmas!

Did you all read the e-mail from Zelia? I could have just cried my eyes out! And I'm still waiting anxiously for more news from Veronica.

Well, nothing quite as exciting is happening around here. The Christmas Eve service went beautifully, and the church gave us a huge pile of Christmas gifts. Apparently, somebody found out that I hadn't had time to do any Christmas shopping, so they took care of Christmas for us! I could hardly believe it. I was so stunned, I just stared at all the packages with my mouth hanging open. One of the church board members joked that they didn't think they'd ever see the day when a preacher ran out of things to say! I've never given so many tearful hugs in my life.

This morning, we all had a wonderful time opening the presents. But Jonathan had a special gift for me. It was a flat shirt box, and when I opened it, there was a stack of papers nestled in tissue. I picked them up, without really knowing what they were. Then, I saw the logos in the upper left corners. Universities. All of them.

"What…" I couldn't even understand what I was looking at.

"They're applications. To the three universities you were most interested in attending. I filled out most of it, but there are some essays and things you have to do yourself."

He'd forgotten to whisper. "You aren't supposed to use your voice," I reminded him, and then realized how stupid that must sound after what he'd just told me.

Then it hit me. He wanted me to go back to school! I threw myself into his arms and laughed with tears in my throat. He hugged me and said that he'd been feeling really guilty watching me teach and then take over his preaching duties in addition to caring for the children. He realized that if I could do all those things, I could certainly handle school, and that it would be wrong of him to stand in my way. He apologized for not being supportive, and promised to help me out any way he could while I went back to school.

The applications are due in only a few weeks, and then I have to wait until next fall to start classes. But that's all right with me, because it will give me extra time to make sure I'm prepared for this.

I don't think it has completely penetrated my brain yet. I'm going back to school! I'm going to get my doctorate, at last! :)

Have a wonderful Christmas, everybody!

Phyllis

From:	VIM <vivalaveronica@marcelloportraits.com>
To:	SAHM I Am <sahmiam@loophole.com>
Subject:	**[SAHM I AM] Stephenie update**

Merry Christmas, y'all!

Stephenie got released from the hospital today. She's such a little trooper, in spite of having inconvenienced Mommy in the extreme. Frank and the kids arrived late last night, so we've all had quite the time getting acquainted with our newest family member.

I'm sure y'all are dying to hear how all this came about. Well, if you'll recall, last Rosalyn had said was that Chad was angry and staying at a friend's house. On Monday, I was finally able to get him and Rosalyn to meet at a restaurant so's we could all talk about this.

It was like trying to mediate between a wolf and a wild-cat. Neither wanted to talk, and if they'd really been wild animals, their tails would've been fuzzed up twice their normal size and their ears would've been flat against their heads.

Rosalyn finally launched the opening attack. "I already know about *Maddy.*"

Chad looked suddenly defensive. "Maddy? What are you talking about?"

"Oh, come on, Chad! Don't play games with me!"

"Look who's talking about playing games!"

Then they both started talking over the top of each other, and guests in the restaurant were staring at us, so I had to clap one hand over each mouth. "Now shut your traps and listen up! Y'all gotta talk to each other, not yell at each other, or I'm leaving."

Well, just then, trouble arrived in the form of Stephen. Y'all probably don't know about Stephen. Well, he's one of Frank's best friends, and he happens to be one of the top private investigators in the Houston area. So when Rosalyn started having serious suspicions about Chad's fidelity, I talked her into letting Stephen come up to Washington and do a little surveillance.

Gals, I'm sorry, I'm going to have to go now. Stephenie wants to eat, and then we're going to take a little nap. I'm exhausted!

Veronica

From:	The Millards <jstcea4jesus@familymail.net>
To:	SAHM I Am <sahmiam@loophole.com>
Subject:	Re: [SAHM I AM] Stephenie update

INFIDELITY? I really *have* been out of the loop lately! What are you talking about, Veronica??? Rosalyn? If either of you are online, please, PLEASE tell us what is going on!!! Jocelyn

From:	Rosalyn Ebberly <prov31woman@home.com>
To:	SAHM I Am <sahmiam@loophole.com>
Subject:	Re: [SAHM I AM] Stephenie update

Merry Christmas, Loopers,

This seems a strange topic for Christmas Day, but it's been a strange Christmas all around this year, so nothing should surprise me now.

Yes, I did fear that Chad was being unfaithful. His behavior pointed to something secretive going on, and the clues I was getting seemed to point to another woman, as ashamed as I am to admit it.

But he thought the worst of me, too, when he saw me with Stephen, and when Stephen showed up at the restaurant with Veronica and me and Chad, I thought Chad might leap across the table and punch him! He ended up chasing Stephen outside, with me and Veronica hurrying after. Veronica was looking really winded after that, and I could tell she wasn't feeling well. But things were unraveling so quickly, there wasn't much I could do.

Chad accused Stephen of having an affair with me, and that made me so angry, I started yelling at Chad. Veronica was trying to keep our voices down, so the police didn't get called. Finally, she stuck her fingers in her mouth and emitted the loudest whistle I've ever heard.

"QUIET!!!"

We all stared at her. She took a deep breath, and said, "Just for the record, Stephen isn't having an affair with anybody. He investigates affairs for a living."

"Then why was he having lunch with MY wife?"

Veronica glared at Chad. "Why do you think?"

Chad's eyes got wide, and he turned to me. "You thought I was having an affair?"

"What else was I supposed to think, with how you've been acting the last few months?"

"And with whom am I supposed to be having this affair?"

"Maddy, of course!"

His face got bright red and he looked as if he wanted to say something, and then he just shook his head. "Let's go."

"Where?"

"To Maddy's house. There's somebody I want you to meet."

Just then, we heard a splash, and a look of horror crossed my sister's face.

"My water broke!" she gasped.

Great. Just great. So much for going to Maddy's house. I ended up putting Veronica in my car, and Chad and Stephen followed us in their cars to the hospital. And the rest is, as they say, history. Stephenie arrived several hours later, and now I have their whole family staying at our house. Stephen left for home this afternoon, after spending Christmas morning with us. Chad was glad to see him go.

Rosalyn

> "She looks well to the ways of her household, and does not eat the bread of idleness."
> Proverbs 31:27 (NASB)

From:	VIM <vivalaveronica@marcelloportraits.com>
To:	SAHM I Am <sahmiam@loophole.com>
Subject:	Re: [SAHM I AM] Stephenie update

My darling sister left out the most exciting part of the story! After we got to the hospital, there seemed to be some confusion. The nurses thought Stephen was my husband! He tried to set them straight, but they thought he was just chickening out on coaching me, so they pretty much shoved him into the birthing room and told him to "be a man about it." Well, not in so many words, but essentially. And in my blind panic about preterm labor, I yelled at him every time he tried to leave, so that reinforced their perception of who he was. He felt very embarrassed to be there, but he *is* Frank's best friend, and so he's practically a brother to me. That's why Frank and I decided to name the baby "Stephenie"—after our good friend Stephen, who stuck by me even in such a ridiculous situation. "Irene" and "Francesca" are for me and Frank, of course, and "Rosalind" is for my sister. Poor baby is going to have a whale of a time living up to all those name-sakes, but she's had a good start for it.

Now, as for Chad and my sister. That's a whole nuther story! I let them in the birthing room with me for a while, and they were STILL arguing. Don't ever let Rosalyn tell you a single other thing about communication, okay? She don't know diddley. They kept at it until I hit transition. Then I just couldn't stand it a single second more.

"BOTH OF YOU SHUT UP AND LISTEN TO EACH OTHER!" I yelled, between contractions. Rosalyn finally noticed that her sister was actually having a baby, and she came over and made herself useful at last. Chad stomped out to the waiting room.

And I have to tell y'all, my sister, Rosalyn, is one terrific birthing coach. She held my hand, got in my face and told me just what to do. It wasn't at all like watching *A Baby Tale* or those nasty videos during Birth Class. It hurt like…well, you know…but my sister was right there to smooth the hair out of my face, grip my hand and tell me I could do it. And when the baby was finally born, Rosalyn cut the cord. She even helped me figure out how to nurse little Stephenie for the first time. We sat there watching her and just couldn't help but cry a bit.

Okay, so it was a *little* like *A Baby Tale*—a sappy, happy ending. Only I'm still not going to forget that it did, in fact, HURT. BAD! That whole forgetting nonsense is a complete myth.

After Stephenie was born, Stephen left to call Frank. Chad returned to the room to have a look at the baby, and then he and Rosalyn actually started having a real conversation.

"How could you think I was having an affair?" he asked.

"What else was I supposed to think? You were always at some meeting or late from work, and Stephen saw you over at Maddy's house all the time."

Chad shook his head and sat down, all hunched over. His shoulders started shaking, and at first I thought he was sobbing. But then I realized he was LAUGHING! My stars, I thought Rosalyn was going to explode!

Just as she turned to leave the room, he caught her hand. "Listen, darling. I love you. I've never had any thoughts about any other women. I wouldn't dare." But he was smiling when he said it. "But you are very intense and hold strong opinions, and I have been changing my mind and making some decisions about things that I knew you would hotly disagree with."

"Such as?"

"Such as I think we've been pressing our kids too much. You need to relax with them, let them be kids for as long as possible."

I don't know about her, but what was crossing *my* mind was Jefferson's coffin pictures—I don't think y'all knew about those—Suzannah's ulcers and Abigail's nightmares. Looked like she might of been having a few of the same ideas. She nodded. "You're right." Then she said, "But that doesn't explain the meetings, the late nights, or…Maddy."

"Ah, yes…Maddy." He poked his head outside the room for a moment and said something. Then, in walked a tall, beautiful brunette…followed by an equally tall, beautiful blonde. Chad gestured to the brunette. "Ros, this is Maddy."

Maddy didn't look too friendly to me. She stiffly offered her hand to Rosalyn, and said, "I've heard a lot about you… Rosalyn."

"Really?" Ros didn't look too impressed with Maddy, either. She turned to Chad. "And your point is...?"

Maddy rolled her eyes. "I am not, and never have been, interested in your husband, okay? Chad seemed to think it was very important for *us* to come down here and explain this to you." Then, before any of us could ask who "us" was, she slid her arm around the blonde's waist and linked her finger through the other woman's belt loop.

Oh.

Rosalyn turned red as a tomato and stammered something about, "Then why...I mean, he was always at your house. Alone..." She glanced at the other woman. "Or maybe not alone..."

Chad grinned. "Maddy is the woman behind...SANTA."

Rosalyn stiffened. "You mean..."

Chad nodded. "I wasn't having an affair. I was the PR guy for SANTA."

Hooo-eee! The fireworks were about to start all over in earnest this time! But before anyone could say anything, I interrupted in my softest, most menacing Texan drawl. "Y'all see this baby here? Shh...listen. That little scritching noise you hear is her *snoring*. If any of y'all start yelling or pitching a fit and make that little old snore go away...well, see now, Mama Ronnie Irene is going to *personally* see that your backsides get thrown out of this here hospital building. So better think REAL carefully before you make a single peep...bless your hearts."

They must have taken me seriously, because Rosalyn burst into quiet tears and said that what Chad did was just as bad as having an affair, whereupon Maddy and her Significant

Other—whose name I never did catch—looked very offended.

"Look here, Ebberly!" Maddy's voice was pretty loud, but I glared at her and gave her a warning "hmm??" and pointed at the baby. She continued shouting, in a whisper this time. "Your GWENCH and Save Christmas nonsense very nearly ruined our business! You talk about charities—did you ever think that maybe we evil retailers DO care about people? Most of the profits from our shop go to an orphanage in Thailand where the children are dying of AIDS because their mothers were forced into prostitution, were infected and had no means of birth control. If it weren't for your husband, we would have not only been unable to send our monthly check and Christmas bonus, but we would have probably had to close up the shop."

Rosalyn stood there, openmouthed. I looked at Stephenie and started crying just at the thought of all those children in Thailand. My excuse is that I've discovered people are very weepy after they've had a baby. And COLD! I could not stop shivering for hours! What's up with that? Oops…focus on the story, Ronnie Irene. None of that new-mommy brain business…

Maddy went on, "You know, there's more than one way to celebrate Christmas." She and the blonde congratulated me, in hushed tones, on the birth of my still successfully sleeping baby and then left the room.

Chad and Rosalyn stared at each other for a few heart-stopping seconds, and then Chad held out his arms. Rosalyn began crying, and he held her. She kept telling him she was sorry, and he kept saying he was sorry, too. And then they both said all these mushy, lovey things that no sister or sister-in-law should have to listen to. In fact, with all their boo-hooing and apologizing and sniffly sweet-nothings, Stephenie woke up! But I didn't throw them out because my baby looked at them and smiled! That's right—smiled before she was twenty-four hours old! Ros and Chad said it was gas, but I think they're just jealous 'cause their kids were never that advanced. Gas? Why would gas make a baby smile, for crying out loud? Sheesh, I may be new to this baby business, but even I know that gas ain't a smiling matter!

But as we say in Texas…it's ALL good! I didn't know having a baby could be so entertaining! Wouldn't have missed a second of it! :)

Veronica

From:	Rosalyn Ebberly <prov31woman@home.com>
To:	SAHM I Am <sahmiam@loophole.com>
Subject:	**Re: [SAHM I AM] Stephenie update**

I'd like to thank my sister for providing such a DETAILED description of my domestic disagreements and reconciliation. It's such a great feeling to have transparency and vulnerability foisted upon me without any say in the matter.

However, I must say, it feels very good to have cleared the air with Chad. And, as you all know, I'm not one who can never admit being in the wrong. I wish Chad had just come and talked to me about his concerns regarding GWENCH, but in all fairness, I may not have listened. I'm listening now, though, and I've contacted Farrah Jensen to run another press release announcing the disbanding and repudiation of GWENCH and its Save Christmas campaign. Chad and I decided to send a donation to Maddy's Thailand orphanage, too. We also are going to make a family appointment with a Christian counselor to talk through some of the concerns about the children. And…I guess some of the concerns about me and Chad, too.

But the most important thing to come out of all this is that I was able to be with my sister and help her through this terrible shock of preterm labor. I'm sure I don't know what she would have done without me. But that's what older sisters are for, and I know she benefited from my expertise.

And, honestly, I feel closer to her than I ever have before. She's proven herself to be a true friend, as well as a sister. It was an honor to be with her for the birth of her first child.

Merry Christmas, everyone,

Rosalyn

P.S. Zelia, by any chance, would "Home For The Holidays" qualify in your little game? Hmm?

"The wise woman builds her house, but the foolish tears it down with her own hands."
Proverbs 14:1 (NASB)

From:	Zelia Muzuwa <zeemuzu@vivacious.com>
To:	SAHM I Am <sahmiam@loophole.com>
Subject:	**[SAHM I AM] Home for the Holidays**

Why, yes, Rosalyn. Yes, it would! :-x By the way—I noticed you changed the verse in your signature line!

Z

From:	Rosalyn Ebberly <prov31woman@home.com>
To:	SAHM I Am <sahmiam@loophole.com>
Subject:	Re: [SAHM I AM] Home for the Holidays

Uh-huh. That's what I thought. You are…sly and mischievous. And in HUGE trouble with your loop moderator. ;)
And yes, it's a new verse. I thought it was time for a change.
And this verse is a good reminder…just for me.
Rosalyn

"The wise woman builds her house, but the foolish
tears it down with her own hands."
Proverbs 14:1 (NASB)

From:	Zelia Muzuwa <zeemuzu@vivacious.com>
To:	"Green Eggs and Ham"
Subject:	Oh. My Goodness. Rosalyn has reformed!

It's like Tigger renouncing his bounce. Or Linus giving up
his blanket. Pigs have officially flown today, girls. You all are
witnesses to this momentous occasion. I feel solemn and
proud and…

Oh, forget all that. IT'S ABOUT TIME!!! Let's celebrate!
Z

From:	P. Lorimer <phyllis.lorimer@joono.com>
To:	"Green Eggs and Ham"
Subject:	Re: Oh. My Goodness. Rosalyn has reformed!

Not so fast, Zelia. Did you see she just posted a schedule of TOTWs for the next month? The first week in January is "Creating Your Family Mission Statement."

Gack!

Phyllis

From:	Zelia Muzuwa <zeemuzu@vivacious.com>
To:	"Green Eggs and Ham"
Subject:	Re: Oh. My Goodness. Rosalyn has reformed!

Uh…well…I guess she's a reformation-in-progress. But, hey, aren't we all? :)

Z

From:	Dulcie Huckleberry <dulcie@showme.com>
To:	SAHM I Am <sahmiam@loophole.com>
Subject:	[SAHM I AM] What a Christmas!

It's a good thing Christmas only comes once a year. I'm not sure any of us could hold up under such excitement all the time! I'm thrilled for Zelia, so glad Veronica's baby arrived okay, excited for Phyllis, and…me? Well, it's been quite a day here in Springfield, too.

After we opened presents this morning, I told Tom and the girls that I had an announcement to make. "I've decided to quit my job," I told them. "Maybe you can call that company back, Tom, and see if the position there is still available, or I'll wait until you can find another job. But I don't want the girls to be unhappy because I'm gone, and I don't want you to feel isolated and unhappy at home."

McKenzie jumped up and started dancing around, singing, "Mommy's gonna quit her job! Mommy's gonna quit her job!" Soon, she had the twins joining in, though they didn't understand what was going on.

Tom, however, didn't look so happy. "You really want to quit?"

"I love what I do, but I can't handle the feeling of being a rope in a tug-of-war between my family and my company. And if it comes to choosing one over the other, I'll pick my family every time."

He still didn't look very happy, which surprised me considering I'd just given the most noble speech of my entire life. At least I thought so! He walked out of the room, and that worried me. Maybe he didn't want to have to go back to a job, either. Maybe I'd just made him angry and ruined our nice Christmas day.

But he returned with a large, flat package in his hand. "If you're going to quit, I guess you won't be needing this." And he handed it to me.

The girls helped me rip off the paper, revealing a large, wooden sign with brass letters. It read The Homemaker: Dulcie Huckleberry, Interior Design Consultant.

I stared up at him. "Did you make this, Tom?"

He nodded.

"It's gorgeous!"

"Thanks. But I suppose we won't need it."

I looked again at the lettering. "You think I should start my own business?"

"Why not?"

"Well, it's not like I can just start tomorrow. And I will have to begin again to build my client base, because I can't take away clients from the company."

"I know. But it's something we can work toward. Together."

I set it down and flew to his arms. Why didn't I think of this earlier? It doesn't have to be either-or. Sometimes the answer can be "both."

Merry Christmas!

Dulcie

From:	Connie Lawson <clmo5@home.com>
To:	Dulcie Huckleberry <dulcie@showme.com>
Subject:	**Your Interior Design business**

Dear Dulcie,

Now that Christmas is over, I wanted to write to you with a business proposition. I would like to suggest that you consider carrying Gadgets for Gals tools as part of your business. I could be your distributor. They'd fit perfectly into a design company. They even come in designer colors, as you know. I'm sending you a complimentary catalog, to look over. I'll even give you a discount, since we're friends as well as business partners. Consider it, okay? This could be the start of a beautiful business friendship.

Blessings,

Connie Lawson

SAHM I Am Loop Mom

From:	VIM <vivalaveronica@marcelloportraits.com>
To:	Rosalyn Ebberly <prov31woman@home.com>
Subject:	**Thank you:)**

Dear Rosalyn,

I wanted to let you know that we all arrived home safely yesterday evening. Thank you for everything the last few weeks. I don't know what I would've done without you, and that's the truth.

Oh, guess what arrived in my mail this morning. A photo of a certain sister of mine perched happily on the lap of a portly old man dressed in a red suit and wearing a white beard. The eyes look suspiciously like Chad's...did GWENCH and SANTA make amends at last? You look *extremely* satisfied... And is that a piece of CHOCOLATE CAKE you're holding??? My, my. Looks like dessert has finally returned to the Ebberly household. I've cleared a place for the photo on my fridge. Every time I see it, I'll remember what lengths sisters will go to for each other. :)

Also, somehow the Grammar Fairy has visited me and erased every vestige of my Texas accent. Don't rightly know how that happened, but I figure y'all oughtta be mighty glad for it. (Okay, maybe there are a few vestiges left…here and there. For nostalgia's sake, you know.)

Happy New Year, sister! I hope it's a good one for you. For all of us.

All my love,

Veronica

From:	Dulcie Huckleberry <dulcie@showme.com>
To:	Connie Lawson <clmo5@home.com>; Rosalyn Ebberly <prov31woman@home.com>
Subject:	A suggestion for the loop

Hi, Connie and Rosalyn,

I was just wondering…what would you think about making SAHM I Am a loop for stay-at-home *parents,* instead of just for SAHMs? I happen to know a couple of really nice SAHDs that would love to join.

Dulcie

From:	Connie Lawson <clmo5@home.com>
To:	Dulcie Huckleberry <dulcie@showme.com>; Rosalyn Ebberly <prov31woman@home.com>
Subject:	Re: A suggestion for the loop

DULCIE!!! Absolutely not! What a crazy idea!

Connie

SAHM I Am Loop Mom

From:	Rosalyn Ebberly <prov31woman@home.com>
To:	Connie Lawson <clmo5@home.com>; Dulcie Huckleberry <dulcie@showme.com>
Subject:	Re: A suggestion for the loop

Not so fast, Connie. Maybe we should consider it. After all, times are changing, and stay-at-home dads need support, too. Besides, just think of all the great media attention we could get. I bet Farrah Jenson would love to do a follow-up article about the new, progressive and inclusive SAHP I Am group. What do you think?

Rosalyn

"The wise woman builds her house, but the foolish tears it down with her own hands."
Proverbs 14:1 (NASB)

From:	Connie Lawson <clmo5@home.com>
To:	Rosalyn Ebberly <prov31woman@home.com>; Dulcie Huckleberry <dulcie@showme.com>
Subject:	Re: A suggestion for the loop

I think it's a "Sappy" idea, but…okay, we'll talk about it. NO PROMISES, though, got it?

Connie

SAHM I Am Loop Mom

From:	Dulcie Huckleberry <dulcie@showme.com>
To:	Connie Lawson <clmo5@home.com>; Rosalyn Ebberly <prov31woman@home.com>
Subject:	Re: A suggestion for the loop

THANKYOUTHANKYOUTHANKYOUTHANKYOU!
And Tom and Flynn thank you, too!
Dulcie

From:	Connie Lawson <clmo5@home.com>
To:	Rosalyn Ebberly <prov31woman@home.com>; Dulcie Huckleberry <dulcie@showme.com>
Subject:	Re: A suggestion for the loop

Hey! I said we'd TALK about it! Sheesh…you're as bad as my kids. Guess that's why I'm the "loop mom."
Connie
SAHM I Am Loop Mom

QUESTIONS FOR DISCUSSION

1) Rosalyn spends a lot of time with her Save Christmas boycotting campaign. What do you think is her motivation for being involved with this? What does she really want to achieve? Is this the same motivation behind the real-life "Merry Christmas" campaigns? Why has using the word *Christmas* or not using it become such a controversy? Do you think it matters?

2) Veronica and Rosalyn constantly take cheap shots at each other. How do you think these sisters really feel about each other? Is there hope for their relationship?

3) Marianne suffers from postpartum depression. Have you or anyone you've known struggled with depression? What helped in that situation? How well do you think Marianne's friends handled her depression? What would you have done the same or differently?

4) Compare the three ways of building a family presented in this story: pregnancy, IVF/embryo adoption and adoption. Were any of these options new or uncomfortable to you? What are some of the advantages and disadvantages of each? Do you know people who have built their families in these ways?

5) Brenna has relatives who disapprove of the embryo adoption. They believe it's silly to adopt an embryo because it's "not a real person." Do you agree or disagree, and why? What are some of the reasons people might choose embryo adoption over embryo donation? How would you have responded to those relatives if you were Brenna?

6) Zelia also faces disapproval from her relatives regarding the choice to adopt from Ethiopia. The concern stemmed from racial issues. Were the concerns valid? Why or why not? Do you think that multiracial couples and families are well-accepted in your community, or is there still needed improvement in that area?

7) The loss of a job is always difficult for a family. How would you have responded if you were in Dulcie's position? Were her anger and fear justified? How has outsourcing to foreign countries hurt the job market in your community?

8) When Dulcie takes a job and Tom stays home, it's quite a role reversal. How is Tom's challenge of being a SAHD different from the challenge of being a SAHM? How is it the same? Do you think this can be a positive role reversal for a family? What factors would need to be in place to make it a success?

9) What did you think about the initial lack of support from her friends for Dulcie's decision to keep her job? Why were her friends so unsupportive? Did this make you more aware of how you respond to your friends' surprising news or decisions?

10) What was the answer to Jocelyn's ongoing Christmas riddle on the loop? Were you able to figure it out? How did knowing or not knowing make you feel? What is it about human nature that makes exclusive or secret knowledge so attractive and desirable?

Dear Reader,

Merry Christmas, Happy Holidays, Season's Greetings...take your pick! I know it can be a stressful time of year, so I hope you take time to relax, laugh a little and thank God for the blessings in your life. My prayer for us all is that we will look to God instead of a holiday or even the warmest family traditions to find the peace, love and joy that only He can provide throughout the whole year. It's tempting as a stay-at-home mom to try to live up to some mythic ideal of what Christmas should be like. Let's give ourselves all a much-needed break and simply enjoy being together and sharing His unconditional love with those around us.

If you are curious about the answer to Zelia's "Holiday Song" game, just go to my Web site, www.meredithefken.com, and find the Special Features section for *@Home for the Holidays*. I want you all to be "in the know"!

If you missed the earlier adventures of Dulcie, Rosalyn and the rest, you can read about them in my first novel, *SAHM I Am*. As I did in that book, I want to give you some additional information regarding a few of the issues in this story. You or your friends may be dealing with these things, and it's nice to know where to find helpful resources. This is by no means a complete list, but it should get you started.

Embryo Adoption: Endorsed by Focus on the Family as an excellent way to combat the use of fetal tissue for stem-cell research as well as to provide frozen embryos a chance to be born and grow up, embryo adoption is an ethical alternative to many of the more controversial infertility treatments. The Snowflakes program at Nightlight Christian Adoptions has more information about this unique, beautiful way to build a family: www.snowflakes.org.

Motherhood: Christian Mommies at www.christian-mommies.com. Extensive site with lots of articles, a discussion board and other resources.

Infertility: Hannah's Prayer Ministries—Christian Support for Fertility Challenges at www.hannah.org. This online ministry includes support for both male and female infertility, as well as miscarriage, the death of a child, etc.

International Adoption: RainbowKids at www.rainbowkids.com. This extensive Web site is a great starting place to begin researching international adoption and related issues.

Stay-at-Home Mothers: Hearts at Home at www.hearts-at-home.org/new. This Web site offers a magazine, conference information, bulletin boards and extensive links.

Women: Her-Wellbeing, an e-mail discussion group, at www.groups.yahoo.com/group/her-wellbeing. "A practical how-to list for Christian women, offering a listening ear, practical advice, and a safe place to talk about women's stuff and share our stories and concerns." Also, Christian Women Today, at www.christianwomentoday.com—an extensive Web site with articles, discussion forums, advice columns and just about any other resources to help and encourage women in all stages of life.

E-mail loops like the one in the story can be found for most of these topics and just about any others through Yahoo Groups (www.groups.yahoo.com) and similar sites. You can do a search for your subject and peruse the list of available groups, then subscribe to the ones you are interested in. Some groups are more nurturing and considerate of people's feelings than others, so you might have to try several before finding one that is a good fit for you.

Visit my Web site, www.meredithefken.com, for more information about me, my upcoming books, additional articles and resources on some of these subjects, and support for writers. I even have a DVD-style Extra Features section for each of my books where you can find deleted scenes, character interviews and other inside info about the stories. I would love to hear from you so please send me an e-mail at meredith@meredithefken.com or snail-mail me c/o Steeple Hill, 233 Broadway, Suite 1001, New York, NY 10279.

Thank you again for choosing my book to read. May God richly bless you this holiday season and in the coming years.

Two inspirational holiday novellas from
bestselling authors

CATHERINE PALMER
and
JILLIAN HART

On sale November 2006.

USA TODAY bestselling author

LORI COPELAND

Yellow Rose BRIDE

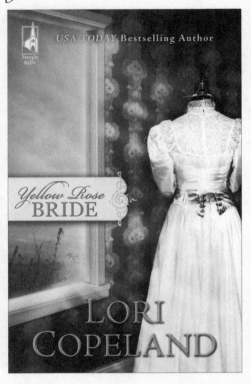

When Vonnie Taylor's husband leaves her, she is doubly insulted when she has to sew the wedding dress for his new bride! As time reveals old secrets, Vonnie just might discover that true love is worth the wait.

*Available from
your local bookseller.*

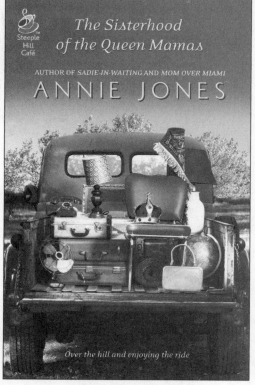

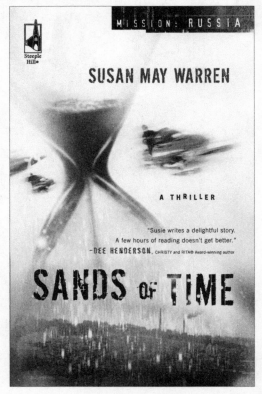